Two women—
One discovering the joys of first love, the other grieving from love's betrayal

Two stories—
Both of intriguing mystery, sensual passion, and the power of forgiveness

One book—
From one of Regency Romance's most beloved talents

For the first time in one volume:

Libby's London Merchant

"Another spectacular novel from the pen of Carla Kelly. This memorable love story will exquisitely catch your heart." —*Romantic Times*

Miss Chartley's Guided Tour

"A milestone of originality. Carla Kelly moves on to yet another triumph in this immensely appealing tale. Superlative." —*Romantic Times*

LIBBY'S LONDON MERCHANT
── *and* ──
MISS CHARTLEY'S GUIDED TOUR

CARLA KELLY

A SIGNET BOOK

SIGNET
Published by New American Library, a division of
Penguin Putnam Inc., 375 Hudson Street,
New York, New York 10014, U.S.A.
Penguin Books Ltd, 80 Strand,
London WC2R ORL, England
Penguin Books Australia Ltd, Ringwood,
Victoria, Australia
Penguin Books Canada Ltd, 10 Alcorn Avenue,
Toronto, Ontario, Canada M4V 3B2
Penguin Books (N.Z.) Ltd, 182–190 Wairau Road,
Auckland 10, New Zealand

Penguin Books Ltd, Registered Offices: Harmondsworth, Middlesex, England

Published by Signet, an imprint of New American Library,
a division of Penguin Putnam Inc.
Libby's London Merchant was originally published by Signet in April 1991,
copyright © Carla Kelly, 1991.
Miss Chartley's Guided Tour was originally published by Signet in July 1989,
copyright © Carla Kelly, 1989.
Excerpt from *One Good Turn* copyright © Carla Kelly, 2001

First Signet Printing (Double Edition), November 2001
10 9 8 7 6 5 4 3 2 1

LIBBY'S LONDON MERCHANT

To Pamela Adams, with love

The two divinest things this world has got,
A lovely woman in a rural spot!

Leigh Hunt
1784–1859

Gentle Reader,

My blushes, but I must lay this matter before you. When I wrote *Libby's London Merchant* in 1991, I—who pride myself on historical accuracy—had not a clue that chocolate candy, as we know and love it, was not developed until 1879. As she was preparing *Libby's* reprise in this two-book format, Hilary Ross, sharp-eyed editor, noticed my error. Alas, it was too late in the production process to do anything about it.

Please forgive my error.

I remain, respectfully,
Your obedient servant,
Carla Kelly

P.S. Heavens, but think the Peninsular War would only have lasted a year or two, if both sides could have mediated with chocolate. On such egregious omissions does history turn.

1

***

"I SAY, Nez, you're not paying a ha'penny's worth of attention."

Benedict Nesbitt, Duke of Knaresborough, grunted, shifted his weight, and rolled gently onto the floor.

"Eustace, you have my undivided attention," the duke replied as he rested his head on the pillow that had rolled off with him.

"Oh, bother it!" Eustace's voice rose to an unpleasant pitch. He picked up another pillow to throw at his friend and succeeded only in knocking down the few remaining bottles that still stood upright on the table. "Here I am, facing the crisis of my life, and all you can do is drink my wine and grunt."

"It's my wine," insisted the voice from the floor, "and it's my house."

Eustace tried to sit up straight. He looked about in surprise as his eyes narrowed. "Well, Lord bless me, you may be right." He nodded wisely and settled lower in his chair again. "I suppose you will tell me that is why the butler did not look familiar."

"That is what I would tell you," said the patient man on the floor, who groped for the second pillow and put it over his face.

Eustace Wiltmore, Earl of Devere, sighed the sigh of a man bereft of all resource and fumbled among the bottles. He picked up the liquor-soaked letter and held it upside down, close to his face. "My father has sentenced me to wedlock, Nez, my dear. You could at least offer condolences."

The man on the floor took the pillow off his face and sat up. He stared owl-eyed at his friend. "There are two of you, Eustace," he concluded after a moment of reflection. "Don't you think that a trifle extravagant?"

Eustace scowled and fanned himself with the letter. "Would that there were, my boy. Then one of me could flee and none would be the wiser." He crumpled the letter and tossed it toward the fireplace, which had winked out hours before.

A bird began to warble outside the window. The Duke of Knaresborough winced and put his hand to his temple. He pressed hard until there was only one Eustace Wiltmore. "Eustace, are you under the hatches again?" he asked.

"As always, Nez, as always," replied the other man, his face mournful. "Have you ever known me when I was not?"

Nez closed his eyes again. "Tell me something. You're not already promised to another, are you?"

Eustace shuddered elaborately. "Good Lord, man, you know I have made it my life's ambition to avoid parson's mousetrap."

"Ah, but Eustace, that is your solution," said the duke, picking his words carefully. "Marry this wealthy woman so long promised in your family, and you'll never have pockets to let again. You don't have to like it; you merely have to do it."

The only sound for several moments was Eustace filling another glass and gulping down its contents. "And now I suppose you will tell me this is rather like Hougoumont or Quatre Bras," he accused.

"I suppose I will, Eustace," the duke agreed. "We none of us had much fun that day, but we did the thing. You need merely to plan your campaign as carefully as Wellington and bring this event to pass."

Eustace was silent again, and it was the same stubborn silence that the Duke of Knaresborough remembered from their shared childhood. He opened his eyes and spent several minutes in close observation of his friend.

Eustace Wiltmore, he of the mournful eye, observed back. "Oh, think of something," he pleaded.

But the duke was busy, taking in Eustace's pallor, studded

here and there with wispy beard. He noted the way Wiltmore's long nose meandered down in the general direction of his too-short upper lip. Eustace's whole face seemed to droop in folds toward his neck with all the grace of a basset hound.

"I think we are getting old, Eustace," the duke concluded.

Eustace groaned. "That is the best you can do?" he cried.

The duke stared back stupidly. "Well, yes, I rather think it is," he replied. "I'm as mizzled as you are, dear boy, and who ever had a good idea at a moment like this?"

"It's a thought," agreed Eustace with reluctance, and turned his attention to the window, which was gradually turning from black to gray. He staggered to his feet and, opening the window, perched himself on the sill. "You are forcing me to think, aren't you, Nez? I call that a rascally thing."

Nez sat up. "I had no idea you were so serious," he said. "This may be the first time since Cambridge that you have been forced to think."

The wounded look that Eustace bestowed on him would have made Nez laugh out loud, except that his head was beginning to throb.

"I told you these were desperate times," Eustace said.

The duke pulled himself upright to the table again and searched about among the bottles and remains of last night's dinner, which had congealed on the plates. He pawed this way and that among the ruins of beef scraps and fish bones until Eustace was drawn from the window to stand over him.

"Whatever are you doing, Nez, rummaging about like a hog in a midden?" the earl asked crossly.

"You said these were desperate times," Nez explained. "I require chocolate."

Eustace let out a sigh that bordered between exasperation and defeat. "Can you never be serious?" he complained.

"No," said the duke. He found a lump of chocolate among the thickened beef juices and helped himself. He rolled the chocolate around in his mouth like a connoisseur of fine wine, swallowed, and gently subsided back onto his pillow.

Eustace made a face. "How you can eat chocolate at a time like this?"

When the duke made no reply, Eustace sat down heavily in his chair. "I am desperate, man. I will run away."

"Don't do it," the duke said from his soft spot on the floor. "How can you uphold the honor of our sex if you are dodging and running from what is obviously the fate of every man?"

Eustace was silent. He lowered himself to the floor and looked his good friend in the eye. "Well then, Nez, I require your help."

The duke opened one eye, suspicion written all over his face. "I still recall our last combined effort. Eustace, doesn't it bother you to know that there is one whole shire in the country where we daren't ever show our faces again?"

"No," Eustace said serenely. "Dorset always was a bore." He prodded his friend. "Seriously, Nez, I think I just had a remarkable idea."

"I don't want to know it," declared the duke as he pillowed his head more resolutely against his arm.

"Oh, yes, you do," Eustace insisted. "You told me only yesterday that you were bored and tired of the prize fillies on the marriage mart that your sister and mum keep trotting around the paddock."

"Umm, so I did."

Eustace Wiltmore was just warming to his subject. He pressed his fingers tight against his skull. "Suppose . . . now just suppose, Nez, and don't look at me like that! Suppose you were to go to . . . Oh, where the devil . . ." He crawled to the fireplace, retrieved the crumpled paper, and spread it on the hearth, smoothing out the wrinkles. "Ah, here it is. To Holyoke Green in—where the deuce—in Kent. Pretend you're a salesman of some sort—it doesn't matter—a regular London merchant."

The duke made a rude noise and Eustace sighed.

"I am continually amazed that you are tolerated in the best circles, Nez," Eustace scolded.

"I don't do that in the best circles," his friend replied. "Been tempted, though."

"Well, never mind. You have an accident in your carriage in front of the house, and they have to take you in, my boy. You don't really have an accident, of course, but you pretend to."

"Thank you," the duke said.

"After you have looked over the girl of my father's dreams, you carry a report to me in Brighton, where I will be enjoying a repairing lease. If the report is too grim, I will pack my bags and head for the Continent. I hear one can live there cheaply on bread and cheese. If the affair seems promising, I will go down in person." Eustace gulped audibly and dabbed at his brow. "I may have to do my family duty yet, but you would ease the way considerably."

"A London merchant? You're daft."

"Not at all," Eustace argued. "Merely drunk. I will be sober in the morning, and it will still be a good idea. Consider its merits."

The duke made another rude noise.

Eustace sighed again.

"You've left something out, Eustace," the duke said.

"What?" snapped Eustace.

"Why should I do this for you? Give me a good reason to do you this—or any—favor."

Eustace sighed again, thought a moment, and pulled out his trump card. "I will remind you of the sow in the headmaster's bed, Nez, and leave your conscience to do the rest."

The duke opened his eyes and raised his brows. "That was breathtaking recovery indeed, Eustace," he agreed. "You did prevent my rustication by taking the rap for that one. I suppose I owe you something."

"You do, my dear, and I have been waiting these five years to collect," Eustace said, his words slurred, but possessed of a certain virtuous tenor that not even a mizzled duke could mistake. "I will merely pause now and allow you to contemplate the virtues of duty and honor to one's friends."

He paused. The duke began to snore. Eustace observed in silence, steeling himself for the ordeal of rising, which he accomplished slowly and in stages. He crossed the room at angles and tugged on the bellpull. When the butler came, he requested his carriage and took one last look at his friend.

The duke slumbered under the table, the pillow on his face again. Eustace waved to his dear Benedict Nesbitt. "Ta, ta, friend," he said softly as he allowed the butler to guide his arms into his coat. "Better that we not meet again for a little while."

Nez opened his eyes, hours later, to total darkness and a great weight pressing on his face. I have died, he thought, and it was not an unpleasant idea.

He felt curiously detached from his body. After a moment's serious thought, he concluded that he could probably not even move a finger, so he did not try. His head throbbed with a life of its own, as if a small animal had climbed inside and was running about from ear to ear, throwing itself against his skull, seeking a way out.

He concluded that he was not dead. Death would have felt better. He had seen enough of dead men on battlefields and worse, in hospitals, and had noted the looks of resignation and the gentle relaxation of the facial muscles to tell him that death was preferable to his present state.

If he were truly alive, there was the matter of darkness. He opened his eyes wider, and it was still dark, which jolted him considerably. I have finally drunk myself into blindness, he thought as he felt cautiously for his face—and then sighed with relief. He took the pillow off his face and blinked his eyes against the exuberant excess of a June morning.

When his eyes grew accustomed to the brightness of the sunlight that streamed in the open window, Nez looked at the underside of his table. I have spent the night under the table in my dining room, he thought, and I am sure I was not alone.

Nez crawled out from under the table and looked around. A wine bottle rested on its side, dispensing its contents a drip at a time. He hauled himself into a chair, surveying the ruins of last night's meal, and sank back to the floor again, nauseated by the sight of drying bones and hard potatoes.

The sight of the open window disturbed him. He had a vague memory of Eustace Wiltmore perched there last night, teetering about on the sill as he rambled on about . . . what? Nez shook his head slowly. He crawled to the window and raised himself up enough to look out. There were no remains of Eustace littering the flower beds, so obviously his friend had not hurled himself to the ground.

But there was something else, something Nez could not recall. He took several gulps of the clean air and felt better. His second attempt to sit in a chair was more successful. Gingerly he propped his leg on a footstool and wondered what it was he had promised Eustace Wiltmore last night when he was three sheets to the wind.

Nothing came to him. He looked down at himself in disgust. "Oh, Lord," he said out loud. "Why do I do this?"

No one answered. The only sound was the ticking of the clock, a sound that crashed about in his brain and kept time with the little animal in there that was still hurling itself about.

His neckcloth was already draped over the bust of an ancestor, so he unbuttoned his shirt, eased himself out of it, and sat there bare-chested, his eyes drooping. The little breeze from the window was cool and felt good, even though he shivered. He moved to another chair in the direct sunlight and sighed. June. June in England.

Someone banged on the door, pounding so loud and long that the hinges shook and the door bulged. Nez put his hand to his head. No, the door did not move. It was someone barely tapping. The animal inside his head stopped to pant and listen for a moment, then whirled around again.

Luster poked his head in. "Sir?" he asked. "My lord?"

"Get my dressing gown."

The butler returned in a moment with the dressing gown, all tapestry and frogs and much too busy for a man scarcely able to comprehend primary colors. Nez closed his eyes against its design and allowed Luster to help him into sleeves that seemed too difficult to maneuver alone.

"What . . . what day is it, Luster?" he asked finally.

The butler permitted himself a smile. "It is the fifteenth, my lord."

"The year?"

The smile broadened and then disappeared as Nez frowned back. "1816, my lord."

The duke managed a slight twitch of his lips. "I know that, Luster," he said. "I was merely testing you."

The butler coughed and held out a cup.

The duke sighed and looked away. "No, Luster. I think I will never drink again."

The butler would not withdraw the offensive cup. "Please, your grace, try it," he urged. "You'll feel much more the thing."

"Do you promise?" the duke asked, eyeing the cup with vast disfavor.

"I do," said the butler. He coughed. " 'Twas my grand-father's own remedy for the Duke of Marlborough."

"Very well, then, in memory of the great duke."

Benedict sipped at the brown brew, wishing that it did not look so awful. He closed his eyes and huddled down into his dressing gown, wishing to pull it over him like the shell of a turtle and retreat from all human contact, particularly the brightness of this June morning.

He took another sip this time, less cautious, and noted that the animal in his brain was slowing down. In another moment, it was sleeping again. He handed the cup back to Luster.

"If this were Waterloo, you would have received a battle-field commission just now, Luster."

The butler bowed and accepted the cup. "Your grace, there is a curious person waiting below who insists upon seeing you."

"Oh?"

The butler raised his eyebrows in unconscious imitation of his master. "I do think he is nothing but a tradesman, and he has the most unusual sample case with him."

"Come now, Luster, you know all salesman are shown the entrance belowstairs."

Luster came closer. "Of course, your grace, but this one might require your attention. Look you here, sir," he said, and held out a card.

The duke took it. "Why, this is Eustace's calling card," he said, turning it over. He peered closer at the words scrawled on the back. "You promised," he read out loud. He looked up at his butler. "I do not perfectly recall . . ."

Hardly had Nez uttered a larger understatement. The last thing he remembered from last night was snatching a garter from an opera dancer at Covent Garden, and even that memory was not as sharp as he would have liked. He reached into his pocket and pulled out the red satin garter.

Luster coughed again and looked away.

"Luster, you old prude," the duke said, the hint of smile in his voice. "Never tell me my father never surprised you with one of these."

"Your grace," the butler declared, his voice shocked. He rocked back on his heels. "But now that you mention it—"

"I rest my case." The duke stuck both hands in his pockets and stretched out his long legs. "This man below. Does he have a card?"

"Indeed, your grace. Here it is."

The duke accepted the card. "Ignatius L. Copley," he read. "Copley Chocolatier, by appointment to His Majesty King George III."

A warning bell began to toll in the back of his brain, right next to the sleeping animal that started to circle about inside his head again. What in God's name did I promise Eustace last night? he asked himself.

"Send him up, Luster. Let's get this over with."

The butler withdrew. Nez lurched to his feet and headed in the general direction of the sideboard, where he was vastly disappointed. Mother must have seen to the removal of the chamber pot that His Grace William Nesbitt, the Sixth Duke of Knaresborough, used to keep there, for situations such as this one. Considering the state of his much-abused kidneys, this interview with the candy man would be a short one. He would guarantee to purchase whatever it was he must have promised Eustace last night, and then beat a hasty retreat to the necessary.

The door opened and Luster showed in a gentleman as round as he was tall, who appeared to be all teeth and handshake. Weakly, the Duke of Knaresborough allowed himself to be greeted like a long-away cousin. He gestured to the chair next to him and looked at the salesman expectantly.

The man stared back just as expectantly. He cleared his throat finally when the duke appeared disposed to remain silent, and leaned forward. "My lord, do you not know why I am here?"

The duke shook his head, a motion he instantly regretted, and waited for his brains to fall out of his ears.

"Pray enlighten me," he said when they did not, and looked at the man's calling card again. "I am overfond of chocolate, to be sure, but I do not know that I require a salesman to look after my needs. A simple trip to the sweet shop will suffice."

"But, your grace, the Earl of Devere said you were needing my services." The little man strained forward, and the duke was compelled to lean forward too, his arms resting on his knees.

"Pray explain yourself, sir," the duke said.

The salesman blinked in surprise. "He told me you would understand perfectly. See here, he paid me for the use of my sample case." The little man winked. "I don't doubt but what the Earl of Devere was a bit to let at the time, but he said you would be borrowing the case for a couple of weeks for a trip to Kent."

Kent. The warning bells went off all at once in Benedict's overtaxed brain. The Duke of Knaresborough could only admit defeat and slump back in his chair. "He paid you money?" he asked. Good Godfrey, Eustace is serious, Nez thought as the salesman nodded so vigorously that his stomach shook.

"If I may venture, sir?" began the salesman.

The duke was stricken into silence by the monstrous perfidy of his nearest and dearest friend.

"He admitted to me that you had made him the happiest man on earth."

"I don't doubt that for a moment," agreed the duke. "Well, sir, let me see your wares."

The salesman opened the sample case, which had double rows of drawers with brass fittings. He opened one drawer and the duke leaned closer.

"Your grace, behold the prize of Copley Chocolatiers," said the man with a flourish. He paused for dramatic effect. "King Charles Revels!"

The duke stared at the gleaming lump of chocolate, which nestled on a bed of white satin. "God bless us," he breathed, his tone reverent. "Is that the one with a nougat center and just the hint of cherry?"

"The very same," Copley said proudly. He opened another drawer. "And for those what like nuts, here is St. Thomas' Temptation."

"I know that one well," murmured the duke. "Ate a whole box once on bivouac, and wasn't I sick?"

Copley clucked his tongue. "Moderation in all things, your grace," he said.

The salesman opened drawer after drawer, displaying his wares. "This would have been my last sales trip," he explained as he lovingly patted each chocolate. "I don't sell chocolate in summer, ordinarily. When Lord Wiltmore said he wanted to borrow my sample case, I was only too glad to oblige him." He permitted himself a giggle behind his hand. "Lord Wiltmore said something about a prank you are playing in Kent involving a lady?" He tittered again and then closed all the little drawers.

The duke groaned as the conversation of last night came back to him again. *I am supposed to disguise myself as a London merchant and travel to God-help-me Kent, where I will conveniently meet with an accident. I will survey the lady in question and give Eustace Wiltmore, formerly my best friend, a report.*

He directed his attention again to the little chocolate salesman. "Yes, Mr. Copley, he did mention a prank. Leave your case, and I will consider the issue."

Ignatius L. Copley got to his feet again. "To complete the disguise, you have merely to drop in on the occasional sweet shop and emporium that you pass in Kent. We are well known." He fumbled in his pocket and handed a handmade card to the duke. "Lord Wiltmore told me that he is having these cards made up for you, and you may stop at Adams in Fleet Street this very afternoon."

"I have never known Lord Wiltmore to act on any matter with such promptness," the duke murmured.

He looked at the proffered card, wavered for another instance between cowardice and duty, sighed, and took it. He looked closer and chuckled, despite his roaring headache. "Nesbitt Duke, merchant for Copley Chocolatiers, et cetera, et cetera," he read, and pressed his fingers to his temple. "So be it, Mr.

Copley. I suppose you have . . . Goodness, what are they called? An order sheet?''

"Certainly, sir. In the top drawer of the case. Fill them out three times, your grace.''

"And how would you recommend I transport myself to Kent?'' asked the duke, dreading the answer almost before he finished the question.

"A gig is best, sir,'' was the expected reply, and Mr. Copley did not fail him. "Of course, this is slow going to one of your equestrian fame, your grace, but it would never do for a London merchant to jaunt about in a high-perch phaeton.''

His own wit sent Ignatius L. Copley into a coughing fit. The duke did not trust himself to render aid and pat the man on the back. He went instead to the window, looked out, and then leapt back, his heart pounding in rhythm with his head.

His sister, Augusta, and his mother were stepping down from a barouche outside his front door, business written all across their faces.

He fingered the mock-up card. "Nesbitt Duke, is it?'' he mused out loud.

"Yes, your grace,'' said the merchant. "And don't you know that Lord Wiltmore was pleased with his own cleverness!''

"Scylla and Charybdis,'' muttered the duke as his sister rang the doorbell with that vigor typical of all Nesbitts.

"Beg your pardon, sir? Might that be a new chocolate I don't know of?''

"It should be,'' said the duke grimly. "Those cards are ready this afternoon, did you say?''

The bell rang again, more insistent this time. Likely Augusta would tell him about the latest matrimonial prize and insist that he accompany her and this paragon driving in the park, punting on some river or other, or dining al fresco amid the ants and wasps. There would be another unexceptionable face to admire, more small talk to suffer through, and another day wasted in the company of a female he couldn't care less about.

"I could pick up the cards on my way out of town, couldn't I?'' he murmured, more for himself than the merchant's benefit.

"Indubitably, your grace. Think what a diversion this will be, your grace!''

The door opened and Luster peered inside again. "Your grace, your sister, Lady Wogan, and the dowager await below."

The duke looked from the merchant to the butler, and back to the pasteboard card in his hand. He contemplated the ruin of his summer and the obligation of friendship and smiled at his butler.

"Luster, show this gentleman out. Tell my sister that you don't know how this comes about, but I have already left the house and have taken myself off to the . . . oh, the Lake District."

"They will never believe me," Luster declared. "You know perfectly well that Lady Wogan will come storming up here."

"Then I will hide myself in the dumbwaiter until she is gone," said the Duke of Knaresborough, who had held off a whole company of Imperial Guards with only ten survivors of his brigade at Waterloo. "This is no time for heroics. Or hysterics. Stand back, Luster."

"Very well, your grace," said the butler as he opened the door to the dumbwaiter and tugged on the rope.

The duke winced as he ducked his pounding head through the little doorway. "A tighter fit since the last time I tried this ten years ago," he said. He looked back at his butler, who was controlling his expression through mighty effort and years of training. "And if you can locate a gig, Luster, do so at once, only do not trumpet it about."

"Very well, your grace," Luster replied as he ushered out the candy salesman and bowed himself from the room. "And should I procure a moleskin vest for you, perhaps?"

"You do and we part company, Luster. There are some lengths to which I will not go, not even for friendship!"

2

AS much as she loved her cousin, Elizabeth Ames knew that when the carriage door shut, when the last instructions were shouted out of the window, and when the frantically waving handkerchief disappeared in a cloud of dust, she would go inside, kick off her shoes, and succumb to the bliss of a cup of tea in the middle of the day.

Such dissipation was rare. Elizabeth rarely found the time for such luxury, but she knew she had earned it.

"Libby, you are absolutely not attending."

Elizabeth looked up from the sarcenet gown she was carefully wadding with tissue paper. "You are absolutely right," she agreed, and flashed her sunny smile at her cousin, who was struggling with the strap of the portmanteau. "Lydia dear, I remember all your instructions. I will water your plants, pet your cats, feed your canary, and revive any would-be suitors who droop on the doorstep." She leapt to her feet and kissed her cousin. "And that's the best you can expect of me."

Lydia hugged her cousin and gave the strap another half-hearted tug. "Oh, Libby, what a pickle this is."

She took exception to her cousin's grin, which went from animated to roguish. "Don't think for one minute that this is easy," Lydia said. She flopped down on her bed and stared at the ceiling, her hands folded across her ample chest in unconscious imitation of vaulted ancestors. "I will miss Reginald."

Lydia paused a moment, as if waiting for the tears to fall. When they did not, she sat up and watched her cousin, who continued to pack. "Libby, not that way! You're wrinkling my gown. Here, let me show you," Lydia explained, and took the offending item from her cousin, folding it inexpertly. "Like that."

"Yes, Lydia." Libby turned away so her cousin would not see that her smile had broadened. "As to Reginald, he will recover, and probably still be here in the fall when you return, my dear."

"I suppose you are right." Lydia sighed and threw herself down again, her hands behind her head. "Oh, Libby, just suppose I meet someone special in Brighton—it happens, you know. I have it on the best authority—and suppose Reginald shows up." She rolled her eyes. "Libby, there could be a duel. Imagine!"

"Yes, just imagine," Libby agreed. "Blood everywhere."

Lydia raised herself up on one elbow. "I don't believe that a more practical human was born than you."

"Likely not," Libby agreed as she closed the trunk and sat upon it. She clasped her hands together and regarded her cousin seriously. "But that is not the issue. You know, my dear, it could be that Eustace Wiltmore is the very one for you."

Lydia groaned. "Eustace! What kind of romantical name is that? I would as lief marry Dr. Cook as someone named Eustace."

The cousins giggled together.

"It would never do, Lydia," said Libby. "Dr. Cook would probably be fumbling about for his glasses at the altar! No, I think Eustace—whatever he is like—would have a bit more address than our good doctor."

Libby went to the dressing table and began to sort through the jumble, throwing brushes and combs into a small bag. "Lydia, do you really think Eustace is coming here this summer? You have not even had your come out yet."

"I told you! Marcia Ravens wrote me from London that she

overheard him at a party talking to that man, Duke something or other. Oh, you remember. The Waterloo hero.'' Lydia sighed. ''I suppose I will have to meet Eustace some day, but not before my come out this winter. Surely Papa will understand.''

Libby sniffed at Lydia's favorite rose scent and dabbed a drop behind her ear. ''Your papa will wonder why you have come to Brighton. You know he will.''

Lydia made a face. ''He will not! Papa is more absentminded than the king in his best moments.'' She giggled. ''He will wonder at the expense, as though he hadn't more juice than a sirloin roast. No, the king is a regular paragon, compared to Papa, I declare.''

Both girls paused in silence for dear old mad George. Libby put her arm about her cousin. ''Lydia, I do thank you for insisting that Mama go with you. It was a stroke of genius, and my uncle will be so pleased.''

Lydia returned the hug and then whirled about. ''Button me, there's a dear. You know my papa requires his creature comforts, and Aunt Ames' occasional jam tart.''

''Which is probably why he got gout in the first place,'' teased Libby, her eyes dancing. ''Hold still! How can I do this?'' She finished the row of buttons and patted her cousin on the back. ''Goodness knows how long it has been since Mama went on holiday.''

''And what better place than Brighton in June?'' Lydia declared. She went to the dressing table and tossed the last brush in her traveling case. ''I only wish you were coming too, dear Elizabeth.''

Libby shook her head. ''Who would watch over Joseph?''

''Who, indeed?'' asked Lydia. She made a face. ''At least with Papa gone, Dr. Cook will not come bumbling around.''

''You are entirely unfair,'' Libby protested, and then laughed. ''But I never did know anyone else trip over a pattern in the carpet. He will be safer with Uncle away.''

''I am only sorry that Father foisted Aunt Crabtree on you.''

''I must have a chaperone, and you know it, Lydia,'' Libby replied. ''I am sure she cannot be all that bad.''

Lydia's lips straightened into an uncustomary thin line. ''You never seem to have any trouble doing all that is proper, so I doubt she will get your back up. I would rather be chaperoned by Lucrezia Borgia, or . . . or . . .'' Lydia groped about for another bad example, but her learning was faulty and she could think of none. "Well, any of those dreadful women. At least they would be interesting. Aunt Crabtree will bore you to death, and make you play cards.''

"Goose! I can deal with Aunt Crabtree.''

Lydia rang for the footman, who loaded the trunk on his back and took the portmanteau in hand. She picked up her traveling case and then set it down decisively. "I still think you should come, too. You would meet someone who would fall amazingly in love with you and—''

"Run for the hills when he discovered my pockets were entirely to let, you silly goose,'' chided Libby, who picked up the bag and handed it back to her cousin.

But Lydia folded her arms, intent upon this new tack. "You're the goose, Libby. Some wealthy man need only look at your face and fall in love and he will forget there is no fortune.''

"Men are more practical,'' Libby assured her cousin, who scowled, picked up the traveling case, and then took one last survey of her room.

"I suppose you are right,'' she said finally, her eyes roving over the bedspread and draperies. "Libby, be a dear while I am gone and have the draperies cleaned. And don't trust it to the laundress. Do it yourself. I want the thing done right.''

"Very well, Lydia, very well,'' Libby said as she pushed her cousin out the door.

Mama was sitting on the bottom step, weeping. Libby smiled and sat down beside her beautiful parent, putting her arm around her mother's slight shoulders and drawing her close. "Mama! We will be fine here.''

Mama only buried her nose deeper into her handkerchief. "I have never left you and Joseph alone for such a time. Only think what your dear papa would think, if only he knew.''

Libby handed her mama a dry handkerchief. "Papa would tease you and wonder why in blue blazes you hadn't done it sooner!''

"Don't be so vulgar, Libby,'' Mama scolded. She blew her

nose and dabbed at her eyes. "I suppose you are right, my dear. You're certain you can manage?"

Libby hugged her mother. "What is there to manage? The servants—most of them—will be on holiday, now that Uncle and Lydia are away. You will be maintaining Uncle, not me. The groom here will see to Uncle's horses." She gave her mother another squeeze. "And I will finally have time to paint."

Mrs. Ames smiled at her daughter and touched her cheek. "I heard what Lydia said upstairs, pet. I wish you could come along and meet someone special." She sighed. "I wish it were possible."

"Maybe someday," Libby said as she tugged her mother to her feet, straightened her bonnet, and retied the bow just under her ear. "There now! You look smashing, my dear!"

Mama pokered up. "I wish you would not use stable slang." She frowned. "Which reminds me. I will depend entirely upon you to keep Joseph and Squire Cook away from each other." Mama stared at her gloved hands. "How that gloomy man could sire someone like Dr. Cook I cannot fathom!" She colored. "Dear me, that was indelicate."

Libby laughed. "But how true. I will keep them far away from each other, depend upon it. I will remind Joseph as many times as it takes that Uncle's trout streams are entirely accessible—and that the fish will swim in our direction, too, if given the opportunity."

Mrs. Ames nodded. "Very good, Libby." She hesitated. "And—"

"—and I will check on Joseph at all odd hours of the day, Mama, you know I will."

"I know you will." Mrs. Ames patted her daughter's arm. "But I worry anyway."

"Don't," Libby said.

Breakfast was a dismal, hurried-up affair, with Mama sniffing in her napkin and Lydia eager to be on the road. Libby abandoned her plate finally and walked the delicate line of curbing Lydia's spirits and raising Mama's. By the time the last drop of tea had been drained, Libby's head was beginning to ache.

With nothing but relief, she nodded when Candlow announced the arrival of the carriage at the front door. Trying not to sound overeager, Libby helped Mama inside the carriage, nodding as her mother told her again what to do with the melons in the succession house, how to make sure the butcher did not cheat her, and to look out for gypsies in the field beyond the hop gardens.

"Mind, we want them in late July when the hops are ready for picking, but not before, Libby. Make sure they understand," Mama said. She sighed and made to open the door. "Perhaps I should stay."

"Mama," Libby exclaimed. "I wish you would not worry. After all, I am twenty."

Mama regarded the upturned face through the carriage window and folded her hands in her lap. "I suppose you are."

"Mama!"

Mrs. Ames rose up again in her seat, a smile at odds with the tears in her eyes. "Joseph," she said.

Joseph Ames hurried from the stable. Libby watched his progress, her eyes alive with amusement. He was wet again, his brown hair curlier than usual from the river. She held out her hand to him and he took it.

"Joseph," she said in her sternest voice, "have you been swimming again?"

He mimicked her perfectly, down to the crease between her eyes, and then tucked her arm close to his body. "Libby, I remembered this time, I remembered! I took off my clothes first this time."

Libby smiled up at her younger brother and touched his dry sleeve. "So you did, Joseph. I am proud of you."

He looked at her earnestly. "You don't think I'm foolish?"

"I never think you are foolish, Joseph," she said quietly.

His expression changed. There was shame in his eyes now as he ducked his head. Libby cringed to see his face fall, and tightened her grip on his arm without knowing it.

"The lads down the road . . . I heard them say I was a moonling as I walked by." He shook his head. "I don't understand how they can be that way. Didn't I help their papa when his sheep had the staggers?"

"You did, Joseph," Lydia agreed. She loosened her grip on her brother and pulled him toward the carriage. "Say good-bye to Mama, my dear," she directed.

Joseph stood on tiptoe and kissed his mother, who was leaning out of the carriage window and sobbing in good earnest now. He looked at her tearstained face in surprise. "Mama, you're not going to America." When she made no reply, except to shake her head helplessly, he kissed her again. "Mama, I will be good," he said simply, and then stepped back as the coachman chirruped to the horses and the carriage set its ponderous course toward Brighton.

Lydia leaned out of the other window and waved to her cousins. "Libby! Tell Reginald I will return!"

Libby stood in the drive, her arms upraised. "And you tell Uncle I hope his gout is better."

"Good-bye, my dears," called Mrs. Ames as the carriage picked up speed and lumbered through the gates.

Brother and sister stood shoulder to shoulder until the carriage was a cloud of dust.

"I like to say good-bye to people," Joseph said at last as they turned, arm in arm, toward the house again.

Libby stopped. "Whatever do you mean, Joseph?" she asked, a twinkle of good humor in her eyes.

Joseph tugged at his ear and engaged himself in thought for some moments. Libby knew better than to interrupt him. He let go of his ear finally. "Libby, when I say good-bye to someone, that means I am staying behind." He looked around him and took a deep breath. "And I like it here."

Libby gazed at her brother. How tall you have grown, Joseph, she thought as she admired his handsome face. No one would know, except for the slight blankness in his eyes, that he "wasna" entirely home there," as Tunley the groom put it. She hugged him.

"I know what you mean," she said.

"And do you know something else?" he asked. He leaned closer and whispered. "I think Lydia is the moonling. Why would anyone be in such a pelter to leave this place?"

Libby burst into laughter. "I couldn't agree with you more. Why, indeed?" She stood on tiptoe to smooth down Joseph's hair, where it stuck up in the back, still damp from his bathe in the river. Her voice became conspiratorial. "Joseph, she is running away."

He laughed. "And taking Mama with her? I call that odd."

He hugged her, pecked her on the cheek, and headed toward the stable, whistling as he meandered along.

"Odd, indeed," Libby said to his retreating back. With a slight smile on her face, she turned toward the sun and took a deep breath, too.

All of Kent was in bloom. She could not remember a June that was more beautiful than this one. The rains of spring had come in timely fashion, and had exited promptly, yielding to the aching loveliness of fields and fields of daffodils and jonquils, dancing about on March winds. The hawthorn and apple blossoms of May had been gracefully supplanted by clover in bloom, and lilies of the valley and wild violets, half-hidden here and there.

I could never leave this place, she thought as she shaded her eyes with her hand and strained for one last glimpse of the carriage. And yet . . .

Brighton. She had been there once before, during one of her father's rare leaves from Spain. She remembered the crowds that frightened her as much as they intrigued her: the soldiers in their regimentals strolling about with their ladies on the Promenade; the painter who sketched her portrait as she sat, and then did another one because he declared to her proud papa that she was too beautiful for one drawing only. She wrinkled her nose and remembered the smell of the pilings when the tide was out, and the sharp fragrance of pomaded gentlemen in crowded Assembly Rooms. And the ladies, oh, the ladies, with their more delicate scents, and rustling silks, and sidelong glances.

"I would like to be someone's lady," she whispered, and then looked about to make sure that no one had overheard the practical Elizabeth Ames talking to herself.

The goose girl was busy organizing her charges down at the pond; the groom had followed Joseph back into the stables. The air was so quiet that she thought she could hear the bees in the orchard, busy about their work.

"But mostly, I want some peace and quiet."

And now the house was empty. Without Mama there to admonish, she could wear her old, comfortable dresses, arrange her hair only if she chose to, and maybe even walk barefooted into the orchard with her box of paints, canvas, and easel tucked under her arm.

She had never been a person who needed crowds about her, or admiration. Libby had learned at an uncomfortably early age that she was a beauty, and there was nothing she could do about the stares and second glances that came her way on the most mundane walk into Holyoke, or a mere look-in at the lending library. It embarrassed her to be blatantly admired for something she had no control over. It struck her as strange that all her defects of character—so obvious to her—could be so generously overlooked in the worship of beauty.

I would like to spend this summer with myself, she thought as she watched the goose girl scold her flock. I need to think about where I am going. She smiled to herself. Papa would have understood. He had been a handsome man who turned heads, and he took as little thought of it as she. His one passion had been the army, and he had soldiered until the day he died.

"But what is there for me?" Libby asked out loud. It was a question that had begun to nag her in recent weeks, particularly as she celebrated her twentieth birthday with no prospects in sight.

She had known all her life there would be no prospects for her, but the issue hadn't mattered until Papa, her dear Papa so impervious to bullets, was struck down by camp fever as Wellington prepared to march from Toulouse to Paris.

They had all assumed she would marry into the army, but Papa's death sent them back across the Channel to a country they scarcely remembered. True, there were offers among the military before they left Toulouse, but the offers were quietly withdrawn when Mama informed the officers that there was no dowry.

"Officers do need to marry well," Mama had said as she closed the door on the last captain of the regiment. "Heaven knows those uniforms are expensive, child."

And so they came home to Kent. It was Papa's home, a place

he was unwelcome as long as he lived and his own papa still breathed. Foolish Papa, with no more sense than to follow his heart and marry a tobacconist's daughter. Grandfather Ames had never forgiven him. Not only was there no provision for Major Ames' wife and orphans in the will, but Uncle Ames was forbidden by that same will to give them any, under threat of losing his own inheritance.

If Uncle Ames was unable to aid them directly, there was nothing in the will that said he could not provide a roof, which he did, and promptly, too.

"Mind, I never could fathom Father's distempered freaks about your eligibility," he had assured Libby's mother when they arrived at Holyoke Green. "And stap me if I'll let my little brother's near and dear starve while there's breath in this body."

Kent it was, then, with Mama soon settling in as housekeeper and Joseph kept busy about the stables. Over Uncle Ames' protests, Libby gravitated to the kitchen, which suited her right down the ground. Uncle Ames had not surrendered willingly. He shook his head the first time he saw her, apron about her waist, kneading bread in the kitchen. "Don't know why we can't find you a husband somewhere," he had muttered to himself, and he had snapped off a piece of dough to tuck in his cheek. "Don't know what's wrong with young men these days." He was still grousing to himself as he climbed the steps, careful to favor his gouty heel.

She had rubbed along happily enough in Kent for the past two years, enjoying her Uncle's obvious affection, and Lydia's gentle tyranny, and doubly pleased with the way Mama took to managing a normal household that didn't have to pack up and move with the army.

The greatest pleasure had been watching Joseph, who had gone from a tongue-tied, bewildered boy who dreaded the stares and pity of others, to a more assured young man, aware of his obvious limitations, but serene in the knowledge that there was a home for him always at Holyoke Green.

Libby stood another moment in reflection, grateful for her good fortune, wondering about her future. Now would be a good time to plan some strategy for the rest of her life. She would do that while everyone else was in Brighton.

She squared her shoulders and walked up the front steps, pausing for one look up at Lydia's bedroom windows. "And I have draperies to clean," she said, and then smiled. "Lydia, you *are* a goose. Joseph is right!"

Her good humor regained, she grabbed up a corner of her apron and polished the brass door knocker. "Someone will have to drop himself upon my doorstep," she said, "and it will be true love."

Libby giggled and put her hand to her mouth. It would likely be Dr. Cook, looking about in his squinty-eyed fashion for his favorite patient. How disappointed he will be when I tell him that Uncle has been in Brighton this past week.

It was prophecy. No sooner had she reentered the house and opened Mama's book of household accounts than Candlow appeared at the book-room door.

"Miss Elizabeth, it is Dr. Cook," he said, and his eyes twinkled in spite of himself.

Libby could appreciate his humor. It was difficult for the old retainer to be serious about a person, even a doctor, who had been rescued from trees as a child and spanked on more than one occasion for disturbing the Ames beehives.

"Show him in, by all means, Candlow," Libby said. She patted her hair and closed the account book.

Dr. Cook filled the doorway, as he likely filled every threshold he had ever crossed. As he stood there a moment, the width of his shoulders an impressive sight, Libby couldn't help but remember her first glimpse of Anthony Cook after her years in Spain. Mama had stared, goggled-eyed, and whispered to her, "Never mind who is it: what is it?"

No one could have called Dr. Cook fat. He was solid, well-built and massive, rather like a ship, thought Libby as she watched him exchange some pleasantry with Candlow in the doorway. He was no flashy man-o'-war or yacht, not by any reach of the imagination. Anthony Cook reminded Libby of a clinker-built coal barge, the kind of sturdy vessel that plied the waters from port to port, year in, year out, in all weathers—totally reliable, utterly dependable.

He was dark like many Kentsmen, with curly hair that never

seemed to be in place, and black eyes remarkably nearsighted. He fumbled with his glasses, settling them more firmly on the end of his nose, as Libby came around the end of the desk and held out her hand to him.

Dr. Cook came forward in a rush, as he did everything, narrowly avoiding a collision with a chair that seemed to reach out to trip him.

"Beg pardon," he said, as though it were animate.

Libby looked away and mentally shook herself. "Can I get you some refreshment, Doctor?" she asked when the danger was averted and he was safely into the room and standing before her.

He shook his head, and the glasses slid down farther, dangling for a moment on the end of his rather indeterminate nose, and fell to the carpet.

"Oh, blast," he said, and dropped to his knees and began patting the carpet.

Libby knelt beside him. He turned suddenly in surprise and they cracked heads. Libby sat back and felt her forehead, hoping that she would not have to explain a bump to Candlow, and at the same time resisting a fierce urge to go off into great gusts of merriment, which would only cause the good doctor further agonies of embarrassment.

When she had command of herself, she got to her feet again and left the search to the doctor. After getting down on all fours and peering under the desk, Dr. Cook found his glasses and hastily replaced them upon his nose.

"Dear me," he uttered, out of breath, as though he had been running. He squinted at her and then touched her forehead in such a professional manner that she did not think to draw away, even though he stood too close and the room seemed to shrink about them. "I trust that will not create a swelling, Miss Ames," he managed finally, when his fingers ceased probing.

"No," she said doubtfully. "I think it will not."

He stood in flustered silence, staring at her, his black eyes magnified by his glasses, the sweat beading on his forehead, even though it was cool for June. As the desperation left his eyes, it was replaced by an expression that mystified her.

To her growing discomfort, he seemed content to stand and gaze upon her. Libby cleared her throat, and the small sound in the quiet room recalled Dr. Cook to his errand.

"I have some powders somewhere here for your uncle," he explained, slapping his pockets until an acrid cloud of white powder heralded the location of the medicine.

Libby coughed and stepped back as the powder billowed out and enveloped her. She threw open the window and leaned her head out, wondering, as her eyes began to fill with tears, if she could survive the doctor's visit this morning. I should have gone to Brighton, she thought. I would be safer.

"My dear," exclaimed Dr. Cook as he patted her back. He grabbed up the account book on the desk and began to fan her with it as loose pages tucked inside scattered about the room. "Oh, blast!"

Libby drew her head in, wiped her eyes, and looked about the room that had been so tidy only moments before. White dust settled on the plants in the window, and the canary began to chitter and scold.

"I am sorry, Miss Ames," Dr. Cook said. He pulled the offending packet out and laid it carefully upon the desk. "Is Sir William about this morning? I have only a few instructions to accompany this medication," he said, his face a flame of red and his eyes looking everywhere but at her.

"I am sorry, Dr. Cook, but he is not here," she said. "He has gone to Brighton this week and more."

"Brighton?" repeated the doctor.

Libby nodded and opened a window by the canary cage. "I will be happy to forward the powders to Uncle, if you think it advisable."

He nodded. "Tell him he is to take a teaspoon in water every three hours." He smiled then as he brushed the powder off his sleeve. It was a self-deprecating smile that took the embarrassment from his eyes. "Mind you tell him he is to drink, in addition, two glasses of water every hour, without fail." His smile broadened and Libby smiled back. "Don't tell him this, but I suspect that the water will do more good than the powders."

Libby laughed out loud. "Then why do you prescribe your powders, Dr. Cook?"

He leaned closer to her in a moment of rare abandon. "Because, Miss Ames, it is expected of physicians." He winked and then blushed. "Do emphasize the water when you write to him."

"I shall." She twinkled her eyes at the doctor, who blushed again and ran his finger around the inside of his collar. "Now, tell me truly, sir, if the waters were nasty, like the water at Bath, would that be even more efficacious, at least, in the eyes of the patient?"

"Indubitably," he agreed, and dabbed at his sweating forehead. "And now you understand doctors. The nastier the brew, the better the cure, eh?" He sighed and then his good humor restored itself. "I suppose now that, as a doctor, I have no secrets from you."

Libby smiled. "None, sir. I am on to you, and all doctors. Water it will be, and so I will tell my uncle."

There was nothing more to say, but Dr. Cook made no move to leave. Libby cleared her throat again, but it had no effect this time. Anthony Cook seemed content to regard her over the top of his spectacles, which were rapidly in danger of falling off again.

As the glasses slid down his nose, he grabbed at them and planted them firmly again. "Well, well, Miss Ames. No one is sick here?" he asked, and the hopeful note in his voice brought the twinkle into her eyes again.

"We're all quite well, doctor," she said.

"You're sure?" he asked.

"Positive." Libby permitted herself a small chuckle. "Mama always did say I had the constitution of a cart horse."

"So I have observed." If he sounded disappointed, Libby chose to overlook it.

Dr. Cook bowed, pushing his spectacles up again, and went to the door, careful this time to circle the offending chair that had nearly cost him grief on his entry into the room. Instead, he backed into the coat tree, which toppled to the floor, striking the bird cage and setting its inmate fluttering and scolding.

Libby grabbed the coat tree and righted it, grateful that Lydia was gone and not standing by, dissolved into a fit of the giggles.

A lesser man would have fled the scene. Anthony Cook threw up his hands—narrowly missing a lamp by the door—and shook his head. "Bull in a china shop, eh?" he asked her, and then smiled. "The wonder of it, ma'am, is that I do not frighten babies."

"I don't think you could frighten anyone," Libby said honestly, and was amazed how quickly the doctor turned red. "It is merely an observation," she added hastily, and felt her own face grow warm. What is the matter? she thought. Being around Dr. Cook seems to rub off in a most disconcerting manner.

She walked with him into the hallway, grateful that there were no buckets or mops or chairs out of place to offer the doctor any danger.

"You did not wish to go to Brighton?" he asked finally as they approached the open door.

She shook her head. "No, I did not. Someone must keep an eye on Joseph, and it has been so many years since Mama has been anywhere."

"You are all kindness," he said.

Libby stole a sidelong look at Anthony Cook. The words from anyone else would have seemed merely a glib utterance, soon forgotten. When Dr. Cook said them, they seemed to mean something. I wonder why he is not married yet, she thought.

3

"WHY am I doing this?" the Duke of Knaresborough asked himself again as he clucked to the modest horse that pulled his gig sedately across Kent.

Augusta had been too quick for him in the dining room. When Luster had announced to his sister that the duke was already on his way to the Lake District, she had uttered an oath that made Benedict blush in the dark of the dumbwaiter, and marched right to his hiding place, flinging the door open. She had stared at him with narrowed eyes, hands on her hips, lips pressed tight together, until he started to sweat.

"Benedict Nesbitt, it is high time you grew up and did your duty by your family," she said to him finally, biting off each word.

Meekly he pulled himself from the dumbwaiter. Augusta jabbed her thumb in the direction of a chair and he sat down, wishing that his head wasn't five times larger than the room and Augusta's voice less debilitating in his weakened state.

He listened with half an ear as she railed on about "choicest morsels on the marriage mart," and "devoting my good time to you," but took exception when she started in on his ancestors and how they must be reeling about in the family vault.

"Now really, Gussie," he had attempted, but she cut him off with a fierce stare.

"Yes, really! Every one of them married and set up their

nurseries." She flung her arms about. "And here you are, rising
thirty, and all you can think about is drinking your next bottle.
You didn't used to be this way."

He sat there and took it all, knowing that she would never
understand how comforting were the moments when the liquor
was inside him and his surroundings were a pleasant blur. He
wasn't cold then, that peculiar battlefield cold that he couldn't
forget. He couldn't hear anything then, when he was full of
Scotch or gin—it didn't matter. There were no sudden sounds,
no stirrings and rustling, none of his dying men, ghosts a year
now, pleading for help that he couldn't render. Augusta would
never understand the way wine allowed the responsibility to slip
from his shoulders and that he could forget, if only for a
moment, the weight of his years and the years stretching ahead.

Augusta would never understand, so he made no attempt to
tell her. He wanted her to go away. If she would only leave,
he could straighten himself around and then begin drinking
again, and he would soon forget that she had ever been
there.

But Augusta was not budging this time. He struggled to listen
to her. She droned on and on about Kensington Galleries and
Lady Fanny Hyslip until he put the two together and nodded.

The effect on Augusta was startling. Without a warning, she
grabbed him and kissed his cheek. "I knew you would not fail
me, brother," she said. "Two o'clock, then? Fanny and I will
be at the Titians."

He nodded and suffered his hand to be wrung. "You'll never
regret this, Nez," his sister was saying, and already he could
not remember what it was he would never regret.

He managed a small wave in her general direction as she left
the room as swiftly as she had entered it. He spent a moment
in muddled reflection, then sank into sleep again.

He woke hours later, wrenched from sleep by his butler,
whose face showed every sign of strain. It was the face of a
man who, in a matter of seconds, could be capable of giving
his notice.

The duke struggled into an upright position, marveling at how
his head throbbed. His throat was drier than a Spanish plain,
and he wanted a drink. He motioned toward the sideboard, but

Luster ignored him, going so far as to clutch the front of his dessing gown and haul him back into the chair.

"My lord, do you know what time it is?"

Nez shook his head and shuddered as his brains rolled from side to side. His eyes started to close again. Driven to desperation, Luster grabbed him by the shoulders.

"Your grace, you were promised to your sister and Lady Fanny Hyslip at two o'clock in the Kensington Galleries."

"Was I?" he asked, struggling to remember his sister's visit, which couldn't have happened above thirty minutes ago. "Ah, yes. I remember now. Well, what of it?"

Luster sank down in the chair next to his master and declared in a toneless voice, "Your grace, it is after three o'clock." He looked suddenly old. "I left instructions with the footman to make sure you were awake. He has failed me."

"Dear me," said the duke. To his credit, he felt a tiny ripple of fear running like fingers along his backbone. "I'll send flowers," he said.

"I rather think it has gone beyond flowers, your grace, particularly since this is not the first time this week you have failed Lady Wogan," Luster replied. Forgetting the dignity of his years and office, he leapt to his feet and scurried to the window. He peered around the edge of the draperies as if afraid of what he might see on the street.

"I have only just received a missive from your sister to inform you that she is coming directly over again." He paused and wiped a mustache of sweat from his upper lip. "And she is bringing your mother." He drew the word out and allowed it to soak into the duke's piffled brain. "The dowager," he added, wiped his hands like Pontius Pilate on Good Friday, and left the window.

"God's wounds," breathed the duke, "I am in the basket now, ain't I?"

"You are, sir," agreed the butler. Luster's right eye began to twitch ever so slightly.

The duke pulled himself to his feet. He looked at Luster and then crossed to the window himself and peered out. He stood there in silence for a long moment.

"We could be facing a crisis of monumental proportions,

Luster," he murmured as he let the drapery fall from nerveless fingers.

Luster nodded, stood as tall as he could, and delivered the final blow of the afternoon. "Your grace, you will face this crisis alone. The cook, housekeeper, your valet, and I have tendered our resignations. You will find them on the desk in your study."

Benedict Nesbitt stared at his old retainer. "Luster, you have been in the family since before I can remember."

Luster took a deep breath. "For the most part, your grace, I have enjoyed our association. Now we part company."

At this intelligence, the duke sank to the chair again and scratched his chest. "I could offer you more money," he ventured.

"You could, my lord. I would not take it."

"I could promise the cook one of those newfangled cooking ranges."

"You could, your grace. The outcome would not satisfy you, however."

The silence that followed stretched into minutes, until the duke sighed. "I know that look on your face, Luster." He spread his hands out on his knees. "What must I do to retain you and my entire household staff?" he asked at last. "What extortion must I surrender to?"

Luster coughed and looked own at his own hands, which shook only slightly. "You must go on that errand you promised to do this morning. If you are truly not here, we can probably rub through this knothole. Lady Wogan will storm and rail, and your mother will require an entire carafe of smelling salts, but we can pull it off. If you are not here," he added, underscoring each word with a wave of a finger.

The duke was silent for a moment, engaged in the almost visible effort of thinking. "I . . . I did promise Eustace soemthing, didn't I?" he asked. "It was something about a young woman, wasn't it?" He paused and frowned at his butler. "But what is this? You just said that you were quitting my service, and now you want to save my bacon. I don't precisely understand."

A slight smile flitted across the butler's impassive features.

"It is this way, your grace. Your father exacted a promise from me that I would look after you." He noted the duke's startled expression. "It surprised me too, your grace, but there it is."

"I wish I had been here when he died, Luster," murmured the duke. "God, how it chafed me to receive the news in Belgium, and then I could not leave." He sighed.

Luster rose to his feet again. "I will keep that promise to your father, my lord, but only if you are away from here within the quarter-hour."

He delivered the last sentence in a loud voice that made Nez wince and clutch at his temples. "Very well, Luster, I will do it." He managed a sickly smile. "Even though I have vowed not to exert myself ever again."

Luster took the duke by the arm. He pulled the duke gently to his feet. "I have managed to arrange for the loan of a gig." When the only response was an upraised eyebrow, the butler smiled beatifically. "A gig, your grace, yes indeed."

"I could never," declared the duke.

"You have promised your friend," the butler reminded. "And if you do not, we will quit your service. If you manage to rusticate a month or so in Kent—and don't roll your eyes at Kent, your grace—it might be sufficient to calm Lady Augusta. Your mother will have other thoughts to occupy her by then. Come, sir, and do your duty."

Luster helped his master toward the door. "Do you know, your grace, Cheedleep found several suits of clothing that might possibly be something a chocolate merchant would wear."

"Not in my closet he never did," declared the duke.

"Ah, but he did," insisted the butler. "In your very own closet. Come, your grace. I have already taken the liberty of packing a bag for you and have authorized a sufficient sum on your bank. It remains for you to pick up your business cards in Fleet Street."

"Luster, this is out of the question," snapped the duke, digging in his heels.

Luster did not blink in the face of obstinacy. "Then you, sir, must face the dowager and your sister alone." He lowered his eyes and his voice was soft. "We will pray for you, your grace, from the safety of the park across the street."

The duke spent a long moment in contemplation of his butler. Dash it all, he thought, Luster is too old to be flinging around his resignation. And who's fault is that? came the other voice from somewhere inside his skull.

"Who's fault, indeed?" he said out loud.

"Your grace?"

"Nothing, Luster." He spent another moment in thought. "I suppose you are adamant, Luster," he ventured finally.

"I am, your grace."

And so, as the clock struck four, Benedict Nesbitt, Seventh Duke of Knaresborough, found himself steering a gig through London traffic. He hunched himself low in the modest vehicle, acutely aware that he was shabby beyond his wildest imaginings. He cast his bloodshot eyes over the equally modest bag that rested near his feet, an artifact of Luster himself and further proof that the butler had no intention of bolting from the family home while his master was flinging himself about Kent.

Kent! Was there a place more unfashionable? For all he knew of Kent, the people still painted themselves blue and bayed at the moon. No one went to Kent, except to board a vessel for France, and that was only coming back into style again, now that Napoleon had taken up residence on St. Helena. He knew that grandmothers and maiden aunts were wont to pop 'round to Royal Turnbridge Wells, that genteel watering hole for the elegantly senile. Beyond that, Kent was a crater on the moon.

Benedict picked up his business cards in Fleet Street, suffering through an interview with the printer, who leered at him, laughed, and wondered aloud what kind of havey-cavey business the gent was attempting. The duke could only manage a weak smile, overpay the man, and beat a hasty retreat.

"Nesbitt Duke, agent for Copley Chocolatier," the cards read. He stuck them in his pocket, closed his eyes, and wished that it would all go away and that he would wake up in his own bed, with a bottle nearby.

When he opened his eyes, there was only the rumble of carts and tradesmen jostling him about on the crowded sidewalks. As he stood there, miserable in the clutch of reality, he heard a voice at his elbow.

"Major? Major Nesbitt?"

He whirled around, surprised, and stared down at a man crouched by the shop entrance. He had only one leg and a begging cup, but he was military from the proud set of his shoulders to the dignity of his voice. Nez knelt beside the man, and a slow smile made its way across his face.

"Yes, Private Yore, it is I."

The man hesitated a moment and then stuck out his hand. Nesbitt took it. "I didn't see you when I went in," Nez said, resting back on his haunches, heedless of the people who growled and swore and circled around him on the busy sidewalk.

The man set down the cup and tried to brush it under the edge of his cloak. "Sir, you had a preoccupied look on your face, sir." He grinned. "I don't think you'd have noticed Father Christmas, from the set of your glims, sir. Like I say, preoccupied. I seen that look before, your lordship, sir."

Benedict grinned back. "I daresay you have. We were both a bit 'preoccupied' about this time last year, if memory serves me."

" 'Deed we were, sir. Glad to see you've recovered, sir."

"Oh, I'm fine, Yore," he said quickly, and crossed his fingers behind his back.

The two men looked at each other. The ex-private lowered his eyes first, and the shame of what he was doing spread up his neck and heightened his rather sallow complexion. "It's a good corner, sir," he said finally.

Nez could think of nothing to say. His mind was racing. *You're the lad who defended my back,* he thought, *and I have allowed this to become of you? When did I become so thoughtless?*

"Sir?"

"Nothing, Private. I was just . . . thinking."

"Doesn't pay to do too much o' that, sir," Yore replied quietly.

"Well, maybe it should," Benedict said. He reached in his pocket and sent a handful of coins clinking into the cup; then he rummaged in his pocket for a pencil and tablet. He scribbled something on the back of one of the Copley Chocolatier order forms, folded it, and pressed it into Yore's hand.

"Take this 'round to Clarges Street, Private. That's an order, lad," he added gruffly when Yore protested.

"Aye, sir," said the beggar, "if the need arises. Thank ye."

The duke stood up. "I should thank you. I wonder that I never did."

"You didn't need to, sir. You kept us alive, and we should be thanking you."

"You're kind, Yore," he murmured, and felt the unfamiliar tears behind his eyelids. "Now, take that note 'round, do you hear?"

The man nodded. He held up his hand and Benedict shook it again, managed a small salute, and strode off down the street.

He had a close call at the corner of Fleet and Barkham, turning away and staring at the colorful message on a beer wagon as a high-perch phaeton bearing two of his best friends careened down the street, scattering pedestrians. He turned to watch after they passed, watched them take their careless way from one side of the street to the other. He thought about following them, calling to them to pull over and make room. He knew the inns they would frequent, the liquor they would drink, the lies they would tell to each other and anyone who would listen. The temptation to catch up with them made him clutch tighter at the reins.

But he had promised Eustace. Even worse than that, he had promised Luster. He smiled in spite of himself and said out loud, "If a man can't keep a promise to his butler . . ."

He turned the gig toward the Dover road.

The duke arrived at Rumleigh after dark, just shy of the county line, but too tired to drive any farther. His head pounded until he could almost hear it, and he had a raging thirst.

He drove slowly down High Street, remembering an inn from one of his earlier visits, where the ale was a mythical color and strength. As he peered at each overhead sign in the gathering gloom, he began to shake, so badly did he want a drink. Surprised, he held his hand up close to his face, watching the fine tremor that had seized him and wondering if he was coming down with something.

The thought cheered him. If he fell sick, truly sick, then Luster would surely take him back. Eustace would be breathing deep of Brighton's sea air and need never know that Benedict Nesbitt had gotten no farther than Rumleigh. He felt his forehead, and it was disappointingly cool. He shrugged, tightened his grip on the reins to stop the tremor, and reined in at the nearest inn.

It was not the place he remembered, but there was a taproom. He sank down in a chair and ordered, snatching the cup from the barmaid's tray when she brought it, and drinking deep.

"Some victuals, sir?" she asked.

He shook his head and held out the cup. With a slight frown, the barmaid disappeared behind the counter and returned with another glass, which he drank more slowly this time, rolling the flavor of it around his mouth, and wondered why it didn't taste as good as he remembered.

When Nesbitt finally dragged himself up to his room, he sank down on the floor by the bed and rested his head against the counterpane, which reeked of tobacco. He closed his eyes and tried to think of a prayer, but there wasn't anything in his mind.

Nez crawled into bed and slept then, slipping immediately into a pit, maws gaping wide, that swallowed him whole. He fell and fell, all the time wishing that he would hit bottom and there would be nothing else.

When Benedict awoke, the sun was up and the cleaning woman was rattling the doorknob.

"Another ten minutes and I charge you for another day," she bellowed through the keyhole as the duke groaned and tried to smother her voice with the pillow.

The pain in his head was a vise slowly tightening, inch by inch. He finished off the bottle he had brought upstairs the night before, lurched to his feet, and found himself face to face with his reflection in the cracked mirror over the bureau.

He didn't recognize the hollow-eyed man with the grim mouth who stared back at him. He resisted the urge to look over his shoulder in the hopes of seeing himself.

With hands that shook, Benedict shaved, changed clothes, and was stumbling down the stairs when the maid came out of the room across the hall, mop and pail in hand. She sniffed as he passed and drew her skirts aside.

The taproom was closed and locked and he nearly wept as he leaned against the door. He settled instead for a pot of scalding tea bullied down him by the landlord's wife, who appeared more than usually eager to have him off the premises. She offered him hard bread and then egg and bacon, but he could only shake his head and turn away, nauseated.

His modest horse was already hitched to the gig, and Copley's precious sample case was right where he had left it last night in his rush to get into the taproom. Remorse stabbed him as he remembered Copley's admonitions to take care of the case. He opened all the little drawers and was relieved to find the chocolate undisturbed, each piece solid and glossy in its compartment.

Benedict asked the ostler for directions to Holyoke, and then Holyoke Green, the Ames estate. The man answered him in some detail, but he might have spoken in tongues, for all the sense Nez could glean from the conversation. Finally the man drew a map, which he tucked in the duke's pocket as he kindly advised that he would not be able to miss the place.

Nesbitt clucked to his horse and started down the road, only to be whistled back by the ostler. He sucked in his breath, clutched at his temples, and turned slowly around, careful to keep his throbbing head level.

"Nay, then, sir, do ye not recall anything I said, think on? That road over there, as I live and breathe."

Benedict turned his horse and gig about, ignoring the catcalls of little boys who shouted to him and jabbed their fingers in all directions for his benefit, pointing this way and that, directing him back to London, north to Essex, south to Sussex.

He drove with his eyes half-closed until he was accustomed to the brightness of the summer morning. The birds that flew about and admonished him from the trees seemed swollen to enormous size, and he ducked in terror several times until they went away.

He sniffed cautiously at the easy puffs of wind that circulated, bringing with them the heady smell of flowers. He squinted in the sunlight, breathing deeper finally and feeling a measure of enjoyment that had eluded him for many more mornings than he could remember. If only his head didn't ache so!

He came to Holyoke before noon, but could not discover the estate. He paid closer attention to the directions he got from a member of the farming fraternity who was broadcasting seed in a newly turned field.

"Back the way ye came, sor," the man was telling him. "I don't know how ye missed it. It's one half mile to the turnoff. You'll see the house set back in the trees, sor, indeed ye will."

And there it was, a pleasant brick edifice of two and more stories, relentlessly old-fashioned and covered with vines, a far cry from the magnificence of his own ancestral estate in Yorkshire, but filled with a quiet prosperity that he could recognize from the road. Thoughtfully, he spoke to the horse and passed in front of the house, down a long slope that likely led to a river. He turned and came back, looking about and seeing no one. He noticed a large black horse in front of the house, but no rider. People were moving about in distant fields.

He walked the horse down the road again and planned the accident. It would be a simple matter to stop the horse by those trees that hid it from the house, and upend the gig. He would lie down by the gig. He could be sitting up and clutching his head when someone came to help. It would be a simple matter to clutch his head, which had not stopped throbbing all day.

The inmates of Holyoke Green would take him in; he could look over Eustace's intended and beat a retreat to Brighton with a full report. When the issue was settled with Eustace, he would find an inn on the coast where both the sheets and the ale were dry, pause there, and regroup while Augusta got over her fury and Lady Fanny Whoever had retired for the summer to the serenity of one watering hole or another.

He made one last jaunter up the slope. The horse looked back at him as if to question him. "Don't stare at me like that," he snapped at the animal. "Blame it on Eustace and his squeamishness."

He took a deep breath and had started down the slope one last time, moving faster, when it happened. A rabbit exploded out of the hedgerow and darted into the road. The horse, city-bred and familiar only with pigeons, shied, reared and began to gather speed as it raced down the slope.

Swearing a mighty oath learned from a sea captain and saved for such a moment as this, Benedict Nesbitt pulled back on the reins. Nothing. The horse only went faster. He tugged again, wondering if his arms would part from their sockets. "Wait until I see you again, Eustace," he muttered through clenched teeth.

And then there was no more time for threats or oaths. The horse lost its footing on a patch of gravel and spun the gig around. The last thing Nez remembered was a pop in his shoulder and a mouthful of Kent.

4

AT the sound of someone running up the steps, Libby turned to the doorway. Joseph threw himself into the entrance, his eyes wide.

"Libby! You must come quickly! There has been an accident on the road!"

Libby could only stare at her brother, but Dr. Cook had no hesitations. He took Joseph by the arm and turned him around.

"Where, Joseph?" he asked, the voice distinct. "Tell me quickly."

"Just a quarter-mile down the road toward your place. I could see it happen from the hayloft." He scratched his head and began to tug at his earlobe. "It was the strangest thing, Libby. He went back and forth several times over the same little bit of road, and then went really fast and tried to stop. I wonder he did not see the gravel. I would have seen the gravel."

"I am sure you would have," the doctor agreed. "Well, Joseph, are you up to a footrace?"

"Sir?"

"We'd better see if there is anything to salvage on the road."

Joseph grinned and the troubled look left his face. "I can beat you, Dr. Cook," he exclaimed.

"You can try, lad," said the doctor.

To Libby's openmouthed surprise, Dr. Cook shoved his spectacles into his pocket and took off after Joseph. She watched them run down the road, Joseph well in the lead but Dr. Cook coming up surprising fast for one so big.

"Lydia will be sorry she missed this sight," Libby murmured to herself, looked about, picked up her skirts, and chased after them.

Her side was aching before she reached the scene of the accident. Joseph had already untangled the horse from the traces and had tied the animal to a tree across the road. He was standing nose to nose with the trembling horse, talking to it, as Libby hurried up, gasping for breath.

The doctor knelt over the lone figure in the road. Libby took a deep breath and came closer until she was peering over the doctor's broad shoulder.

A man about thirty lay stretched out on the gravel, his face skinned and already starting to swell, blood dripping from a cut over his right eye. His shoulder was oddly twisted under him and his pant leg below his right knee was torn. Libby gulped and rested her hand on the doctor's shoulder to steady herself.

Dr. Cook looked over his shoulder and touched her hand. "You'll be all right, Miss Ames," he said.

Libby nodded and knelt beside the doctor. "We're not the branch of the Ames family that faints," she said, her voice thin, but determined in a way that made Anthony Cook smile at her, despite the concern in his eyes.

"I didn't think you were. Move around here, Libby," he said, calling her by her name for the first time. "Let's rest his head in your lap."

She did as she was told. Gently the doctor rested the unconscious man's head against her legs. She hesitated only a moment before she dabbed at the cut over his eye with her apron. In a moment, the bleeding had stopped.

"It's not as bad as I thought," she said.

"It rarely is," the doctor replied. From the deep recesses of his coat pocket, he extracted a pair of scissors and began to cut up the man's sleeve. "Seems a shame to do this," he said out loud. "Good material. I wonder . . ." He glanced at

Libby. "Feel around in his breast pocket. See if he has any identification."

"Oh, I couldn't," Libby said.

"Of course you can," the doctor said.

"If you're sure he won't mind," she said finally, and reached toward the man's coat.

"Libby, how will he ever know?" Dr. Cook asked, his voice alive with amusement.

Slowly, carefully, as if she expected the unconscious man to reach up and seize her, Libby slid her hand down his chest and into his coat. She felt about, noting how well-muscled his chest was, but did not turn up a wallet.

"Try his pants pockets," said the doctor as he resumed snipping away at the coat.

"I will not," she declared. "It's improper."

Dr. Cook sighed, and there was a touch of asperity in his voice. "Don't be a goose, Libby. I'd like to know who this is."

"I shouldn't, you know," Libby said. "Mama would never approve." After another moment's hesitation, Libby slid her hand into the man's pocket and pulled out a wallet.

She held it between thumb and forefinger and then opened it. It was stuffed with bank notes. She pulled out a card and held it out so Dr. Cook could see it, too.

" 'Nesbitt Duke,' " she read. " 'Merchant to Copley Chocolatier, by appointment to His Majesty George III.' "

"We seem to have a candy merchant here," said the doctor as he finished cutting around the sleeve. "He must be a good one. I wish I could afford a suit of this quality. Copley's, eh? I've bought a few pounds from them before."

"You and everyone in England," Libby said.

She watched as the doctor cut the last of the fabric and gently lifted the sleeve from the oddly twisted arm. "What are you going to do?" she asked finally, and would have preferred that he not answer, because she thought she knew, and the prospect was not pleasing.

The doctor didn't answer for a moment, so intent was he on cutting through the shirt and exposing the man's arm and chest. He sat back on his heels.

"It is as I thought," he said to Libby, who stared, wide-eyed, at the dislocation. "Dear me, how I dislike these presentations." He touched the man's forehead and smoothed back the mechant's rumpled hair with that same gentle gesture that so intrigued Libby. "Why could you not have done this in someone else's backyard?"

Libby shivered in spite of herself and clutched the unconscious man closer to her. "What are you going to do to him?" she quavered. "Oh, I do not think I like it."

The doctor grimaced. "Joseph," he called. "I need you."

Libby closed her eyes and bowed her head over the merchant, who chose that moment to open his eyes.

"My God, you are beautiful," he said, his voice faint and faraway. "An angel? Have I died?"

Libby sucked in her breath and scooted closer to the doctor, who leaned over the man and opened his eyes wider with his fingers.

"A pardonable mistake," he murmured. "She will introduce herself later, sir." He pulled down the skin below the man's eyelids and then passed his hand slowly across the merchant's face. "Ah, excellent, sir. Pupils in equal alignment and movement."

The doctor took a deep breath and gently manipulated the merchant's shoulder. Nesbitt Duke sucked in his breath and held it so long that Libby began to fidget. When she was about to cry, he let his breath out slowly and drew a shuddering breath, and another. He shifted his weight and groaned. "My leg . . ."

" . . . will wait," finished Anthony Cook. "We will worry about it after your arm has rejoined your body."

In spite of her growing agitation, Libby stole an admiring glance at Dr. Cook. Something had happened to the awkward, formal man in the bookroom. Dr. Cook knew precisely what he was doing. Libby held the candy merchant closer and forgave Anthony Cook the entire mess in the book room.

"Joseph, you are just the man I need," the doctor was saying. "Take Mr. Duke, is it? Take him by that arm. Gently, gently. When I tell you, start pulling on it slowly and evenly. Can you do that?"

Joseph turned white and started to back away, but Anthony

Cook fixed him with a stare that stopped him where he was. Without a word, Joseph took the merchant by the arm. Libby made an inarticulate sound in her throat.

"Just hang on to him," the doctor said as he rose up on his knees.

"Yes, by all means," the injured man murmured. He smiled at her. "Libby, is it? I am in the right place, then," he added, more to himself than to her. He closed his eyes resolutely and set his jaw.

"All right, Joseph, begin," said the doctor quietly.

Libby braced herself as the injured man cried out. Joseph pulled steadily, even as tears streamed down his cheeks, and Dr. Cook guided the arm back into the shoulder socket. There was an audible click, and the man fainted.

Libby felt remarkably light-headed. She swallowed, shook her head, and made no complaint when Dr. Cook pulled her away from the injured man and without any ceremony pushed her head down between her knees. She stayed that way until her head cleared and the humming went away, and then she raised her head, embarrassed.

Dr. Cook paid her no attention. He had cut away Mr. Duke's pant leg below the knee and was surveying the ruin. Joseph took one long look and directed his attention to Nesbitt Duke's horse again.

The man was still unconscious. Libby cleared her throat. "That was foolish of me," she apologized.

Dr. Cook rubbed his hand across her hair, the gesture careless and comforting at the same time. "Don't give it a thought. You should have seen me the first time I watched that piece of work. I thought you came through very well." He smiled. "Although I don't doubt you wish you had gone to Brighton after all."

She could only agree silently to herself. Libby forced herself to look at the man's injured leg. "What are you going to do?" she asked.

"Carry him to Holyoke Green, if you think that will do," he said.

"Of course, of course," Libby said at once. "Your place is a bit closer, but I doubt . . ." She paused, her face red.

"You doubt that my father would be sufficiently interested

to nurse a gentleman of the merchant class?" the doctor finished. He laughed at her evident chagrin. "You are entirely right. Mr. Duke of Copley's will fare better at your place. Let us leave Joseph to see to the horse."

With scarcely any effort, Dr. Cook lifted the injured man in his arms and started down the road with his burden, cradling him close. Libby snatched up the worn bag that had burst open in the road and stuffed the clothes back inside. She hurried to catch up with the doctor. Libby tugged at the doctor's sleeve. "You're not . . . you're not going to have to amputate, are you?" she whispered.

Anthony Cook looked down at her and smiled as though he were out for a Sunday stroll and had nothing more serious than dinner on his mind. "Lord, no, you goose," he chided in his good-natured way. "What I do think is that I will be spending a good portion of this day picking out the gravel."

Libby blinked back her tears. "I'm not very good at this, Dr. Cook," she said. "He looks dreadful."

"And so would you, if you had just graded up the road with your body. Hurry on ahead like a good girl and find a room for this poor purveyor of chocolate."

She did as she was bid. Candlow, never one to succumb to nerves, took one look at the doctor coming up the steps with the man cradled in his arms and led the way upstairs. He looked back once and shook his head, but there was just a tinge of satisfaction in his eyes. "This reminds me of any number of scrapes your father found himself in, Miss Ames," he said fondly. "Ah, but your uncle is devilish dull."

"Candlow," Libby exclaimed. "You have never spoken of my father."

The butler managed a slight smile in her direction. "I don't know that we were allowed to speak of him, miss, at least while your grandfather was alive. Indeed, it became a habit, something I have not thought about until the arrival of this person."

"Perhaps that will change now?" Libby asked, her voice soft.

"It might," the butler answered, his voice equally quiet. "May you give way now for the doctor, miss."

Libby hurried ahead and stripped back the bedspread, smoothing out the pillow and then standing aside as Dr. Cook lowered the man carefully to the sheet. He stood silent then, towering over the man on the bed, just regarding him, his lips pursed, the frown line between his eyes quite pronounced.

"Doctor?" Libby asked when he appeared not to be attending to the matter at hand.

He started visibly and then shook his head. "Just wondering where to begin, Libby . . . Miss Ames," he said, correcting himself. "I don't suppose your uncle ventured all the way to Brighton without his valet?"

"Oh, no, Doctor. I couldn't imagine such a thing."

"Nor I," he agreed, "but I had hopes. Well, let us summon Candlow again. Miss Ames, I suggest that you find other matters to occupy you." He started to unbutton the unconscious man's shirt. "In fact, take his bag into the hall and see if there is a nightshirt within."

Libby did as she was bid. She opened the bag but could not bring herself to put her hand inside and rifle through the stranger's belongings. After a moment spent in serious contemplation of the sad fact that she was going to ruin, and Mama scarcely out of sight, Libby plunged in her hand and pulled out a handful of clothes.

She found a nightshirt straight off, a cheerful blue-and-white affair that reminded her of mattress ticking, and a dressing gown that looked more valuable than the Bayeux Tapestry.

Libby fingered the rich material. Chocolate must pay beyond my wildest imaginings, she thought. Robe in hand, she spun a story to herself, imagining that Mr. Nesbitt Duke must be no mere salesman, but part owner at least.

Her speculations were disturbed by steps on the stairs. Joseph was coming slowly up the stairs, hand over hand on the railing like an old man.

"Joseph, are you all right?" she asked as he sat down beside her and wrung his hands together.

"Will he die, Libby?" Joseph asked, his voice a monotone, his eyes suspiciously red.

Libby put her arm around her brother. "Oh, Joseph, I think not!"

He allowed her to hold him, and he clung to her, even when the door opened and the doctor came into the hall.

If Dr. Cook was surprised to see the two of them holding on to each other, he did not show it. Without a word, he put a large friendly hand on Joseph's head and rested it there until Joseph looked up.

"That's better, now, Joseph," the doctor said. "You did a capital job back there on the road. His shoulder is fine. Now if Libby will spare me that nightshirt . . ."

She handed it to the doctor. "Can I help, Dr. Cook?" she asked, half-hoping that he would say no. She glanced at her brother, who sat so still beside her. "And Joseph will help too, won't you, dear?"

He thought a moment, his hand straying to his earlobe. "If you are there, Libby," he managed at last.

"Then it is settled," she said decisively, and got to her feet, holding out her hand for Joseph. "You will tell us what to do, Doctor."

"Joseph, you and Candlow will get him into his nightshirt. I will go downstairs and send the footman for my bag. Deuced foolish of me to leave it home, but then, we didn't expect to find a chocolate merchant plowing up the road in front of Holyoke Green, now, did we? You can get us a basin and some tweezers."

When she returned with the basin and tweezers and enough gauze and cotton wadding to upholster a chair, Joseph was inside the room. He stayed close to the wall, but the fear was gone from his eyes. Dr. Cook had removed his coat and was rolling up his sleeves.

"Very good, Miss Ames," he said, and took the basin and tweezers from her. He sat on the bed, draped a towel on his breeches, and pulled the man's leg into his lap. He perched his glasses firmly on his nose, picked up the tweezers, and began to extract little bits of gravel. In a moment, he was whistling tunelessly to himself as he plinked the gravel into the basin. Joseph began to grin, and Libby smiled in spite of herself.

The doctor looked up and noticed the amusement in her eyes. "Miss Ames, Mozart is efficacious for more than the concert hall, don't you know?"

"I prefer a little Bach now and then," she teased, and they laughed together.

"Well, when it is your turn, you may whistle Bach," he said generously, and reapplied himself to his task until the bottom of the basin was covered with the stony fragments. He paused then and rubbed his eyes. "Now it is your turn, Miss Ames. I haven't the eyes for this."

They changed places. The man stirred and muttered something when the doctor moved his leg into Libby's lap, but he did not appear alert. She took the tweezers from the doctor and continued the search for gravel. In a few moments, Joseph seated himself across from her. Libby looked up long enough to nod in his direction.

"I am sure that if you held his hand, when he woke he would not be so frightened, my dear," she said to her brother.

"Then I will do it." Joseph took the man by the hand, his eyes on his face, anxious for the first signs of returning consciousness.

Libby bent over her work again, pulling out the fragments and dabbing at the blood with the cotton wadding. Dr. Cook loomed over her as he carefully ran his hands through the man's hair, searching for futher injury.

The man looked as though he slept, so relaxed did he appear.

"A candy merchant?" Libby asked out loud, and then glanced at Joseph, who was subjecting the man to intense scrutiny. "Joseph, I should think that a candy salesman would be round and jolly, rather like . . ." She paused in embarrassment.

"Like me?" supplied the doctor, and then chuckled as she blushed.

There was an awkward pause as Libby devoted all her attention to the man's leg. The blush left her cheeks in a moment, and she turned to the doctor.

"You are right to tease me," she said, and then smiled. "But I will say this, Dr. Cook: you were a fierce competitor in the footrace."

He bowed. "I will depend upon you never to let the medical faculty at Edinburgh know that I had to run after a patient."

She giggled behind her hand, her good humor restored.

"Beg pardon," said a faint voice from the bed. "If I'm not asking too much . . ."

The chocolate merchant's eyes were open and the pain in them made Libby wince. Impulsively she leaned forward and laid her hand upon his chest, and then touched his face. "You are in excellent hands, Mr. Duke," she said.

"Oh, I am well aware," he murmured, turned his face toward her hand, and kissed it. "Now, is there a doctor, too? My joy would be complete."

His eyes closed again.

Libby snatched her hand away and stared down at him in astonishment. "Dr. Cook, he is a shocking flirt. One would scarcely think he would feel like jollying the ladies."

"Shocking," murmured the doctor as he gazed at Libby, then shook his head, cleared his throat, and shoved his wandering glasses more firmly upon his nose. "Let us continue. Oh, thank you, Candlow. I was needing that."

The butler held out his black bag and whispered in the doctor's ear. "Mrs. Weller said your father had a particular message for you, Doctor. Said to make sure the merchant had money in his pockets before you even put so much as a stitch in him."

Dr. Cook sighed. "Do you know, Miss Ames, I think that my father and Hippocrates would never have seen eye to eye on the matter of payment for hire." He touched her arm. "Those are embedded rather deeply, Miss Ames. You dab now and I will tweeze."

The stones cut deeper around the man's knee. Dr. Cook worked one out before the merchant opened his eyes again, reached down, and grasped the doctor's hand.

"Hold him, Libby," said Dr. Cook.

She took his arm and held it tightly in her hands. "Now, now, sir," she said. "He'll be through soon."

To her horror, the man began to cry. Joseph let go of his other hand and retreated from the room. "Anthony," she gasped, forgetting her manners, "what do we do now?"

Dr. Cook dropped the tweezers and reached for his black bag, drawing out a vile of amber-colored liquid. "A drop of this will simplify things," he murmured as he reached for a cup. "Now, then, sir."

Tears streaming down his cheeks, the merchant struggled to sit up. He knocked the basin off the bed and the stones rolled across the floor.

Libby took his face in her hands. "Oh, please, sir. Dr. Cook only wants to help," she said.

The man ignored her, reaching for the doctor again. He grasped Cook's arms. "No. Not any of that." His hand began to tremble. "If you would, I could manage a drink."

The doctor looked at him thoughtfully and put the cork back in the bottle. "As you wish, sir. Candlow, can you concoct a mild cordial for our guest?"

"I'd rather have whiskey," said the merchant.

Dr. Cook shook his head. He lifted the man's hand gently off his arm and held it steady, watching the slight tremor. "I think a cordial will be more than sufficient, Mr. Duke, is it? Doctor's orders, sir."

When Candlow returned, Libby raised Mr. Duke up and tipped the glass to his lips.

The man took a surprisingly strong grip on the glass and downed the cordial. "More, please," he gasped, tugging at Libby's hand. "Oh, please!"

Without a word, Dr. Cook poured another glass, this one larger.

The man drank without a murmur, closed his eyes, and slept.

"My stars, but he is thirsty," Libby said. She wiped the corner of the merchant's mouth.

"Yes, isn't he?" agreed the doctor, a thoughtful expression on his face. "Let us continue."

Dutifully, Libby dabbed at the wounds, her lips pursed in concentration. She heard Dr. Cook heave an enormous sigh. "Doctor, you must be weary of all this," she said, without looking up.

"Me? Oh, well, yes, I suppose," he said, and he sounded embarrassed.

He continued his work and Libby heard no further sighs until he finally sat back, rubbing at his neck. She noticed that his shirt was damp with perspiration. His glasses slid off his nose and she caught them expertly and handed them back.

"Thank you, Miss Ames." He rose to his feet and stretched, going to the window and leaning out for some moments. In a moment he was back at the bed again, looking down at his patient. "He will have gravel working out of his leg for some time, I think,'' he said. "But you will have nothing to do with landanum, will you, sir? I wonder . . . '' he mused.

He ran his hand over the man's other leg, which showed bare from the knee down. He touched a pit mark that Libby had noticed, and another, and traced his hand up a long scar, faintly red, that meandered from ankle to knee by a jagged route. He raised the man's nightshirt and Libby looked away.

"Really, Dr. Cook,'' she exclaimed, and devoted her attention to the cotton wadding again.

"Yes, really, Miss Ames,'' he said, a touch of asperity in his voice that surprised her. Alert now, the doctor leaned forward and unbuttoned the man's nightshirt, looking at his chest with clinical interest, and uttering "H'mms'' and "My words,'' until Libby sighed in exasperation.

"Dr. Cook, what are you doing?'' she whispered as the chocolate merchant stirred and muttered something imperative.

The doctor didn't answer right away. He buttoned the man's nightshirt again and then reached in his bag for a jar of salve, which he smoothed on the leg. He stepped back to survey his handiwork.

"It would appear to me, Miss Ames, that selling chocolate is a damned dangerous line of work. So glad I am a physician, instead.''

"Whatever do you mean?'' Libby asked. The man moaned in his sleep and she rested her hand alongside his cheek for a moment until he was quiet.

"I mean that this man has been in battle, and not overlong ago. I wonder, do you suppose he might have been engaged in last year's little tiff in Belgium?''

"Waterloo, do you mean?'' she asked, her eyes wide. "Oh, surely not.''

"Then we can only surmise that London is a singularly dangerous place,'' said the doctor. "Or can it be that people there take exception to chocolate?''

After another moment in silence, Dr. Cook draped a long strip of gauze over the merchant's leg and pulled up the sheet. "Perhaps we will learn something tomorrow,'' he mused out loud. He looked toward the lawn, which was in shadows, now that the sun was behind the house. He returned the vial of laudanum to his bag. "He should sleep soundly enough."

"If he wakes?" Libby asked.

"I've left some sleeping powders on the night table, Miss Ames," he said. "If he should come around, try to get him to eat something." He held out his hand.

She took it formally and then blushed as he enveloped her hand in both of his.

"I'm sorry this has fallen your lot," he said.

"It is I who should apologize to you, Dr. Cook," she insisted as she tried to work her hand out of his warm grasp.

Dr. Cook blinked and pushed up his spectacles. "Whatever for?" he asked.

She couldn't look at him. Libby freed her hands and put them out of reach behind her back. "I didn't mean to call you . . . Well, you know, I called you Anthony a while back."

"It is my name," the doctor said.

"Yes, but you are a physician," Libby said stubbornly. "And I hope you will overlook my rudeness."

He leaned toward her for a brief moment and winked. "My dear Miss Ames, contrary to popular opinion, at least that which is noised about by physicians, being a doctor does not make me God. You may call me Anthony anytime you choose."

She shook her head. "It won't happen again. Please believe me."

He smiled faintly at her reply, but there was little humor in his eyes as he sighed and bowed himself out of the room, setting the glass ornaments shivering on the table as he passed by.

With a smile of her own, Libby went to the window and looked down on the front drive, where the doctor's horse had stood so patiently. She watched as the doctor heaved his considerable bulk onto the animal, gratified to see that he was more agile than she would have suspected.

As if he knew she was watching, the doctor turned in the saddle and waved to her. She waved back and then rested her elbows on the windowsill, wondering at the strangeness of her mood, wishing that he had not left her with this sick person, and suddenly fearful for the peace of her summer.

She watched the chocolate merchant a moment more, smoothing the tangle of straight hair across his forehead. "Poor man,'' she whispered. "How can you earn a living from a sickbed?''

Libby hurried downstairs. The maid was lighting the last of the lamps and Libby was wondering about dinner when Joseph came into the room.

He was tugging at his earlobe and she knew something was wrong. When the front door slammed open and she heard heavy footsteps coming down the hall, Joseph hurried to the other side of the room.

The voice was loud now, an angry voice that made her stomach turn over, even as she flashed a reassuring smile at Joseph and held her hand out to him.

"I forgot where I was, Libby,'' he said simply.

She nodded and kissed his cheek.

The door banged open and Squire Cook stalked into the room, pointing his riding crop at Joseph.

"If that simpleton trespasses on my land again, I'll flog him,'' he shouted. He pointed his whip at Libby. "And if I find you're making sheep's eyes at my son, I'll flog you, too.''

5

LIBBY gasped at his accusation and then burst into delighted laughter. She laughed until the tears came to her eyes, and then struggled to a seat as she dabbed at her face. She raised her smiling countenance to the squire's fury and watched as his expression changed from rage to a certain mystified agitation.

"Dear me," she began when she could speak, "that was fearsome rude, but, sir, be aware that I have no evil designs on your son. I am convinced that he is an excellent physician, but I am equally sure that we would never suit." She gestured toward the chair opposite her as Joseph retreated to the door. "Please have a seat and let us discuss this matter."

Joseph ducked out the door. For a moment, the squire wavered between rushing after him and taking the chair instead. He just stood where he was, jerked off his hat, and slapped it against his knee.

"Dash it all, Miss Ames, doesn't that chucklehead have any sense of boundary?"

She gestured toward the chair again and he threw himself into it. The chair creaked and Libby held her breath, but it did not crack.

"No, I fear he does not, Squire. I wish that he did, and I am equally sorry that his presence is such an agitation to you. I can only reassure you again that he is completely harmless."

The squire refused to be mollified. "That's not the half of it. Do you know where I found him?"

Libby shook her head. Candlow came into the room on tiptoe and set a tea tray at her elbow. She poured a cup for the squire, who frowned at it and then accepted some refreshment. He took one sip and then another. An expression less forbidding came into his eyes for the smallest moment, but then he recalled the matter at hand. He set down the cup with a decisive click.

"Miss Ames, you cannot distract me with tea," he said. "Your brother was in my horse herd again. Again! I always find him there."

"Surely he causes you no trouble, Squire."

He snatched up a biscuit from the tray she offered, and chomped down hard on it, glaring at her through bushy brows. "That is hardly the issue, Miss Ames, but trust someone of your sex to obfuscate the problem. He has no business among my herd."

Libby counted to ten in her head, poured another cup of tea for the squire, and handed it to him. "I cannot disagree with you, sir, but Joseph loves horses and you have a particularly fine herd. Certainly the best I have ever seen." She took a sip of her tea and allowed that bit of mild flattery to settle in.

The squire drank his tea and did not object when she offered him another biscuit.

Libby watched him in silence, wondering to herself how it was that such a cantankerous old rip would have fathered such a good-natured son as the doctor. She was moved to empathy for Dr. Cook. *I wonder, Doctor, did he bully you to ride to hounds?* she thought. She reminded herself that the doctor did sit a horse rather well, and concluded, in all fairness to the squire, that there was likely no childhood tyranny. But how different they were.

"I ask you again, Miss Ames, and beg you to attend me: what do you propose to do?"

The squire's voice penetrated into her thoughts. She looked up from a frowning contemplation of her hands. "I do not know, sir," she said at last. "Joseph loves it here. I think he would suffer anywhere else. And there is no questison that he cannot be sent away to school."

The silence hung heavy for a moment as the squire chewed and swallowed some more. "Do I gather from your less-than-satisfactory answer that you intend to allowed him to roam tame across my lands?"

"I do not know what else to do, Squire, short of locking him up," she said simply. "I nag, scold, and admonish him, and it does little good."

He stared back at her and she did not allow her glance to waver. "This may eventually become a matter for the constable, Miss Ames," he said finally. "There are places for people like your brother."

"I know there are, sir," she replied, and had the small satisfaction of watching him break away eye contact first. "But I trust to merciful providence that you are too kind for that, Squire."

Her calm words hung in the air and he made no reply, other than to brush the crumbs vigorously from his coat and rise.

Libby stood, too, thinking to herself what a tall race the Cooks were. A mere mortal could get neck strain in that family, she thought, and her lips curved into a smile.

Her smile seemed to recall the squire to the other reason for his visit. He slapped his hat against his knee again.

"I warn you, Miss Ames. Do not try that smile on my son."

She stared at him in surprise and felt that warmth rising up her chest to blossom on her face. "But, Squire, I—"

"Pretty is as pretty does, miss," he said, and waved his riding crop at her again. "My Anthony can look much higher for a wife than a penniless brat whose mother is a shop owner's daughter."

The words stung. For a fleeting moment she thought of her beloved grandfather, now deceased, and his tobacco shop. "Yes, I suppose that renders me completely ineligible for this county's society," she said softly. "You may rest assured, Squire Cook, I would never do anything to encourage your son. I have been raised better than that." She marched to the door and resisted the urge to fling it open. "And now, sir, if you will allow me? I needn't take any more of your valuable time. Your son is safe, and I will do what I can with Joseph."

The dignity of her reply left the squire wordless, for once.

He jammed his hat upon his head, bowed to her curtly, and took his leave.

When she heard the front door close, Libby sat down to wait. In another moment, Joseph stuck his head in the parlor door. "Is he gone?"

"Yes, dear," she replied, and was unable to hide her exasperation. "Joseph, what possesses you to bother that man's horses?"

Joseph sat down beside her. "He has beautiful horses, Libby," was all he said.

The anger left her as quickly as it had come. "Yes, he does," she agreed. "Joseph, perhaps you could just admire them from the other side of the fence from now on."

"They always come up to the fence when I am there," he said. "I think that angers him, too, Libby."

He was silent. After another moment, Libby patted his hand and left the room. She mounted the stairs slowly. Her first instinct was to summon Dr. Cook and pour out her woes to him and ask his advice with Joseph. Her second thought convinced her of the utter folly of her first thought. She smiled in spite of herself at the thought of the overpowering Dr. Cook kneeling before her, offering marriage.

She giggled. "Oh, dear. Such a picture!" she said out loud as her practical nature took over. No, Dr. Cook, you and I would never suit, she thought as she peeked in the room where the chocolate merchant lay.

He was wide awake and staring at the ceiling, shivering in the room, which was still warm from the lingering effects of the afternoon sun, long gone from the sky.

"Are you cold, sir?" she asked in surprise.

He nodded. His eyes followed her as she hurried to the blanket chest at the foot of the bed and pulled out another coverlet, tucking it over him, high up under his chin.

"There, now," she said, her voice gentle. "You'll feel much better in the morning, I daresay."

He sighed and settled himself more comfortably in the bed, while Libby smiled down at him. "Would you like something to eat? You must be famished."

He shook his head. "I would like another drink, Miss . . . Miss . . . "

"Ames. Libby Ames. The doctor left that bottle of cordial here."

She raised him up and he drank, uttering sounds of pleasure deep in his throat that startled her. "I don't know how you stand that brew," she said when he finished and lay back. "Mama bullies me to drink it when I am feeling peaked. And I hold my nose."

"Thank you, Miss Ames." He shivered again involuntarily.

Libby smoothed the blanket across his chest. "People do that when they have suffered a severe shock, Mr. Duke. I have seen it before in Spain."

She stood by the bed another moment. "Do you want me to sit with you for a while?" Libby asked. "Just until you fall asleep?"

He nodded and she pulled the chair closer. "I don't have any clever stories to tell," she confessed. "There isn't much that happens around here. I suppose your London is much more exciting."

The merchant did not answer. He had closed his eyes. She thought he slept, but in another moment he opened them.

"It can't be too dull here, Miss Ames. Didn't I hear angry voices below?"

"You did, but it was only one angry voice. It was the squire. Joseph was trespassing again." Libby giggled. "And the squire never forgives those who trespass against him."

She was rewarded with a smile from the chocolate merchant. "I would suspect that you must have managed him admirably."

"I try, sir, but I am running out of ways to placate him." Libby hitched the chair closer. "You see, Joseph is continually trespassing on his land. He loves the squire's horses, and strange to tell, they follow him about like Mary's little lamb."

Libby wanted to say more, to pour out her troubles to this stranger, but she closed her lips in time and managed an embarrassed laugh. "See here sir, you should not allow me to burden you with our difficulties. I suppose that wrangles among neighbors are common enough in London, too."

He smiled slightly as his eyes began to close again.

Libby peered at him. "Oh, I shouldn't be talking so much."

He shook his head. "I enjoy it."

"I cannot imagine why. We country folk are a decided dull lot," she declared, and then allowed herself to twinkle her eyes at him. "But, then, we rarely have captive audiences." She tucked the blanket up higher and, after only the slightest hesitation, felt his forehead. "Ah, very good! Dr. Cook will be pleased if you are not running a fever in the morning. And I, too," she added softly as she blew out the candle.

Nez held out his hand to her as she rose to leave the room and she grasped it.

"You will sleep well, sir, I know you will. And I will see you in the morning."

He did sleep well all night, his thoughts untroubled by dreams or anything more menacing than the deepest reluctance to move. When he woke in the morning, his shoulder ached, but it was a pain he could live with. His right leg was on fire, but he gritted his teeth and slowly moved his ankle, noting with relief that it was still attached.

I seem to have all parts and accessories still assembled, he thought as he opened his eyes and looked about the room, wondering only briefly where he was and then remembering that he had sacrificed considerable dignity and skin the day before on one of Eustace's whims.

The room was bright with morning sun that streamed in through lacy curtains just now being drawn back by the loveliest woman he had ever seen.

He remembered her from the day before, but he had seen her through such a haze of pain that her beauty had not fully registered in his mind. Now it filled all his senses, and he wondered that such a creature really drew breath.

Her hair was deep brown or black, and curled about her head. She had attempted to twist it into a knot on top of her head, but must have given it up for a bad job. The tendrils curled about and the disordered effect was so endearing that he smiled, despite his aches and pains. He was glad that her hair was not cropped in the current fashion. As he gazed at her in frank admiration, the duke wondered how all that riot of curly brown would look tumbled about her shoulders. The thought stirred him as nothing had in recent memory.

She was a perfect assembly of exquisite parts, from the proud way she carried her head to her elegant deep bosom, to the trimness of her ankles, which just peeked out from under the muslin dress she wore. Her waist was tiny, and he wondered if he could span it with his hands.

As he watched in admiration, she opened the window wide and perched herself on the window ledge, looking out at the morning. She waved to someone below and then clasped her hands together in heartfelt delight at one more summer day. He thought her eyes were blue. Her high-arched eyebrows and prominent cheekbones gave her face an inquiring look. She seemed to the duke the kind of woman who would just naturally look interested in everything about her, because nature had designed her face that way. Even her lips had a natural curl to them.

As she sat so still on the window, her hands clasped together in her lap, something about her spoke of endless, tireless energy, a vitality that made him feel older than old and then suddenly young again.

He sighed. No, he did not sigh; someone else did. The duke, still holding his head still, shifted his eyes to the door, where the doctor stood, his glance fixed on the woman in the window.

Dr. Anthony Cook wore a good suit, but it was rumpled, as though he slept in it. Possibly he had, the duke decided. Perhaps he had spent the night at another bedside. He certainly looked the part. His hair was rumpled, even as his suit. On closer observation, the duke realized that it was curly rather than rumpled. The shade precisely matched his black eyes in hue, eyes that appeared slightly enlarged behind the gold-rimmed spectacles perched on his nose.

The doctor's whole face seemed to beam out benevolence and a quiet capability that spoke louder than words. For no real reason, the duke felt a sudden twinge of envy as he regarded this massive, rumpled, good man. He used the measuring stick on Dr. Cook that he had used on every man for the past year. Could you have kept your men alive at Waterloo? It was a mean thought, and for the first time in a year he wished he had not considered it. As he surveyed the doctor's calm, rather placid face, the duke decided that Dr. Cook would have managed very well, indeed. No matter how unprepossessing, the physician appeared to be a man with enormous reservoirs of strength. It showed in his face.

And my strength is almost gone, thought the duke.

There was more to the doctor's expression as it rested on the charming young lady in the window. Libby? Was that her name? Never had the duke seen so powerful a glance of love cast in anyone's direction, and the scope of it almost took his breath away.

The duke enjoyed a tiny moment of superiority and resisted the desire to call out to the besotted physician in that bored voice he reserved for London parties: "Doctor, oh, dear doctor, don't you know that love is decidedly unfashionable? One dallies, one plays about, one pretends, but one does not love. That sort of nonsense is not seen in the best circles these days. Did no one tell you that we are living in an epoch of cynicism right now?"

He said no such thing, but merely enjoyed the spectacle of a man in love staring at the totally oblivious object of his admiration. It delighted the duke; it enervated him; it made him envious.

Poor sod, he thought. The only way someone as tame as you are could possibly win this prize would be by incredible subterfuge or unthinkable default.

At the thought he shifted himself and groaned as the sheet rubbed against the gauze on his leg.

The involuntary murmur from the chocolate merchant recalled Libby to the moment. "Oh, you poor man," she said as she hurried to his bedside, her eyes filled with concern.

She glanced up at the doctor and looked away quickly. His face was red. She had a terrible feeling that his father had been scolding him about his visit to Holyoke Green last night.

"Good morning, Miss Ames," said the doctor. "And you, sir, how did you sleep?"

"Well enough," said the merchant. He pulled himself into a sitting position.

"Shall we see then if you are well enough?" asked Dr. Cook. He pulled back the bed covers and examined the chocolate merchant's leg. He gently worked off the gauze and stared at it some more. "You'll do," he said at last. "I would prefer for the air to get at it now." He glanced at Libby's expression. "And don't look so shocked. We learned the latest methods in Edinburgh."

"We do live in a modern age," Libby said. "Very well, sir, I will see that his bed is pulled closer to the window."

"Very good, Miss Ames." He turned from his contemplation of Libby and regarded the merchant again. "I doubt you'll be bounding about for a few days."

"I hadn't planned on it," Nez agreed. He winked at Libby and felt himself vastly rewarded by the returning twinkle in her eyes. "I will trust to my charming hostess to tolerate my distempered convalescence."

The doctor raised expressive eyebrows over his spectacles. "Yes, I suppose you will," he said in a different tone of voice, a proprietary tone that sounded to Libby remarkably like the squire.

The doctor sat on the bed and unbuttoned the merchant's nightshirt. He felt the man's shoulder. "Be careful with that," he said finally. "They have a habit of slipping out again, once it has happened." He peered closer at the man in the bed. "And this is not the first time, is it?"

"No, sir," said the merchant promptly. "It has happened once before."

"At Waterloo?" ventured the doctor.

Startled, the merchant nodded. "Hougoumont, to be more specific. How the devil did you know?"

"You carry sufficient souvenirs of battle on your person to make you highly suspect," said the doctor mildly as he buttoned the man's nightshirt again. "But how did you dislocate your shoulder?"

"Dangling off the roof of a burning farmhouse," the merchant replied, and then closed his lips in a firm line.

The doctor returned the merchant's gaze. "And that, I take, is all you choose to say about it." When Nez made no reply, the doctor touched the man's head in a gesture oddly protective. "I'll not pry further."

There was an awkward silence. For some reason, the merchant appeared to be wavering on the edge of tears. Libby looked away, troubled by the strange tension between the two men. She thought about leaving the room, so palpable was that tension, but she stayed where she was.

The doctor patted the merchant's good leg and stood up. The cordial bottle caught his eye. He held it up to the light and shook it, then set it down. Without a word, he grasped the duke by the wrist and raised his hand, watching the fine tremor. Deep in thought, he held the man by the wrist, then grasped his hand and squeezed it.

"Well, sir, you could use some breakfast, I am convinced," Dr. Cook said at last. "The rumor circulating about the neighborhood testifies that Miss Ames is an excellent cook, so you could be in for a beatific experience."

Nez shook his head. "I do not doubt you, but I'm not hungry. What I really would like—"

The doctor did not allow him to finish the sentence. "A bowl of oatmeal with cream, and an apple tart." He bowed to Libby. "Could you produce such a menu?"

"No . . . I—" began the duke. His voice became sharper then, querulous. "Now, see here, I know what I want and it is not oatmeal."

Dr. Cook stuck his hands in his pocket and walked to the window. "But, sir, that is my prescription. I wasn't in Edinburgh for four years for nothing. Oatmeal, Mr. Duke, oatmeal."

Libby observed the merchant's evident agitation. "Dr. Cook, it would be no trouble to locate another bottle of cordial," she said. "Indeed, Uncle often takes it with his breakfast."

He froze her with a look. "No."

She stepped back in surprise. "Very well, sir," she said, her voice frosty. "But I am not a very good hostess, then, am I?"

"You'll have to run that risk, Miss Ames," said the doctor, his voice serene again. He nodded toward the bed, where the merchant was making sputtering sounds. "And if Mr. Duke does not like it, why, he can get out of bed and leave this place."

"Only get me my clothes, and I will be off," shouted the duke.

The doctor stuck his glasses more firmly on his nose and looked elaborately about the room again. He picked up the bag in the corner, carried it to the window, and threw it out. Libby gasped in surprise.

Her surprise deepened as the merchant threw himself back against the pillow and stared at the ceiling. As she watched in amazement, sweat broke out on his face.

But Dr. Cook was watching her. He nodded to her. "Miss Ames, I have a matter to discuss with you."

Without a word, she followed him from the room. In silence, he tucked her arm in the crook of his elbow and steered her down the hall. She hurried to keep up with his long stride, wondering what possessed him to behave in such a cavalier fashion, and grateful, at the same time, that the squire could not see them so close together.

He sat her down on the top of the landing and seated himself below her several steps. He seemed at a loss for words and looked at her hopefully. When she only stared at him, he sighed and began.

"Miss Ames, the chocolate merchant is a drunkard."

"What?" she shrieked, and then clutched his arm and lowered her voice. "You cannot be serious. He seems so nice."

The doctor shrugged and patted her hand. "My dear, you must disabuse yourself of the notion that all drunkards look like Hogarth's rake. I am sure he is nice. Tell me, did you leave that bottle of cordial on the night table? I distinctly remember putting it on the bureau."

She thought back to the night before. "I did pour Mr. Duke another cordial," she said. "And I must have left the bottle on the night table. Could he have drunk the whole thing?"

"It is a distinct possibility, unless you have extremely agile mice in this house, and I cannot imagine your mama would ever permit that!" He smiled. "Ah, that is more like it, Miss Ames.

You really have a fine dimple." He took her by the hand
absently.

"But a drunkard, sir?" she asked, her eyes wide.

"I am sure of it. He is not hungry, and he should be famished.
His hands tremble. Did you notice the sweat on his face?"

She nodded. He held her hand gently and began to massage
her knuckles. He was obviously troubled, so Libby allowed him
to continue.

After another moment's reflection, he looked down at her
hand and let go of it quickly. "Beg pardon, Miss Ames," he
said.

She refused to let the moment embarrass her, but scooted
down another step until they were at eye level with each other.
"I suppose it would be a simple matter to let the man rest here
a few days, give him his cordial, and then send him on his way."

"It would be," he agreed. "I could overlook all this. We
could keep him well lubricated and then wave good-bye to him
and let him become someone else's problem." He fastened an
inquiring eye upon her.

"Or we could keep him here a few weeks and sober him up,"
Libby said. "Uncle would have a fit. You know how he feels
about the consumption of excessive spirits. And Mama . . .
Mama would be aghast."

"They are not here," the doctor reminded her.

"Oh, but, Doctor, my Aunt Crabtree—Uncle Ames' aunt,
actually—she will be arriving today. I fear she will take great
exception to this little scheme."

"Surely she will not dump out an invalid who is already in
residence."

She felt a flash of irritation at Dr. Cook's calm reason. "I
think you could cajole me into keeping Napoleon himself in the
best guest room."

"I could try, if he were a patient of mine, my dear," he
replied. "Now, throw out your other objections and let us get
them aired and out of the way."

"I had planned to spend the next few weeks in blissful
solitude," Libby mused, "painting and subjecting myself to
absolutely no exertions." She jabbed a finger toward the

doctor's ample chest. "Surely Hippocrates does not cover this in his oath."

"You are correct, of course, Miss Ames. But I might also add that nowhere does it say in the Hippocratic oath to leave well enough alone, so I do believe I will meddle in this man's existence."

"He won't thank you for it," Libby pointed out.

"Not now, he won't, but he may someday." The doctor rose to his feet and pulled Libby up after him. "We may be doing him a greater good than he could ever have expected from an accident." He chuckled. "Poor Mr. Nesbitt Duke! He had the misfortune to overturn his gig in front of a most meddlesome house. Someone should have warned him about selling chocolates in this part of Kent."

The doctor looked at his pocket watch. "And now I must be off. Lord Lamborne of Edgerly Grange in convinced that if I do not lance a carbuncle this morning, he will likely cock up his toes by evening, although why this has not bothered him anytime in these past six weeks, I cannot tell you. Good day, Miss Ames."

Libby clutched at the doctor's arm. "You cannot leave me like this. What am I do with my chocolate merchant?"

Dr. Cook threw back his head and laughed. Libby stamped her foot and shook his arm. He pried her fingers from his sleeve. "Careful, my dear, or you'll rumple the superfine," he said, and was rewarded with a laugh.

"And you, Doctor, must resist the urge to sleep in your suits," she scolded. "What you need, Dr. Cook, is a wife."

"So I do, Miss Ames, so I do," he agreed. "I also need patients who have babies during daylight hours or who do not stumble into trees coming home late from the public house." He touched her cheek. "Don't worry, Miss Ames. He won't bite. He may growl and snap a bit, but just bully him into some food, keep him warm, and hold his hand."

Anthony Cook rubbed lightly at the little frown that appeared between her eyes. "You know where to get in touch with me, my dear, uh, Miss Ames. Now, go do your good deed for the summer and rescue this chocolate merchant from himself."

6

"RESCUE the chocolate merchant, indeed," Libby grumbled after she saw Dr. Cook out the door, warned Joseph strictly to stay out of the squire's fields, and took her reluctant way back up the stairs.

Candlow had left a covered tray with breakfast on it outside the door. Libby armed herself with it and knocked.

There was no answer. She sighed and knocked louder, and was rewarded with a gruff, "Oh, Lord knows you're coming in anyway," from the inmate within.

She squared her shoulders. "Indeed I am, Mr. Duke," she said in her cheeriest voice, and was rewarded with a frosty glance that reminded her forcefully of her father with new recruits on parade.

She set the tray alongside the bed. "You must be hungry," she said, and took the lid off the oatmeal.

The chocolate merchant screwed up his face and looked with vast distaste at the offering before him. "I only require some more cordial," he said after a thoughtful perusal of the treat before him.

"What you require is food in your stomach, sir," she replied.

He fixed her with that frosty stare again, and her toes curled in her shoes. One would think you had commanded a regiment at Waterloo, she thought as she returned his stare. You must have been a sergeant major at least.

"I ought to know what I need," he said slowly, drawing out each word and clipping it off.

He raised his hand to his hair to smooth it back and Libby noticed again how his hand shook. The sight gave her heart and strengthened her own resolve.

"Until the time comes when you do know what you need again, I think you will dance to the doctor's tune," she said, her own voice soft but just as precise as his.

"Dance," he roared. "I can barely walk!"

Libby tightened her grip on the tray of oatmeal and resisted the sudden urge to dump it on his head. "Do you want this oatmeal?" she asked.

"No. Not now, not ever. If you won't give me some cordial to ease the pain a bit, I want my pants."

Libby shook her head. She set the tray back on the night table within easy reach. "Candlow has retired your bag to regions unknown in this house."

"You could ask him," came the comment, barely under control.

"But I am not curious, sir," she replied.

"Damn your eyes," he roared, but the fire had gone out of his voice. The merchant threw himself back on the pillow and closed his eyes. He shivered involuntarily.

Libby took a step closer to the bed. "Can I help you?" she asked.

He opened his eyes and glared at her. "You can bring me something to drink," he insisted.

"I will not."

"Then go to the devil." His voice was quiet, but she could tell he meant it. The gooseflesh marched down her spine as she walked to the door and then paused for a last look.

"Very well, Mr. Duke," she said, her voice matching his, calm for calm. "If you need help, you need only summon me."

She left the room, closing the door quietly behind her. She ducked instinctively as the bowl of oatmeal hit the other side of the door. Libby pursed her lips tightly together. "Dr. Cook, I will beat you about the head when I next see you," she declared out loud, and then shook her head. "Providing I could reach your head. Sir, you are safe."

There was no other sound from the room. Libby stood there
a moment, wavering, and then went to her own room. She
grabbed up her chip-straw bonnet, the old one Lydia had judged
unfit, and tucked her box of paints under her arm. The orchard
had lost its bloom, but she knew she was still in time for the
flowering of red clover in the meadow. She could spend the
day sketching and absorbing the sun, and return in the late
afternoon, refreshed and ready to join battle again with the
imperious chocolate merchant.

She picked up her easel and went into the hall. She almost
made it past the door to the guest bedroom, but she stopped
to listen.

There was no sound within. The silence should have satisfied
her, but it did not. With a sigh, Libby set down her easel and
paints and quietly entered the room.

Oatmeal smeared the door. She pushed the bowl aside with
her foot and peered closer at the man on the bed. He lay on
his back, staring up at the ceiling, his hands clenched at his sides,
the knuckles so white that she feared they would burst the skin.
The chocolate merchant was sweating, even as he shivered.

As she watched in amazement, his mouth opened in a soundless scream. The hair rose on her neck, as if she heard it. Libby
hesitated only one moment more and then put the clover and
the meadow from her mind. She took a deep breath and cleared
her throat.

Slowly, almost painfully, the man on the bed turned his head
toward her and then looked away, as if the sight was more than
he could bear.

Libby felt her anger return in a rush that left her breathless.
Hot words rose to her lips, but he spoke before she could.

"Miss Ames, I wish to God that you would hurry away from
the door," he said, his voice tight with strain. "Please, Miss
Ames, I beg you, step lively and you'll be safe enough."

Mystified, she did as he said.

He still would not look at her. "Miss Ames, it is only that
there is such a cluster of snakes on the door frame that I feared
for you. And do watch your step. The floor is writhing."

Startled, she looked back at the door, gleaming white and
cheery in the morning sunlight that streamed through the

curtains. She looked down at the floor, which admitted of nothing more terrifying than an old Persian carpet of intricate design.

"Sir, there is nothing here, nothing at all."

He shook his head, still not looking toward the door. "I wish you would come away from there."

Without another word, she hurried to the bedside and sat down. She poured him a drink of water. As the water dribbled into the cup, he opened his eyes hopefully and turned toward the sound. When he saw it was only water, he sighed, but did not look away. She raised his head up and he drank enough to wet his lips.

His tone was more conversational then, reasonable. "I merely need a small drink, Miss Ames," he said, his voice smooth, except for a slight tremor that did not escape her ears. "That is all."

"No."

Libby looked on in horror as he began to cry, sobbing out loud, begging for a drink. She wanted to leap from the chair and run from the room, her hands over her ears. Through it all she lay there rigid, his hands clenched into tight fists as he wailed and begged. Libby stared at him a minute more and then tentatively reached out her hand and touched him on the arm.

In another moment, she had worked her fingers into his closed hand, which she clasped in a firm grip. Libby scooted her chair closer. She stroked his arm with her other hand until he began to relax, little by little. When his tears stopped, she dabbed at his eyes with her apron, all the while holding tight to his hand.

He slept finally, and she relaxed in the chair, wishing that Candlow would come with a pillow. When the door opened, she looked toward it expectantly and then felt her stomach plummet to her shoes.

It was a little woman with a big nose and a red face and could only be Aunt Crabtree. Uncle Ames called her "the family aunt," the impoverished member of the family who lived from relative to relative, depending on the needs of the respective households.

"Aunt Crabtree?" she whispered.

The bonneted head nodded vigorously, but came no closer. "Is he contagious?" Aunt Crabtree asked.

Libby almost said no, when a wonderful idea filled her mind. It was a stroke of genius that Lydia would chortle over, were she here.

"Oh, Aunt Crabtree, he is fearsomely contagious."

The woman leapt back into the hallway with a little shriek that made the chocolate merchant twitch and shift about.

Libby freed her hand and tiptoed to the door. The old lady, the rest of her face as red as her nose now, sat and fanned herself from a chair halfway down the hall. Libby hurried toward her, gave her a peck on the cheek, and took her hand.

"How grateful I am that you did not go in there, my dear. Uncle Ames would never forgive me." Libby steadied her voice and looked about in conspiratorial fashion. "Aunt, it is culebra fever."

She paused for dramatic effect and also to assure herself that Aunt Crabtree was unacquainted with Spanish. The woman, her hat on crooked now from her strenuous exertions to get far away from the still-open doorway, nodded seriously, her eyes wide, and Libby continued.

"It is highly contagious. I had it in Spain when I was a child and I am immune." She paused and dabbed at her dry eyes. "We can only be grateful that the man happened to faint practically on this doorstep, Aunt, or else no one could have tended him."

Aunt Crabtree gulped. "How merciful are the ways of providence, child," she said.

"Merciful indeed, Aunt," said Libby, crossing her fingers and hoping that God was far away from Kent at the moment. "I recommend that you keep away from this hallway until I tell you it is safe. And even then, well, who knows?"

Aunt Crabtree was already heading for the stairs. "I will direct Candlow to put me in the housekeeper's old room downstairs," she said as she scurried down the steps. "If you need anything, my dear . . ."

The rest of her sentence was gone with the slamming of a door.

Libby stayed where she was another moment, wondering

where her scruples had vanished. "It is merely that I cannot deal with you right now, Aunt Crabtree," she excused herself.

Hours passed. She was mindful of Candlow peering into the room and then sending a maid to quietly clean the oatmeal off the door. A steaming pot of tea appeared at her elbow. She sipped gratefully as she held tight to the chocolate merchant and watched him drift in and out of restless sleep.

He woke once with a start as the afternoon shadows were climbing across the bed. He looked around in alarm at his surroundings and closed his eyes again, as if he feared what he saw. Libby wiped his forehead dry of sweat and did not relinquish her hold on him.

After the sun went down, she tried to let go, but the man whimpered and stirred about restlessly in the bed until she gave up the attempt. Joseph brought her dinner on a tray and cut up the beef roast for her while she ate with one hand.

"Is he going to die?" Joseph asked when she finished, his voice a loud whisper.

"No, my dear, I think not. He will be better in a few days," she whispered back.

Joseph shook his head, his eyes wide. "I hope you do not catch what he has," he declared.

Libby smiled at her brother. "I do not think it is contagious."

Joseph peered at the man in the gathering darkness. "He doesn't seem to be throwing out any spots, Libby. That is a good sign."

"No, no spots," she exclaimed, and then patted her brother on the knee. "It is nothing for you to worry about, so do not exercise your mind."

Her answer satisfied Joseph. He sat with her until he began to yawn, then kissed her on the cheek and took himself off to bed.

Libby yearned to follow, to go down the hall to her own room, throw herself down on her bed, and not even worry about removing her shoes. Instead, she remained where she was, holding tight to the chocolate merchant's hand as he mumbled in his sleep, perspired, and shook.

She had never seen a man so destroyed with liquor before,

not even among the hard-drinking officers of her father's regiment in Spain.

"What have you been doing to yourself?" she murmured as she toweled off his sweating face and neck where the perspiration had puddled on the sheets. "What is so bad that you must see it through the bottom of a bottle?"

He did not answer her, but only opened his mouth again and again in that soundless scream that so unnerved her, his eyes opened wide upon some nameless horror that she could not see. In desperation, she put her hand over his eyes until she felt his eyelids close under her palm.

What a shame your commanding officer has taken so little interest in your plight, she thought, remembering the care that her father took to know the whereabouts of each man discharged from duty. When she was old enough, he had pressed her into service as he dictated letter after letter to hospitals and places of employment, seeking help for his soldiers invalided out of the service.

Libby removed her hand from the merchant's eyes and touched his face, noting the fine bones in his cheeks and the handsome shape of his lips. What a pity you did not soldier for my father, she thought as she rested the back of her hand against his neck for a moment. He would have seen to your welfare, as any good commander should.

Libby was lost in contemplation of her father when the door opened and Dr. Cook stuck his head in. She motioned him closer, rubbing her eyes with her free hand and wondering why the house was so still and what the hour was.

The physician loomed over the sleeping man and then gently felt for the pulse. When he seemed satisfied, he unbuttoned the merchant's nightshirt and knelt down, head on his chest, to listen to his heart beat.

"Good steady rhythm," he murmured at last as he got to his feet. "The man must have the heart of a Hercules."

"I don't know why it is you must always sound so bereft when you discover people in good health," she observed, but not unkindly.

"Hush," he commanded, and then weakened the order with the self-deprecating smile she was coming to appreciate. "It is merely a hazard of the profession, Miss Ames." He touched the man's pulse again. "Be aware that I did not rend my garments and sit among the ashes."

She smiled back, despite her exhaustion. "Why did you stop? It must be terribly late. And I wish you would not sleep in your suits. You must be the despair of your housekeeper."

"Which inquisition shall I respond to first?" he asked, his voice alive with good humor. "I stopped because I noticed the light in the window. It is past midnight. I put this particularly handsome suit of clothing on fresh since I last saw you this morning, but I sleep when I can, and it is rumpled. Excuse it. Father's housekeeper gave me up long ago, and I have never been able to maintain a valet, for obvious reasons."

Libby giggled, but did not relinquish her grip on the chocolate merchant.

"Won't he let you go?" the doctor asked.

She shook her head. "Poor man! I wonder how much in his life he has been solitary. He looks so wretched, sir, as though he were used to seeing himself through difficulties alone." She searched for understanding in the doctor's face, and found it. "No one should be alone in desperate situations."

"I couldn't agree more," said the doctor. "He sleeps soundly now. Try turning loose."

Libby did as he said, and the merchant slumbered on.

"I could sit with him now, Miss Ames," Dr. Cook said.

She leaned back in the chair, free of the merchant, but shook her head again. "No. You keep far worse hours than I do." Libby twinkled her eyes at him. "Besides, Dr. Cook, I would not forgive myself if you could not return to your house and rumple up another suit."

"Silly nod," he said mildly.

Libby was surprised at this side of the staid, clumsy Dr. Anthony Cook. *Lydia will be amazed when I tell her that Dr. Cook is human,* she thought.

After a long moment spent in idle contemplation of her face, which should have discomfited her, but did not, the doctor turned to his patient again. "Has he eaten anything, Miss Ames?" he asked, his voice all business again.

"No, nothing. I asked him this evening when he was lucid,

and he said he feared he would throw it back up. I did not press him.''

"He is probably right. It is often that way with drunks," the doctor said.

"Oh, pray don't call him that," she said quickly.

The doctor regarded her again. "Oh, and has our mysterious candy merchant taken your fancy?" he asked. "That is what he is, my dear, a drunkard, and destined to remain so unless we can dry him out."

Idly, he placed his fingertips against the merchant's neck for another check of the pulse. "And so he will remain, more like. I wonder what it was that started him drinking? He appears to be a merchant of some substance, if one can credit the quality of his suit."

"A merchant at very least," said Libby. "Sir, you should have heard him order me about. He sounded like a duke. Or at least a sergeant major." She laughed. "How he reminded me of Papa's sergeants, especially if I did something to disturb the calm of the regiment."

"You miss those days, don't you?" Anthony Cook asked as he pulled up another chair and sat beside her.

"Oh, I do," she said, the animation unmistakable in her voice. "I miss the marches, the cantonments, even the food sometime. And the sound of Spanish, and the little children, the smell of camp fires . . ." Her voice trailed off and she looked at the physician shyly. "But I am boring you."

"You couldn't, Miss Ames, you couldn't," he murmured. He touched her wrist, his fingers going to her pulse without his even being aware of it. "When the gypsies arrive for the hop-picking this summer, you will have to visit their camp fires."

"I shall," she said, and moved slightly. He was sitting too close.

The physician remembered himself and laughed softly. "Good, steady rhythm! Beg pardon, Miss Ames. It is a habit. I suppose I would feel for the Prince Regent's pulse, if I were ever to shake his hand."

She smiled in the dark, charitable toward the hulk of a man

who seemed so at ease beside her. "Well, it is comforting to have a professional opinion that my heart beats."

"Yours and others, too," he said enigmatically, and then proceeded directly onto another tack. "I have been asking in Holyoke about our candy merchant. No one in the public houses or the food warehouses has heard of our own Nesbitt Duke, although all are familiar with Copley's Chocolatier. Indeed, the food brokers tell me that as a rule, Copley's does not venture on selling trips when the weather is warm."

"How odd." Libby could think of nothing intelligent to say. She felt a great stupidity settle over her that she could only credit to exhaustion.

The doctor stirred beside her and Libby roused herself sufficiently to remind him that the hour was late and he needed to be home.

In answer, Dr. Cook snapped open his watch and stared at it. "So it is," he agreed. "I will take myself off if you will go to bed. Tomorrow, our mysterious chocolate merchant should be hungry enough to eat oatmeal. It is what I hope, at any rate."

He stood up then, the chair protesting as he left it. Dr. Cook shoved his hands deep in his pockets and stared down at his sleeping patient.

"Do you know, Miss Ames, I have wondered if drinking is a disease," he said.

He looked at her quickly, ready to gauge her reaction. When she made no comment, but only dabbed at the merchant's forehead, he continued, his voice less tentative.

"You're a rare one, miss. Most people laugh me out of the room after a statement like that."

She smiled and shook her head, her heart warming to this strange and open man. "After Joseph's accident, Papa used to say to me, 'What a mystery is the human body.' " Libby sighed and leaned back in her chair. "For all that we live in a modern age, sir, there's much even doctors don't know."

She heard his chuckle. The doctor rattled the keys in his pocket and started for the door. "True, indeed, Miss Ames. You need only ask any lawyer and he will tell you how little

doctors know." He sighed and fiddled with the door handle.
"Or you need only ask any honest doctor in practice. How little
we know about anything. Do get some sleep, Miss Ames."

He paused again. "I hear that he has snake fever. Despite
the lateness of the hour, I was met by a curious little woman
who told me to be very careful. I promised her that, I, too, was
immune."

He winked and left the room. In another moment, Libby heard
the crash of the little hall table, victim of Dr. Cook's late-night
blundering, followed by a markedly unprofessional oath. Libby
clapped her hand over her mouth to stifle her laughter. Dr. Cook
strikes again, she thought.

Libby's plans to remain at the merchant's bedside were
disrupted an hour later by Candlow, who sat himself down
across from her and fixed her with such an expression of
sorrowful unease that she bowed to the pressure and retired to
her bed. She had only the faintest memory of sinking into the
welcome feather mattress.

Her own unease was replaced by optimism with the rise of
the sun. Libby lay in bed, hands clasped behind her head, and
thought of her father. "I disremember anyone ever made so
glad by the mere rising of the sun," he had declared to her on
more than one occasion. "How simple you are, child."

He was right, of course. She felt her spirits rise higher as
she went to the window, leaned her elbows on the sill, and gazed
out on as perfect a morning as Kent ever lavished on its
inhabitants.

She sat in the window then for a moment, relishing the sun's
warmth. Perhaps the merchant would agree to some nourishment
today. Perhaps he would disclose something about himself. And
even if he did neither of those things, Libby knew she had the
heart to get through the day, because the morning was so fair.

She dressed slowly, taking more time with her hair than her
usual quick twist of the heavy braid and poking of pins here
and there. She stood in thought a moment, a generous handful
of shining brown hair in her hand, and wondered if she ought
to take a deep breath and cut it. "You're dreadfully far from
the mode," Lydia had told her only days ago as she patted her
own shorn locks and coaxed the little curls around her fingers.

But the weight of it felt good on top of her head. She decided to postpone the event and wait until Lydia returned from Brighton with new ideas about what was fashionable and what wasn't. "For all I know, if I wait long enough, I will be *à la mode* again," Libby said to the mirror. "Not that it matters."

Her toilet quickly accomplished, she paused outside the door to the guest room, knocked, and then pressed her ear at the panel.

"Come in," said the merchant, and he sounded remarkably clear.

She turned the handle.

"On one condition."

She stopped.

"Sir?"

"Promise me that you do not have any oatmeal. I hate oatmeal." His tone was conversational and there was a bantering quality to it that was new to her.

"Cross my heart and hope to die, sir," she said.

"Then you may enter."

The room was still gloomy, the draperies pulled, but Libby saw the merchant sitting up in bed. His face was pale and unshaven, but his eyes were open and alert.

She approached the bed, her hands behind her back. "How do you feel, Mr. Duke?" she asked cautiously.

He frowned at her. "Rather like someone has used my body to beat out a camp fire. Not that it's any interest of yours."

"My, but you're a rude one," she declared, secretly pleased right down to her shoes that he was not shaking or crying.

"I certainly am," he agreed, "and I'll get a great deal more rude if you don't bring me . . ."

He paused. Libby held her breath and crossed her fingers behind her back.

"Some tea and toast."

Libby exhaled her lungful of air and clapped her hands together. The chocolate merchant winced and she put her hands behind her back again and started to edge out of the room.

"I'll be only a moment, sir," she said.

"You'll be less time than that, Miss," said Candlow behind her, and she whirled about to see the butler in the doorway, bearing a covered tray. "I was here before you, miss."

Candlow was dressed impeccably as usual, but there were dark smudges under his eyes and his well-lived-in face had settled further.

Libby eyed him, her hands on her hips. "I would suspect, Candlow, that you were here all night."

"He was," said the duke, a touch of irritation mingled with amusement in his voice. "Is no one ever left alone in this house to suffer in silence?"

Libby considered the question in some seriousness before her own good humor surfaced. "I suppose not, Mr. Duke." She came closer and gave the merchant the full force of her smile. "Be grateful that Mama is not here. It would have been hot bricks at your feet, a poultice for your chest, and possibly a leech or two, if Joseph had been prevailed upon to visit the pond."

The merchant shuddered in mock horror. "And chamomile tea and sal hepatica?"

Libby nodded. "You obviously have a mother, sir."

"Doesn't everyone?" quizzed the merchant. "Although I do not know that she would have done those things . . ." His voice trailed off.

"Who, then, sir?" Libby asked.

"Oh, others," he replied vaguely.

Her eyes wide, Libby hurried to his side. She touched his arm. "Oh, sir, I never thought. You have a wife. Only tell me her direction and I will inform her of your accident. Candlow, why didn't we think of that? I am distressed."

The merchant reached over and stopped the agitated movement of her hands by grabbing one in a firm grip. "There is no one to tell, Miss Ames, no one."

Libby let him hold her hand. "Surely there is someone, Mr. Duke. Everyone has someone."

The duke eyed her thoughtfully in silence, as if he were considering all those near and dear. Libby watched his face.

"There is no one really too interested in me, my dear," he said finally.

Libby felt tears welling in her eyes. She looked away and brushed at them.

The merchant tightened his grip on her hand. "See here, Miss Ames, are you really that concerned?" he asked, his voice soft. He leaned back against the pillows and attempted a joke. "I suppose that the emporiums I supply with chocolate would miss me."

Libby sobbed out loud and dabbed harder at her eyes. The chocolate merchant stared at her in amazement.

Candlow cleared his throat. "Miss Ames has a soft heart," he said.

"So I gather," Benedict murmured. He raised her hand to his lips and kissed it. "You can't imagine the compliment you have paid me," he said.

Startled, Libby withdrew her hand from his and wiped her eyes. "Heavens, Mr. Duke, you must think I am a silly nod," she said.

"You certainly are," he replied. "Now, where is my tea and toast?"

His bracing words, delivered with a wink, dried her tears and recalled her to the business at hand. Libby rose, curtsied deep, and flourished her hand toward the butler. "Very well, sir, since you are waxing imperious again, ta-dah, breakfast!"

With a flourish of his own, Candlow settled the tray across the chocolate merchant's lap and whisked off the lid.

"Well done, indeed, Candlow," said the duke. "You're as good as any I have seen in noble houses." He paused, cleared his throat, and recovered. "Or at least, what I imagine those butlers to be like."

"Indeed," said the butler.

The chocolate merchant gagged on the toast and only sipped at the tea, but there was a grim, determined look in his eyes that encouraged Libby more than she would have thought possible, considering the paucity of his intake.

"That will do, Candlow," he said finally when the toast— after a second attempt—proved insurmountable. "Just leave the tea, please."

"As you wish, Mr. Duke."

"I would still prefer a cordial," he complained when the butler closed the door behind him.

"You'll not get it in this house," Libby said. "And I shall not return your trousers, either."

"When I am old and gray, eh, madam?" he murmured. "I may be forced to wrap a sheet about my middle and set off that way to seek my fortune, if you will not oblige me with my pants."

Libby laughed out loud at the thought, and was rewarded with an answering smile. "Sir! Whatever would the neighbors think?" she teased.

"Who cares? I am sure I do not."

"Sir, you may spout off like a duke if you choose, but here in Kent we must behave ourselves to suit the neighbors."

"What did you say?" he asked suddenly, his eyes intense.

Libby stared back in some confusion. "Oh, I don't know. Something about coming on the lordship. Nothing that signifies. And you do have that air about you, sir," she concluded, and then rushed on. "And I have to wonder how you manage to sell much chocolate that way."

"Sell much . . . Yes, yes, it is a deplorable way I have," he agreed. "I suppose there are many far better merchants." He paused a moment and then perjured himself without a blink. "How fortunate that I am the nephew of Charles Copley."

Libby nodded. "Aha! That does rather explain the excellence of your suit, Mr. Duke."

"I thought it a rather drab one, myself, Miss Ames," he said without thinking, and then attempted a recovery. "But of course, I would bow to your obviously superior knowledge of men's clothing, but I don't bend too well right now, especially in a nightshirt. Only give me a day or two."

"And so we shall," Libby said. She blushed for no discernible reason and turned with relief at a familiar knock on the door.

"Dr. Cook, do come in," she said.

Dr. Cook, looking no less rumpled than he had the night before, came into the room, peering at them over his spectacles. He gazed at Libby in admiration for a moment and then remembered the object of his visit and turned to his patient.

"Hold up your hand, sir," he asked, and nodded in approval.

"Much steadier, Mr. Duke, much steadier." He observed the toast crumbs on the merchant's sheet and eyed the teapot. "What, no oatmeal?"

"Not now, and not ever, Doctor," said Nesbitt Duke. "I'd rather sip my own phlegm."

Libby laughed out loud and then put her hand over her mouth.

"Oatmeal does have that quality about it," the good doctor agreed. "Possibly that is why the Scots are so dour."

"I am certain of it, sir," replied the merchant. He pulled back the sheet and exposed his legs. "I think I will mend rapidly, Doctor."

Dr. Cook smiled, pushed his glasses up higher on his nose, and poked and prodded. "Not a pretty sight, Mr. Duke, and destined to scar, but then, how often are your limbs bared to view, anyway?"

The duke shrugged. "Since I don't swim with the Brighton crowd, I think it a matter of concern to me alone."

After another careful perusal, the doctor replaced the sheet. He put his hands in his pockets and went to the window. "I don't suppose we have any real reason to keep you here, sir."

Libby sighed and the little sound seemed to fill the room. He needs longer than this, Dr. Cook, she pleaded silently with the physician's broad back. How is he to stay off the bottle if he is turned out into the world again so soon? Oh, please.

She looked at the chocolate merchant, who folded his hands across his lap and appeared to be deep in thought. When he said nothing, Dr. Cook turned to him.

"Really, sir, it is your decision. We cannot force you to stay here against your will. As much as I would like to," he added softly.

"Why?" asked the duke. "What possible interest can you have in me?" His tone was not belligerent. It was a serious question. He regarded the doctor with real interest.

Dr. Anthony Cook removed his spectacles and polished them with the tail of his coat. "Dear me, lad," he replied, as if startled anyone would ask such a foolish question. "How can you ask such a question? I care. That is all. Libby—Miss Ames—does, too."

The merchant looked from Libby to the doctor. She held her breath as Benedict appeared to waver.

"But you don't even know me."

"Hardly matters, Mr. Duke," the doctor said brusquely. "If you were the archbishop of Canterbury or a peer of the realm, it would make no difference to me."

"No liquor?" the duke asked, his voice soft.

"None, lad. Not a drop. Not even a whiff."

The chocolate merchant sighed and sank lower in his pillows. "The issue is settled, then, sir," he declared. "Besides that, no one seems to know where my pants are." He gestured toward Libby. "And we care what the neighbors think, don't we, my dear Miss Ames? I am yours, sir, and yours, Miss Ames. Do your best."

"Oh, I shall," Libby declared.

7

SHE was as good as her word. Without a complaint or murmur, Libby Ames set about her task of stitching the Duke of Knaresborough's broken body and spirit back together. Somehow she seemed to sense that there were deeper wounds that she could not salve away with Dr. Cook's marvelous "Mystic Soother," a balm he had concocted during his Edinburgh days and used on everything from tooth canker to saddle sore.

Morning and night, she smoothed on the balm, humming softly to herself, completely unmindful that young ladies as gently born as she usually didn't set eyes on hairy masculine legs until marriage. The duke mentioned something about that to her once and she just laughed.

"I suppose you are shocked, Mr. Duke," she agreed, wiping her hands on her apron and placing one layer of gauze over the worst of his gouges. "I spent too many years with Wellington's army to let a little thing like that bother me."

He was aghast, and his face showed it. "Surely you didn't tend the battlefield wounded?" he asked, irritated with himself that his voice came out in such an undignified squeak.

She stared at him in equal surprise. "And was I to stand by, wring my hands, and faint when there was so much to be done, Mr. Duke? 'Tis no wonder you didn't last in the army beyond Waterloo." She was silent a moment, her face set as she finished her gentle task and covered his legs with the sheet again. "Oh, forgive me," she said at last, "but that was unkind." She stood up straight and looked him right in the eye. "It was some small way that I could help. That's it, simply put, sir. I never begrudged a moment of it."

He could tell from the conviction in her voice that she did not, and he had the sudden, heartening thought that there probably wasn't anything horrible that she had not seen and dealt with. And how have you managed to survive so unscathed? he asked her, but only silently. He hadn't the courage to put his thoughts into words, because they would only mean more questions he wasn't prepared to answer.

"We could have used you at Waterloo," he said finally.

Her eyes clouded over and she sat down on the bed, almost without realizing it. He shifted himself obligingly to give her more room.

"I would have been there, too—at least in Brussels, Mama and I—if Papa had not died in Toulouse," she said.

Her voice was calm, composed, and he sensed, more than heard, the great sorrow behind her words. He took her hand and held it for a brief moment.

"What happened to your father?" he asked.

"It was camp fever," she replied. "Imagine how strange, Mr. Duke. He had soldiered all through Spain for years and years with scarcely a scratch, and here we were at peace at last, and on our way into Paris itself . . ."

Her voice stopped and she remained in silent contemplation, swallowing hard several times, until she could speak. He wanted to reach for her hands again, but she had placed them out of his reach.

"He had a sore throat and a mild fever one night, and then next afternoon he was dead," Libby continued. "I don't understand it, not at all." She made a gesture of dismissal, as if to brush away the memory. "I wanted to ask Dr. Cook about it, how a man so healthy could die so fast, but there isn't much purpose to that now, is there?"

It was a question requiring no answer. She sat another moment in silence, in that perfect, self-contained repose that seemed as much a part of her as her boundless energy. She sighed, and

Nez felt an almost overpowering urge to pull her close to him. He stayed where he was, propped up against his pillows, hands clasped together, and allowed her that moment of calm grief.

"And so we came home to Kent," she said at last, and the spell was broken. "And we lived happily ever after."

He looked at Libby quickly, worried for some hint of bitterness in her voice or face, but saw none. She smiled at him then and reached forward suddenly to poke his chest. "And don't be so gloomy. I'm not entirely sure that peace would have been entirely to Papa's liking."

"My God, but you are a brave soul," he said, not meaning to, but not stopping the words.

She smiled again. "You're a goose, Mr. Candy Merchant. We Ames always take life on whatever terms it is offered to us, sir. There is nothing heroic about that. Our experiences have made us practical. You may ask my cousin, sir, and so she will say. I am a dull dog indeed."

He laughed and she poked him again.

"Very good, sir! You have not done that before." She sprang to her feet then, her energy restored, her mind clear, and poured him a glass of water. "Now, sir, Dr. Cook said you were to drink at least four cups of water before luncheon, so be quick about it, else I shall have a great peal rung over me when he arrives this afternoon."

He made a face, but accepted the goblet. "I will float away, Miss Ames. Does the good doctor believe in nothing but water and oatmeal?"

She considered his quiz of a question a moment in that mock-serious way that he was finding so endearing. "As to that, I do not know. I am never sick. It is Dr. Cook's great despair, although he is vehement in denial. He so loves to fiddle with the sick."

He would have liked for her to have stayed close by and jollied him some more, but she was at the window, pulling wide the draperies and raising the window sash to let in the summer. She took a deep breath. "Don't you just love it, Mr. Duke?" she asked.

As a matter of fact, he did. Nesbitt Duke, candy merchant for Copley's Chocolatier, decided that he could easily lie there all day and admire her beauty. But she was gesturing toward the window, where the June breeze played with the curtain. "Not me, silly. Take a deep breath. It's good for you," she challenged, and then grinned at him. "Better than oatmeal."

"If you say, 'It is good for you' one more time, I will throw my pillow at you," he muttered.

"Good for you," she whispered softly, and then shrieked when he hauled back and heaved his pillow at her. Libby danced out of reach and the last thing he saw was the wave of her hand as she skipped out the door.

With one pillow gone and feeling sleepily disinclined to get out of bed and retrieve it, the duke resigned himself to a nap. He folded his hands carefully across his middle and lay there listening to his brain tick and feeling Dr. Cook's Mystick Soother working its magic on his legs. He thought for a moment about a drink, rolling a phantom wine about in his mouth and then swallowing. There was no pleasure in it, but old habits die hard, he was discovering.

The agony of his withdrawal from alcohol had lasted for several days, and when he could make some sense of things again, he could only wonder at first at the intensity of the pain. Did I drink that much? he asked himself several times. Oh, surely not. After two days of enforced abstinence, he was compelled to admit that the answer to that question was an emphatic yes.

He didn't surrender gracefully to his sudden removal from Blue Ruin, malt, and whiskey, but his own rudeness wasn't borne home to him until the afternoon when, his head throbbing and his stomach heaving, he swore at some commonplace tidbit of news or gossip—he couldn't remember what—that Libby had brought his way. She had delivered it in her usual lighthearted fashion and had gasped out loud when he swore at her.

He regretted the words the moment he said them because they were so rude, some detritus from army life that he never would have uttered, drunk or sober, in a woman's presence. He inwardly cursed his impulsive tongue.

She fell silent and turned pale at the vulgarity he had uttered. The silence lay thick about the room. As he watched, in sick disgust at himself, she had come closer, until her face was just inches from his.

"Grow up, Mr. Duke," she said, speaking the words slowly and distinctly so there could be no mistaking her meaning. "Grow up."

He had not complained since that awful afternoon. She had never referred to his rudeness again, but he liked to remind himself of it in moments of quiet as further guarantee that he would never repeat such impetuosity.

And then he turned to his favorite task of late: calling Libby Ames to mind and cataloging her great beauty in his brain, storing away the facts in a calm, rational manner so he could recite them to Eustace in the future.

"Eustace, she is a beauty like none I have ever seen, or you either, and how many years have we been dangling after the choicest morsels on the marriage mart? I hesitate to recall. Libby Ames is just tall enough, and just shapely enough in all the appropriate places. A trimmer ankle I have never gazed upon, and I have seen a few, mind you. But I cannot adequately explain her graceful ways. You will have to see them for yourself."

That consideration never failed to irk him, however momentarily. "Eustace, I hope you never set eyes on this paragon. She is much too good for such a fop as you."

And she was, of this the duke had no doubt. Truly, how could he describe Libby Ames' gentle movements, her exquisite poise, particularly when contrasted—as it so often was—with the bumbling charm of Dr. Anthony Cook. Libby Ames made the clumsy physician look much better than he was. The duke had decided, after a moment's thought, that she would make any man appear a far superior being than reality would dictate. That was Libby Ames' particular gift to the world.

She would even make me look good, he thought as he closed his eyes. Eustace, there are some things in life you are destined never to know. With any luck at all, you will never focus your glims upon Miss Ames, no matter how illustrious her fortune, or by virtue of whatever scheme your papa and her papa concocted so many years ago.

And then the duke would sleep, peaceful, undisturbed sleep,

carried beyond dreams by the memory of Libby Ames' beautiful face.

When he woke, later in the afternoon, his leg paining him, she would be there in his room, her chair pulled up close to the bed, busy at needlework, her tongue between her teeth in concentration, or gazing off into space, thinking her own thoughts. If his face showed any of the pain he felt, her hand would be resting on his arm, her warm grasp better than whiskey.

"Where do you go all morning?" he complained once when his legs were particularly painful and he wanted gin more than he wanted breath. "It seemed to me that you can't wait to dash out of here each morning."

He hadn't thought he was a whiner by nature, but the duke was also discovering that he wasn't much of a patient, either.

Libby put her hands on her hips and shook her head in mock exasperation. "Are we feeling left out?" she asked. "Abandoned? Cast upon the muddy beach of life?"

"Cut it out," he growled, and then winked.

"My days are busier than you think," Libby said. "I find myself compelled to fabricate another story about the progress of your illness to Aunt Crabtree."

The duke nodded, appreciative of the effect of culebra fever on his system. "Am I getting better?" he teased.

"Indeed you are, sir," she replied with aplomb. "Soon you will be well enough for whist with Aunt Crabtree."

He made a face. "I dislike cards, but if that is the sacrifice I must make in order to be completely cured of this loathsome disease, I will chance it."

"Sir, you are all condescension."

He took her by the hand. "Seriously, my dear, what occupies you? I wouldn't mind a few more hours of your time."

She withdrew her hand. "It is scarcely mysterious. I snatch what remains of my time to go into the orchard and paint."

Encouraged by his look of interest, she continued. "I'm not very good, but I did promise myself at the start of summer that I would get much better."

"And have you?" he asked, his pique forgotten.

"You may judge that for yourself," she replied as she pulled up his sheet from the end of the bed to expose his knees. "I shall ask Dr. Cook this afternoon if he thinks a little orchard air would be good for you tomorrow."

That he, the Duke of Knaresborough—who had experienced all of life's pleasures and most of its extravagances—should be so thrilled by the thought of a toddle in the orchard, would have astounded him only a week ago. He lay there, gritting his teeth as she carefully removed the gauze, eager for a glimpse of the orchard, that elysian field.

"Yes, put it to Dr. Cook, by all means," he said as she patted on the Mystick Soother. His comic demon took possession. "He can visit me there in safety. Nothing to trip over," he said, and was rewarded with Libby's smothered laugh.

And soon it was Dr. Cook's turn. His arrival was generally heralded by Candlow, who had such a gleam in his eye that Benedict could only wonder what the good doctor had stumbled over, fallen into, or run up against on his perilous journey from the front hallway to the upstairs guest room. And bedbound as he was, the duke took a certain unholy glee in the doctor's meanderings.

Libby Ames would greet Dr. Cook with that same brilliant smile that she bestowed on everyone—now why did that make him grumpy—and withdraw from the room, allowing privacy for doctor and patient.

Dr. Cook would begin by feeling his pulse. This particular afternoon, Anthony Cook felt the duke's wrist, frowned, and then chuckled to himself.

"My pulse amuses you?" the duke couldn't resist asking.

"No. I do believe that in future I will take it just before I leave your room, and not just as I enter it. Miss Ames does make one's heart beat faster, doesn't she?"

The two men smiled at each other in perfect accord.

The doctor proceeded with his examination, even to the point of making him rotate his shoulder several times.

"Do have a care with that in future, lad," the doctor said. "I am discovering that there is no guarantee of eternal youth, after age thirty."

Usually at this point, Dr. Cook would comment on his eating habits, as faithfully reported to him by Candlow or Libby, remind him to drink water, water, and more water, and then take his leave.

This day was different. The doctor went to the window and rattled the keys in his pocket, prelude, the duke already knew, to some bit of business. "Have you had a drink in the past week?" he asked finally.

The duke snorted and hunkered himself lower on the pillows. "And how would I engineer that, I ask?"

"Anything is possible, lad. I was curious."

"The answer is no."

The doctor opened his mouth to speak, but the duke waved him to silence. "No, no, and let me guess? Your next question: do I want a drink? God, yes, I do. There have been moments in this past week when I think I would have killed for one lick of a cork." He let that bit of intelligence sink in and shrugged. "Then the moment passes, until the next one, and then I deal with that. And so my day goes, Dr. Cook."

"An honest appraisal, Mr. Duke," the doctor said. "I suppose there is nothing to prevent you from taking up with the bottle again when we finally spring you from this place."

"Nothing, Dr. Cook, not a thing in the world."

"Do you want to leave?"

The queston was blunt and, unlike the doctor somehow, totally professional and cold, almost. It was bracing in the extreme and somehow unwelcome. Did he want to leave? No, he didn't. What he wanted more than anything was to take a stroll in the orchard with Libby Ames.

"Not yet."

Dr. Cook grinned at him then, the formal spell broken. "Then don't. I don't know how well your chocolate business will fare if you linger in Kent, but it can only rebound to your advantage, I am sure."

"Yes, likely you are right." The duke hesitated. "Dr. Cook, she promised me a stroll in teh orchard tomorrow, if you think it advisable."

Before he answered, Dr. Cook pulled back the bedclothes and examined the duke's legs. "You're already up and about to the necessary, aren't you, lad?" he asked as his fingers probed the deeper lacerations.

"Yes, of course."

"Then I can't see how a stroll about the orchard can do you any possible danger, particularly as the orchard does not intersect at any angle with a public house or a wine cellar."

The two men laughed.

"You don't really think that Lib—Miss Ames— would permit me within a league of a pub, now, do you?" the duke asked.

"No, I do not," the doctor agreed. "You've already observed that she doesn't object to ordering people about."

"Bossy little baggage," murmured the duke.

"She does tend to make her opinions known." The doctor patted his coat, brushing off imaginary lint. "Please observe that I have arrived here unwrinkled for once, strictly to impress her."

"She is rather a nag about your sleeping and dressing habits, Doctor," the duke replied. "I wonder that you tolerate her."

"I wonder, too. Do you think she will notice my new suit?"

The duke doubted that Libby took much notice of the doctor. "I am certain she will," he prevaricated.

Once the subject of Libby Ames had been introduced, words failed both men. The doctor twiddled with his spectacles as the duke collected his thoughts and finally recalled one pressing concern.

"I will relish this stroll about the orchard, Doctor, but until Candlow recovers from amnesia, I am afraid that I cannot oblige either you or Miss Ames."

"What's that?" the doctor asked, caught off-balance. He dropped his glasses and fumbled after them on the floor.

"Candlow seems to have forgotten where he stowed my traveling case, after you, uh, jettisoned it from that very window."

"Is that a fact?" the doctor asked, when, red-faced, he finished foraging for his glasses and put them on again. "I predict he will undergo a remarkable cure in only a matter of minutes, Mr. Duke."

"What a relief for him," said the duke.

There was a knock at the door, a familiar knock. Both men turned toward the door expectantly. Libby flung the door open, her eyes on the doctor. She was out of breath, as if she had taken the stairs two at a time. "Dr. Cook, Jimmy Wentworth waits below and he says his mama needs you right now."

The doctor nodded absently. "I can't imagine why, really. This will be her seventh, Mr. Duke," he explained. "I think she could find the resource to weed her garden, play a game of whist, and still have the time and energy to tell me how to go about my business. Thank you, my dear."

Libby came into the room, standing well back from the doctor, as if wondering what piece of furniture would be in jeopardy as he made his ponderous way across the room. The duke grinned in appreciation as her eyes widened and she clapped her hands.

"Dr. Cook, that is a magnificent suit," she declared. "I didn't know you were a Bond Street beau!"

Touché, thought the duke. Miss Ames, you are more observant of the good doctor than I would have thought possible, or do I flatter myself?

Dr. Cook blushed, turned aside, and would have stumbled into a potted plant if Libby had not darted in front of him and borne it to safety. She hurried to the window with the rescued plant. "Needs sunlight," she said, still breathless.

The doctor nodded, his face pink. He bowed with a flourish that impressed the duke, who would have thought such an exercise beyond the doctor's talents. "Miss Ames, the inmate in this room needs sunlight, too. You have my permission to take him on a stroll about the grounds tomorrow. He may exert himself only to the extent of picking up your handkerchief, should you drop one."

"You know I never do that, Doctor," Libby teased. "I am not a flirt."

"Miss Ames, you are a managing female with no scruples about wrapping both of us around your little finger," the doctor said, while the duke stared at him.

Libby merely laughed at both of them. "Dr. Cook, you know I never have anything like that in mind," she protested.

The doctor bowed again and waved his hand to the duke. "She is incorrigible, but not without heart. Good luck to you both." He sighed, remembering the task before him. "*Adieu.* Mrs.

Wentworth is probably even now waiting to make a mockery of my obstetrical skills.'' He shook his head. ''Delivering babies for these farm women is rather like having someone behind you telling you how to steer your gig.'' He closed the door behind him.

The duke look at Libby, who had gone delightfully pink at the doctor's words. ''A most interesting man, Miss Ames.'' He looked at her a moment until he was sure he had her attention. ''He's in love with you, of course.''

His heart went out to her, so adorably confused did she look at his statement. ''Mr. Duke, that is absurd!'' Libby pulled some dead leaves from the plant that balanced so precariously on the window ledge. Her agitated motions piqued his own interest.

''It's not so absurd, Miss Ames,'' he argued.

Libby grabbed the plant from the window and plunked it back down on the floor. ''The doctor and I would never suit, sir,'' she said properly, and then ruined the effect by making a face, ''Besides, sir, Squire Cook is looking for a much better match for his only child, and so the squire told me so himself only last week.''

The duke lay back against the pillows, finding it difficult to imagine what possible defect an alliance with Libby Ames presented. *Good God,* he thought, *Eustace tells me the Ames are as heavily laden as Croesus. This squire must be high in the instep indeed.*

''This is a strange place, Miss Ames,'' he said finally, at a loss. ''I cannot understand the squire, then.''

Liby's face grew serious. ''Perhaps you do not know everything about us, sir.''

''Perhaps I do not, Miss Ames,'' he was forced to agree.

His words must have put a crimp in her nose, because she did not visit him after dinner as she usually did, laughing and making fun of the clumsy way he played solitaire, or reading to him from one book or another, it didn't matter which. That he had embarrassed her was obvious. He had thought she would make light of his words. Instead, it was as though his words about the squire, lightly spoken, had reminded Libby Ames of . . . what? He did not know.

I wonder, Libby Ames, do you really love that buffoon of

a doctor, he thought as he lay in restful peace in the silent room. The idea was so absurd that he laughed out loud, rolled over, and composed himself for sleep.

He was dozing off at last when there came a timid knock at the door. He knew at once that it was not Libby, but he raised up on his elbow, curious.

"Come," he said.

Joseph entered the room, and he carried Copley's missing sample case.

As a sample case, it was almost unrecognizable. The shining leather box with its cunning drawers lined with watered silk was dull from mud and rain, and what looked like as thorough an encounter with the road's gravel as his own accident. The drawers were all smashed to one side, as if the case had been struck at full speed by an army of carts. Some drawers sagged out, some sank in, and the rest were gone.

The duke sat up as Joseph came closer. "It appears that my sample case has fallen on hard times," he said at last when Joseph did not seem disposed to fill the silence with words of his own. "Ah, well. So it goes."

Joseph blinked in surprise at his flippant words. To the duke's horror, tears welled in the young man's eyes and he began to cry silently. Nez flung back his bedclothes and stood up, taking Joseph by the arm and guiding him to a chair.

"See here, lad, it's not so bad," he said in a rallying tone. "Honestly, Joseph," he said, his voice less reassuring, when Joseph continued to sob, clutching the sample case to him and caressing its battered sides.

The duke's feeling of helplessness subsided as quickly as it had come, and it was replaced by a new emotion—or at least, one that he had not felt for so long that it seemed new. He felt sorry for someone besides himself.

In another moment, his arm went around Joseph's shoulders. "It doesn't matter, lad, truly it doesn't."

Joseph stopped crying and wiped his eyes with his sleeve. "But how will you earn a living?" he asked at last. "I am worried for you."

It was the duke's turn to struggle with himself as he tried to remember the last time anyone had worried about him to the point of tears. He couldn't recall such a moment, if there had ever been one, and here was this young man, practically a stranger, this moonling, worried about how he, the Duke of Knaresborough, would find bread for his table, now that his means of livelihood was gone. Benedict Nesbitt was touched to the quick.

In silence he rubbed the boy's neck until the tears stopped, and then he offered the handkerchief from his night table. "Blow, lad," he ordered.

Joseph did as he said, and then looked away in embarrassment. "Libby said I was not to trouble you with this, but I know you are concerned about your sample case."

Benedict Nesbitt had not given it a thought since he had heaved it in the gig and beat a hasty retreat from London, but the duke would have allowed the Grand Inquisitor himself to yank out his tongue and use it for bait before he would have ever admitted this fact to Joseph, who cared very much.

"Well, yes, indeed, I was worried about it and wondered where . . . what . . . had become of it. How good of you to find it, Joseph."

The boy smiled then and relaxed. He allowed the duke to take the case off his lap and set it on the floor.

"I knew you would be wanting it, especially after Libby said you were a merchant and that you surely had a sample case about somewhere. I looked and looked until I found it."

Again the duke had to turn away for a moment to examine the intricacies of the carpet pattern until his own vision cleared. "Is that what you have been doing? I have not seen you in several days," he said, his voice husky.

Joseph nodded, his eyes shining, his voice eager. "It took me a week, sir, but I found it this afternoon, just as the light was growing dim. I think it must have fallen off when your gig turned over the first time, and then bounced on down the hill. It was under a bramble bush. I got scratched up, but Libby said she was proud of me."

His face pokered up then, and Nez feared Joseph was going to cry again. With an effort that raised the sweat on his forehead, the boy mastered his emotions. "I'm truly sorry it is in such wretched shape, sir. I don't suppose there is any hope for it."

Nez clapped his hand on the boy's shoulder and gave him a rallying shake. "But I can get another, easy as pie, now that you have restored this one to me," he said, perjuring his soul with no remorse whatsoever. "Copley would have cut up stiff if I had come back empty-handed. Thanks to you, Joseph, I can turn this one in and receive another just like it." He leaned closer. "There is probably a reward in it for you, too."

Joseph shook his head. "I couldn't accept anything, but . . . Well, I do like chocolate. We all do, sir."

"Chocolate it will be, then," said the duke, "as soon as I return to London."

Joseph grinned. "I'm glad, sir," he said softly, and then added, "Do you know I wish I had employment like you. Libby and Mama tell me that I am not a burden to them, but I know I am." His cheeks burned with sudden color. "I wish I could support myself, as you are doing. It must be a very satisfying feeling, Mr. Duke."

Benedict Nesbitt, whose only exertion—after Waterloo—consisted of betting on the horses at Newmarket, nodded in perfect understanding. "Yes, there's nothing as satisfying as earning a living. No feeling quite like it. I really can't even describe it."

"I thought that was how it would be," Joseph said simply. "I would like more than anything to lift the worries from Mama's shoulders, and Libby's too."

What possible worry can you have with thousands in the funds? the duke thought, remembering Eustace's breathless admiration of the Ames fortune. What earthly difference can it possibly make if you never earn a farthing of your own? He nearly asked the question out loud and then realized it would be pointless. Obviously some little corner of Joseph's mind harbored the absurdity that the Ames household teetered on the brink of financial disaster.

He returned some inanity that seemed to satisfy Joseph, who bid him good night and retired, leaving behind the ruined sample case.

"And now I suppose that dratted sample case will just stay there as a reproach to me," he said out loud. "Well, you deserve it, Nez." He flopped back in bed and stared at the ceiling. "Nez, old boy, I wonder if any of your tenants at Knaresborough and wherever-the-hell-else have any idea what a lazy chufflehead you are?''

It was a good question, and one that he had never bothered to ask himself before. Whenever he had been troubled by matters weightier than which waistcoat to wear, or what horse to buy, he had reached for the bottle. Now he lay in bed thinking about himself and wondering where the Benedict Nesbitt he vaguely remembered had really gone after Waterloo.

As he lay there, considering his own flaws, he heard Libby Ames crying.

It could have been a housemaid, but surely the maids slept in the attic or belowstairs, he told himself. It wasn't Joseph, who had left his room in a decidedly more cheerful frame of mind. It could only be Libby.

He got out of bed, tugged down his nightshirt until it covered his ragged knees, and went into the hall. A single lamp glowed at the end of the hall near the stairs. He walked toward it in his bare feet, careful to stay on the carpet runner that traveled the length of the hall, listening at each door until he found Libby Ames' room.

He raised his hand to knock, but only stood there and listened to Libby Ames crying as if her heart were being squeezed dry.

He stood outside her door until she blew her nose, sniffled a bit more, and the room was silent. Without a word, he tiptoed back to his own room and crawled into bed again.

''What can you possibly have to cry about, my dear Miss Ames?'' he asked the ceiling, until his eyelids drooped and he slept.

8

❧

AS she lay in bed the next morning, Libby Ames took the time to give herself a silent scold and a mental shake.

I am turning into an air dreamer, she thought, recalling with some embarrassment her noisy tears of last night and wondering again why she had spent the better part of the evening flung across her bed, sobbing like some character out of one of those feverish novels that Papa had always growled about.

She had been too agitated then to attempt an analysis of her mood. As sunlight spread its warmth across her bed, she attempted to understand her own mind.

With a sudden smile, Libby quickly dismissed the crackbrained notion that she was in love with Dr. Cook, as the chocolate merchant had said. The very thought made her roll her eyes and laugh out loud.

Her misery was wrapped up in her own words, her announcement to Mr. Duke that she wasn't good enough for the squire's son. Not that she wanted the squire's son, she reminded herself quickly, for she did not. It was just the idea that burned.

I am a pooor match for anyone, she thought. The words did burn, so she said them out loud, letting her ears and heart get used to the blunt reminder.

It would be so easy to blame Papa, cheerful, handsome Papa, who always looked so grand in his regimentals, even if the cuffs were twice-turned, the gold braid faded, and his trousers too shiny. He was one of the few officers in Wellington's army forced to support himself and his hopeful family entirely on army pay, and it was never enough, even for the most careful economizers.

Libby sighed. Dear Papa was the dashing kind of man who would catch the eye of any number of susceptible females, even a tobacconist's daughter. No one but impetuous, thoughtless Thomas Ames would have courted her and married her, secure in the knowledge that because he loved beautiful Marianne Gish, others would, too, his father included.

But Grandfather Ames had turned them away from his door. Mama used to tell the story, and her dark eyes would flash with anger at the memory, then cloud over with the humiliation that still burned like phosphorus, long after the event was past. "He just took me by the collar and pointed me toward the door," Mama had said during their Channel crossing with Papa's coffin in the ship's hold and Joseph lying seasick across both their laps. "As though I were a dog that had wandered on the place by mistake," she finished softly, the pain no less, even though the incident was twenty years gone.

The rest of the story Libby had heard from Uncle Ames, dear Uncle Ames, who had witnessed the blow that Thomas Ames struck his father. Uncle Ames, in hushed tones, had told how the old man, dabbing at his broken nose, had risen from the floor as though pulled by invisible strings, and ordered his son and daughter-in-law from his presence forever.

After Papa's shocking death in Toulouse, Mama had sat up all night by the camp fire, burning all letters and papers. She had shown Libby the lawyer's documents detailing her father's disinheritance. "I don't know why he kept these all this time," Mama had remarked as she tore the infamous document into tiny bits and sprinkled them in the fire. "Take that, you evil man," Mama had whispered.

Libby had seen her Grandfather Ames once when Papa, nearly destitute and on half-pay while recuperating from a wound, had taken her and Mama to Holyoke Green to ask for no more than a place to stay until he was recalled to active duty. She was only six, but Libby remembered watching through the bars of the gate as the fierce old man with the shock of white hair rode right past his son without even a glance in his direction.

They had scuttled away in embarrassment to Portsmouth and the little flat over the tobacconist's shop, where they had remained for three months before Papa was recalled to Spain. Libby remembered with painful clarity the relief they all felt to return to that land of war that seemed so much more friendly than Kent.

It was at her late Grandpa Gish's crowded flat where the second set of lawyer's documents had reached Papa, this set a copy of the one Uncle Ames had signed, declaring that now that he was the legal heir, he would never give any money, property, or goods of any sort to Thomas Ames or his wife and child, on pain of losing his own inheritance.

"My father never said in writing that I could not take you up as a housekeeper," Uncle Ames had told her mother years later when they returned to bury Papa in the family graveyard. Grandfather Ames was long cold there, too, and Mama had hesitated before putting her beloved Thomas in the same soil. "If I could have afforded a plot elsewhere . . ." Mama had murmured as the coffin was lowered in the ground. She had stood in silence until the grave was covered, then turned and accepted Uncle Ames' offer.

But there would be no dowry for Libby. Marriage to anyone of similar background was out of the question.

Libby's thoughts wandered to the chocolate merchant. "Too bad you are a cit," she said out loud. "Mama would never allow me to align myself with a cit, no matter how refined you seem."

Another thought followed, one more chilly, that made her sit upright and hug her knees, as though the June air had suddenly turned to February.

"Dear Chocolate Merchant, you would expect a dowry too, wouldn't you?" she said. "How silly of me to think it would be otherwise."

The realization that she belonged in neither class settled on her shoulders like a clammy blanket, and she shivered and hugged herself closer. Mama had never put it into words, but Libby understood her own future. She could only learn her mother's duties well, and someday hope to inherit her set of keys. She would likely spin out her days in the service of others, too genteel for the one half of her family, and not genteel enough for the other, the impoverished daughter of a disinherited son.

And when Mama died, the burden of Joseph would rest squarely on her shoulders alone.

"Joseph, what will we do?" she asked. Libby thought of the squire's threats and resolved anew to keep Joseph in sight as much as possible. I suppose if the squire truly wanted, he could declare Joseph a public nuisance and have him put away. Libby closed her eyes tight against the thought and felt a great anger rise at her own powerlessness. Tears smarted behind her eyelids again, but it was time to get up.

She snatched a hasty breakfast and gave her orders for the day to Candlow, who assured her that Joseph had risen earlier and was busy in the stables.

"And do you know, I have remembered where I put the chocolate merchant's traveling case," he said, his face perfectly composed.

"Candlow, you are a wonder," Libby teased.

He cleared his throat. "I took the liberty . . ."

"Yes?" Libby prompted.

"His one trousers were ruined during the accident, of course, and he has only one other pair, so I found some of the major's old pants," the butler said. "Sir William had been keeping them in his own dressing room. I think they might fit the merchant."

"Good of you, Candlow," Libby said, only the slightest quiver in her voice. "Papa always did hate to see things wasted."

Before she went upstairs to visit the merchant, her guilty conscience compelled her to scrawl a hurried note to Lydia and Mama, telling them of the candy merchant's precipitate arrival in their household. She assured Lydia that her draperies were clean now, and told Mama that the maids had been released for a well-deserved holiday, with only Candlow remaining of the house servants, and the cook, who refused to leave, as usual. She inquired about Uncle Ames' gout, told Lydia to breathe deep of the sea air for her, and closed it all with affection unbounded, theirs truly.

She sighed and rested her chin on her hand. *And now I must deal with Aunt Crabtree.*

Libby went downstairs to the servants' quarters and paused outside the housekeeper's door. Inside, she heard the faint slap of cards on the table. Two more slaps were followed by silence and then an unladylike oath. Aunt Crabtree was losing at solitaire.

"Aunt?" she called through the door.

"Yes, my dear," her aunt inquired, opening the door almost at once. She peered closer at Libby's face. "Tell me, is something the matter with your chocolate merchant?"

"Oh, no, Aunt. Actually, I have come to announce that he is much improved. In fact, we can pronounce him almost cured," she concluded in her most casual tone, looking everywhere but at her aunt.

"Almost?" Aunt Crabtree asked, her suspicion deepening.

"He is well enough to walk in the orchard," Libby said, and then sidled closer and lowered her voice. "And I do not believe he is contagious anymore."

"But you are not sure?"

"No, I am not sure," Libby replied, amazed that her conscience gave her not a twinge. *I am turning into a hardened prevaricator,* she thought as she smiled sweetly at her aunt.

"Well, I will wave at him from a distance, dear Libby." Aunt Crabtree kissed her. "You are a dear child to be so concerned for my welfare."

Libby blushed and could not look at her aunt. She kissed the air near her ear and backed out of the room.

Libby went upstairs and knocked on the chocolate merchant's door. She inclined her ear toward the panel out of habit and nearly fell into the room when he opened the door.

"Whoa, there, Miss Ames, are you taking clumsy lessons from Dr. Cook?" he asked as he grabbed her. "Or do you always listen at keyholes?"

"I never listen at keyholes," she said firmly, pressing her hands to her face to tame the sudden color there. Her eyes lighted on the sample case. "I see Joseph has been here this morning," she said, grateful for this excuse to change the subject.

"Last night."

"I told him not to bother you so late," she said in dismay. "But he was so proud that he found it. I hope he did not disturb you."

The merchant shook his head. "Not a bit. He provided me with some intriguing food for thought."

"Joseph?" Libby asked, her eyes wide.

He opened his eyes wide in imitation of her, and grinned. "The very same. I shall not tell you any more, madam. You have promised me a walk in the orchard, and I am eagerness itself."

"Very well," she agreed. "What must I do to find out more? Joseph is not noted for his scintillating conversation."

"No, he isn't, is he?" the duke agreed. "He is blunt and to the point, and would never make a splash in London society."

Libby frowned, and he took a step back, clutching his chest as though he had been wounded.

"And now you are going to give me a bear garden jaw because I have been making fun of your brother," he said.

"Well, I was, too," she admitted, "so I will be generous this time."

Libby scooped up her paints and easel on the way downstairs, and her bonnet off a convenient shelf by the door that led into the gardens. "I am attempting weeds and small rocks this week, so we must go into the orchard," she explained breathlessly as she hurried along. "Do tell me if I am going too fast for you."

"I shall," the merchant replied promptly, took the easel from her, and strolled along beside her with scarcely a limp.

They traveled the formal gardens in silence, Libby stopping every now and then to pluck a few weeds in the stone-lined beds and then hurrying to catch up with Mr. Duke, her hand tight to her head to keep the bonnet from flopping off.

When she reached him, he took her by the shoulders and pulled her closer to him. Libby stared up at him. She automatically closed her eyes and raised her face, and then opened them in surprise when he tied the strings of her bonnet, gave her shoulders a pat, and turned her loose, chuckling to himself.

"There now. If you must dawdle at every flower bed, at least you will not lose your hat. You must have been a charge to your mother when you were younger.''

She laughed out loud. "Do you know, they used to tether me to the flagpole when they were in garrison?"

"I don't doubt it for a minute," the merchant replied. "The temptation must have been great to leave you there when they marched away."

Libby joined in his laughter.

"Much better, Miss Ames. You seemed a trifle down-pin earlier, and I am glad to know that you have not forgotten how to make merry. I could ask you why the melancholy, but you would not tell me, so I shall save my breath."

They continued in silence, passing through the formal garden and into the kitchen garden, where Libby stopped again and tackled the weeds among the radishes.

The merchant watched her, a smile on his face. "I am wondering how you ever manage to make it to the orchard for your painting," he exclaimed at last when she finished the row of radishes and cast her eyes upon the peas.

"Sometimes I do not, sir," she replied, and started toward the peas.

Nesbitt Duke grabbed her by the arm. "Miss Ames, you have promised me the orchard, and I have been looking forward to this event. I tolerated the radishes, but I do not care for peas."

"Very well, Mr. Duke," she said, and gently disengaged herself.

"And another thing, Miss Ames—can I not call you Libby?" he asked. "After all, you have been tending to my hairy legs this past week and putting up with my alcoholic fidgets. Surely we are on close-enough terms to call each other Libby and Nez."

She considered the issue. "I suppose we are, although you have not seen me at my worst yet, and perhaps *I* should still insist upon Miss Ames."

"Scamp."

He set up the easel for her in the orchard, moving it several times to suit her and then plunking it down and glaring at her when she suggested another location. Libby laughed and moved the easel herself, waving him toward a boulder where he could perch in relative comfort. He sat down carefully, his look of pained concentration warning her that he had probably walked enough for one day.

"Will you be all right?" Libby asked, and he was dismayed to think that some of the pain must have registered on his face.

"I will be fine," he said firmly.

Libby nodded, her mind already on her task, and turned to her paints. She selected the browns and yellows she wanted, and applied them to her well-used palette and then raised her brush, only to set it down, and exclaim, "Drat!"

He looked up from his idle perusal of her trim ankles. "H'mmm?"

She pointed into the distant field. "It is Joseph, and he is much too close to the squire's land. What is the fascination, I would like to know?" she asked herself out loud. "Some days he is worse than a two-year-old."

They both watched in silence, Libby tense, a frown creasing her forehead, and the duke, interested and curious about Joseph.

Libby relaxed finally. "That's right, Joe, go back into the woods," she said softly, and then looked at the duke. "It appears he is heading into our woods now, thank the Lord."

She picked up her brush again and approached the canvas on the easel as the duke made the decision to meddle a little.

He considered the matter. If he asked no questions, if he did not become involved in these lives, beyond an appreciative glance now and then at Libby's ankles, or her trim figure, he could leave this place in a few days, report to Eustace, and return to London.

But he had to ask, and somehow he knew it would make a difference.

"Libby, has Joseph always been . . . well, slow?"

There. He had asked. In some inscrutable fashion, at least in his own mind, he had become involved at last with the Ames family.

Libby seemed not to realize the momentous quality of his question. She merely sighed and sat down beside him on the boulder. He obligingly moved over to make room, but he didn't move too far.

She fiddled with her bonnet strings, as if forming an answer in her mind, and then turned to him.

"Do you know, Mr. Du—Nez, sometimes I wish he had always been slow. Then it would bother him less because he wouldn't remember other times. No, he has not always been the way you see him now. There was a time . . ." Her voice wandered off and he could tell by her expression that she was somewhere far away.

"Once upon a time . . ." he offered helpfully, and she laughed, recalled to the present.

"No! Where you ever in Spain?"

He shook his head.

"I did not think so. You could never mistake Spain for a fairy tale. No, Joseph was thrown from his horse during the retreat from Burgos, four, five years ago. He was twelve." She paused again, remembering. "The path was icy and we were being harried rather close from the rear." She shuddered at the memory. "He hit his head on a stone. It didn't seem to be anything serious at first, but he did not regain consciousness and his head started to swell."

"Was there a doctor?"

"No. He had been killed in the retreat, and in any case, we could not stop until nightfall."

Libby got off the rock, as if the memory were hurrying her along, too. "Poor Joseph! Poor Papa! He had just given Joe the horse for his twelfth birthday. Papa cried and blamed himself, and Mama, oh, how she carried on."

"What did you do?" the duke asked.

"I found a Spanish doctor," she said briskly, as if his question was a silly one. "Papa never was much good in domestic crisis. And Mama?" Libby shrugged. "They were so much alike."

He looked at her with new respect. "You couldn't have been over fourteen or fifteen yourself."

"I was sixteen. The doctor came and was able to drain off some of the fluid. In a few days, the swelling went down, but Joseph was never the same again."

Libby went back to the easel and picked up the brush again. "Poor Joe. For the longest time, he couldn't remember anything. Gradually, some of his memory came back, but he

doesn't reason well anymore; emotionally he is very young."
She dabbed at her eyes. "It isn't too bad, if you just don't allow
yourself to remember how he used to be . . ."

She just stood there, her eyes on the distant field, where
Joseph had disappeared into the Ames' wooded park. "But I
have come to paint, sir," she said at last, closing the subject
beyond his powers to open it again without appearing a complete
rudesby.

He had heard enough. He gazed at her with admiration,
wondering at her strength, wishing there were some way to tap
into it.

The rock was warm, and Libby had seriously come to paint,
he decided after his few attempts to restore conversation failed
to elicit more than a grunt and a "H'mm?" from her. The duke
eased himself off the rock and sat down on the ground, leaning
back against the boulder, letting the sun warm his shoulders.

He sat there, his mind engaged in no more intricate task than
trying to decide which, out of an embarrassment of riches, was
Libby Ames' best feature. He admired her profile, the way her
improbably long eyelashes swept her cheeks. Her mouth was
formed in a pout as she concentrated, and he wished again that
he had kissed her in the garden when she had expected him to.
He liked the way she carried herself, head high, shoulders back.
You look like a duchess, he thought. By God, but you do. She
was not very tall. This first walk together into the orchard had
shown her head to scarcely reach his shoulder. She was a tender
little morsel who would fit quite handily under his arm, and
probably be simple to pick up and carry away when he felt more
like such a venturesome enterprise.

With that pleasant idea circulating in his brain, he dropped
off to sleep.

When he woke, she was still painting, but she had moved
the easel out into the sunshine, away from the shelter of the
apple trees. Her bonnet dangled down her back and the pins
had come out of her untidy hair until it spread around her face
like a dandelion puff.

He smiled to himself, wondering again why she looked so
good to him, in all her dishevelment and fierce concentration.
After a moment's thought, he realized with a start that she was

the first woman he had admired in over a year that he wasn't looking at through the fog of liquor. Everything about her was beautiful, and he was sober enough now to realize that his estimation of her would not change, because he saw her truly as she was.

"Eustace, I think you are about to be cut out," he said, and didn't realize he had spoken out loud until Libby gave him an inquiring look.

He got to his feet slowly, carefully, impatient with the pain in his legs, but grateful suddenly that he had crashed the gig and practically dismembered himself on the road in front of Holyoke Green. *We can tell our children about this someday, and laugh a lot,* he thought as he came closer and set Libby's hat back upon her head.

"You'll be brown as a Hottentot, and look, your cheeks are already pink," he warned, touching her cheek.

She stuck her tongue out at him and turned back to the painting, but he took her in his arms and kissed her before she had time to take another breath or sketch another weed.

She smelled of sunshine and lavender, and her lips were wonderfully soft. She kissed him back with as much fervor as he dared hope for, and then she stepped back suddenly, her hands on his chest.

His hands went to her waist and stayed there. "I know why Dr. Cook rescued me from the road and the bottle," he said quietly. "I am interesting to him. But why have you gone to this trouble?"

She did not move from his grasp. When he embraced her, the paintbrush had slashed a brown streak down the front of her muslin dress. She dabbed at the dress and then met his eyes. "I did it for the chocolate lovers of Kent," she said, without a smile, but a gleam in her eyes that made him laugh out loud and turn her loose.

"It could be that I care," she added softly, and seated herself on the boulder he had vacated.

He sat down again on the ground beside her and plucked a long-leafed wig. An ant was crawling up the stem. He turned the leaf this way and that. "Be serious, Libby," he said.

She touched his head, and the gesture brought sudden tears

to his eyes, so gentle were her fingers. "I hate to see waste, Nez." She waited a moment and folded her hands in her lap. "Was there something at Waterloo that made you take to the bottle? I've known of such things."

How simple. He knew that she would understand better than most young females because she had been raised in war. He also knew that he would not tell her much. He wouldn't describe that nauseating sensation that filled his whole body when the smoke cleared off the battlefield and just before dark covered the land. She didn't need to know that he had raised up on his knees and looked over the dead bodies of his entire brigade, strewn here and there, with only three other exceptions.

"There were only four of us left, Libby," he said, keeping his voice deliberately toneless. "The brigade major, God damn him, a sergeant, and two privates. That was all."

She was silent. Her hand went back to his head. "And it's your fault?" she asked.

He looked at her, a question in his eyes.

"I mean, are you blaming yourself because you survived and they did not? Is it your fault you lived?"

He understood at last, for the first time in a year, and shook his head slowly, unable to speak.

"It's such a small thing, Nez," Libby said. "I hardly know how to say it, because it seems so simple. It's time you forgave yourself because you survived." She moved closer to him and he leaned against her leg. "Maybe it just comes down to that. Maybe it's time you just let it alone."

He could think of nothing to say because she was so absolutely right.

She sat beside him for another moment and then slid off the boulder, kissed the top of his head, and moved off gracefully from the orchard without a backward glance, giving him time to be by himself.

He leaned against the boulder again, feeling almost light-headed with relief that washed over him like a warm summer shower. He could not excuse the fact that he had ignored the three other survivors, following their return and discharge, but he knew that it was within his considerable powers to make it up to them now. He had been granted a reprieve from his personal hell by a little bit of a girl so practical and wise that he could only look at her with renewed admiration, and some other emotion that felt suspiciously like love.

He watched her with renewed interest, a smile on his face, as she walked slowly toward the open field that led to the edge of the Ames land. The bonnet still dangled down her back; he would have to remind her to wear it to save her skin.

The smile left his face. She stood still now, tensed, and then she threw herself into sudden motion, grabbing up her skirts to her knees and running toward the fence, waving her free hand and shouting something that the wind picked up and tossed away.

9

SHE would leave him alone to think about what she had said. Libby walked toward the pasture that bordered upon the squire's land, her mind on her father. She remembered one night years ago with Papa, teasing the camp-fire coals with a stick and listening as he consoled one of his sergeants, the sole survivor of a sudden raid on his file by the French. "Let it alone, lad," Major Thomas Ames had said. "You survived and it's not your fault. Let it alone."

Funny how his words should come back so clearly. And now I understand them, she thought. Libby looked behind her at the candy merchant, who still sat on the rock, his head bowed. Maybe things will be easier for him.

She was distracted from thoughts of her father by a whinny at the edge of the oak grove that marked the outer reach of the Ames land. Libby looked toward the sound, knowing that Joseph and Tunley, the groom, seldom exercised the horses so close to Squire Cook's land. The Ames stallions had been known to jump the fence, which had caused all manner of ill until Uncle Ames had thrown up his hands in disgust and ordered the area beyond the pale of his own horses. "Though I do not suppose Squire Stiff-in-the-rump should object so loudly to free servicing," he had complained once before his sister-in-law, her face scarlet, could hush him up in front of his daughter and niece.

Libby smiled at the memory of her mama, more genteel than
the genteel, and her plainspoken brother-in-law. She waved to
Joseph again and cupped her hands around her mouth.

"Joe, you know you should not be so close to Squire Cook's
land. Uncle will not be pleased."

She watched as Joseph shrugged his shoulders elaborately so
she could see the motion from a distance, and then stood behind
the horse to the side. Libby frowned. She shaded her eyes with
her hand this time and stood still as her brother petted the
panting, heaving animal.

That can't be one of Uncle Ames' horses, she thought. She
started walking again, faster this time, until she was running
toward her brother and the horse.

She arrived, out of breath, full of questions, to watch, wide-
eyed, as the animal strained, grunted, and gave birth to a colt.
Libby clapped her hands in delight as the dark wet creature no
larger than a dog, but with long, long legs, lay still a moment,
sneezed, and began to struggle to its feet.

"Joseph," she exclaimed, her voice softer now. "Oh, won't
Uncle Ames be so pleased. What a beautiful sight!" Libby
reached out and touched the colt, laughing as its wet body
twitched and it turned to nose her hand.

Joseph only smiled and stroked the mare. The horse
whickered softly to him as he pulled his shirt off and began to
wipe down the colt.

"Mama would have a screaming fit if she saw you doing that,
Joe," Libby warned. "Even if it isn't your best shirt."

"Mama is in Brighton," Joseph replied, his eyes full of the
colt, which rested under his brisk application of the shirt. "And
I do not think Aunt Crabtree will look up from her solitaire long
enough to see what I am about. If you don't tell her," he
murmured, and then sat back. "And besides, Libby, this isn't
Uncle Ames' mare."

Libby sucked in her breath, all pleasure gone from the sight
of the animal that even now struggled upright, wobbled, and
fell over in the grass. "Joseph, you don't mean . . ."

He sighed and nodded. "Squire Cook's," he said, and
wadded up his shirt, tossing it from hand to hand.

"Joseph! Sometimes I wonder what possesses you," she said,

and then stood back as the mare nudged at the colt in the grass.

Joseph did not answer for a moment. He watched as the colt slowly rose again, wobbled forward toward its mother, and began to suckle. "I do not understand how they always seem to know what to do, Libby," he said.

Libby took her brother by the shoulder and shook him. "Don't you dare change the subject, Joseph."

He looked at her, his eyes mild, and she knew there was no sense in arguing with him. "Libby, don't be a goose," he said. "She followed me."

Libby sat down suddenly and drew her knees up to her chin. "Rather like Mary and her little lamb, I suppose you will tell me," she grumbled.

Joseph laughed. "Exactly so! There is a weak spot in the fence and she must have come through."

Libby flopped back on the grass and contemplated the clouds overhead while she counted to ten. "I suppose you could not have convinced her of the error of her ways and led her back?"

"Silly," Joseph said. He sat down beside her. "Libby, I did lead her back, honestly, but do you know, the squire's groom is drunk." He looked over at the mare and colt again, each absorbed in the other. "I did not think it safe." He was silent another moment. "Do you think Squire Cook will be angry?"

There were both silent. What would be the use of a full-strength scold, Libby thought as she regarded her brother. As simple as Joseph is at times, I know he is right on this occasion. Libby sat up and absently tugged at the grass, strewing it across her skirts. She thought of the squire's angry face as he had sat fidgeting in her sitting room only a week ago, stirring his tea into a maelstrom and glowering at her.

"Well, perhaps when he sees the outcome, he will give us a chance to explain," she said, her voice hesitant. If he doesn't lock us up as public nuisances, she thought, unwilling to speak her fears out loud.

Joseph nodded and got to his feet. "I am sure you are right," he said, "and look, here he comes now. I suppose we will have our opportunity."

Startled, she turned around, stared, and gulped, wondering why her hands felt so wet all of a sudden and her throat so dry.

The squire raced toward them at a gallop, liberally working his riding crop on his beast, hunched low over its neck, shouting something that they could not hear. Joseph smiled and waved to him, motioning him closer.

"No, Joseph, don't," she said, her voice urgent as she tugged on his arm. "I do not think he is pleased at all."

She gasped as the squire came to a sudden stop in front of her brother that sent his horse back onto its haunches.

The squire quirted the animal upright again and rose in his stirrups. "Get away from my animal, you looby," he shouted to Joseph.

The boy did as he said, but instead of retreating, he came closer to the squire, a smile on his face. "Sir, your mare has a beautiful colt. Isn't that a fine thing?"

Libby cried out as the squire, his face a study in fury, struck her brother across the chest with his riding crop. Joseph gasped, more from surprise than pain, and stared at the man on horseback.

"You don't understand, sir," he cried, and then sank to his knees, trying to cover his head and his bare shoulders as the squire struck him again and again.

With a cry of her own, Libby sprang into action. She darted closer to the squire's rearing, plunging horse as she tried to drag Joseph away.

"Joseph, please," she urged. "Let us go. Stop, Squire Cook. We mean no harm."

Libby tried to haul Joseph to his feet as the blows rained down on them both. She could hear someone shouting from the fence, but still she tugged on her brother's arm as he tried to protect his head, the squire's horse dancing dangerously close.

"By God, you Ames are a nuisance," the squire shouted. He pushed at Libby with his booted foot and, when she would not retreat, struck her with his riding crop.

She staggered and fell down in the deep grass, practically under the horse's hooves. Someone grabbed her around the waist and she struck out blindly in protest, kicking her feet.

Her rescuer shoved her to one side and she stayed where she fell as the candy merchant, a set look on his face more frightening than the squire's blows, stepped in front of the bleeding boy and grabbed the reins.

"I wouldn't lift that crop one more time," he said, his voice soft but with that steely edge of command that Libby had wondered about before.

The squire's hand shook as he slowly lowered the riding crop. The vein in his neck stood out and Libby stared at it in horrified fascination, almost as if she could hear the pulse pounding just under the skin.

As she kept her eyes on the squire, Libby touched her fingertips to her face. The skin felt hot and her cheek was swelling already, but there was no blood.

No one spoke. The only sound was the squire's labored breathing. Libby looked more closely at Joseph then and cried out in dismay. The crop had lifted the skin off his temple near his ear. The blood mingled with the sweat that glistened on his neck. Libby reached for his hands and pulled him toward her, clutching him close as they knelt together in the grass.

The candy merchant, his knee stained bright red through his trousers, did not take his gaze from the squire, who glared back.

Libby held her breath. Some instinct, surfacing through her own personal fear, warned her that if the squire made a move, Nesbitt Duke would pull Cook off his horse and kill him with his bare hands.

She had no doubt that he could do it. Murder was in his eyes and on his face. Have you forgotten where you are, sir? she thought even as she looked away, unable to stand the sight of what was nearly inevitable.

Through the soles of her shoes, Libby felt the thundering presence of another horse and rider. She looked around to see Dr. Anthony Cook's horse take the fence in one graceful motion and race toward them. She sighed and closed her eyes for a moment, relieved all out of proportion to see the doctor's familiar person coming toward them.

The doctor, his face registering shock and high color, rode more slowly toward the strange tableau in the pasture. Without a word, he knees his horse between the candy merchant and the squire, forcing the duke to drop his death's hold on the reins. In silence, he held his hand out to his father for the riding crop.

Squire Cook will never surrender that crop, Libby thought as her hand strayed to her cheek again. She held her breath as the doctor sat his horse so calmly and waited.

With an oath that made the hair prickle on Libby's neck, the squire slapped the quirt into his son's hand. He made to grab up his reins again, but the doctor was too quick. Anthony Cook held the reins tight in his gloved hand.

"No, Father," he said, his voice scarcely audible over the squire's labored breathing. "Stay where you are until I find out what is going on."

The squire pounded his hand upon his saddle. He pointed a shaking finger toward Joseph. "That imbecile was trying to steal my horse," he shouted.

"I think that hardly likely," Dr. Cook said, his voice dry and clinical and utterly without emotion. "We could ask Joseph, sir."

"The boy is an idiot," the squire screamed, unable to contain himself any longer.

Dr. Cook sighed and dismounted. He slapped his horse away, but he did not leave his position between his father and the others. He motioned to Joseph, who looked at the squire, hesitated, and gave him a wide berth as he came closer to the doctor.

"It's not your horse, lad," the doctor reminded him as he touched Joseph's face, turning it toward him. He ran his hand lightly over the gash by his ear.

"I know it is not my horse," Joseph said as he twisted out of the doctor's grasp. "The horse followed me into this pasture. I swear it. She was only trying to give birth." He gestured toward the mare again and the colt that had finished nursing and lay practically hidden in the grass.

After another long look at his father and the candy merchant, who still eyed each other with considerable distaste, the doctor crouched in the grass, looking at the little animal. He smiled for the first time and looked at Joseph.

"Maybe you should have run for my father's groom," he suggested as he ran his hand down the mare's leg and then stood up. "This is too expensive a piece of blood and bone to throw a colt in a pasture like a carter's hack."

Joseph shook his head. "I tried, Doctor, but the groom was drunk."

"That's a lie," shouted the squire.

Dr. Cook turned to his father suddenly and raised his eyebrows. Libby watched in fascination as the squire subsided. She looked back at Dr. Cook with new respect. Gracious, she thought, I would never have dared level such a look at my father.

Apparently the candy merchant had similar thoughts. He nudged Libby and whispered in her ear. "A cool customer, eh, Libby?"

She nodded and whispered back. "He tends to come through in emergencies in the most astounding way, so I am discovering."

"Who would have thought it? Surely not I," the duke murmured, his eyes on Dr. Cook.

"Go on, lad," said the doctor.

Joseph shrugged. "I don't know what else to tell, sir. The mare followed me back into this pasture. I didn't think I could keep her from throwing the colt, sir, no matter whose field it was."

"I can understand perfectly," agreed Dr. Cook, a touch of humor back in his voice. "Females of most species seem to know what to do at times like this."

The squire swore another dreadful oath and looked away. He gathered up the reins and dug his spurs into his horse, guiding the animal closer to his son and the colt. He sat in silence for a long minute, looking down at the colt.

"I suppose you will tell me I should be grateful this moonling was here to witness the blessed event," he growled.

"I wouldn't presume to tell you anything, Father," Anthony Cook replied, "although a little charity would not be out of place."

The squire turned to Joseph. "I make no apologies. Your uncle will have a letter from me in the morning."

They watched him go, cantering across the field, pausing to look at the fence, which was in ill repair, and then continuing on until he was gone from sight.

Joseph looked up at the doctor, who stood watching his father. "Sir, should I lead them back to your stables?"

The doctor shook his head. "Best not, lad. My father is in rare ill humor. He will probably pour a bucket of water on that worthless groom of his and send the poor wretch on the errand." Dr. Cook shook his head and nodded to Libby. "I think I will take dinner at your place tonight, Miss Ames, if it is agreeable. I do not imagine there will be overmuch conversation of an uplifting nature around my own table this evening."

Libby nodded. "Of course you may eat with us, Dr. Cook. Sir, what will he do?"

"He will call me an unnatural son for siding with you and dredge up all the arguments he has thrown at me for the last eight years since I first mentioned my plans to seek a medical degree—no matter that this has no bearing on anything that has happened here. He will rail on and on about a man of the leisure class engaged in such dirty business. Father rarely forgets a good argument. When he feels better, he will stamp off to bed."

"How do you tolerate him?" Libby burst out, close to tears.

The doctor did not answer for a moment. He petted the colt one last time and rubbed the mare's long nose. "He is my father, Miss Ames. I owe him that, surely." He peered at her more closely then for the first time, and the color drained from his face. He touched her inflamed cheek. "Merciful heavens, Miss Ames, I had no idea. Did he—"

"I fell down," she lied, devastated by the look in Anthony Cook's eyes. "In all the excitement, I must have tripped."

"Onto your face?" The doctor tugged at his coat, his knuckles white on the lapels. "I am so ashamed," he said.

Libby's heart went out to the doctor. Without a word, she stood on tiptoe, put her arm to his neck, and pulled him down. She kissed his cheek. "Please don't be," she whispered in his ear. "I will be fine."

He put his arm about her waist for a brief moment and then motioned to Joseph. "Well, lad, you have earned yourself a place in the annals of midwifery."

Joseph's face fell. "Oh, I am sorry," he said.

The duke smothered a laugh, and Dr. Cook glared at him over his spectacles.

"No, lad, it is a good thing. Maybe sometime you can really help a mare throw a colt."

"Do you think I could do that?" Joseph asked.

"I expect you could, with the right instruction," the doctor replied. "But let us endeavor in future to see that you practice on your own patients."

Joseph nodded. "I know, sir. You are right. But I meant no harm, and nothing went wrong, sir? Cannot your father see that?"

The doctor shook his head. "I don't understand it, lad. For some reason, you rub him raw." He looked at the others. "Let us go indoors and see if there is some Mystic Soother for your back, Joseph." He peered at the duke again. "From the looks of his trousers, our chocolate merchant could use some, too." He peered next at Libby, and his eyes softened. "And maybe there is a dab for your cheek," he said. "Where you fell down."

The Duke of Knaresborough took his mutton that night clad in his dressing gown, his knee covered again with Mystic Soother and bandaged. Libby had insisted that he join them in the breakfast parlor for his meal.

"If you do not, the doctor will feel uncomfortable, and if he is uncomfortable, there is nothing in the room that is safe," she had teased, tugging on his arm when he seemed inclined to resist.

"Surely your Aunt Crabtree will object," he said even as he winked at her.

"Aunt Crabtree is almost as famous for her nearsightedness as she is for her solitaire," Libby said.

"I wonder that your mother left her to chaperone," the duke murmured as he allowed himself to be pulled along.

"You may blame Uncle Ames," she said. "He has any number of female relatives who would leap at the opportunity for a summer of free room and board."

His resistance was only token, although he would not have told her that, not yet. The thought of dinner by himself was unthinkable, especially with Libby Ames below, entertaining the doctor. He wanted to be part of their conversation, wanted to sit there in peaceful silence and enjoy the society of people who were rapidly become indispensable to him.

"I have no pants, Libby," he had offered as his only excuse.

"No matter. Wear that robe of yours. After dinner I will hem my father's pants for you," she had said. "We have suffered this long with the sight of your hairy legs and I do not see how you could ruin our appetites."

He wanted to keep her longer in his room, but she had grabbed up her papa's pants and danced out of his reach, intent on other errands. *You will probably keep going at a dead run until you collapse in exhaustion over your plate of soup,* he thought. It puzzled him that she had no abigail of her own, but he did not question it. He knew that most of the servants had been dismissed for a summer holiday of their own. Still, it was odd that an heiress of her scope would deign to shoulder the burden of housekeeper, for that was what she was. He put it down to the eccentricity of the Ames household and considered it no more.

Dinner was as pleasant as he had dared hope, Joseph cheerful but quiet, his attention riveted on the marvelous courses that kept coming from the kitchen; Dr. Cook was also closely involved with the plate in front of him. Aunt Crabtree sniffed at the cook's art, called for bread and milk, and slurped it noisily. She darted little glances at the chocolate merchant and hitched her chair far away from him, to his amusement. Libby managed to put away a respectable meal in jig time, and still find time to see to the comforts of her guests.

It was refreshing to see a female eat so well, Benedict thought, remembering only two weeks ago a dreary, endless dinner with Lady Claudia Fortescue, his sister's latest project. He had watched that paragon consume a piece of fish the size of a farthing, a thimble of wine, then roll her eyes, dab her dainty lips, and declare herself replete. It was a hum, and he knew it.

Nothing about Libby Ames was a hum. She ate with relish, cried if she felt like it, fought like a tiger for her brother, and laughed with her head thrown back and all her marvelous teeth showing. Lady Fortescue would have slid under the table in a faint over such female enthusiasm. The duke, on the other hand, was delighted.

"Divine, Miss Ames," Dr. Cook exclaimed after Candlow removed the squab skeleton that he had picked clean. He managed a discreet belch behind his napkin. "How grateful I am that your cook is too devoted to abandon your household when Uncle Ames goes to Brighton.''

"So am I, sir," she said. "Uncle Ames would have cut up stiff if Mama had not consented to accompany him and fulfill his wildest culinary dreams."

"Your mother cooks?" the duke asked. "You are a talented family. I suppose now that you will tell me you are a seamstress of renown and also make your own hats!"

Libby laughed and leapt to her feet. She twirled around, showing off the pretty primrose muslin he had been admiring with sidelong glances throughout dinner. "One shilling, sir, and the ribbons off an older dress."

The doctor applauded, shouted, "Hear, hear," and Libby curtsied and beamed at him. No wonder the Ames fortune is reputed to be bulging at the seams, the duke thought as he admired the dress and the pretty girl in it. His own fortune was respectable enough. Think how it would benefit, placed alongside that of an heiress who knew how to make a guinea dog sit up and beg. Libby Ames is much too good for you, Eustace Wiltmore, the duke thought as he raised his glass of water to her and winked.

No one felt like lingering over port, particularly as the doctor had waved it away immediately, before the duke had time to form an opinion on the subject himself. And there was the daunting prospect of Aunt Crabtree, sound asleep and snoring softly. Libby helped her aunt to her feet and took her upstairs while the men sat at the table and contemplated nothing more strenuous than coffee.

"Very good," said Libby when they joined her in the sitting room. "I get so impatient when men linger in the dining room, as if they are afraid to come out." She threaded a needle and stuck it in her dress front, ordering the duke to try on a pair of her father's pants in the next room.

When he returned, she made him stand on the footstool while she circled about the floor, pinning here and there and casting a critical eye on her handiwork. He was content to move about at her order as he listened to the groans of anguish from a corner table where Joseph appeared to be defeating Dr. Cook at checkers.

Libby looked up at him, a twinkle in her eyes. "I think Anthony Cook lets him win. Isn't he kind?"

The duke nodded. Kind to a fault. He thought again of the horrific scene in the pasture and the capable way the doctor had handled all of them, horse included. He felt a twinge of envy, wishing that Libby would look at him that way, as though he could do no wrong.

"But then he will stumble over his own feet, or the carpet pattern, and I must confess to the giggles," Libby said, bursting that little bubble. "Dear man. I wonder what woman will ever have him?"

The duke sighed in spite of himself. Safe. In another moment he was comfortably ensconced in his chair again, ankles crossed on the footstool, while Libby sewed new hems in her father's pants and hummed to herself.

It was all so domestic and peaceful, and Benedict Nesbitt found himself contented right down to his toes. If I were to tell these people that I used to grace four and five parties, routs, and balls each evening, they would stare at me as if I were an Iroquois in Westminster Abbey, he thought, and chuckled at the idea.

Libby lifted her eyes from her needlework and raised one eyebrow at him.

"I was just thinking how pleasant this is," he said hastily, "and contrasting it with . . . with Waterloo."

"I already told you we are dull dogs," Libby said mildly, and turned her attention back to the pants in her lap. She raised her eyes again suddenly. "But perhaps that was what you were needing, Nez?"

How she could get so unerringly to the heart of the matter continued to astound him. The duke nodded, struck by the fact that never before in his entire life had he ever felt part of a family like he did here at Holyoke Green. His father had died young, and he remembered him only as a dimly seen figure on the edge of his growing up. Life had been a succession of nannies and then boarding schools with early hours, hard beds in cold rooms, hazing by the upper forms, and loneliness that had doomed him to painful heartache, until he became sufficiently cynical. His mother and sisters had paraded through his life at appropriate intervals, but never when he needed them.

None of them had sat with him through long hours like Libby Ames, holding his hand, as if it were the most important task that would ever fall her way. No one had ever allowed him to talk and talk, the way Anthony Cook had encouraged him. He thought of Candlow's numerous solicitous kindnesses, and of Joseph's genuine pleasure at seeing him up and about, and he knew that he owed these people more than he could ever repay.

But the doctor was speaking as he fumbled with his watch. "And now, Miss Ames, I had better take my courage in hand and see if Father has changed the locks on the house. Good night, Nez. Joseph." He sighed and stretched, coming dangerously close to the glass figurines on the whatnot shelf.

The duke noted with some amusement that Libby had set aside the pants and was poised to spring to the rescue of the glass ornaments, even as she smiled and held out her hand to the doctor.

He held it longer than the duke thought necessary, but Libby didn't appear to mind. "With any luck, my dear, my patients will be two-legged tomorrow."

Joseph followed him to the door and Libby took her brother by the arm. "My dear, did I leave my paints and easel in the orchard? Would you be a love and fetch them?"

"Of course," he said promptly, and darted out the door ahead of the doctor.

She saw Dr. Cook to the door and just stood there, watching him walk into the night, her shoulders shaking as he tripped over the flower bed bordering the driveway and uttered a mild oath obviously learned at his father's knee. In another moment, she closed the door and dissolved into silent laughter before straightening up, and catching the duke's eyes, and collapsing into laughter again.

"Oh, dear," she said, wiping her eyes.

"If you were ever to kiss him, I expect he would fall into a fit from which he would never recover," the duke said.

"We will never know, will we?" she said, her eyes merry. She went past him into the sitting room for her father's trousers and returned to the duke in the hallway. "Here are you, sir," she said, and fixed him with a stern look that didn't fool the duke for a minute. "When you have run through these, it will be time to return to London."

She hesitated then, and the duke knew she had something else on her mind. "Nez, I have been meaning to tell you . . ." Her face turned red. "I really don't go around kissing people in orchards."

He looked at her face, rosy with embarrassment, and thought to himself, You should, Libby dear. At least, as long as it is I. Instead, he shook his head. "No apologies, Libby. Let us just say I was overcome with the idea of being outside again."

She sighed with relief. "Thank the Lord. I don't want you to think I'm not what I should be. And besides . . ." She hesitated again.

Besides what he did not know. He thought for a minute she was going to tell him what he already knew about the long-standing promise between her father and Eustace Wiltmore's father, but she did not.

He said good night and started upstairs.

A thought struck him, and he looked back at Libby where she stood in the hallway, watching him.

"My dear, do you know, I have just realized that I have not wanted a drink all day?"

She raised laughing eyes to his. "I do not know that we can promise so much excitement every day, Nez, to distract you, but we will try."

He nodded, climbed another step or two, and realized that he was in love with Libby Ames. He started down the steps to say something to her—what, he really didn't know—when the door opened and Joseph came in with the paint and easel tucked under his arm. His eyes were alive with excitement.

"Lib, only imagine what I saw."

"I cannot, Joseph," she replied.

"The gypsies have returned!"

10

THE GYPSIES had returned to Holyoke Green. Benedict noticed the pinpoints of light from the flickering camp fires as he paced about his room, unable to sleep.

Long after the house was quiet, he had walked back and forth from the door to the window, glanced out, and returned to the door to begin again. From the door to the window, he thought of Libby Ames and saw her in his mind. At the window, he paused and thought about the gypsies. From the window to the door, he wondered what Libby would think when she learned he was a duke instead of a purveyor of chocolate. It could only further his cause in an amazing way, he decided, if she didn't cut up too stiff when he confessed all and told her that he had been sent originally to spy upon her.

The more he paced and the more he thought about it, the more muddled he became in his mind. There would be trouble with Eustace, of course, particularly if his friend ever got a glimpse of Libby Ames. He would never call me out, thought the duke, but he will be a trifle miffed. That the promise between the fathers could be circumvented he had no doubt. These were modern times, not the Dark Ages.

A place would have to be found for Joseph eventually, too. He didn't know Libby Ames well, but he knew her well enough to know that Joseph's welfare would always be a prime consideration when she contemplated marriage. London would never do, he thought as he took another turn toward the window. Suppose the duke's friends saw him? No, Joseph would have to content himself elsewhere.

The duke stopped at the window finally and leaned his hands on the sill, looking out at the June-scented darkness. He would write to Eustace first thing in the morning and tell him that the affair held no promise for him and that he might as well remain in Brighton. It was not the truth, but Benedict Nesbitt did not think he could deal with Eustace right now. He would smooth his own path with Libby and make all things right before he took her to London to meet Eustace Wiltmore and the other lions that awaited.

Soon even the gypsy camp fires flickered out. With a sigh, the duke went to bed and surprised himself by dropping into a sound sleep.

"The gypsies have returned," Candlow said when he came to open the draperies and bring a can of hot water.

Nez lay with his hands behind his neck, deriving some amusement from the evident fact that Candlow did not seem to bear his news with the enthusiasm obvious in Joseph last night.

"Joseph was quite pleased with those tidings last night," the duke said.

Candlow sniffed. "That's what comes from living in foreign parts for so many years, I don't doubt. We as are Kentsmen born and raised know better than to get exercised by the notion of smelly gypsies." Candlow looked out the widow and frowned, as if he expected to see them camped on the front yard and washing their persons in the fountain. "They are early this year."

Benedict rolled over and propped himself up on his elbow. "What do they come for, Candlow?"

"The hops harvest, Mr. Duke, and that is still six weeks away." Candlow turned away from the window. "They come to trade for horses, more like steal some. If you have anything of value, do not leave it lying about."

"I shall not, Candlow," said the duke, barely able to suppress a smile. "Are Joseph and Libby about yet?"

This apparently was a sore subject to the butler, but he was too well-bred to show his disapproval, beyond the raising of one eyebrow. The duke was forcefully reminded of his own retainer.

"They have collected several pans that want mending and have taken them to the gypsies already," said Candlow. He cleared his throat and rocked back and forth on his heels. "Miss Crabtree retired to her bed again at the news."

"I do not doubt it," the duke said as he sat up. "I understand the necessity of a figurehead of Miss Crabtree's talents, but she is a singularly ineffective chaperone. That reminds me, Candlow. Does not Miss Ames have an abigail to do things for her of the pan-mending variety? Is her maid away on holiday with the others?"

The butler forgot himself enough to smile. "Miss Ames with an abigail? I don't think so." He leaned closer in conspiratorial fashion. "Such independence comes from too many years following the army about, I am sure, but the Ames will do as they choose, will they not?"

The duke nodded in solemn agreement. He knew enough about the eccentricities of the titled and wealthy to have augmented Candlow's text.

And speaking of text . . .

"Candlow, can you get me my pen, ink, and paper? I have some correspondence that cannot wait."

Candlow nodded. "With pleasure, Mr. Duke. Miss Ames has been wondering when you would feel good enough to inform your relatives of your mishap."

His relatives. He had not thought of them in some time, and the matter did deserve some rational contemplation. Mother would not object to Libby. The Ames name was a good one, despite whatever deficiencies—real or imagined—that Mother could dream up. Benedict Nesbitt felt sure that the Ames fortune would more than recompense for the fact that Uncle Ames was only a baronet.

Augusta would be charmed, too, at least until she realized that Libby Ames—no, Lady Nesbitt, Duchess of Knaresborough —was not one to be lead by anyone. By then, Gussie's opinion would scarcely matter. Libby would have stormed the battlements of society with that beauty, sweet nature, and indescribable charm the good duke himself was rapidly finding indispensable to his happiness.

He spent the better part of the morning at the escritoire in his room, considering what to say to Eustace and discarding mistake after mistake. He finally decided on the simple expediency of the truth, telling Eustace that he had at last found the girl of his dreams and that by the time he received this missive, Eustace would probably want to return a letter of congratulations.

"The truth hurts a bit, Eustace," he said out loud with some satisfaction as he affixed a wafer to the letter and pocketed it.

Libby and Joseph had not yet returned from their visit to the gypsies, which suited him. He would take the time for a stroll into Holyoke, where he would post the letter himself.

He considered the matter of his leg for a moment, and then decided that a genteel stroll would do it wonders. I could continue to coddle myself, he thought, but to what end? He smiled to himself as he started out, remembering much longer forced marches through terrain more arduous than a Kent neighborhood. And with snipers shooting at me, too, he added to himself. I can rest if I get tired, and not have to worry about death around the next bend in the road.

The walk would be long enough for him to think of his next course of action. I will confess all and throw myself upon her mercy, he decided as he started back from the village, hands in his pockets, the sun warm on his back. I don't suppose any woman alive would be disappointed in a duke. She knows that I have dipped too deep in liquor, but it did not seem to disgust her, and besides all that, I am a reformed man. She will laugh when I tell her about Eustace's harebrained, rum-sodden scheme to scout her out in Kent and see if she was a fit vessel for the Wiltmore aspirations.

His fancies occupied him so fully that he did not hear the doctor's horse until the animal's hooves struck a stone beside the path. He started in surprise and then looked up with some amusement.

Dr. Cook was seated correctly atop his mare, his gloved hands poised precisely and capably over the pommel, his eyes closed, his spectacles barely lodged upon his lengthy nose. He was sound asleep. Nez thought he snored.

The duke cleared his throat and the doctor's eyes snapped open. He jerked his head up and watched in dismay as his glasses slid off his nose. He grabbed for them, but Benedict was quicker, catching them in midair and returning them, with a flourish, to their owner.

"Dr. Cook, do you always sleep in the saddle? Surely your father didn't banish you to the stables for championing us yesterday."

"Oh, no, nothing like that," said the doctor. "A paucity of dialogue passed between us last night, but by then he had vented his spleen on the groom and I got only what was left."

The doctor dismounted, his horse trailing along behind him like a large dog. He rubbed his eyes. "It has been a long night, Nez, that is all. One of many long nights. I disremember when I last slept the night through."

They walked along in silence. The doctor seemed distant, uncommunicative, and the duke rose to the challenge. "Well, I trust the outcome was to your liking."

"The patient died."

An awkward silence stretched out along the path the two men followed. The doctor blinked his eyes several times, and the duke saw that he was dangerously close to tears. "Well," Nez said heartily, even as he wished he would keep his mouth shut, "I suppose you are better equipped to deal with death than the rest of us."

"I never deal well with death, particularly when the patient is a child," the doctor said, slapping the reins in his hands in agitation. "Death of a young one is such an affront to nature."

The duke found his attention captured by a lark on the wing as the doctor whipped out a handkerchief, blew his nose, and pocketed it again, his eyes straight ahead, his lips set in a firm line. He sighed then and managed a slight smile. "I brought her into the world three years ago, only to usher her out of it this morning, poor honey. I hope to God I never grow used to such events, Mr. Duke."

"Indeed, no," Nez murmured. "I didn't mean to sound so flippant. I must remind myself not to speak until I think."

The doctor seemed to come out of himself then. He touched the duke's arm. "It is a tendency we all have, lad, that propensity to speak where we should not. I didn't mean to trouble you with my woes. No one forced me to go into medicine." He laughed then, a rueful laugh with little humor in it. "Indeed, it was quite the opposite."

The doctor grew more expansive and his mood seemed to lighten as he talked. The duke was wise enough to be silent and give Anthony Cook free rein of the conversation.

"Father still does not understand why I wanted to be a doctor. I can't tell you how many times he said, 'But you are a gentleman's son,' until I wanted to crack his head." The doctor stood still and took the duke by the arm. "I am certain you, of all people, must understand. There is little value in doing nothing, is there?"

"None at all," agreed the duke, hoping that he sounded convincing.

"I mean, you understand the value of work—you, a purveyor of chocolates," said the doctor, warming to his subject, enthusiasm evident in his eyes again. He laughed at his own earnest tones and shook his head. "I suppose some of us are not meant for a life of leisure, eh?"

I shall be smitten on the spot by a just God if I continue prevaricating, thought the duke as he laughed along with the doctor.

They walked along in companionable silence, the horse nudging his master until the doctor gave the animal a slap on the flank and sent him home. Cook looked at the duke then, as if seeing him for the first time.

"See here, sir, should you be out jauntering along? I must admit, however, that you do seem cheerful for one who must have his budget of aches and pains. How are you feeling?"

"Quite fine, thank you."

" 'Quite fine,' and nothing more? Sir, you appear to have a gleam in your eye," teased the doctor, whose own eyes were red with late night, badly drawing fireplaces in crofters' cottages, and the general anxiety of his calling.

"Well, yes, I suppose I do," replied the duke, gratified, flattered even that his love showed on his face. Perhaps with this guileless man he could try the waters now, test out this great, remarkable truth he had learned, and see how it flew with Dr. Anthony Cook. The man had a right to know.

"Sir, I am in love. I have discovered that I cannot live without Miss Libby Ames close by."

If he expected something more than raised eyebrows and silence from Dr. Cook, he was disappointed. News of this import demanded herald angels at least, or so Benedict reasoned. But Dr. Cook merely looked thoughtful, even a trifle down-pin, truth to tell.

"You are certain?" the doctor asked at last when the gates to his own estate came into view.

"Never more certain of anything," Nez replied stoutly. "Sir, why do you look at me like that?"

He could not have described the look, not even under oath, that Dr. Cook fixed on him then. It was as though someone had struck the portly physician a sound blow between the shoulder blades and he was trying to regain his breath without appearing too startled. Where his expression was habitually kindly, avuncular even, it was now desperate, as if the man longed for breath and saw no hope of getting any. It was the look of a drowning man on a sunny road in the middle of Kent.

"Are you well, sir?" Nez asked in surprise, putting his arm around Dr. Cook.

As quickly as the curious look had come, it was gone. Dr. Cook straightened himself around, managed a little chuckle, and smiled. "I am quite well, thank you." He hesitated and then plunged ahead. "Sir, how do you think the Ames family will regard your suit?"

Benedict laughed out loud, his head thrown back, a wonderful laugh that he had not attempted in over a year. "Oh, Dr. Cook! There is more to me than meets the eye."

The doctor nodded and settled his hat more firmly upon his head. "So we suspected," he murmured.

It was the duke's turn for surprise. Good God, did Libby know? And had she said nothing?

But the doctor was still speaking. "She rather suspected that you were a partner in the firm."

The duke nodded, relieved to find his secret still his own.

He would tell Libby when the time was right, when he could smooth it over and not risk her sudden disgust at his dissembling. "Oh, I am that and more," he replied quixotically.

They walked a little farther in silence, each man absorbed in his own thoughts. If the doctor was a little slower, if he seemed more deeply involved in his own private conjectures, the duke could only put it down to Anthony Cook's all-night exertions.

Benedict owned to a small twinge of conscience. He knew the doctor loved Libby; that was obvious for all to see, except to the doctor himself. He was as clear as water. The duke gave himself a mental shrug. Libby had assured him that such a notion on the doctor's part was ridiculous.

He looked sideways at the doctor. The notion was far from ridiculous. A man would have to be chipped from stone or carved of wood not to be drawn to Libby Ames, of this Nez had no doubt. But did Libby Ames return the doctor's feelings? Never. She had even laughed at Anthony Cook behind his back and told the chocolate merchant in that artless way of hers that she and the doctor would never suit.

And so he would leave the matter. The duke looked up then from his own silent contemplation of the road and turned around. Both of them, deep in their personal musings, had continued some distance beyond the gates of the doctor's estate.

Nez laughed softly and put his hand on the doctor's arm to stop him. To the duke's amazement, Anthony Cook tensed and made a fist, as if he were about to turn on him. The duke drew back, startled, and the two men stared at each other.

The moment passed quickly. The doctor took a deep breath and rubbed his eyes. "Dear me, I must be more tired than I imagined. This pace I have been keeping of late begins to remind me of the worst days of my training in Edinburgh, when working straight through for seventy-two hours was not unknown."

If the doctor could recover so well, so could he. "Doctor . . . Oh, dash it all, surely I can call you Anthony. You would greatly benefit from having a driver. Then you could nod off in safety between calls."

"It is a thought."

You could also use a wife, the duke thought, but it isn't going to be Libby Ames. He smiled at the doctor. "Sir, retrace your steps and go to bed."

To his relief, the doctor grinned. "I should think of these things myself. Good day to you, sir."

If Cook's smile hadn't reached as far as his eyes, the duke chose to overlook that fact. With a wave of his hand, Nez continued down the road, hands deep in pockets again, whistling to himself. When Libby returned from the gypsies, he would put the question to her. He looked back at the doctor, who was met inside the gates by his horse. The animal nudged him down the lane and the duke felt another twinge of sadness. Poor fellow. Too bad he will not win this one. He is deserving of all good fortune.

But not *that* much good fortune, he thought, and smiled in spite of his philanthropic regard for Dr. Cook.

Libby would never have admitted her disappointment over the gypsies to anyone. When Lydia—with much gyration of face and obvious disdain—had told her about them last winter, Libby had taken her cousin's unflattering description with a grain of salt and had resolved to see them for herself before she passed judgment.

She remembered gypsies from her years in Spain, those inhabitants of the caves of Granada, with their proud eyes, their arrogant carriage, and the magic way they stamped the earth with their feet and stirred the soul. She recalled the time Papa had taken her—without Mama knowing—to have her fortune told. Libby remembered sitting on his lap, her eyes wide, her mouth open, as the woman with gold hooped earrings and an improbable beauty mark had predicted wealth, love, and leisure to enjoy them.

These gypsies of Kent were nothing like she remembered. The sullen-eyed man had snatched away her pots to be mended, as if she would change her mind at the last minute, and Joseph had gone off happily enough to look at the horses. She had been left to sit on a log and wait in solitude, a stranger among those with nothing but suspicion in their eyes, when anyone bothered to glance her way.

It was a small encampment, with only two wagons once painted extravagantly but now shabby, the paint chipped and flaking. There were no older women about, only a young one with small children. The little ones were ragged beyond any poverty she could remember from Spain. They crouched on their haunches watching her, until their mama called them away, and they vanished as silently as they had come.

Libby amused herself watching a small baby in the distance, slung in a blanket in the low branches of a tree. The wind blew, the tree moved, and the little one raised its hand to the leaves dancing overhead. The baby chortled, and Libby smiled, wishing she had leave to come closer to look at the child. Instead, she sat where she was, her hands folded primly in her lap.

Nesbitt Duke. She thought of their kiss in the orchard, her cheeks growing pink again at the mere memory. Last night, as he started down the stairs, she had been sure he would kiss her again, if Joseph had not burst in the door with his news of the gypsies.

A kiss from a gentleman, especially one as handsome as the chocolate merchant, was not an everyday occurrence. She had been kissed before by some of Papa's officers and the sensation had always been a pleasing one, but never before had she wanted to follow any of those men to their rooms.

She sat up straighter. Her thoughts were leading her down paths better left untrod for the moment, no matter how enticing they were. Better not think about how much she wanted Nesbitt Duke, for that was what it boiled down to.

Libby admitted to an unwillingness to consider the subject, even in the privacy of her own brain. She had schooled herself since Papa's death and the realization of her own poverty that there would likely never be anyone willing to engage her affections on a permanent basis. Her long experience with the army had taught her that men needed dowries more than they needed pretty faces.

And here was Mr. Nesbitt Duke, as handsome a man as she could remember, dumped on her doorstep. It seemed to Libby as though kindly providence had chosen to intervene in the planned course of her life, and she was never one to disregard providence.

"Well, Mr. Duke, if you can overlook my complete lack of fortune, I can likely disregard your less-then-genteel background," she whispered as she watched the baby.

That they would suit well together, Libby had no doubt. She had no experience with men, but some instinct told her that she could make this man happy and he would never look elsewhere for company. She would welcome him home from each chocolate excursion, and he would never want to be anywhere but with her. She knew this as fervently as she knew there was a Trinity and that the sun would rise and set and rise again.

She sighed again and smiled to herself. Lydia would declare this turn of events better than a novel from the lending library. In recent months, they had spent nights crowded in the same bed, giggling over the lads of the county and their bumbling efforts at romance.

Even as soon as she had that thought, she dismissed it, and felt her cheeks grow pink again. She did not want to giggle and speculate about Nesbitt Duke, or make foolish wagers with her cousin. She wanted to think about him in private and not subject her feelings to Lydia's well-meant but foolish imaginings. There was only one person with whom she could discuss her feelings, and that was with Mr. Duke himself.

Libby stood up, in a pelter to be off, looking about for Joseph. A little wind had picked up and the leaves were rustling louder now, turning over and showing the underside of their green veins. She frowned and glanced at the sky. She could smell the storm coming, that musty, earthy odor that set cattle lowing and kittens searching about for shelter.

There was Joseph at last, coming slowly toward her across an empty field. The gypsies had tethered their horses in the distance, and squatting in the dust, gesturing to one another, they were grouped about the animals. Joseph looked back once, twice, as if he wanted to stay with them and absorb their strange Rom language, even though he could not understand it, because he knew the subject was horses.

Libby lost sight of him for a moment as he entered a copse

of birch trees, and then she saw him again. He had stopped, and she sighed in exasperation. As she watched in growing curiosity, he straightened up suddenly and stripped off his nankeen jacket, spreading it over something or someone she could not see, not even as she stood on tiptoe.

He gestured toward her then, short, urgent motions of his arm that started her walking toward him and then running as he knelt down again and disappeared from her line of sight.

At least it wasn't likely to be one of the squire's horses, she thought grimly as she hurried toward her brother. And he will befriend every wounded thing and then look at her askance in that mild, vaguely reproachful way of his if she attempted to disrupt his philanthropy. The hot words that rose in her throat subsided as she took a deep breath and hurried on, wishing that her stays were not laced so tight. That was Joseph, and there wasn't any changing him. He would never comprehend her agitation.

Libby came close to the copse as the rain began, a drop at a time, and then many drops pelting down. She sniffed appreciatively again and then stopped suddenly at the edge of the thicket, her mouth open in astonishment.

A young girl sat on the ground, her hands clutching Joseph's thin jacket around her. Her right leg—bird-bone-thin and muddy—was twisted at an odd angle.

"*Marime*," called a woman from behind Libby.

Libby snatched her hand back. It was the gypsy woman who had hung the baby in the tree. The child was clutched in her arms now, wet.

Libby got to her feet. "We were only trying to help," she began.

"*Marime*," the woman said again, her voice more emphatic. She jabbed the air with her finger, motioning Libby away, as the silver bangles on her arms rattled. "Unclean!"

Libby stamped her foot and the woman retreated with her baby to the trees, as if afraid to come closer. Libby stared at her hard for a moment and the gypsy put her hands to her face, covering her eyes.

Libby sighed and turned back to the young girl, who was

whimpering now even as she tried to draw closer to Libby as the rain pelted down.

"Dear me," Libby said, and put her arm around the girl. "It appears that we could use some help." She looked up at her brother, who hovered close by, his eyes on the woman in the trees. "Joseph, hurry and run to Dr. Cook's house."

He shook his head. "The squire will beat me if he sees me. I don't think I would like that."

Libby gritted her teeth to keep from shouting. "My dear, you'll have to chance it. This girl needs a physician. Only look how strangely her leg appears. I wonder, do you suppose she fell out of that tree?"

Joseph looked at the tree that swayed in the wind, the leaves turning over in agitation. "I know that it is a tree I would have fallen out of."

Libby resisted the urge to shout at him, to hurry him along. Angry words would only confuse him. "You probably would have, my dear," she agreed. "And now I really think you should run for Dr. Cook."

He looked over his shoulder again at the gypsy woman, who had set her baby down and was rocking back and forth in agitation, keening a low tune that raised the hairs on Libby's arms. "If they do not want us, they won't want the doctor."

He was right, of course. Libby stamped her foot. "Do it anyway, Joe. We need Dr. Cook."

Without another word but several backward glances, Joseph started across the field on a run. Libby returned to the girl, who only stared at her out of pain-filled eyes and tried to move her leg.

Libby touched the child's arm and the gypsy woman threw the first stone. Libby sucked in her breath and whirled around as the rock landed against her skirts.

"Unclean," the woman shouted, and threw another stone. This one landed short of the mark. Libby released her hold on the young girl and the woman put her arm down.

"So that's how it is?" Libby murmured out loud. She looked at the little girl, who huddled close but did not touch her. "Usually it is not so hard to do a good deed for someone, my dear. If that is your mother, she does not perfectly understand my intentions.''

Libby brushed the tangle of hair from the girl's eyes and was rewarded with a handful of pebbles thrown harder against her skirts. Pointedly, she turned her back on the woman in the trees and looked toward the direction Joseph had disappeared.

Hurry up, Joe, she thought. And for goodness' sake, bring the doctor.

11

❧

EACH minute seemed like an hour as Libby waited for Joseph to return with Dr. Cook. Libby shivered in the rain, wishing she could hold the girl closer to her. Another attempt had resulted in a rock that nearly struck the little girl. After that, Libby folded her hands in her lap, gritted her teeth, and speculated on the perversity of human nature.

The girl had settled down to an occasional whimper. She would catch her breath and sob out loud and try to move her leg. Her mother stayed where she was in the trees, unwilling to leave her child, even to run to the gypsy encampment, where the men watched their horses.

Perhaps I should be grateful for that, Libby thought, shivering at the unwelcome idea of stones thrown by men. She kept her hands to herself and willed the doctor to hurry.

And then he was coming over the little rise and down toward her. He appeared in no great hurry and Libby felt a rush of irritation. She started to stay something to hurry him along when she looked at the trees again and noticed that the woman was running back and forth in greater agitation, calling to her daughter.

The doctor stood still, coming no closer. He squatted on his haunches and Libby let out a sigh of great exasperation.

"Dr. Cook, I need you," she said, her voice raised in agitation.

To her further dismay, he put his finger to his lips. "Hush, Miss Ames. We have a delicate situation here."

She shook her head at the understatement. "I am sure this girl has a broken leg. Can't you do something for her?"

"I wish to God I could. If I touch her, that woman will run for the men and we will be in for it." He held up his hand to ward off Libby's hot words. "Hush, now! There is some strange taboo about a man looking upon a woman's legs, even one as young as this." The doctor regarded the little girl, who watched him with wary eyes and edged closer to Libby, the lesser of two evils.

"Surely you can do something."

"My dear, I have been frustrated for years by gypsies," he said. "I have watched them die when I could have saved them, and I have watched them driven from town to town because they are so strange." He sighed and looked at the woman in the trees. "She is like a mother bird, trying to attract our attention away from the nest. It makes me shudder to think what treatment in our good British towns compels people to behave this way."

He sat in silence in the driving rain, as if trying to make up his mind. "Well, Libby, are you game for a stoning? I am not, but let us try something. Pull up her skirt so I can see her leg."

Libby did as he said, pointing to the place below the child's knee where the leg bent at an odd angle. A shower of pebbles struck her on the cheek.

The doctor started forward, his face red. "I won't do it. Libby, get away from her."

"No. I couldn't possibly leave her," she said.

He sat another long minute until the woman in the trees was calmer. "Well, then, my dear Miss Ames. Hold the inside of her leg steady and push slowly and carefully against it from the opposite side. It looks to me like a mere greenstick break. You should feel it click into place."

Without thinking about anything except the task before her, Libby hunched her shoulders to protect her head as much as she could, took a deep breath, and did as Dr. Cook told her. She shut her mind to the terror of something more than pebbles thrown her way, disregarded the fear of what would happen if she couldn't hear a click and the bone remained as displaced as ever, steeled herself to do something so serious that she knew nothing about.

To her overwhelming relief, the bone offered no resistance but straightened exactly as the doctor had said it would. She looked up at him gratefully and then smiled to feel the tiny click as the bone came together. The child stopped whimpering. Libby hugged her and then let go quickly as the rocks rained down.

To her surprise, in another moment the doctor was beside her. He pushed her to one side and whipped out two splints. "She'll run for the men now, Libby, but we dare not leave it like this. Get the bandage out of my pocket while I position these splints. Joseph told me what to expect, bless him, so I brought these. Ah, very good."

Libby pulled out the bandage and unrolled it in a trice. While she held the splints in place, he expertly bound the leg, spent a swift second in examination of his handiwork, and then jerked Libby to her feet.

"Ready for a footrace, my dear?" he asked as he pulled her out of the little depression. "The interests of medicine are strangely served upon occasion. Oh, God, here they come."

He grabbed her hand and set off running. Libby looked back once to see the men chasing after them, some of them carrying sticks, others rocks. The sight, softened as it was by the hazy rain, still made her pick up her skirts, throw gentility to the wind, and race for the fence.

The doctor panted along beside her. "I could be a gentleman's son and give up all this," he said between gasps.

The stones pelted around them. "What, and lead a boring life? Ow!" she exclaimed as a stone struck her back.

The doctor tightened his grip on her hand and ran faster. They were at the hedgerow that ran alongside the road. A wagon filled with animal fodder lumbered by.

The farmer, still grasping the reins, had raised up off the wagon seat to watch the unusual sight of Holyoke Green's portly physician squeezing his considerable bulk through the hedgerow and tugging Miss Elizabeth Ames along behind him. He grinned in appreciation of Miss Ames' tidy ankles and well-shaped knees as the doctor threw her into the wagon, jumped in after her, and commanded him to drive for all he was worth.

Libby heaved a sigh that came all the way from her toenails, and leaned back against the hay. She shook her skirts down around her ankles again. To her mind, the wagon wasn't going any faster, but the gypsies had stopped at the fence. They threw a few more stones and made some strange gestures with their hands, but came no closer.

"H'mm, we have likely been cursed with boils or piles, Miss Ames," said the doctor as he took off his glasses, wiped the rain from them with the wet corner of his shirt tail that had worked itself loose, and put them back on.

Libby laughed. "You can't talk about piles and call me Miss Ames. My name is Libby."

The doctor joined in her laughter, even as he had the good graces to blush. "I suppose I can't, Libby." He raised up on his knees. "Thank you, Farmer Hartley."

The farmer touched his hand to his hat and chuckled. "Will you charge me less now, sir?"

"You and all your descendants," the doctor declared, "right down into the twentieth century. I will put it in my will. Make it an act of Parliament."

"Very well, sir. Done. I am going in the wrong direction for you, though."

"Any direction away from the gypsies is fine with us," Libby said. She started in surprise as the doctor began to unbutton the back of her dress. "Doctor!"

"Be quiet," he said. "H'mm. The rock broke the skin. Quit fidgeting! Surely you are not a worse patient than our Mr. Duke. I probably have a gum plaster somewhere for that."

He kept his hand on her bare shoulder while he fished in his pockets. In another moment he put the dressing over the little wound. "You can take it off tonight. Be sure to wash the cut well." He buttoned up her dress again. "And stay away from the gypsies."

Libby nodded, sober again. "What will the gypsies do to the little girl?"

The doctor was silent a long moment. "I do not know. I hope they will leave the splint on, but I don't know that they will.

If she will only be allowed to stay off that leg for a month, it will likely heal. Children are amazingly resilient.''

To her amazement, Libby burst into tears. Without a word and with no apparent discomfort at the aspect of a watery female, the doctor put his arm around her and held her tight. She burrowed close to him and sobbed into his soaking wet jacket.

''Did anyone ever tell you that you are a remarkable young woman?'' he asked finally, his voice gentle and close to her ear.

Libby shook her head. ''I don't believe the subject ever came up before,'' she sobbed.

''Strange,'' he murmured. ''What is the matter with the men of Kent?''

''Nothing,'' she wailed, and he threw back his head, laughed, and then kissed her.

Elizabeth Ames amazed herself by letting him. She clung to him with all her strength, kissed him back, and then gasped and sat up straight.

''Doctor, I can't imagine what you must think of me,'' she whispered, her eyes on the farmer's back. Farmer Hartley's shoulders were shaking, and she almost wished herself back with the gypsies.

Completely unrepentant, Dr. Cook loosened his grip but did not let go of her. ''Well, a year ago I thought you were the most beautiful woman in the world. When I finally met you, I learned that you were also intelligent. Now I suspect that you are endowed with supreme good taste in men.''

''I don't do that every day,'' was all she could think to say in the face of his own good humor, and then blushed when she remembered her trip to the orchard with Mr. Duke only yesterday.

''I never suspected that you did,'' he replied as he got off the wagon and held out his arms to her.

The rain pelted down. She let him take her properly by the arm and walk her along the road. The humor of the situation overcame her overloaded scruples, and she laughed in spite of her embarrassment.

''We look like two escapees from a lunatic asylum,'' she said as he turned her way, a question in his eyes, when she laughed.

"I wouldn't know, Miss Ames," he said. "I think you look quite fine. A bit wet, maybe a little muddy." He paused and took her by the shoulders. "In fact, the sight is so awe-inspiring that I am compelled to ask you to marry me."

She stared at him, charmed because it was her first real proposal and dismayed because she could only turn him down. "Sir, we would never suit."

He took his hands off her shoulders and continued ambling along. "Oh, I think we would suit famously."

"I think not," Libby replied, her eyes straight ahead of her on the road. What would Lydia say? she thought as she walked in silence beside the doctor. She would laugh and laugh if I ever told her that our bumbling Dr. Cook had declared himself. This conversation will go no further. Good heavens, he must be crazy to think that I would ever marry him.

Libby held out her hand to the doctor and he took it between his own. "Sir, let us be friends. I don't love you."

Her words sounded dreadful, spoken out loud. She regretted them the instant she said them, but there was no remedy for that. He had to know that the whole idea was absurd.

To her acute embarrassment, the doctor regarded her thoughtfully in silence. He shook her hand finally and continued down the road, speaking more to himself than to her. "Well, it seemed like a good idea at the time." He turned to her again and bowed. "We will pretend this conversation never happened and carry on as before, Miss Ames."

"Very well, Dr. Cook," she agreed, and wondered why she felt vaguely let down.

And then she was acutely aware of the fact that her sodden dress clung to her in disgraceful folds, her hair was tumbled around her shoulders and dripping rain, and her face was smudged with mud.

"Oh, dear, I am a fright," she said, too embarrassed to look at the doctor.

"Yes, you are," he agreed. "I suppose now I have seen you at your worst."

The way he said it, so serious and with just that hint of a twinkle in his eyes, made her laugh. Obviously he had reconsidered his foolish proposal. "You're not much better," she joked.

He grinned back, ran his long fingers through his sopping hair, and then smoothed his lapels as elegantly as if he stood in a ballroom, dressed in his best. "Miss Ames, that takes no effort at all. I've never been burdened with high good looks, so the contrast is less remarkable in me than in you."

They continued in companionable silence toward the house, which appeared out of the haze and the misty rain.

"You're a great gun, Miss Ames," he said finally. "I don't know one woman in a hundred who would have come through like you did."

She shook her head. "I must differ, Anthony," she said as the image of the young girl rose before her eyes again. "I don't suppose there is a woman alive who wouldn't have done what I did. Poor child." She looked up at him in confusion again. "I am so rude! Do you mind that I have called you Anthony?"

He grabbed her by the elbows, picked her up, and smacked a wet kiss on her muddy forehead before setting her down again. "You goose! Even if we are destined to be no more than friends, you may call your friends by their first name, Libby. I intend to." He patted her cheek. "And I promise not to kiss you again. It just seemed like a good idea."

"You and your good ideas," she declared.

As they neared the house, she thought of Joseph for the first time. "Did he really summon you, Anthony? I was afraid he would not. He is so afraid of your father."

Anthony chuckled, "A most interesting reflection, now that you mention it. I was just about to lie down—I was up all night, Libby—when I happened to glance out the window. There was Joseph, pacing up and down in front of the gate, as if he could not quite decide what to do. I waved to him, and he called to me, and you can guess the rest."

"Thank goodness," she said, and gave his hand a squeeze.

They walked in silence to Holyoke Green. Libby wondered how Candlow would receive her in all her mud. If there was a merciful providence, Aunt Crabtree would be lying down, recovering from the exhaustion of an afternoon of solitaire. She was only grateful that Mama—a high stickler if ever there was one—would not be standing in the entry, tapping her foot.

Libby thought of the chocolate merchant then and hoped that he was involved somewhere in the house and would miss her less-than-auspicious entrance. Mr. Duke, if only you had rescued me from the gypsies, I think I would have accepted your proposal.

She glanced at the doctor and blushed. Anthony, she thought, I could never marry you.

It was time to let him go on his way. "I shall sneak in the side door," she said. "With any luck, I shall avoid everyone."

"Why sneak in?" he asked. "If we mention the events of this afternoon to the right people, soon it will be evident that you are a bit of a heroine. Even if they were gypsies."

She shook her head. All she wanted was a long soak in a hot bath and the opportunity to reflect on what they had accomplished that afternoon, and put Dr. Cook's proposal to rest somewhere in her brain where her rudeness would not come back to chastise her.

"I think I understand," he said. "I remember that first case in Edinburgh where it all depended on me. Let me just see you in the house and I will go. I could use some sleep, too."

She took a good look at Dr. Cook, noting how red his eyes were and how his shoulders drooped. Surely I could have found a kinder way to let you down, she thought.

Candlow saw her first. He threw up his hands and his mouth opened and closed like a nutcracker. Libby could feel Dr. Cook's amusement as they stood shoulder to shoulder. She hurried forward.

"Candlow, I am all right," she said. "We had to splint a gypsy girl's leg in the field and nearly got stoned for our pains. Imagine that!"

Candlow could not. He leaned against the wall and slid into a chair, staring at Libby. The doctor hurried to his side and felt his pulse and then backed into one of Uncle Ames' vases that teetered a moment and then crashed into a thousand Oriental fragments.

Libby heard rapid footsteps in the hallway, familiar footsteps.

Her heart surged into her throat and then sank to her shoes. She looked into Lydia Ames' startled face.

"Heavens, Libby, what has happened?" her cousin shrieked, her face as pale as the butler's.

Libby hurried to her cousin, careful not to touch her and painfully mindful of her dishevelment. "It is a long story, cousin, but one perfectly reasonable when you hear it all."

"I say, Lydia dearest, such a racket disturbs that bucolic calm you promised me. We can't be under seige from Napoleon's army. What have we here?"

The speaker was a tall gentleman, bereft of most of his hair but dressed in the latest stare of fashion. He was finely muscled and his bearing and manner were without fault, but his voice—high and reedy—already grated on Libby's raw nerves.

His eyes, slightly pop-eyed, stared out of their sockets at the sight of her, muddy and dripping wet in the hall. He raised a quizzing glass with shaking fingers and examined her.

Libby drew herself up and glared back at him as Lydia recovered, gulped, and pulled him forward. "Libby dearest, I have the greatest pleasure to introduce you—you will not believe how droll this is!—to my own dear Eustace Wiltmore, the Earl of Devere."

Libby's jaw dropped as she stared at the elegant man, who stared back at her through one overmagnified eye.

Lydia came closer to her cousin, careful to stay out of reach but close enough to lower her voice. "And aren't you the sly one, Libby?"

Oh, Lord help us, I will die of embarrassment if she suspects that Dr. Cook proposed, Libby thought. "Beg pardon?" she asked.

"Naughty, naughty Libby, and who has been hanging about here for weeks with the Duke of Knaresborough?"

Libby shook her head to clear it as Nesbitt Duke strolled around the corner, as if on cue, and stopped short at the sight of her.

Eustace Wiltmore turned from his openmouthed perusal of Libby to cast his magnified eye upon the duke. He dug him in the ribs. "Nez, you quiz! *This* is your paragon? How droll you have become here in Kent."

Libby stared from one man to the other. "The Duke of . . ."

"Knaresborough," said Nez, his voice low, his eyes hopeful.

Libby whirled about to face her cousin, whose attention was fixed upon Eustace Wiltmore with an expression not far removed from adoration. "Lydia. Lydia, pay attention! Are you telling me—"

"Yes, my very dear Libby," the duke interrupted. "I was the spy. Do let me explain."

12

THE PEACE she had expected to find in the quiet of her room was not there.

The hot bath had been welcome. With a sigh of relief, Libby had scrubbed off the grime and mud until her skin glowed pink, and she washed her hair until it squeaked.

"It does wash off, Dr. Cook, just like you said," she said out loud.

And yet it didn't, at the same time. As she thoughtfully scrubbed at skin already clean, she knew that the experience would never rub off. In idle moments, when all other subjects had been worked over and exhausted, she and Lydia used to speculate why someone as well-born and wealthy as Anthony Cook had felt the need to soil his cuffs with medical school.

She understood now, and it had changed her. Libby sighed and ran her hands under the water, creating whirlpools and undertows. It was unlikely in the extreme that she would ever have the opportunity to talk to Anthony about her feelings. She had already come to know that he would only blush and stammer and bump into something in his hurry to get away, as he had done after the chocolate merchant had made his startling revelation. Anthony Cook was remarkably efficient in an emergency, heroic even, but he was not a man readily accessible to earnest conversation. A pity, she thought. I would like to have known him better.

She drew up her knees and rested her forehead against them. "As it is, Dr. Cook, I will not joke about you anymore," she vowed.

Any hopes of further contemplative time deserted her while she still sat in the tub. Lydia, her face animated, her eyes bright and brimming over with good humor, had eased herself into the bedroom, pulled up a hassock next to the tin tub, and waited for her cousin to ask her about Eustace Wiltmore.

That Libby had already taken a high dislike to the balding man with his ever-present quizzing glass, she would never have admitted to her cousin. Libby sat in the cooling water while Lydia, in that breathless way of hers, went through the chance meeting at the Pavilion, the dance when she stood up three times to waltz with Eustace, much to Aunt Ames' discomfort.

"Oh, but your mama is a high stickler," Lydia said, rolling her eyes. "I do not know when I have been so thoroughly wrung out and hung up to dry."

"You should have heard her with Papa's lieutenants when they did something she disapproved of," Libby said, her eyes lighting up at the remembrance of those fearsome dressings-down. "I don't believe she ever knew—such a conspiracy we had!—but she was known as Tommy's Little Captain among Papa's troops."

"I do not doubt it," Lydia said. " 'How does it look?' 'What do you owe your family name,' " she mimicked. "If I heard it once, I heard it dozens of times."

She was silent then. Libby stirred the bathwater about with her finger, watching the circles widen. "Did you know he was *the* Eustace? I remember your telling me at least once that you would never get within drawing-room length of anyone named Eustace, on the off chance that it was 'That One,' as you referred to him."

Both cousins laughed. Libby got herself out of the tub and wrapped a large towel about her.

Lydia made a face. "It is a dreadful name, is it not?" Her eyes softened. "But he is a darling, Libby, simply a darling. Eustace Wiltmore is all that is elegant and slap up to the mark." She giggled. "And, no, I had no earthly idea. I can only suspect that he thought it better to save the revelation of his name until later. Silly boy! He told me that he found out who I was, and decided then to pursue an acquaintance he had been dreading.''

"I can understand," said her cousin. "Who on earth wants to marry someone that fathers have schemed over and decided is the right choice? Even if he is," she added, hugging her cousin. "I'm happy for you, Lydia."

Lydia beamed. "At our first meeting, the dear boy told me that his name was Barnaby Hackwell, and I suppose he is. Those are two of his names. And he said he was the Viscount Clonmel, which he is, but it is one of those Irish titles. Clever, clever lad."

Libby nodded, thinking to herself that Eustace Wiltmore, with his pop eyes, his air of infinite superiority, and his silly voice, looked anything but clever. But he had fooled Lydia. Libby shivered and drew the towel tighter about her. And the Duke of Knaresborough obviously fooled me.

"Clever lads," Lydia amended, her thoughts the same as her cousin's. "When Eustace told me, as we were coming here, that he had sent his friend the duke to Kent to spy me out, oh, how I laughed."

Libby managed a weak chuckle and wrapped her arms about herself. There was nothing funny about being duped so thoroughly. Her cheeks burned at how readily she had believed the chocolate merchant. She gave the matter rational thought a moment and decided, in fairness to the duke, that the issue rubbed both ways. He had assumed she was the heiress. She had no doubt that he had mistaken Lydia's name for her own when Eustace had hatched the deception back in London. He had probably been foxed at the time, she thought. He had probably planned a minor accident on the road in front of Holyoke Green that would have been just enough to get him into the house and then out again in a day. Surely he had not intended to hurt himself so badly.

But perhaps he had every such intention. Libby stalked about the room, her towel tight around her. I do not think it would have mattered greatly to him if he had died then, she thought. How sad. Tears came into her eyes again, and only the greatest force of will made them go away. It would never do for her cousin to know how deeply involved she was. Maybe she had not really known it herself until now, when the duke was suddenly far removed from her sphere by Lydia's artless disclosure of his title.

Libby rested her forehead against the window glass, savoring its coolness. She knew that she and Anthony Cook had done the Duke of Knaresborough a great favor. Anthony had doctored him and counseled with him, and she had held his hand through gloomy days and nights. They had helped him chase away the banshees that had followed him, shrieking and swooping, since Waterloo. She knew he had only told her the smallest part of his miseries there, and she realized with a sudden shock that he must have been the major commanding, and not the sergeant, as he had led her to believe.

"Libby, come away from the window," Lydia scolded. "If you aren't behaving like the funniest stick." Lydia was beside her at the window. "I still haven't told you why we are here. Eustace is taking me to London tomorrow to meet his family. Can you imagine? Me in London." She whirled about the room and threw herself on Libby's bed, arms outstretched. "He has told me I shall have a town house, a country estate, and carriages. And, Libby, imagine the parties. Think of the quarterly allowance. I shall go distracted with the mere thought."

"He stopped here to collect his friend?" Libby asked, keeping her voice casual.

"Oh, I suppose," Lydia said, her dimple showing. "And isn't the duke a handsome devil? I wonder that you have not fallen deep in love with him, Libby. But then, you were already so practical, and besides, we know it would never do."

Libby looked sharply at her cousin, who was examining her fingernails. Lydia, you are so heartless, she thought, even if you do not mean to be. You have no idea how your words wound. You would be appalled if I told you.

She said nothing, but pulled on her nightgown quickly as Lydia lay on the bed, listing all the treats in store for her that Eustace would provide. "We shall see all the sights in London, he assures me. His mama knows all the dressmakers and Papa has given me leave to spend and spend."

Libby did smile then. The idea of Uncle Ames making such a statement was so far removed from the truth that she could only marvel at Lydia's gift of imagination. As she listened with half an ear to Lydia's list of elegant necessities, Libby could only hope that when the bills from the milliners and cobblers and modistes and mantua-makers avalanched into the book room, her mother would be on hand to provide Uncle Ames with the restorative jellies and soups that his enervated constitution would require.

I have to change the subject, she thought. It becomes too painful.

But Lydia had already chosen another tack. She rolled over and rested her chin on her hands, her eyes bright with merriment. "Libby, I told Eustace how quiet things were around here. 'Dead dog dull,' I told him. And there you were, soaking wet and filthy, with that ridiculous doctor. I do not know when Anthony Cook has appeared to less advantage. I wonder that you could stand there with a straight face."

"I wonder, too," Libby said, her voice soft.

Lydia stared at her. "Libby Ames, what is the matter with you? You would have been in whoops on any other occasion."

"I think I must put it down to the fact that we did something rather extraordinary this afternoon, cousin," Libby said as she sat down at her dressing table, her back to Lydia.

Lydia groaned and made a face. "I can only hope that bit of news doesn't travel from here to Brighton. That you should have anything to do with gypsies makes my knees turn to jelly." She looked at Libby, suddenly concerned. "You're sure you brought no lice or fleas into the house? Your mama would cut up stiff."

"No lice, no fleas, Lydia."

"Thank God for that!"

Silence followed Lydia's heartfelt pronouncement. As they sat regarding each other, it felt to Libby like the end of a friendship. Something had happened, but she did not entirely understand what it was. Whether it had to do with Eustace Wiltmore, or with the duke's deception, Libby did not know. Maybe it had to do with Anthony Cook and the gypsies; Libby could not tell.

As she watched the cousin she loved and had confided in and joked with only a few short weeks ago, she knew that a page in her book of life had turned. There was a gulf between them now that had not existed before, and once Lydia was in fact Lady Wiltmore, the gulf would only widen.

Libby smiled at her cousin, put on her dressing gown, and started to brush her hair, the crackling sound filling the silence. They would always be polite to each other, and likely neither would ever mention the well-mannered estrangement that was taking place even as they sat there in Libby's cozy room. They would nod and smile at each other at infrequent family gatherings to come and ask how they did and maybe even listen to the answer, but the damage was done. Libby had the wit to notice, but Lydia would probably only wonder why things weren't the same and then move on quickly to more pleasant topics.

As it was, there was nothing to say. In another moment, Lydia rose, kissed her cousin on top of the head, and left the room.

"Libby?"

Libby sighed and turned around. Joseph stood in the open door. She held out her hands to him and he took them.

"I found Dr. Cook like you said," he reminded her.

"I know. You did splendidly, Joseph. Mama will be so proud when I tell her."

Joseph grinned in real pleasure. "Do you think so?"

"I know so."

He let go of her hands and perched himself on the edge of her dressing table. "I went back to the gypsy camp, Libby."

"Would they talk to you? I am surprised they did not stone you, too. Did you see the little girl?"

There were too many questions for Joseph. He nodded, as if surprised. "Of course they talked to me. I helped them shoe a colt."

Trust Joseph, she thought. She could see him standing around with the gypsies, minding his own business, saying nothing, and then rushing forward to help. They probably found him useful. She touched his hand, her heart wrung out with love and misery. *You would have no place in Lydia's society, either. Perhaps it's just as well that things have fallen out this way for us. We have always known they would.*

"Good for you, my dear. Did you see that little girl?" she asked again.

He shook his head. "No. I think they were a bit suspicious by then."

"Did they ask you to return?" she teased, amused at his understatement and grateful that the child did not appear to have been abandoned, or at least left out in the rain.

He regarded her seriously. "Libby, they said I could follow them to the next town, where there is a horse fair."

She shook her head. "That would never do, Joseph."

"I thought you would say that," he replied, and left the room quietly.

When he shut the door behind him, Libby rested her elbows on the dressing table and stared into the mirror. "Elizabeth Ames, you have the perfect knack this day of putting people off. One could say you were a genius at it."

She thought again of Anthony Cook. As they had stood shoulder to shoulder in the hallway, she had caught the amused glances that passed between Eustace and Lydia and she knew they were intended for the doctor. Deeply aware of their pointed amusement, she had moved closer to the doctor. He had touched her sleeve and then shook his head slightly, bowed, and made his ponderous way from the house, dripping water at every step like a sheepdog. No one had tried to stop him, offer him tea, or even a towel to dry his hair. She certainly had done nothing. The memory burned.

Tears stung her eyelids, but she brushed them away as someone else knocked on the door. She sighed. "Come in."

Nesbitt Duke entered the room. Libby blinked at him in surprise and pulled her robe tighter about her.

He carried a small tray, which he set on the little table by the window. He glanced at the storm that threatened on her face and began to whistle softly to himself as he arranged the chairs closer to the table. He motioned to one of them.

Mystified, Libby came closer and sat down. Still without saying anything, he poured her some tea. She took a sip. It was scalding and strong and precisely what she needed. She sipped slowly, her eyed on the duke as he sat down beside her and took up his cup.

She set down the cup finally. "That's the worst tea I ever drank," she said.

"Yes, it is, isn't it?" he agreed, and continued sipping. In another moment he put down his cup. "I used to have my batman brew me a pot like this right before we went into battle."

She laughed out loud, the significance of his words not lost on her. "Battle, is it? I scarcely feel like loading a rifle, my lord, but I must admit that you have considerable cheek."

He leaned forward and possessed himself of one of her hands. "Libby, you will have to forgive me. I did come to Kent with the intent of reconnoitering the terrain for Eustace." His face reddened right down to his collar. "I suppose I will not surprise you when I admit that it was something I agreed to when I was cross-eyed and feeling no pain."

She nodded. "I suspected as much. Was that why you mixed up our names?"

He chuckled, obviously feeling himself on higher ground. "You will have to agree that 'Lydia' and 'Libby' sound somewhat alike. Imagine how they sounded to someone half gone." He took her hand to his lips. "And Eustace never mentioned a beautiful cousin."

Flattery, flattery, she thought. "Why on earth did your friend think he needed to resort to such a stratagem? Surely the agreement between the fathers had no actual binding force."

The duke released her hand and restored himself with another sip of tea. "Although he is a friend of mine, and has been since Eton, I do not equivocate to state that Eustace Wiltmore is a frivolous, flighty fellow, somewhat suspicious of the married state. He just wanted to make sure the Lydia Ames didn't have spots or gap teeth or a squint-eyed stare." He leaned back in his chair, not taking his eyes from her face, as if gauging her reaction to his words. "Even with his pockets empty and the creditors scratching at his door, Eustace is fastidious about appearances."

Libby rose and went to the window seat. How odd men are, she thought. Eustace is no beauty, and besides, it sounds as though he has not a feather to fly with and needs a wealthy connection. And he was concerned that Lydia would not suit? She turned to regard the duke, who was watching her carefully.

How mercenary men are, and how vain. She felt a cool breeze cross her face and she shivered.

"I trust that he is agreeably surprised at his good fortune?" she asked, unable to keep the bitterness from her voice. "Does Lydia Ames suit? Should he open her mouth and count her teeth? Perhaps when they hurry to London he can duck away long enough to audit Uncle Ames' worth on the Exchange? Does no one marry for love?"

"I do," said the duke impulsively, as though her own angry tirade had jolted the words from his brain. "Libby, when does your uncle return?"

"I . . . I have no idea," she stammered, caught off-guard and vastly mistrusting the sudden light that had come into his eyes. "I believe he plans to continue in Brighton, at least until the hops harvest."

It was on the tip of her tongue to commit the ultimate folly and inquire why, but she knew she did not need to ask. She could see the reason in his eyes. He loves me, she thought suddenly. He knows that I am not the heiress and he loves me anyway. Without another thought in her head, she held out her arms to him and found herself tight in his embrace.

"Libby, Libby," he murmured, "you cannot imagine how I have wanted to do this."

She kissed him and rested her cheek against his chest. "I seem to recall that you already did this in the orchard yesterday."

He took a firmer stance and wrapped his arms around her, enfolding her in a possessive embrace. "That was only practice. This is for real. I cannot imagine returning to London—and I must, my dear!—without some sort of sign from you that my suit will not be entirely unwelcome."

He kissed her. His fingers traced the outline of her jaw and then found themselves caught in her unbound hair. He kissed her neck and throat, and with only the deepest strength of will, Libby put her hands against his chest and pushed him gently away.

"That will do for now, my lord," she said breathlessly. "I am still somewhat out of charity with you for the joke you have pulled on me, and I may remain this way for some considerable time."

He kissed her solemnly on the nose. "At least until I have the opportunity to speak to your uncle, eh?"

"Probably until then, sir."

"Brighton, you say? I can be there tomorrow."

"So you can," she said, and turned her cheek toward him for one last chaste peck. "Sir, what *is* your name?"

"It is Benedict Nesbitt, so I was not far wrong, and my friends do call me Nez."

"And what should I call you?" she teased.

"Oh, I am partial to 'my lord,' or perhaps 'your grace,' " he said. "We have time to decide on a name, dear Libby, something suitably grand to puff up my pretensions."

"And you have no connections with Copley Chocolatier?"

"None beyond the fact that I am one of their more ardent customers." He kissed her hand then and looked up into her laughing eyes. "Will you see me off in the morning, my dear? I go on an errand of considerable importance to both of us."

"I wonder what it can be?" she said, her dimple showing. "While you are there, I suggest that you get acquainted with my mother, too. Her word has considerable weight in our household. Oh, I love you, Nez."

The duke left the room with such a surfeit of exhilaration that if he had put his mind to it, he surely could have walked upon water. He rubbed his hands together, relishing the moment when he would present Elizabeth Ames to his mother and sister, who had schemed so long and hard to find him a wife suitable for a duke. He would present his dear Libby with a flourish—if she would let him—and just for once, perhaps Gussie would tell him what a capital fellow he was and applaud his judgment.

He went slowly down the stairs, noting how soft the lamplight was in early evening, how rosy the sunset through the wavy glass of the stairwell landing. Everything about him looked more vivid because he loved and was loved.

True, the bulk of the legendary Ames fortune would reside in Eustace Wiltmore's pocket; the Earl of Devere was marrying the heiress. But surely any brother of Sir William Ames would have been sufficiently juicy to settle an ample cushion on such a daughter. Not that the duke required a transfusion; revenue from the Knaresborough estate alone would have maintained them in elegant comfort, and that was not his only investment. It was just the idea that pleased him and made him break into song as he descended the stairs and threw open the library door.

Eustace and his ladylove were sitting close together, ignoring the books that lined the walls. The earl had removed his elegant coat so that Lydia would not wrinkle it as she nestled in his arms. Eustace stared in surprise at the duke's peremptory entrance and took immediate exception to it.

"Dear boy, must you burst into a room as though it were a new discovery? Lud, I could easily be frightened out of the rest of my hair."

"Egad, I am all atwitter," replied the duke, flopping himself down across from them. He clapped his hands together and leapt to his feet again, leaning against the fireplace mantel in what he hoped was a studied, casual manner, no matter how fast his heart raced.

"Wish me happy, Eustace," he said simply, and waited for the contratulations to lave over him.

He was met with silence. His friend stared at him, his pop eyes more pronounced than usual. Lydia Ames sat bolt upright, a look of real bewilderment on her face. "Beg pardon?" she asked when Eustace seemed unable to supply the text.

"I am going to Brighton tomorrow to ask your father's permission to marry Libby," he told Lydia.

Lydia stared at him and then burst into laughter. As he watched in amazement and growing irritation, she threw back her head and roared, clutching her sides and drumming her feet on the floor.

"So glad you are amused," he said finally, and looked to Eustace for help.

After a moment, Lydia regained her control over herself. She wiped her streaming eyes and fought down the laughter that continued to bubble to the surface.

"I had no idea my marrying Libby would bring you such amusement," the duke said.

Lydia shook her head, waved her arms helplessly, and sailed off again in another gust of glee, while Eustace rose to his feet and carefully straightened his neckcloth, examining the damage in the fireplace mirror.

"Nez, dear boy, have you seriously got something against your mother, sister, and six generations of dukes?" he asked, his voice casual.

"What can you possibly mean?" snapped the duke, his patience gone. "I only want to marry Libby Ames. Surely that won't cause any heartburn."

His angry words hung in the air. Eustace turned around slowly to face him.

"Can it be that she has not told you?" he asked.

"Told me what?" said the duke, biting off his words and resisting the urge to grab his friend by the neckcloth he was so carefully adjusting.

"Libby doesn't possess a single penny, and her mother's father sold chewing tobacco to sailors in Portsmouth," Lydia said, her eyes merry. "She will be a duchess that no one in London ever forgets."

The silence that settled over the library was so heavy with tension that it seemed to suck the air from the room. Lydia sidled toward the door while Eustace ran his finger around his collar. The duke felt the blood drain from his face.

"How can this be?" he asked finally when the quiet in the room threatened to settle all around them like Holland cloths. He looked at Lydia, who stopped moving toward the door and stood still as if nailed there. "The Ames fortune is about as well-known as your father's charming eccentricities."

Lydia had nothing to say. She stared at him out of frightened eyes as Eustace scuttled to her side and took her hand.

"Really, dear boy," the earl murmured. "One mustn't shoot the messenger, must one?"

Nez shook his head, made a futile motion with his hand, and sank into the chair again. When Lydia, watching him carefully, remained rooted to the spot, he motioned her closer. "Forgive me, Miss Ames, but please tell me what is going on. I am obviously in the dark here."

Lydia tiptoed to the sofa she had deserted and perched herself gingerly upon it. "Libby's father met her mother in Portsmouth before he shipped out to Spain for the first time. He eloped with her, and his father disowned him. The title was to have been his. My father is the younger son. Papa only gave them a place to live last year because they were destitute and had nowhere to go. Libby told you none of this?''

The duke made another impotent gesture and then rested his head in his hands. ''I never asked. Why should I have done so? I assumed from the first that she was you, and even after I found out differently this afternoon, I assumed that because she was an Ames, there was still the family fortune to spread about, and a good name in the bargain. A tobacco merchant's granddaughter, eh? Good God.''

''Hmmmm, yes, dear boy,'' Eustace said. ''Rather less distinguished than a purveyor of chocolates, I suppose.'' His feeble joke passed unnoticed by the duke, but the earl did not let that stop him. ''And when word gets about, as these things do, I doubt that anyone will give you the time of day, at least not without a giggle.'' He patted his friend on the knee. ''Better give it a miss, my boy.''

Without a word, the duke jumped up and left the room, slamming the door behind him.

He didn't know how far he walked that night. The country was dark and still unfamiliar to him. He recognized Holyoke when he strolled through after midnight, hands deep in his pockets, head down. The lamps were lit, the few streets deserted. His knee began to pain him, but he walked on, passing the Cook estate. There was a light on, and he nearly turned in, wanting a word with the doctor but not sure what to say.

He walked until his body was exhausted and his mind equally tired. Still he walked, his stride automatic and well-remembered from days of soldiering through Belgium. He walked to a cadence of ''You fool, you fool, you fool,'' that repeated endlessly through his whole body and made him sob out loud.

There had been no deception on Libby's part, of this he was sure. Like a dunce he had assumed too much, and now he would have to go to her in the morning, look into her loving face, and take it all back. He would have to find the words to tell her that he had been an idiot and they would not suit and would she please forgive him, et cetera. There wouldn't be any visit to Brighton, and no trip to London with Libby Ames at his side.

He would never have the contentment of seeing her face first thing each morning for the rest of his life. As much as he loved her, there wasn't any way he could ever marry her, no way on earth. Such things happened only in vulgar novels, and he knew it.

When the sun rose, he found his way back to Holyoke Green. He sat quietly on the lawn, watching the smoke begin to rise from the chimneys as the house came to life again. He startled the goose girl when she tiptoed barefoot across the lawn to turn loose her charges. She eyed him suspiciously and made a wide detour around him, her switch clutched tight.

Are you a tobacconist's daughter? he thought as he watched her hurry through the wet grass. Oh, God, what was I thinking?

That he loved Libby Ames, he had no doubt. That he owed her his life, and more, of this also he had no doubt. He also knew that she would never be the Duchess of Knaresborough. That title would have to go now by default to one or another of the bloodless little bits of blancmange that Gussie found for him, with titles to match his own. It scarcely mattered which woman he chose. He would marry well and do his duty and grit his teeth and raise his family and wish himself to hell every day of his life.

He heard a window open and looked up, his heart in his throat. Libby stood framed in the sill, leaning out as she had done every morning she came into his room, looking with appreciation on another June day in Kent. She rested her elbows on the sill, her long brown hair a glory around her face.

Instinctively, he moved farther back into the shadow of the trees so she could not see him, and cursed himself for cowardice. How could he possibly look into those blue eyes and tell her that he had made a dreadful mistake? He knew that he could not.

An idea drifted into his skull. It buzzed about inside his head like a fly intent on a midden, and then settled quietly somewhere while he considered its merits.

That Libby Ames loved him, he knew as surely as he knew his own name. And more than that, she had loved him when there was no more promise than that he would be selling chocolate for the rest of his life. There was nothing in her of the well-turned-out beauties he was used to, the young ladies

trained since babyhood to flirt and tease, always with an eye
to titles and investments. He could have been doddering, bald,
and without a tooth in his head, and those paragons would not
have looked upon him with any less affection. Or any more.

He considered the matter, worrying it around in his mind,
looking at it from all angles like a horse at an auction. Libby
was intelligent; surely she must realize that a duke was
completely out of her reach. She could no more become a
duchess than hope to succeed Pius VII.

He got to his feet, brushing the leaves off his buckskins, his
eyes still on the window. Libby had turned away now, but her
presence was almost as palpable as if she still stood there, her
eyes on the morning, thinking of him, perhaps?

He foresaw some difficulty with the mother, but he knew he
could win her around, too. Mrs. Ames was probably one of
those shabby genteel women he had seen hanging about the
fringes of the army, pretty once, with a face at one time palatable
enough to catch the fancy of a cornet or ensign green as grass.
And if the family's situation was as desperate as Lydia Ames
had hinted at last night, it was unlikely that Marianne Ames
would look with disgust on his plan.

He would broach the subject with Libby and then proceed
to London to drawn up papers with his lawyer. For all that her
origins were questionable, she was not friendless in the world,
and Uncle Ames would require careful handling, too.

"I will move with all deliberate caution and endeavor to get
over heavy ground as lightly as possible," he said, smiling at
the memory of the Iron Duke's favorite military dictum reduced
to the terms of romance. "And so I shall succeed."

It remained only to find Libby and tell her of his brilliant idea.
He went into the house, calling her name.

In another moment, she looked down on him from the upstairs
landing, a smile of welcome on her face that made his heart
lift and turn over.

"We wondered where you were, Nez," she scolded, and she
descended the stairs, coming toward him on light feet. "The
others are nearly done in the breakfast room, but I believe there
are still toast and eggs."

She took him by the arm and tugged it until—a smile on his

face—he bent down so she could kiss him on the cheek. For the briefest moment she rubbed his cheek with hers. "Lydia said it would be fine if you took one of Uncle's horses to Brighton, unless you prefer a post chaise, and they are available in Holyoke. But do come to breakfast now."

He shook his head and took her by the hand, pulling her down the hall toward the book room. He answered the question in her eyes with a wink and a kiss of his fingers at her.

He took her in his arms in the book room and kissed her, touched and gratified at the same time to feel the trip-hammer of her heart against his chest. He rested his chin on the top of her head, breathing in the fragrance of lavender that would always mean Libby Ames to him.

"I am not going to Brighton, after all, my dear," he said finally, still holding her close.

Libby pulled away from him slightly to look up into his face, a question in her eyes.

He cupped her face in his hands. "I have a much better plan."

The look that she gave him was full of so much trust that he felt another tug, this time to his conscience. He ignored it and pulled her close to him again.

"Really, your grace," she teased, out of breath, as he kissed her neck and ears. "Ought we to at least close the door?"

"Libby, you told me everyone was at breakfast," he murmured, and then reminded himself of the next step in his clever idea. He picked her up and set her lightly on the desk.

"How would you feel about a little house in Half Moon Street?" he asked, suddenly at a loss how to introduce the subject and trusting that his charm would carry him through.

To his relief, Libby smiled back and placed her hands on his shoulders. "Anywhere you are would be home to me," she whispered, and touched her forehead to his. "You know that."

"And I suppose you would like above all things to have a high-perch phaeton of your very own?"

"But of course I would," she replied promptly, her eyes merry. "And it must be painted white with gilt trimmings. I shall cut quite a dash."

"So you shall," he agreed, laughing. "And you shall have furs and jewels and a box of your very own at the opera."

"And you will introduce me to Florizel himself?" she asked, twinkling her eyes at him.

"Oh, no! Suppose he should decide to make you his own dollymop? I shall never introduce you to the prince," he said firmly. "Come to think of it, I shall never introduce you to anyone, my darling. You're much too tender a morsel, and some other friend of mine will think you are his for the taking. No, we will be together whenever we can, just you and I."

A curious look came into her eyes, less trusting, more wary. He ignored it and hurried on, pleased with his success. "I shall go to London with Eustace and Lydia and make all the arrangements with my lawyer. You will be well provided for, Libby, and never have a moment's regret."

There was a long pause as Libby looked deep into his eyes. As he watched in growing discomfort, the color sailed away from her cheeks, leaving them the dead white of circus clown makeup. She took her hands off his shoulders.

"Why should I have any cause to regret, Nez?" she asked quietly.

The tone of her voice should have warned him. There was something in it of curious great control, even as a muscle began to twitch below her eyes. She looked at him steadily and he stared back in fascination at the little tic.

He looked away first. "Well, Libby, sometimes these arrangements can be awkward," he said as he reached for her hands again.

She put them behind her back. "What 'arrangements' are you referring to?" When he did not answer, she got off the desk, still not taking her eyes from his face. "What arrangements, Nez?" she asked again, her voice soft.

He knew she was a girl of great good humor, so he laughed and flicked her cheek with his finger.

"Libby, my love, surely you never thought I meant to marry you?"

13

I ABSOLUTELY refuse to faint, Libby thought as she stared at the duke. She ignored the little flickers of light around her eyes and the drumming in her ears and clutched at the desk to keep her balance in a world suddenly upside down.

"The notion of marriage had crossed my mind, Nez," she said when he seemed disposed to make no further comment. "I rather thought that was what we were referring to last night."

She wanted to say more, to scream at him and cry and stamp her feet and dig at his face with her fingernails, but she clutched her hands tight in her lap and struggled against the tears that spilled down her cheeks anyway.

He took her by the shoulders. "Libby, you didn't seriously think that a duke would ever marry the granddaughter of a tobacco merchant? And wasn't there some scandal about your father's disinheritance? Good God, Libby, be reasonable."

She felt as though she stood miles away from him and that she listened to his voice from the top of some distant mountain. "I assumed you were already aware of all that when we spoke last night," Libby said.

He shook his head and made no move to touch her again when she brushed off his hands. "My dear girl, I thought you were Lydia, and then I thought that . . . Well, I never imagined that you weren't . . . well, you know, Libby, eligible." He shrugged his shoulders. "I suppose we both assumed too much," he concluded.

"Or not enough, my lord," she said.

"Libby, be reasonable! You know I can't possibly marry you."

She did know. She shook her head when he offered her his handkerchief, and she wiped her eyes on her sleeve instead, wishing he would go away and close the door behind him. Incredibly, he was still speaking to her, his voice soothing as though he addressed a cranky child that must be brought to reason.

"What do you say, Libby? I love you. Only think how well we will suit. Any marriage I make will only be one of convenience. You, I love."

His words seemed to roar in her ears and she sobbed out loud. It gave her no pleasure to see the helplessness creep into his eyes. He is only upset because I am crying, she thought. He has no idea of the insult he has heaped upon me, as if it were a favor.

Libby took a deep breath and held out her hand to him. "My lord," she began, her voice loud so she could hear herself over the roaring in her ears. "I am deeply appreciative of the great condescension of your offer, but I am equally certain that we would never suit. Do not let me detain you a moment longer."

"Libby, don't be a fool," he said quietly.

"In future, I shall try not to be, sir," she said. "I've learned such an excellent lesson and can only be grateful to you for that, I suppose. Good day, my lord."

He shook her hand and stepped back as she swept from the room, her face set, her eyes straight ahead.

Joseph stood before her in the hall. He looked on in silence as the duke left the book room and stalked down the hall without even a glance of recognition in his direction. He turned back to his sister, openmouthed.

"I—I didn't mean to listen. Libby, did you turn down his proposal?" he asked, his voice filled with amazement.

She nodded, afraid to trust herself with words.

Joseph leaned against the wall as though he could not hold

himself upright anymore. "It was because of me, wasn't it?" he asked at last.

Libby flinched. "Oh, no, Joseph, never that!"

"I disgust him, don't I, and he doesn't want me in London. Libby, I am so sorry."

Mastering her own emotions, she reached for her brother, even as he wrenched himself away from her, turned, and ran out the back door. Her face a mask of pain, she watched him run with his curious loping gait to the stable. She closed her eyes and leaned her forehead against the door frame. In another moment, she heard the sound of horse's hooves.

Joseph was gone.

She watched him ride away, hunched low over Uncle Ames' horse. He took the fence toward Fairbourne with his usual ease and disappeared in the trees. Libby just stood there, knowing that he would return later in the day, hungry and tired and with only a sketchy memory of what had gone on before. The only danger was that he would ride too far and forget where he lived. And then what do I tell Mama? she thought as she rubbed her arms.

She longed to throw herself on her knees in front of Mama and pour out the whole dismal story into her lap. It would be such a relief to cry herself out and to feel her mother's gentle hand on her hair. She would take the next mail coach to Brighton.

And the next moment, Libby knew she would do nothing of the kind. Mama must never know of any of this. It would only shame her and deepen her mother's own sense of failure. Mama had suffered enough at the hands of her father-in-law. They had not roamed Europe for years and years not only because Thomas Ames had been a dedicated soldier, but because there had never been a home to return to in England, no kind welcome from relatives on either side.

Libby turned away from the door. Mama would never have to know that this same rejection extended to her beloved daughter and son. I owe you that, Mama, she thought. She would swallow the misery all by herself and count herself lucky that she had not got any deeper into the mess.

But now the only thing that remained was to sneak upstairs, plead a sick headache, and stay there until Eustace, Lydia, and the Duke of Knaresborough left for London. Aunt Crabtree would chide her for her inhospitality, but that couldn't be helped. She started for the stairs on tiptoe.

"Ah, Miss Ames, I have been looking for you," Candlow said, coming toward her on the half-trot that usually indicated catastrophe. "The cook is in an uproar over some remark that the Earl of Devere made about his croissants, and I need you in the kitchen. Your aunt tried and has retreated to the card table."

She sighed. "Won't it wait?"

Candlow's sigh was louder. "No, it will not, Miss Ames. This is serious." He paused for breath and then threw in his weightiest argument. "And didn't Sir William expect you to keep house for him this summer?"

Yes, this summer, and all the summers to come, and then when Mama died, she would be housekeeper for life. She would be the one to welcome the Earl and Countess of Devere to Holyoke Green for the occasional holiday, standing with the other servants, but slightly apart, for she didn't belong with them, either. And when the Wiltmores had their friends down from London, she would be there, too. Oh, God.

I only hope I do not become the family joke, like poor Aunt Crabtree, Libby thought as she followed the butler belowstairs. I hope they do not point me out as the one who had pretensions. Pray God they will not laugh about me after I have served them tea, and twitter among themselves that I thought myself good enough for the Duke of Knaresborough. Silly woman, she thought to snare a duke. I wonder that the Wiltmores keep her on.

Several cups of tea and a tumbler of Uncle Ames' best smuggled brandy convinced the cook that the Earl of Devere wouldn't know a muffin from a croissant it if leapt off the plate and smote him across the chops.

"But I won't cook for him again," the cook sniffed, tipping the brandy glass for the last drop.

"I believe they are leaving this morning."

"And good riddance to rubbish, is what I say," declared the cook.

This was certainly not the time to tell the cook that the Earl of Devere would likely have his feet under the dining-room table for more meals to come. She took another sip of her tea and wished it were brandy. Some things shouldn't have to be faced all at once.

When she could gracefully escape from the cook, who grew more garrulous the lower the level in the bottle dropped, Libby tiptoed up the back stairs. With any luck she could avoid the other inmates of Holyoke Green until the moment of departure. If they did not linger long with farewells and instructions, she could maintain her composure and then go about the arduous and unwelcome task of putting the Duke of Knaresborough from her mind.

The maid and footman were hurrying down the hall with the bandboxes, portmanteaux, and hatboxes that Lydia considered essential for a London stay. From the look of resignation evident on the footman's face, this was not his first trip down the stairs.

The duke was nowhere in sight. Libby knew how limited was his wardrobe. Probably he was already packed and standing by the carriage, eager to be off, relieved to put behind him the embarrassment she had caused. By the time the carriage rolled into London, he would likely have forgotten she ever lived.

And then Lydia was hurrying from her room, tying the bow of her chip-straw bonnet under one ear, calling to her abigail in breathless tones to hurry up or be left behind.

"Do you know, cousin, I think I will procure a dresser when I get to town," she said as she tucked her arm in Libby's and pulled her along to the landing. "Dear Eustace says I am to throw myself on the mercy of his mother for these details. He says she is a frivolous lady, but that we should deal admirably."

Libby was not surprised that the irony of her statement flew over Lydia's head. She could only pat her cousin's hand and descend the stairs, keeping her peace.

At the bottom of the stairs, Lydia laughed. "Libby, I must tell you the most delicious thing. You will go into whoops when I tell you, but last night . . ." Lydia put her face close to her cousin's. "Last night the duke said he was going to offer for you. Isn't that amusing? How I laughed when I heard him!"

She laughed again, a merry peal that was almost painful to Libby's ears. "Naturally, I set him straight, and wasn't he surprised! Men will do the strangest things when they think they are in love."

"I suppose they will," Libby agreed, winking back her tears.

Lydia looked at her cousin. She dabbed her handkerchief at Libby's eyes. "You dear thing! I will miss you, too." She danced out the door, calling to Eustace.

Libby walked out into the open doorway and watched as the footman, his collar dark with sweat and his mouth set along grim lines, poked bags and boxes here and there at Lydia's command. The duke stood apart with his friend the earl. He looked back at Libby once and there was scarcely a flicker of recognition in his eyes.

She urged the footman on silently and was grateful beyond measure when Candlow found a pressing matter of house business to occupy Lydia so the man could finish his task in peace. In another moment, the coachman was in his seat and Lydia hurled herself into her cousin's arms for one last embrace.

"I'll write, Libby dear, but it may be easier for you to write me," she said, hugging her cousin close. "I think you will likely have more time than I will. Do take care, my dear."

"I'll write, Libby dear, but it may be easier for you to write me," she said, hugging her cousin close. "I think you will likely have more time than I will. Do take care, my dear."

"That I shall do, Lydia dear," Libby said, and kissed her cousin. "If Uncle Ames should send you one of his famous letters of good advice, do take some of it."

Lydia pinked up and flashed her dimples at her cousin. "Only some of it, silly! What does Papa know of the *haut ton*? He spent all his life avoiding it. I shall do this family proud."

And then it was Eustace's turn. He bowed over her hand. "Charming, charming," he murmured. "Do come see us."

And then Nez took her by the hand. He looked in her eyes as if searching for something there. For just one moment, she held her breath.

The moment passed quickly as he pressed her hand and leaned

closer. "If you should change your mind, Libby . . ."

She withdrew her hand and stepped back as the coachman gathered the reins and the horses moved. She smiled for Lydia's benefit, Lydia who was even now edging closer to hear what was passing so quietly between them.

"I promise you, my lord, I will not change my mind. Safe journey to you, sir."

She stepped back and the duke had no choice but to hand Lydia into the chaise and climb in after her. She blew a kiss to Lydia and waved until the vehicle was out of sight on the road that ran past Holyoke Green. The same road that had brought Nesbitt Duke, the chocolate purveyor, into her life so precipitately carried him out.

When the carriage was gone from view and only the dust cloud remained, she sat down on the front steps and rested her chin in her hands, ignoring the stares of the butler and the footman, who had never seen her do such an unladylike thing. The footman started to say something, but Candlow took him by the arm and pulled him inside, shutting the door behind him.

Libby sat there until the urge for tears left her. Her heart booming in her chest, she looked up in surprise once to the sound of a carriage. Nez had thought better of his words and was returning to her.

But it was only a farmer's cart full of produce in kegs that rumbled down the road, bound for the great open-air markets of London. The duke was not going to come back. Men like that don't look back, once they have made such a decision, she decided.

Libby, you are a wonder, she thought, chin in hand. Only think of all the wisdom you are acquiring this summer. Dr. Cook taught you how to set a bone yesterday, and today a peer of the realm showed you handily your place in life. I wonder what else there is to learn today?

She looked up then from her contemplation of her shoe tops and gazed across the road. And where was Joseph? The thought propelled her to her feet and she started around the house. Perhaps he had returned and was helping Tunley in the stables. Her steps quickened until she was almost running, her eyes hopeful that he would be there, mucking out the old straw in that awkward but methodical way of his. Or perhaps he was just sitting there watching Tunley, absorbing each simple task that the groom lavished on the animals they both loved so well.

He was nowhere in sight. Libby sighed and went into the stable, blinking her eyes against the sudden gloom.

If she had thought to find edification from Tunley, her hopes were quickly dashed. He hurried toward her.

"That brother of yours! He must have borrowed Sir Williams' best hunter. I do not think your uncle will be overly pleased if he learns of it. Where do you think he has got to, miss?"

"I was rather hoping you could tell me, Tunley," she said.

He shook his head. "Then we are two ignorant people, miss." She turned to go, but Tunley called her back. "Miss, I almost forgot. Do come and see what wandered into our stable this morning."

She followed him to one of the loose boxes and rested her arms across the top rail, her eyes dancing with delight, her miseries shoved to one side for a moment. "Oh, Tunley!"

A wisp of hay in its mouth, the horse looked up when she spoke. The mare was small and delicate-boned, a deep chestnut that fairly glowed with good health. Libby reached out slowly and let it smell her hand and then she touched its neck. The animal whinnied and moved closer as she patted it.

"Oh, you're practically a house pet," Libby praised. "Tunley wherever did you get this little beauty? I don't remember this one."

The groom scratched his head and then tipped some more oats in the manger. "She was here when I came down from the loft this morning, just as sweet as you please, in that very box." He reached in his pockets and fumbled through the nails, bits of wire, scraps of paper and lint until he found a piece of bark. He held it out to her. "This was twisted in her mane."

"Why, I do believe it is my name," Libby said as she ran her finger under the crude letters that spelled LIBE. She smudged a letter with her finger. "It must be charcoal from a camp fire. Oh, Tunley, do you think it is from the gypsies? And how do they know my name?"

"Witchcraft, miss," he said seriously. "Potions and charms and such like that a Kentsman never mentions."

Libby stoked the animal again, noting the little chips of shining beads that someone had taken great care to lace into the mane. "I am amazed. It must have been the gypsies," she said, "or perhaps that gypsy mother. I would not have thought it possible. Tunley, what should I do?"

The groom grinned at her. "I don't suppose you have any choice but to ride her, miss, and a sweet goer she looks."

"I wouldn't, Miss Ames, I really wouldn't. This could be a matter for the law."

Libby jumped in surprise and whirled about, moving closer to Tunley. His legs planted wide apart, a riding crop in his hand, Squire Cook stood in the doorway. He tapped the crop in his gloved hand and Libby pressed her lips tight together. It was the same crop he had used on Joseph the other day. And now he has come for me, she thought irrationally, more angry than fearful.

She swallowed her irritation and forced herself to walk toward him with a smile on her face, her hand extended. She marveled how little Anthony Cook resembled his light-haired, blue-eyed father, except in height. Father and son could have been strangers jumbled together on the planet, so little did they resemble each other.

To her amazement, he took her hand, his fingers surprisingly gentle. "Good day, Miss Ames," he said as he released her hand. "I did not mean to startle you, but I heard voices and thought to investigate, considering that this was my destination."

"Sir?"

The mare whinnied and the squire peered over her shoulder. He came closer to the loose box, his face without expression except for his lively eyes, which even now were frowning at the horse Libby found so beautiful.

"I—I think it is from the gypsies," she began. "It appears to be a gift to me."

The squire let out a crack of laughter that startled Libby and caused the horse to sidestep to the other side of the box. "I wouldn't have thought a gypsy brat to be worth so much," he said. "Remind me to tell my son that he has been cheated through countless country visits."

Libby said nothing, but she did not back away as the squire

came closer and she repeated her earlier pose, draping her arms on the rail.

"I am missing two of my best hunters, Miss Ames," he said, his words casual, as though he discussed this year's price for hops.

His voice was not loud; he did not accuse, but as he pursed his lips and peered at her out of the corner of his eye, she felt a little chill travel up her spine.

"I am sure I know nothing about them, sir," she said, wishing that her voice was more steady. "I don't make a habit of horse knavery." Her chin came up. "And neither does my brother."

He put the riding crop under her chin gently, but there was a threat in his eyes as he forced her to turn in his direction. "I do not accuse you of thievery, ma'am, or your simple brother. I merely came by as a friendly warning."

Tunley started forward. "See here now, sir," he said.

The squire lowered his crop. "My cousin in Wilverham is missing a horse something like this one." He sighed and peered into the gloom. "But it is a mare with a blaze on its forehead and two white stockings. A beautiful animal, trained to a sidesaddle for his wife."

Before she could protest, the squire vaulted the railing and moved toward the animal, which had retreated against the far wall.

Libby thought to object, but she watched the squire, surprised at his agility in the same way that Anthony Cook, for all his clumsy ways, always brought out her admiration when he rode by on horseback.

Tunley took exception. He began to sputter and protest with dire mutterings about "his stable," and "wait until Sir William returns."

Libby touched his sleeve and shook her head. "Let us see what he is about, Tunley," she said. "I don't know that we could eject him anyway."

"I can try, miss," Tunley returned in a fierce whisper.

"And end up in jail," she reminded him. "Let us be discreet here."

They watched as the squire moved closer to the horse, his voice gentle now and coaxing. The mare came toward him and he stroked her nose, talking softly, crooning to the skittish animal.

He reminds me of Joseph, Libby thought, and then put her brother from her mind. It would never do for the squire to know that Joseph had bolted from here in a pelter and was roaming the countryside.

"Miss Ames, toss me a rag, please?"

She wadded up a bit of sacking and threw it in a slow, gentle arc, so as not to upset the animal, which by now nuzzled the squire's hunting jacket. Traitor horse, she thought mildly.

Still talking in gentle tones to the mare, the squire smoothed out the sacking and began to rub the animal's forehead. In a moment, a white streak appeared.

"God love us," Tunley murmured.

Libby sucked in her breath. The squire looked at her and raised his eyebrows. He turned back to the business at hand and ran the sacking down the horse's forelegs, exposing the perfectly matched stockings there.

"This animal appears to have suffered a sea change," he declared.

As Libby stared at the horse, her mouth wide open, the squire sauntered across the loose box, rested his arms on the railing, and bent down, his face just inches from hers.

"Never trust a gift from a gypsy, Miss Ames," he said. "Lesson Number One for the day."

Lesson Number Two for the day, she thought as she stood her ground and smiled back at him. I am becoming so well-educated that I will astound myself. "Thank you, sir," she said. "I will remember this lesson."

"See that you do." With a light hand, he vaulted back over the railing. "I do hate to see a woman cheated."

Tunley shook his head. "Well, sir, better send your groom over, or I can return the horse to your cousin, whichever you please, sir."

"I sacked my groom."

"Gor, you never did," exclaimed Tunley in surprise, forgetting himself so far as to add, "And high time, I say."

"Gor, I did," said the squire as amusement flickered in his eyes. "It was rather forcefully brought home to me the other day that I had been suffering a fool gladly. If you know of anyone about in the neighborhood, Tunley, do drop a bee in his bonnet.''

As she watched the squire, Libby smiled in spite of herself. That was likely as close as the squire would ever come to an apology for his treatment of Joseph. She stepped up to him boldly. ''Squire Cook, you could hire my brother. He would suit you right down to the ground.''

The squire threw back his head and laughed, and then chucked her under the chin again with the crop. ''Miss Ames, you are not only a beautiful baggage; you are also a cheeky one. I'd see you in hell first before I'd hire a simpleton to tend blood stock. Tunley, loan me a halter for that animal. I'll take her to my cousin now. Lord, Miss Ames, that was a rich one.''

He was still chuckling to himself as he mounted his own horse outside the stable and led the little mare away.

Libby let out her breath slowly.

''You can relax, miss.''

She followed the direction of Tunley's glance and saw to her surprise that she had doubled her hands into fists. She dropped her arms to her sides. ''He gets my back up. What a strange man!''

''Stranger than we know, more like, miss.'' Tunley turned back to the stable and pitched up the pitchfork and stabbed it into the old straw. ''If you see Joseph, tell him to hurry in here with Sir William's horse, and I'll overlook it this time.''

She nodded and walked slowly toward the house, pausing once or twice to shade her eyes with her hand and scan the fields again. Where was Joseph?

There was still no answer to her question by the time the maid removed the luncheon tray that Libby had taken into the library with every intention of eating. As she maneuvered the food about from one flowery design to another on her plate. Libby considered all the places Joseph could have taken himself to. She was none the wiser when she gave up on her cold meal and pushed it aside.

He had never been gone this long before. She could only assume that he was even now sitting somewhere, wondering why he had ridden so far and wondering when his sister would come for him. He will be too shy to ask anyone for directions, she decided. He always went to some length to avoid strangers who might make fun of his stilted way of talking.

She admitted to herself that there was a certain relief in having to worry about Joseph. It kept her from thinking about the other man who had ridden out of her life only that morning.

"Candlow, what do I do?" she asked the butler when he let himself into the library to bully her for her neglect of luncheon. "I am afraid Joseph is lost."

Candlow looked at her inquiringly and she gave him leave to sit. "None of us knows his habits as well as you, Miss Ames, else we could go searching."

She shook her head. "I'll have to find him, Candlow, if I can."

"By yourself? What a pity, miss, that the Duke of Copley's Chocolatier is not here to help us," he said, permitting himself a little smile over his joke.

Libby smiled too, because she knew he expected it. "He doesn't know the country any better than I do, really."

They sat in silence for a moment, and then the butler leaned forward. "Miss Ames, I recommend the doctor."

"Oh, I could never," she exclaimed. "I could not be such a bother, Candlow. The man never sleeps as it is."

They sat in silence for another moment and then Libby rose. "I'll go for the doctor," she said quietly. "I don't see that I have any choice."

"He won't mind, Miss Ames," said Candlow, another smile in his eyes.

"Well, he should!"

She walked across the field to the Cooks' estate, looking about her for the squire. It was eight miles and more to Wilverham; likely he had not returned yet from his cousin's house. She didn't relish the thought of his crop across her back for trespassing, even as she scolded herself and knew he would never strike her. "It is always easiest to expect the worst of someone," she said out loud as she strode along, arms swinging, hat dangling down her back. "Wasn't that another of your little bits of wisdom, my lord duke?"

She hurried faster the farther she went, and by the time she arrived at the door, she was breathless. She leaned against the door frame to gather herself together before ringing the bell.

Libby looked about her with interest. She had never been to the squire's house before, although she had often admired the stone building from the road. She examined it up close with a critical eye, noting the limp curtains inside the windows that wanted washing. I think this looks like a house that has been tenanted too long by men only, she thought. I would replace those old-fashioned tapestry draperies with something more modern. White lace would look so nice and airy. And that trim! What can they have been thinking to paint it that unbecoming gray? White would be so much more the thing. How well it would set off the honey color of the stones.

Libby rang the bell and straightened her bonnet back on her disheveled hair, tying the strings more firmly. She waited for the butler to appear, wondering what he would look like. He will likely be an apparition, beanpole-thin and funereal, with baggy stockings and hair growing out of his ears.

The woman who opened the door was none of those things. She was round and short, with dancing black eyes and an apron covered with flour. As Libby stared in fascination, she dusted her hands off over the open doorway and onto roses that looked as though they had suffered this indignity before.

"Come in, Miss . . . Miss Ames, is it?" She grinned into Libby's surprised face. "God love us, Doctor said that you were pretty, but he were mistaken, he were." She searched about in her brain for the right word. "You're a regular Adonis, Miss Ames!"

Libby coughed and turned her head to hide the twinkle in her own eyes. "Well, yes, ma'am—er, no, ma'am," she stammered. "I need to see the doctor. Is he about?"

The woman—she could only be the cook—clucked her tongue. "And hasn't he only just got himself from bed, his eyes looking like bits of liver, so red they are?" She leaned closer in conspiratorial fashion until Libby could smell the yeast on her. "Farrell Frink tumbled down a well, he did, and wasn't Doctor up until all hours, putting him back together like Humpty-

Dumpty?'' She giggled behind her hands, dusting flour across her face. '' 'Can't but be an improvement on the original,' says I to Doctor.''

Libby laughed out loud. "Farrel Frink! I doubt the doctor will get a ha'penny for all his stitching.''

The cook joined in the laughter. "More like he'll get a poached deer, dumped at the back door in the dead of night, and then won't we all be in trouble? When Doctor heard who had fallen down the well, Lord love us, he rolled his eyes and muttered something about 'damn that old Hippocrates anyway!' ''

Libby heard heavy footsteps in the hall. She looked behind the housekeeper to see Dr. Cook standing there.

He was dressed in buckskin breeches and a shirt without a neckcloth, which he held in his hand. He ran his fingers through his curly dark hair with the other hand and managed to boost his spectacles higher on his nose, all in one gesture.

"Miss Ames," he exclaimed. He came closer to feel her forehead. "You're not ill?''

"No, sir, I am not," she said, feeling suddenly shy to be standing on Anthony Cook's doorstep. "I need to talk to you, though. Have you a moment?''

He smiled and somehow the exhaustion left his eyes. "I have more than a moment, Miss Ames. Do come in. That will be all, Mrs. Weller.''

The cook seemed reluctant to leave what promised to be an interesting interview. "Can I bring you some biscuits, Dr. Cook?'' she asked.

He nodded. "And a little sherry, if the maid hasn't drunk it all." He gestured down the hall. "Come to my surgery, Miss Ames.''

"Libby," she corrected. "Didn't we decide on that the other day?''

"So we did," he agreed. "I had wondered if you would remember.''

They passed open doors on the way to the back of the house. Libby couldn't help but peer into rooms either empty of furniture or stuffed with furniture and shrouded in Holland cloths. What a curious house, she thought.

Anthony must have understood the process of her mind, for he grimaced. "We have been without the services of a house-keeper since the last one took umbrage. 'Twas in 1813, I believe." He gestured with his head in the direction Mrs. Weller had dis-appeared. "She's a dreadful substitute, but can she cook!"

He opened the door to his surgery and she stepped in, looking about her in delight.

It was an oasis of calm in an untidy house. The room was as neat and clean as the rest of the house was chaos. One wall was lined with books, each carefully in place but all bearing the unmistakable look of volumes well-read and much-thumbed-over. There was a large desk by the books, and a diploma with many seals and elaborate scrollwork framed on the wall. A handsome screen stretched across one corner of the room. Libby could see an examining table behind it, and rows of instruments, all gleaming, under glass.

"I wish we had a hospital hereabouts, like in Edinburgh," he said, gesturing to a chair. "As it is, I dream that I will chance upon a nabob in need of a good physicking, whom I will heal of an incurable illness, and he will build me a hospital to show his deep gratitude."

Libby laughed and removed her hat. "And all you get is Farrell Frink!"

He reached out impulsively, ruffled her hair, and laughed along with her. "Do we ever get what we want, Libby Ames? I doubt it."

"I suppose we do not, Anthony, but, how we try," she said, and sat down.

She thought she would be embarrassed to bother Anthony Cook with her trouble, especially if he sat behind that intimidating desk. Instead he pulled up the other chair opposite her and relaxed himself into it.

"What's troubling you, Libby?" he asked quietly.

She took a deep breath. "Joseph has run away, and I don't know where to look. I hate to bother you, but I am afraid he might be in trouble."

There was a scratching on the door, and Mrs. Weller opened it and peeked around, carrying a tray laden with biscuits and sherry.

The doctor held up a glass, sighed, and wiped it out with his neckcloth. He poured in silence, his face red. "I wish we had a housekeeper, Libby." He offered her a biscuit.

She selected a promising morsel and bit into it, uttering exclamations of delight. "You certainly don't want for a cook, Anthony."

He downed two biscuits to her one. "That's why we keep her on, Libby, and, yes, let us go find your brother." As she nibbled on the biscuit, he took her hand. "There is something else troubling you, isn't there?" he asked.

"No . . . no," she stammered, her face as red as his. "That is, nothing of any great importance."

He let go of her hand and leaned back in his chair, eyeing her carefully. "Do you know, some of my best patients only come to talk?"

I cannot tell him about the duke. It would be too painful, she thought as she looked into his kind face.

After another moment of silence, he got to his feet, putting a hand on her shoulder to keep her in the chair. "Stay where you are and I will arrange for the gig. Have another biscuit." He patted her shoulder, gave up on his neckcloth, and tossed it on the desk. "It will be dark soon enough. We'd better find the wanderer."

14

LIBBY was still eating biscuits, drinking sherry, and feeling very much better when the doctor returned to his surgery. By then she had propped up her feet on the other chair and had sunk down further in the overstuffed armchair, on the verge of a nap. Libby sat up quickly when he came into the room and began to dust the crumbs off her lap.

Anthony merely stood there looking at her, a slight smile on his face. "Here, here, my dear. I leave you alone for fifteen minutes and return to see such dissipation. And see here, you left me no biscuits. I shall have to live off my fat for the duration of this adventure, obviously."

Libby brushed the wrinkles from her dress and put her hat back on, tying it in the reflection of the glass-fronted bookcase. "If I came here too often for Mrs. Weller's remedy for depression, ennui, and general lethargy, I would have to be lifted out of that chair with a block and tackle."

The doctor patted his stomach. "I daresay we should let her go. Then I could get down to my fighting weight again." He rubbed his chin, his eyes merry, the fun in them infectious. "Of course, I never was much of a fighter, and Father, on the other hand, has never added so much as a stone to what he took to Cambridge years ago. Life, Libby, is not fair."

She could only agree with this sentiment, particularly when

they ventured outdoors to a gray day. The blue sky and cotton-puff clouds had metamorphosed into something less congenial.

The doctor lifted her into the gig as though she weighed nothing, and climbed in after her. A quiet word to the horse set them on their way down the long drive from the house. Libby turned around to look behind her.

"Do you know, Anthony, you really should plant a row of flowering crab apple or hawthorn along either side of this lane," she said. "It would be a delight in the spring and would afford such shade in deep summer."

He nodded, his eyes on the road. "I'll give it some thought. Which way do we go, Libby? I am yours to command."

"I think we should find the gypsies," she said, her voice decisive. "Joseph may have decided to throw in his lot with them. You know that he is horse-mad."

"Very well." He tugged on one rein and the gig turned away from Holyoke.

They rode in silence for a considerable distance. Libby could feel him glancing at her every now and then. She could sense that he was on the verge of saying something, but some reticence kept him bereft of speech.

One mile passed, and then another, and then he gathered the reins in one hand and turned to her. "Why did he run away, Libby? It seems so unlike Joseph."

She could not look at him, but replied in a small voice. "We had a misunderstanding. He felt himself at fault. I tried to explain, but he would not listen."

She twisted her hands together in her lap, longing to spill out the whole story of the duke's infamous offer and her rejection, but the subject was too delicate. She sat in silence and flogged herself for her lack of courage. Hen-hearted, Libby, that's what you are, she thought. He's giving you a perfect opportunity to unburden yourself, and you sit here like Lot's wife.

Another mile and then they passed beyond the boundaries of the Ames estate. Another mile, and the doctor stopped the gig. The cart creaked as he turned sideways to face her. "I really have to know something, Libby, and I am sorry if it is none of my business, but tell me this: am I to wish you happy?"

She couldn't even look him in the eye, but merely shook her head and tried to make herself small on her side of the gig. This proved to be no easy task, because the doctor filled most of the space.

Libby wanted to speak, but she could only sit there in miserable silence.

The doctor touched her shoulder. "And here I sit probing away at what seems to be an open wound. I am sorry, my dear, truly I am, but I was certain that the duke would offer for you." He sighed. "It seemed inevitable."

Libby looked up then and spoke without thinking. "Oh, he made me a generous offer, Anthony. He offered me a house in Half Moon Street, a high-perch phaeton, jewels and furs, a box at the opera, and everything but his name."

She blanched to see the anger rise so fast in his face. In his rage, he suddenly looked older and very much like the squire. While she watched in alarm as his high color became even more vivid, Libby wondered that she had never noticed the resemblance before.

"It doesn't matter," she assured him. "Please don't get into a taking about it."

"I will call him out," he said in a voice of deadly calm. "How could *anyone* take such advantage of a young women with really no one to stand up for her? Damn his eyes."

Anthony's anger made her forget for a minute her own misery. "You'll not call him out," she declared, flinging off her hat and throwing it behind her so she could see him better. "He would likely drill you through."

"He probably would," the doctor agreed, his anger receding as quickly as it had come. "I would have to be my own surgeon, and I am squeamish about physicking myself." He looked at her, bewildered. "I do not understand why he would do such a thing."

"I suppose it is a matter of pride," she said, grateful that she was not dissolving into tears as she feared she would, and thankful for the doctor's matter-of-fact air. "Anthony, how would it look? A duke married to a penniless nonentity who knows how to use the right fork and never scratches in public, but whose father was disgraced and whose grandfather sold tobacco to tars?''

''And I suppose he was surprised when you turned down his perfectly reasonable offer.''

''I do believe he was,'' she replied, considering the matter.

The doctor took up the reins again and the horse moved on. ''Tell me now where Joseph fits into this picture, and then I will back out of your affairs, Libby.''

''I think he must have overheard my refusal only, and blamed himself,'' she said, the frustration back in her voice again. ''Oh, Anthony, Joseph feels his lacks too acutely. I wish it were not so. He thought that I turned down the duke because Nez would have considered him an embarrassment in London. I tried to reason with Joseph, but that is never easy to do. And now he is gone, and he is probably lost.''

She began to sob in good earnest. Without a word, the doctor stopped the gig again and took her in his arms. ''Go ahead and cry, my dear,'' he said when she tried to push him away. ''You'll feel better soon enough. You need your mama at a time like this, and I am but a poor substitute.''

Libby raised her tearstained face to his and shook her head. ''I daren't breathe a word of this to Mother. She would be so ashamed that it is her background that makes such an alliance so impossible. I would never hurt her that way. And Aunt Crabtree?'' Libby rolled her eyes. ''She would fall prostrate upon the carpet, and how would I ever explain that to Uncle Ames?''

''For the Lord's sake, then, don't carry your burdens around any longer,'' the doctor said. ''Have a really good washout, Libby dear, and then let us find this stubborn brother of yours.''

''You don't mind?'' she sniffled, groping unsuccessfully in her reticule for a handkerchief.

''I don't mind.''

She took the doctor at his word and sobbed until her nose started to run and her eyes felt raw. The doctor made no comment other than to tell her to blow when he held his handkerchief to her face. His arms were tight about her, and she wept out her misery on the most comfortable shoulder she could have hoped for.

When her tears had subsided to an occasional hiccup and then one more strengthy session with the handkerchief, Libby pried herself from the doctor's arms and sat upright again. Her hair had come loose in a tangle about her shoulders and there was a nest of hairpins in her lap and on the seat. She began to gather them together.

"I must look a fright," she said.

"You are—" he paused to consider a moment—"a veritable antidote." He had released her, but his arms still rested across her shoulders. "I cannot but wonder about the fact that for two days running now, I have surely seen you at your worst, and find you not in the least disgusting. I must be in my dotage."

Libby managed to chuckle as she attempted to twist her hair back up on her head again. "What you are is extremely obliging and much too kind, sir, for your own good. All your patients will cheat you and watery damsels will destroy your coats. What you need, sir, is management in your life, and then you would be too well-organized to be forced to listen to sad tales from silly women."

"You are describing a wife, Libby," he said mildly as he unwound the reins and started the horse in motion again.

It was on her lips to say something amusing, but she could think of nothing, particularly in light of her recent refusal. *Why does that plaguey proposal not disappear from my mind?* she thought, irritated with herself and embarrassed at the same time.

Libby tucked her hair here and there, deeply conscious of the fact that Anthony had deliberately left the conversation unfinished. She looked away from him across a meadow flowered with yellow daisies and lupins. *Yes, by all means, find yourself some sensible woman who will not be afraid to bully you and your father, clean up that midden of a house, plant some flowers, and raise your children.*

The silence that stretched between them should have felt strained and difficult, but it did not. Libby replaced her hat as the doctor slowed the gig again. He pointed to the next field. "See there, Libby, they have gone away."

Libby clutched his arm. "Oh, could you just look and make sure they have not left that child behind? Maybe there will be some sign of Joseph."

He got out of the gig and vaulted over the fence in that same easy fashion as his father. He walked on until he was out of sight in the copse of trees. He emerged on the distant side at the place where she had sat with the child in the driving rain.

It all seemed so long ago, she thought as she watched him reappear and grow larger again. Anthony Cook walked with an easy stride that reminded her of her own father. Funny, she thought, he has not bumbled into anything lately, or stumbled over his feet, or cracked his head. Lydia would be amazed to see him. She giggled, her hand to her mouth. I suppose like Kate the Shrew he is merely cursed in company. This must mean that we are friends now and he feels easy with me. He must have forgotten that ridiculous proposal. Thank the Lord for that.

He leapt the fence again and held up his hands to her. "Nothing. They're gone as though they had never been." He leaned against the fence. "What now, my dear?"

"No tracks to follow?"

"None." He shrugged. "I must amend that. Perhaps if I were a Mohican, I could find a bent blade of grass." He climbed into the gig again. "I vote that we go to the next town and just look about." He sat a moment in thought and then brightened. "What day is it, Libby?"

"Friday, I believe."

"Silly, I know that! The date, please."

"June twenty-fourth. Oh, Anthony, is it the week of the midsummer fair in Dewhurst?"

"Precisely. If we cannot find gypsies at a horse fair, then we obviously should send others on our errands."

They found gypsies in Dewhurst, camped on a woody knoll by the river. They were her gypsies, but they had been joined by others in more elaborate wagons. After several glances full of suspicion, and whispered conversations, the gypsies ignored them.

"Do you see Joseph anywhere?" Anthony asked, keeping a firm grip on the reins.

"No," she said, and then glanced down when someone tugged at her skirts.

It was the little girl from the field. She hobbled on crutches and the splinted bandage was dirty, but it had not been removed. She could almost feel the relief that seemed to flow from Anthony.

With a helping hand from Anthony, Libby left the gig and stood beside the child, careful not to touch her.

"Your brother was in our camp."

"Oh, you do speak English!" Libby exclaimed. "Where is my brother now?"

"I do not know. He came into our camp around noon, talked to our men, and then rode away. My sister Iviva saw him sneak back and steal two of our best horses." She paused and then added scrupulously, "Horses that we had traded for fairly." She looked over her shoulder at her mother, who stood close to the wagon, afraid to come closer. "Mama said I was to say that."

Libby thought about the stolen gift she had received only that morning. "My brother is a scoundrel. Will your father and the other men track him?"

The little girl glanced again at her mother for reassurance. "Mama says that would depend on which direction he is traveling."

Libby nodded. "Thank you, my dear." She leaned closer. "Stay off your leg all you can."

The girl smiled then and hurried away.

Libby let Anthony help her into the gig again.

"I wonder whose animals Joseph recognized and is bearing away?" he asked when they left the village.

"Your father's, I think," she said. "The squire told me only this morning that he was missing two horses."

The doctor managed a thin smile, his eyes troubled. "My father doesn't deserve such kindness from Joseph."

They drove from Dewhurst, no wiser than before about Joseph Ames' whereabouts. "All we really know is that there are two more horses now," Libby said, taking inventory. "I doubt Joseph knows the way back to your father's estate. Oh, Anthony, and now it is getting dark."

It should not have been dark so soon, on this week of the midsummer's fair, but the sky was gray with clouds that grew blacker as they traveled in the general vicinity of Holyoke, trying little-known paths the doctor barely remembered from his childhood, and backtracking when they thought they saw something among the trees.

The rain began as they backed out of yet another dead-end path that had appeared so promising. Without a word, Anthony stripped off his coat and wrapped it around her. It could have gone around her twice, but Libby pulled it close, thankful for the warmth.

"I should have done that sooner," he said, his eyes squinting into the gathering gloom. "You've been shivering this past half-hour and more. Sprig muslin is not fabric suited for adventuring, although it is remarkably attractive on you."

She moved closer to him. "In the Peninsula, Mama dressed me in wool and flannel, but that never seemed adventurous to me. Only think what a dull life I lead now."

Anthony held up his hand. "Hush! Did you hear that?"

Nerves on the alert, she listened. At first there was only the sound of rain and leaves blowing about on bending branches, and then she heard it. Someone sneezed again and again.

Anthony cupped his hands around his mouth. "Joseph! Joseph!" he called.

Libby strained to see through the rain. She gripped the doctor's arm. "Look, there he is. Joseph, over here!"

"Can't see a thing," the doctor muttered. "Spectacles all wet."

Libby leapt out of the gig and splashed along the road to the figure that was coming toward them, head down, arms slapping his chest to keep warm. Behind him trailed three equally sodden horses.

Libby grabbed her brother and hugged him.

"Libby?" he said, and then threw his arms around her. "Libby, I was so lost. And here are these horses and I can't remember when I got them, or where they are supposed to go, and they keep following me."

He was on the ragged edge of hysteria. She turned around

to call for the doctor, but Anthony was right beside her. He took a firm grip of Joseph's shoulders and shook him gently.

"You're fine, laddy. These horses belong to my father and you are returning them to him. The other horse is your uncle's hunter. Laddy, you're just blue with cold."

Libby took off the doctor's coat and wrapped it around her brother, who was looking back at the horses, recognition in his eyes. "That's it," he exclaimed, pumping the doctor's hand in gratitude. "I remember now!" His face fell again. "But I really am lost."

The doctor put one arm about Joseph and the other about Libby. "Laddy, you are in luck. I know precisely where we are."

Joseph burst into tears and the doctor tightened his grip on his patient. Libby started to cry, too, tears of relief, and Anthony laughed. "Here I stand, a soggy petunia in the midst of the Ames watering pots."

The idea of the portly physician as a petunia captivated Libby's tired brain and she laughed along with him. Joseph did not join in, but his tears stopped. The horses trailed along behind them like large, bedraggled hounds.

Anthony helped Joseph into the gig and then handed Libby up to him. "Here, lad, she'll have to sit on your lap. I would graciously volunteer, but I am busy with the reins."

Whistling to himself as the rain drummed down, the doctor tied the horses to the back of the gig and started off again, moving faster down the lane and keeping up a spanking pace until they saw the glow of a single lamp in a crofter's cottage. The doctor pointed. "Maud and Wallis Casey," he said. "We'll be six in a bed tonight, but won't we be warm."

The door was flung open wide to the doctor's knock, and they were pulled inside. Wallis sized up the situation and led the horses off to the barn, which made up the larger half of the cottage. He was followed by three or four little Caseys, laughing, dodging the puddles, and hollering that they wanted to help.

Almost before he knew what was happening, Joseph was stripped of his wet clothes, tucked in someone's nightshirt, and dropped into the middle of a large bed that filled one side of the cottage. At Maud's command, another two or three Caseys leapt into bed, too, cuddling close to Libby's brother. Joseph looked about in amazement, accepted his fate without a murmur, and closed his eyes.

"Better than warming pans," was Maud's comment as she turned to Libby. "You're next, miss," she ordered, and then looked at the doctor, absolutely fearless. "You're a big looby to bring this little bit of a thing out in such a storm. Where are your wits, Dr. Cook?"

He backed off, a smile on his face. "This little bit assures me that she has the constitution of a horse. She's even healthier than you are, Maud, and that's going some. But I will turn my back while you do your best."

He turned around, shoulders shaking, as Libby was led off to a darker corner, taken from her wet clothes, enveloped in a nightgown as large as the doctor's coat, and tucked into the other bed.

By this time, Maud was running short of children. She carried the baby to the bed and placed him in Libby's arms. "He's a regular little camp fire, is John," she boasted. "Will you have your bread toasted or plain, miss?"

"Toasted," she said, startled, and then hugely pleased with herself as little John regarded her, burped, and snuggled into her arms. In a moment she felt warm. In another moment, her eyes closed.

When she woke later, the doctor was sitting close to the fire, eating her toast dipped in milk. His breeches dangled in front of the fire and he was wrapped in a blanket. Maud was laughing about something, Wallis pulled on his pipe, and the littlest Casey girl leaned against the doctor's knee. He put down his cup, picked her up, and fed her every other bite as she nestled in the crook of his arm.

Careful not to wake little John, who slumbered beside her like a banked furnace, Libby raised herself up on one elbow and watched Dr. Cook make himself the perfect guest. He chuckled over Maud's tales of children and animals, nodded at John's cryptic comments about corn prices and unemployed soldiers, and told the Caseys grouped around him about the gypsies. The cattle lowed in their pen on the other side of the wall.

Maud noticed that she was awake. "Come over to the fire, Miss Ames," she said. "Likely John'll never budge." She poked her husband in the ribs and he grinned. "Like his dad he is!"

Libby crawled out of bed and grabbed up the robe at the end of it, hugging it tight about her as Anthony Cook made room for her on the bench. He set his spectacles up higher on his nose. "You don't appear any the worse for wear, Libby. I could recommend pills and potions to ward off the devil, but the best specific I know of is Maud Casey's hot milk and toast."

In another moment she was warming her hands around a huge mug and wondering how she would drink it all. It was gone before Wallis finished his longish story about the excisemen and the rum found buried in the pasture.

"I tells him, whisht man, how do I know how it got there? He didna believe me, but, laddy, I don't know anything about it." He drew out the word "anything" in such droll fashion that Libby laughed. Wallis drew on his pipe again and crossed his heart.

Anthony tucked the little girl on his lap in closer and gestured with his free hand. "I am remiss. Miss Libby Ames, these are the Caseys—Wallis and Maud, who command this army, and Rebecca, Louis, Russell, Brian with the red hair, little Maudie here, John you have met, and a bed full of Thomas, Lisa and William."

"Goodness," said Libby in awe. "Did you deliver them all?"

Anthony shook his head. "No. Maud is usually quite well in charge of that herself. Only little John, right, Maud?" He smiled at Libby. "Cork in a bottle, was John."

Anthony finished his story about Libby and the gypsies, adding a few embellishments that she intended to take him to task about when they were alone again.

When he finished, Maud looked at her with respect. "Weren't you afraid of them dirty beggars?" she asked, brushing away the chickens that had moved closer to peck at the crumbs the doctor and little Maudie had dropped.

"She needed me, Mrs. Casey," Libby said. "You would have done the same."

Maud tucked her arm through her husband's. "I would have more like, but first that little'un would have had a good wash."

They sat a long while in companionable friendship before the fire. Another Casey found his way onto the doctor's lap and Libby smiled at Anthony, her eyes heavy. "I never cared much for my doctor when I was their age," she said. "Of course, he was the regimental surgeon and believed in chewing tobacco for all ailments." She was silent a moment, thinking about her grandfather, dead these ten years. "I sometimes think that chewing tobacco is good enough."

Maud looked at her with a question in her eyes, but Anthony understood. He gathered her under his arm with the Casey chldren. "Sometimes nothing else will do, Libby. I have been known to recommend it, on occasion."

Tears came suddenly to her eyes, and he flicked them away with his finger. "Let it go now, Libby."

She nodded, sleepy again, and closed her eyes. When she woke, it was much later. Mrs. Casey snored beside her in the bed, with a smaller Casey snuggled close by and a large one draped across the foot of the bed.

Libby looked at the other bed. Anthony Cook, pants on, but his shirt half-buttoned with the tails out, stood over her brother. As she watched, he felt Joseph's neck for his pulse and pulled the blanket up higher. He stood there then, just watching his patient.

After a long moment's contemplation, he went back to the fireside, stretched until his hands touched the ceiling, and then sat down. Libby lay watching him and then got quietly out of bed, careful not to wake John.

She sat down beside the doctor, who was staring at the fire. He seemed not to be aware of her for a moment and started in surprise when she cleared her throat.

"I did not mean to give you the jitters," she whispered. "I just wanted to thank you for . . . for everything today. When Joseph didn't come home, I had no one to turn to." She looked deep into the fire, too. "And thank you for hearing me out about . . . Well, you know."

He smiled faintly, but did not look at her. "Do you love him, Libby?" he asked when a log crashed and settled on the glowing coals.

"I suppose I do," she said. "Right now, I just feel confused, rather out to sea, and I'm not quite sure why." She didn't pull away when he put his arm around her. "I think I will go to Brighton, after all, and visit my mother."

"An excellent idea, my dear."

He was silent a long time then, even as he sat so alert beside her, tense even, as though he had something to say.

Libby cleared her throat finally. "If you have something to say to me, I wish you would do it. I suppose I deserve a bear-garden jaw for being such a gapeseed about Benedict Nesbitt."

"Not a bit of it. He's an engaging man, and I, for one, wish him very well." He paused. "I was thinking along other lines."

Again the silence. She poked him. "Really, Anthony, if I didn't know better, I would think you were trying to work up the courage to propose again."

She regretted the words the moment she said them. *I am so stupid,* she thought, dredging that up again.

"That's it, Libby," he said, the words surprised out of his mouth as though she had struck him on the back. He took off his spectacles, polished them on his shirt in one nervous movement, and replaced them as she stared at him. "Would you even consider making me the happiest man in the world by marrying me?" he asked. "I know I asked before, and I thought I would not again." He shook his head and regarded her mildly. "And so I ask you once more."

"Your father would be so disappointed," was the first thing she thought of, even before she thought of "no" this time. Her heart began to pound and she felt the blood rush to her face.

"He wouldn't be marrying you; I would," the doctor replied, warming to his subject. "Go ahead and list all your objections."

"I can think of many," she said in exasperation. "I don't have any money. Not any, Anthony," she declared.

"Did I say I needed your money? As my wife, you'll not have the elegancies of life, but with Mrs. Weller as our cook, you'll never starve. Well?"

She giggled. "You can't possibly be serious! My papa was

disgraced in the family. No one receives us in Holyoke."

He shrugged. "Your Uncle Ames likes me, except when I bother his gouty foot, and that's good enough. They'll receive the doctor's wife or look elsewhere for services."

"Well, how about this?" she said. "The man who marries me will have to take Joseph sooner or later. I could never abandon him and Mama will not live forever."

"I like the lad, and I think we can find plenty for him to do."

Libby was quiet then, leaning forward and watching the flames as they flickered and then died. The doctor rested his hand on her back. The feeling was pleasurable beyond words and she knew she should sit up. She did, and his hand dropped away.

"There is this, Anthony. You needn't offer for me because you feel I have been compromised by this situation tonight. There," she concluded, triumphant.

"Silly nod," he whispered. "The thought never entered my head. I doubt even Aunt Crabtree would make exception to our arrangement tonight. How on earth could I compromise you in a room filled with eleven Caseys, one brother, a handful of chickens, and through the wall, two cows and four horses? No, I think that is not an issue."

She laughed out loud and then clapped her hand over her mouth and shook in silence.

"You'll have to do better than that, Libby," he said finally.

She stared into the fire again and then turned to face him. "I do not wish to have to say this, Anthony, but I still do not love you. It's as simple as that."

He rubbed his chin. "That is an obstacle indeed, now that you mention it." He thought a moment more. "Do you think you ever could?"

She considered the merits of the question. Only yesterday I had my answer so ready. What is there today that makes this same answer impossible? She looked at him. He was too big, too nearsighted, too busy, and too homely for her. No, she reconsidered, he is not at all homely, setting aside the spectacles that never stay where they belong. That could be remedied. And his face, although fleshy and inclined to redness, was frank, honest, and appealing in a way she was hard put to explain. He was kindness itself. Perhaps she could like him someday, but love him? She did not know.

She said as much as he bent closer to hear her reply. "I don't know, Anthony. I never really considered it before."

"I know that well enough. I love you enough for both of us," he said, and put his arm around her waist, drawing her close. "I think that eventually we would deal very well together. Whether it was early or later in our marriage, I would never force your hand, Elizabeth."

He had never called her by her given name before. No one did, and she liked the sound of it. Her name had never seemed so pretty as when he spoke it.

"You would marry me without even being sure that I loved you, or would ever love you?" she asked.

"Oh, yes," was his prompt reply. "I am a patient man."

"Then I will do it," she said suddenly, astounded at herself even as the words left her lips and could not be retrieved. "My answer is yes."

He leaned forward to kiss her then. I will not like this, she thought as his face came closer, but she did. In fact, she liked it even more than his kiss the day before in the hay wain. Libby closed her eyes as their lips touched. His spectacles plummeted down onto her face, but without missing a moment, he set them on the floor and cupped her face in his hands as he went on kissing her.

She began to be short of breath, but found that she could breathe quite handily through her nose, if she only turned her head a little. His hair was curly under her fingers and still slightly damp from the rain, or perhaps he was sweating. All of a sudden she wanted him to touch her body.

He seemed to read her thoughts, gripping the skin of her waist through the heavy nightgown. And then he stopped, out of breath, his eyes slightly out of focus, and took her hands off his neck.

"You have made me a happy man," he whispered, his lips on her ear. "You'll have no regrets, I assure you. Go back to bed now. We can talk tomorrow."

She did as he said, crawling back between sheets still warm from little John. She lay quietly in the dark until she heard Anthony's steady, even breathing by the fireplace.

What have I done? she thought. What have I done?

15

MORNING came much sooner than Libby wished. Little John began to root about, hunting for his mama. When he began to whimper, Libby picked him up, kissed him, and trundled him over to his mother on her other side, who soon satisfied his restlessness.

It was quiet for a moment and then the rooster in the loft of the stable took a dim view of the silence and added his rider. Wallis grumbled and slid out of bed on the other side of the room, tugging on his breeches and tucking in his nightshirt.

Libby rolled over and resolutely shut her eyes again. She heard a sharp crack from the vicinity of the fireplace, followed by a heartfelt "Damn," and she sat up in bed to see Anthony on his feet and rubbing his head where he had forgotten about the low beams. He looked at her with a sour expression.

" 'Tis a good thing I do not physick myself," he said to her, "else I would diagnose that as rampant stupidititis."

She laughed and he threw his pillow at her. She threw it back, and that was the signal for Caseys large and small to tumble out of bed, pelting the doctor as he stood there in his bare feet. Libby lay on her back and laughed until the doctor whispered to the Caseys and they turned the attack on her.

Maud Casey attempted to restore order but was seriously hampered by little John, who took exception to the sudden disappearance of his breakfast. He set up a squalling that Wallis

Casey heard on the other side of the wall as he milked. "If this cow gives sour milk this morning, I will smite you all," he roared. "You, especially, Dr. Cook."

The Caseys looked at one another and burst into laughter. Mrs. Casey lay back down again and relieved John's misery.

Libby looked at her over the pile of pillows on top of her. "I should apologize for disrupting your morning," she said as she pulled off the pillows.

Maud only winked. "My dear, this is a typical morning, only more so."

Libby laughed again and looked over at her brother, who was sitting up in bed, a puzzled expression on his face. The doctor sat beside him, listening to his lungs with his ear pressed against his back.

"Ticking like a well-wound clock," Anthony said, a satisfied expression on his face. "I worry about pneumonia, laddy, especially after that drenching we all had."

Joseph gestured toward his sister. "Doctor, I wish that you would listen to Libby. She got a fearful drenching, too."

"Oh, no, I . . ." Libby began, pulling the blanket up higher on her chest.

"I suppose you are right, laddy, although Libby claims she is healthier than all of us," replied the doctor, his face redder than usual. He came to Libby's side and sat on the bed. "Turn around, my dear. You needn't bare your back. My hearing is acute enough through flannel, heaven knows."

She did as he said, leaning forward and resting her forehead on her knees as Anthony laid his ear against her back. He was silent a long time.

"Well?" Joseph demanded, a frown on his face.

" 'Tis not an easy matter to listen for crackles when your sister's stomach is growling," the doctor said.

"Wretch! Now go milk a cow or something, and take Joseph with you, while I dress," she said, not looking at the doctor.

She dressed quickly, her clothes warm from the fire, and held little John while Maud prepared the simple breakfast of milk and bread again. The Casey girls made the beds and then grouped themselves about the table while their mother buttered the bread, carefully scraping off any excess and applying it to the next piece.

"I am sorry we have taken up so much of your space," Libby said. Little John had appropriated her locket, passing it from hand to hand and chortling as he leaned against Libby.

"Well now, Miss Ames, we couldn't be more delighted to do the doctor a good turn, so many has he done us. Wasn't little Maudie nearly dead last winter after she fell through the ice? That was after Wallis' bad spell last fall and we had no money to pay him, but there he was." She smiled proudly. "I give him vegetables every week now. No, lassie, it's we that should thank you." She replaced the butter crock on the shelf. "Isn't he a fine one, Miss Ames? He's a bit of a bumbler, is Dr. Cook, but what one of us doesn't lack somewhere?"

Libby sipped at the warm milk Mrs. Casey handed her, ashamed to remember all the times she and Lydia had giggled over Dr. Cook and his clumsiness. And now I have promised that I will marry him. The idea seemed alien in the morning, stripped of all the mystery of the dark night and the crackling fire. I wonder why I did that, she thought. Is it because I am disappointed that the duke didn't offer for me?

It was a notion to reflect upon, Libby decided as Anthony and Joseph came back into the cottage, each carrying a bucket of milk, which Maud Casey deftly strained, covered with cloth, and left for the older Casey boys to remove to the milk house.

"He's a better doctor than he is a milkman," Wallis declared over breakfast as his children sat on the floor and ate their portions. "But, Maud, he has good hands. He calls 'um surgeon's hands, but gor, he can squeeze a teat." He winked at the doctor, who grinned back. "If physicking ever gets slow, I'll take you here on sufferance."

"Obliged," said the doctor. "One never knows, and we do live in an uncertain world."

After the dishes were done, they left, Joseph mounted on Sir William's hunter, amid the general clamor that was part and parcel of the Caseys' daily lot. Maud Casey stood in the doorway with little John on her hip and insisted that they return soon and often.

"She means it, Libby," the doctor said as he called to his horse. "I've sat in drawing rooms in London without invitations half so sincere." He shook his head. "Father wonders why I did not choose to hang out my shingle on the same street with the likes of Starnley, Croft, and Knightson, but I would rather be here. Others can specialize in diseases of the rich."

He glanced at her, trying to gauge her reaction. "Of course, maybe that sets differently with you, considering that one of these days, in the fall, more like, you'll become part of the Cooks' traveling circus," he said, in his best imitation of Wallis Casey.

She did not smile, but merely looked thoughtful. *Why did I say I would marry him?* she asked herself again.

"Regrets, Libby?" he asked then, his voice gentle.

"I would be lying if I said no, Anthony," she replied, her chin up but unable to look him in the eye. "I mean, it is no one day, and yes the next. Am I so fickle?"

"I said I was a patient man, my dear," he reminded her.

"So you did. So you did."

Joseph rode ahead of them on the tree-shaded path that led from the Casey holdings, careful not to get out of their sight. They traveled the lane past two more isolated holdings, where children came out to wave as they went by, and to jump up and down when they saw it was Dr. Cook.

Libby watched the excitement at each crofter's cottage. "You are a popular man among the infantry," she commented. "What is your secret, sir?" she asked, teasing him, atoning for her second thoughts.

"Lemon drops," he said, reaching into his pocket and extracting a linty clump of candies all stuck together from last night's rain. He pulled one off the wad, dusted away the lint, and handed it to her. She popped it in her mouth.

Joseph waited for them at the next rise, his eyes dancing with excitement. Libby smiled to see him sitting so straight on her uncle's horse. *I wish Papa could see you,* she thought. *He would be so proud.*

"What are you so exercised about, Joseph?" Anthony asked as he reined in beside his father's horses.

"Dr. Cook, I think I know where I am!"

"Tell me then, Joseph," said the doctor.

Joseph pointed. "Isn't that your house? The one with the stone facing and four chimneys?"

"The very same," said the doctor. "Well done, my lad. Libby, I think Joseph has found our way home."

She clapped her hands and Joseph beamed. He dug his heels into the horse's flanks. "Race you!" he shouted over his shoulder.

"Rascal," said the doctor. "How can I win, think on?"

They watched Joseph ride toward the house. Libby sighed and touched Anthony's arm. "Do you suppose his memory will ever come back completely?"

The doctor considered the question and then shook his head slowly. "I do not. It will like come and go. He will probably have to be told over and over, and we will always have to know precisely where he is. A lowering thought, Libby?" he asked.

"Well, yes, in a way, but . . ."

She stopped. Her thoughts were becoming too tangled. How could she tell Anthony yet how good it made her feel when he said, "We will always have to know," instead of "you." She realized for the first time how much easier her responsibility for Joseph would be if she shared it with another. But is this really the one I am to share my life with? she asked, and stole a glance at the big man seated so tall beside her.

She watched his face, surprised that he did not notice how hard she was staring at him. After a moment's bold contemplation, she realized that he was intent on the meadow before him. She sucked in her breath as his face paled and he rose up in the gig.

"Joseph," he was whispering. "No! Go back!" And then he was shouting at her brother, waving his arms, as she stared at the field in sudden fright and wondered what he was looking at.

Libby clutched his arm and he shook her free, sat down, and slapped the reins smartly on the horse's back. She grabbed the seat as they lurched off the main road and down the little-used track that led into the Cook estate.

Joseph looked back once, waved, and continued on his way, unaware of Anthony's shouts. It was then that Libby noticed a quick movement to the side of the field by the hop gardens. Squire Cook sat on his horse, statue-still, a musket pointed at Joseph as he ambled along, unconcerned, unaware.

"Oh, God," Libby breathed. "Anthony, does your father think he has stolen those animals?"

Anthony was beating the horse with the reins now, unmindful of her, his eyes full of Joseph, who had stopped now, as if he finally sensed danger but could not locate the source. He looked back at them over his shoulder, uncertain what to do.

"Get off the horse," the doctor said, his voice low and intense, as if he were willing Joseph to do as he said through some telepathy between man and boy. "Just do it, lad. Ah, God!"

Libby screamed as the gun smoked and Joseph jerked backward, clapped his hand to his face, and toppled from his saddle, a spot of red blossoming on his cheek. Libby tried to leap out of the gig, but Anthony grabbed the back of her skirt and jerked her down. "He may have another gun. Hold still. Hang on."

He whipped the horse into action again and raced to the fallen boy, who had not moved from where he lay. He barely spared a glance for the squire, who still sat astride his horse, the musket across his lap now. He noticed his son for the first time and gestured triumphantly.

"He was thieving my horses, son," he shouted. "I will have him put away, if he is not dead."

The doctor jumped from the gig while it was still in motion and threw himself down beside the boy, heedless of the horses that moved about his head restlessly. Libby ran after him and grabbed the reins of Joseph's horse. Not daring to look at the ground, she led the horse to a tree, tethered it, and led the others after.

She ran back to her brother and knelt by his body. Blood was everywhere, staining the grass, covering the doctor's lap as he ripped off his neckcloth and pressed down firmly on the wound. Libby held Joseph's hand, feeling for his pulse. To her infinite relief, it was faint but steady. She let out her breath slowly.

Joseph lay on his back. Libby's eyes caught something shiny

in the sodden grass, not far from him. She peered closer and picked up the ball.

"Look, Anthony," she said.

He nodded. "Thank God! I was afraid it was lodged somewhere in his head." He touched the wound, feeling the track where the ball had grazed his cheek. "Well, Joseph," he said, his voice shaky, "you don't have any choice but to get better. Thank God Father's aim was off."

A shadow fell across the doctor and Joseph. Libby looked up into the squire's smiling face.

"I got the little beggar, didn't I?" he said, barely able to contain the excitement in his voice. "He won't steal my horses again, because he will be in an asylum."

With a cry of rage, Libby leapt to her feet and threw herself on the squire, scratching him and kicking him. "He was bringing your horses back," she screamed at him, pounding his chest with her fists. "He learned that the gypsies had stolen them and he was bringing them back."

She sank down in the grass again, covering her face with her hands, shivering in the warmth of the summer's day.

"That's the biggest faradiddle I ever heard," said the squire, dabbing at his face where she had scratched him. "Son, are they both daft?"

"Libby, tear off a string from your bonnet," was the doctor's only comment.

She did as he said. Deftly the doctor tied the satin ribbon around Joseph's face and knotted it securely across the bloody neckcloth. "I'll do it better in a moment, lad," he assured Joseph, whose eyes were wide open now, wild like an animal's, as he tried to speak. "Don't, laddie, don't. Let's get you into the house. Libby, bring the gig over here."

She did as he said. Anthony picked up Joseph, wincing when Joseph moaned. He set him in the gig and commanded Libby to climb in the small space behind the seat and hold him up. The squire watched the proceedings and then stepped in the path of the horse as Anthony prepared to climb into the gig.

"Not to my house," he said, his voice deadly quiet.

"Yes, to your house!" Anthony shouted, his face pale.

"Elizabeth was right, you old fool. We found Joseph yesterday with your horses. He was bringing them back from Dewhurst, where the gypsies had taken them to trade in the horse fair. He was lost."

"It can't be true," said the squire in a hollow voice as the words finally sank in. He shook his head as if to clear it. "You're both lying."

Wearily, the doctor shook his head. "Another inch and you would have killed a lad who was doing you a favor."

The squire sank to the grass as though his legs had lost all power to hold him upright. He was still sitting there as Anthony started the horses forward and Libby held Joseph upright in the gig. She looked back once as they made their painful way across the field. He was slumped there, head bowed.

In the surgery, Dr. Cook worked silently and swiftly, his face set, his eyes rock-hard. Libby addressed several questions to him, but he seemed not to hear her as he worked, pressing against the wound until the bleeding stopped and then cleaning it carefully. With a shudder, Joseph fainted when the doctor began to sew the underlying muscle of the wound together.

Anthony sighed with relief. "It's easier this way," he muttered, working faster to take advantage of Joseph's respite.

While he worked, Libby sat huddled small in the armchair in front of the desk. She went to the window once. The squire sat where they had left him.

When Anthony finished, he dropped the needle in the porcelain basin and sat down in the stool beside the examining table, his head between his knees. Libby came closer and touched his hair, suddenly fearful. He looked up, and the pain in his eyes made her step back as though he burned. He held out his hand to her, but it was flecked with blood and she came no closer.

"He should heal well. It was a clean wound." He shook his head. "When I think how close . . ." His voice trailed off. He washed his hands and stood by the window, drying them. "How long will he sit there, do you think?" he murmured, more to himself than to Libby.

"Till he rots, I hope," Libby said suddenly, and then put her hand to her mouth, surprised at her own vehemence.

To her further amazement, the doctor reached out and gave her tumbled hair a sharp yank. "Enough of that," he ordered, and then bent and kissed her cheek swiftly. "I'm sorry, but really, Libby, there has to be more here than we are aware of. I wonder . . ."

Libby dabbed at her eyes. Her scalp ached, but she was alert now and not sunk in the bitterness that had enveloped her since she had knelt in the bloodstained grass. She reached out tentatively and put her hand on Anthony's shoulder. "Perhaps you had better go to him."

"Perhaps I had better," he agreed. He turned to her suddenly. "Elizabeth, I am so ashamed."

She was silent for a long while, and they just stared at each other. Libby spoke first. "Come, Anthony, help me get Joseph back into the gig. I am taking him home."

He took issue with that at once, but she would not hear of anything else. Joseph was fully conscious by now. He looked about him, his eyes heavy with pain, but nodded when Libby asked him if he wanted to go home.

"I'll be over in the morning to check on him," the doctor said, handing her a black bottle. "Two drops only of this for the pain, and no more than three times a day."

She pocketed the bottle. "I am coming back as soon as he is in bed," she said. "I have to know what is going on. I want to know why your father holds so much hatred for my brother." She paused, searching for the right words. "It is as though he had a grudge against Joseph, but he never knew us before last year."

"Do not come back tonight, Libby," Anthony said finally, after he had helped her lift Joseph into the gig and tied her uncle's hunter on behind it. "I'll be after my gig in the morning. I think this evening will be a matter between my father and me."

She did not argue, but took the reins from the doctor; steadying her brother, she turned toward home.

Candlow and the footman, full of questions, helped Joseph from the gig and carried him to his room. When Joseph was comfortable and his eyes closing in sleep, Libby took Candlow and the footman aside and told them all that had happened. She spoke calmly, dispassionately, and when she finished, she shook her head against their questions and went to her room.

Aunt Crabtree sat there. Without a word, Libby went to her side and knelt beside her on the floor, telling her the whole story.

"My dear, this is grim, indeed," Aunt Crabtree said.

Libby nodded, amazed at the calmness of her aunt.

"I wish you had confided in me sooner," was all Aunt Crabtree said. She rested her hand on Libby's head and Libby closed her eyes in gratitude.

Aunt spoke finally, clearing her throat in that precise way of hers that for once did not irritate her niece. "Should I write to my brother, or your mother?"

Libby shook her head. "I will do it in the morning. Mama should know, of course. Perhaps I will send Joseph to her in Brighton. I have not proved much help to my brother this summer."

"Should you go, too, my dear?"

"No," Libby said emphatically. "I think that Dr. Cook needs me here."

Aunt Crabtree was silent. In another moment, she kissed Libby and told her to go to bed.

She fell asleep at once, even though the sky was still light with midsummer.

Joseph was much better in the morning, sitting up in bed, eating the gruel that Candlow brought him. He spit out a tooth on the spoon, and his cheek was still swollen, but he could speak.

"Dr. Cook said that I would have a great scar, one of the marvelous, romantical kinds," he said as Libby tugged out a pillow from behind his head and he lay down to rest. "Won't Mother be amazed?"

"Amazed is not the word I would use, Joseph," Libby said. "We'll be fortunate indeed if she does not chain both of us to the front steps on a short leash."

She finished her early-morning duties, picked up her long-neglected mending, and sat down to wait for Dr. Cook.

He did not come. After staring in exasperation at the clock, she went to the mantelpiece and gave the timepiece a therapeutic shake. After another hour of pacing back and forth and spending much time at the window, staring hard at the road, she rang for Candlow.

"Would you please ask Tunley to hitch up Dr. Cook's gig? I think I had better return it. He appears to have been detained."

The noonday sun was warm on her back as she drove slowly down the road. "How unlike you to forget an appointment, Dr. Cook," she said.

She rang the bell several times before Mrs. Weller, her eyes red with weeping, answered it. She opened the door only a crack at first, then flung it wide when she saw who stood before her. Mrs. Weller pulled Libby inside and began to sob in good earnest. Libby clutched her hands.

"Oh, Miss Ames, I am glad you are here."

"Is something wrong with Anthony?" she asked, her voice faraway in her ears.

Mrs. Weller nodded. "Something is wrong with everyone in this house, miss."

Libby listened no more. She ran down the hall to Anthony's surgery and threw open the door.

He sat in his chair, his stockinged feet on the desk, his eyes wide open, his expression more grim than she had ever seen before. "Libby," he said, and held out his hand to her.

She was on her knees at his side in a moment, holding tight to his hand, taking in the exhaustion on his face—nothing new to her now, but somehow worse, because there was no hope in Anthony Cook's always hopeful eyes. She stared at his rigid profile, thinking to herself that if he were to drive by any country lane like that, and wave to the children playing there, they would run from him.

She rested her cheek against his hand. "What has happened?"

He made a visible effort to collect himself, freeing his hand from hers and putting his feet on the floor. He had not changed his shirt or breeches. They were the same bloodstained garments he had been wearing the afternoon before. His face was unshaven, his hair wild, as though he had been tugging at it.

Suddenly the room was too close, too airless. Libby rose to her feet and opened the windows by the examination table, averting her eyes from the bloody basin and wads of crimson cotton waste still scattered about. She pulled the draperies farther back and leaned out, grateful for fresh air, dizzy with the odor of blood and disinfectant.

When her head was clear, she turned around, found a clean glass, and poured the doctor a drink of water. She took it to him and put it in his hand. "Drink that," she ordered.

He did as she said, still staring straight ahead. He leaned forward then and rested his elbows on the desk, as if he had not the strength to sit upright. To her relief, he smiled briefly and handed her the glass again. She refilled it and he downed it quickly.

Anthony looked about him then. "Place is a mess," he said. "Sorry, Elizabeth."

He looked down at himself in disgust. "And I am worse." He sighed. "This begins to remind me of the worst days in Edinburgh, except that I cannot put in my seventy-two hours and leave the hospital."

Libby sat on the desk in front of him. "What happened, Anthony? You have to tell me."

"I do?" he asked.

"Yes, you do," she insisted. "You spend days and nights listening to everyone's problems. Now it's your turn. Where is your father?"

He passed his hand in front of his eyes and all the weariness returned.

She thought for a moment that he would cry, but he did not. He sagged back in the armchair again and then leaned forward, pulled the chair closer to her, and rested his head in her lap.

Her legs tensed in surprise, and then she put her hand on his head. "Tell me, Anthony," she urged, bending close to his ear, smelling again the rank odor of blood and sweat about him, but not repulsed this time.

He was silent, his breathing regular, and she thought he slept. She continued to stroke his hair until he sat up again.

"My father is upstairs. We spent a long night together, my dear."

He sat there and she got him another glass of water, which he drank dutifully. She wanted to shake the words out of him, climb in his lap and beat on his chest until he talked, but she merely regarded him.

"Libby, I learned something most interesting last night." Again the silence. Again she wanted to scream.

"I learned that I had a brother." He paused and looked at her for the first time. "A brother like Joseph."

16

"NO!" Libby shook her head in disbelief.

The doctor took her hand. "You are a perfect mirror of my own reaction last night. Why do we always deny what we do not wish to hear? I have puzzled about this for some years."

He stood up then on unsteady feet. "Elizabeth, I am so weary, but I cannot sit still and talk of this."

He went to the window and leaned against the frame, not looking at her, but out at the field where she had last seen his father, slumped in the grass. "We sat outside there and Papa talked until the cock started to crow." He looked away. "It seems I have been doing my best work lately out in fields."

Libby gritted her teeth. Get to the point, Anthony, get to the point, she thought, and then was instantly ashamed of herself. He would tell her when he was ready, and not a moment sooner.

When he walked back to the desk finally, she took him by the arm and steered him to one of the armchairs in front of it. He sank down with a sigh. Without a word, she pulled up the other chair and propped his feet on it, brought him one more glass of water, and made him drink it.

He handed back the glass. "Tyrant," he said with a slight smile.

"It's about time someone tyrannized over you," she retorted, and pulled his desk chair closer. "Now tell me, and then you can sleep," she coaxed.

He did as she ordered, his voice flat, monotone at first and then becoming more animated as his own clinical discipline took over.

"He was born in 1776, so he dates me by ten years precisely, my dear. Papa carried a miniature of him on his watch fob." He leaned back and stared at the ceiling. "I have seen it many times, but he never would say and I never would ask."

"How strange," Libby murmured.

He looked sideways at her, not moving. "Not if you know the squire. One didn't ask needless questions."

"But he is your father!"

Her outburst elicited no response, and she was ashamed, thinking of the myriad questions she had pelted at her own father and his elaborate discussions of tactics and weapons with a child who adored him. *And to think that I have been feeling angry of late because Papa was not wiser, or that he left me in uncomfortable straits,* she thought as she watched Anthony's agony. *How foolish I have been.*

"As far as I could glean from what my father said, they knew right away that the boy was not normal. He was slow to do things and resistant to change in routine." He reached over and took her hand, pulling it back to his chest where he rested it. "A pillow fight like the one at the Caseys would probably have been beyond his ken."

She scooted closer, resting her hand more comfortably on his chest. "Surely they tried to work with him. Joseph has learned so much since his accident."

"Apparently they did not, my dear." The doctor shifted restlessly. He tensed to rise again and continue his fruitless pacing, but Libby pressed her hand down firmly and he stayed where he was. He looked at her sharply, then relaxed. "You are a determined minx, aren't you?" he asked, half in exasperation, half in amusement.

"Oh, yes, Dr. Cook. Now lie still. You are exhausted."

He removed his spectacles, handing them to her, and rubbed his eyes. "Oh? Is that why I feel so tired? Bless my soul. No, Libby, no one seems to have given my father very good advice. And Father was—is—a proud man. You know him. You have seen him. He is a handsome devil with a quick wit and a shorter fuse. The knowledge that a child of his loins could be less than perfect must have been a real abomination." He grimaced. "When I came along later, I suppose he was more prepared for the shock."

"Anthony . . ."

He kissed her fingers and placed them again closer to his heart. "Well, Father was, shall we say, somewhat incoherent last night, but I gathered from what he said that one of my uncles, mercifully long dead now, suggested that the boy be placed in an asylum in Tunbridge Wells. And so it was done. That was when my parents moved here."

"That would explain . . ."

" . . . why no one around here ever chose to enlighten me. No one knew. This estate was one of Papa's from his mother, and he apparently had long been contemplating such a move. The timing was perfect."

"How old was your brother then, do you know?"

"As near as I can gather, around eight."

"Oh, God," she said, unable to keep the sadness from her voice. "He must have been terrified."

His hand tightened over hers. "An active little lad who was slow in the head, sent to asylum in Tunbridge Wells." He rested his other hand on his eyes, as if to shield them from a glare that only he could see.

He slept then suddenly, as if sleep was something he could no longer put off. Libby did not waken him, did not remove her hand from his chest. She tried to keep her mind a deliberate blank, but all she could see was a small boy being led to an asylum, the gates clanging shut behind him.

In fifteen minutes the doctor woke, looking about him in surprise and some embarrassment. "My apologies, Elizabeth," he said, his voice rusty, "but the physiology of the body is such that if you put one in a comfortable position that has not slept for a long time, it will sleep." He patted her hand. "At least you did not take advantage of the lull to escape."

"Of course not," she said calmly, considering. "I think the time to escape was back when we set that gypsy child's leg, Dr. Cook."

He stared at her, an arrested look on his face. "I suppose it was," he agreed. "Never thought of it that way."

He settled himself more comfortably in the armchair. "Two years after my brother's incarceration—Father never visited; he could not bring himself to visit—he received a letter from the asylum's director, advising him that the boy was near death. Papa went immediately to Tunbridge Wells."

Anthony swallowed convulsively several times. "Libby, I feel so cold!" His heart pounded rapidly and sweat broke out on his forehead.

"Tell me," she urged, "tell me!"

"When Father got there, riding all night in the rain, my brother was dead. He went into the room . . ."

Anthony leapt to his feet, unable to remain seated any longer. He went to the window, leaning out for a long moment as she had done earlier.

Libby did not move, fearful of breaking his concentration. She stared at him, dry-eyed, her heart in her throat.

Anthony was crying now. He wiped his eyes and forced himself to continue. "For two long years he had been chained to that bed and kept in the dark. Good treatment, his keeper said, for lads who kept trying to escape. Father said . . . Oh, Libby, he said that my brother's fingers were worn down to bloody stubs where he had been scraping at the wall, trying to get out."

Libby ran to the doctor and threw her arms around him, burying her face in his chest, as he sobbed and held her close. Tears streamed down her face and she forced herself to think of Joseph in such a place—Joseph a little slow, never to be normal now, but harmless, likely as harmless as Anthony's brother must have been.

They clung together for a long time, and then he freed himself and drank the rest of the water directly from the carafe. His eyes looked like two coals in his dead-white face.

"He's buried in Tunbridge Wells, God rest his soul."

He allowed her to lead him back to the chair and sat down again. "Well, Papa had to have an heir. I gather that my mother wanted nothing more to do with him after the boy died." He shook his head to clear it, unable to meet her eyes. "Father's a big man, and strong. He got what he wanted from an unwilling wife. God, I only hope that my mother conceived quickly. Imagine the torture, if you can.''

Why are some people so cruel to those they love? she thought, embarrassed at the intimacy of what he was telling her. She said nothing, knowing that he would continue when he was ready. His wound needed no further stretching or poking about. It bled freely enough already.

"She died when I was born. Except for my height, I am her image. We can safely say that Father was disappointed and draw a curtain over that little episode.''

Libby sat in troubled silence, hands tight together in her lap. The doctor, astute even in exhaustion, noted her puzzled expression. "You are wondering where all this leads with Joseph, aren't you?"

She nodded. "Joseph never did your father a harm.''

Anthony relaxed in the chair again, his feet up. "Father managed to carry on through the years. I suppose he would still be normal enough, if you and your brother and mother had not moved in with Sir William. Father was reminded all over again of his son.''

"So that's it," she said.

"There's a rub to it, of course, my dear. Isn't there always a rub to life, a little bit of sandpaper where it grates the most? He saw how happily Joseph fit in your family, how devoted the two of you are, and how everyone found simple tasks that Joseph could do quite well. I think it harrowed him up, knowing that perhaps he could have done the same for his boy. He's taking out his punishment on your brother. I'm sorry, Elizabeth, but that's the story, as near as I can gather it together.''

"Where is he now?"

"I finally convinced him to go upstairs to bed, along about dawn. He was talking wildly then, intent upon suicide, so I have sedated him heavily. I sat with him until I couldn't stand it anymore and came in here. The scullery maid sits with him now." He closed his eyes, and she thought he would sleep, but after a struggle with himself, he opened his eyes again.

"How long can you keep this up?" Libby asked. When he did not answer, she stood up. "I'm going to help you upstairs now to your own room," she said, "and when you are comfortable there, I am going to sit with your father so the maid can go about her duties."

"I can't ask you to do that," he protested.

"You didn't ask me; I told you," she replied, and was gratified when he managed a weak grin. "When the maid finishes her duties, I will send her for Candlow. Come now, stand up, sir."

He did as she said, leaning on her for a moment before he found his balance. "I feel like a baby," he grumbled as she helped him up the stairs.

"You would probably be a dreadful patient," she replied. "See that you stay healthy, sir, and spare the world."

They walked slowly down the hall to the room where the door was open and his father lay sleeping. Anthony stopped in the doorway watching the squire out of bleary eyes suddenly alert through sheer force of medical habit.

"Should he come around while you are sitting with him, another two drops will put him under for an hour or so, and that will be enough for me," he said.

"It is not enough," Libby said indignantly. "You can't do this to yourself."

"I can and will," he said firmly. "The first rule of medicine is, 'You must attend.' Don't be a snip, Elizabeth."

He motioned to the next door and she opened it, not at all surprised to see the same order and neatness of the surgery downstairs. Her quick glance took in more books, piles of books, old dark furniture smelling strongly of polish, shabby and lived-in, and a bed with a homely sag in the middle.

The doctor sat down on the bed, opened his mouth to say something, and closed his eyes before anything came out. He sank back wearily on the bed.

His shoes were downstairs, so Libby covered his legs with the light blanket at the end of the bed and unbuttoned his waistcoat with the blood caked on it.

"You are a great lot of trouble, Dr. Cook," she said out loud, and stepped back in surprise when he opened his eyes.

"So are you, my dear," he said, and then closed his eyes. In another moment he was snoring.

Libby laughed softly to herself and went to the escritoire by the window, rummaging about for paper, pen, and ink. Sitting in the chair with a padded seat conforming to the doctor's ample contours, Libby composed a note for Candlow that briefly outlined the events. She begged him to hurry over and, while he was at it, to think of a steady couple who could be prevailed upon to restore order to a household at sixes and sevens for years and years.

She folded the letter and affixed a wafer, her eyes straying to Anthony Cook, who lay as though dead in the middle of the bed. She came closer, peering at him, amazed how completely he could abandon himself to sleep. She touched his hair. *I wonder when you last had a good night's sleep with no interruption*, she thought. *I suppose that is the unenviable lot of physicians.*

The scullery maid was relieved to see her. She jumped up and darted to the door almost before Libby could grab her by the arm, shove the note at her, and urge her to hurry. The maid took the note, curtsied, and paused in the safety of the doorway for one last look at the squire. She crossed herself and ran down the hall.

Libby allowed her eyes to adjust to the gloom and came closer to the bed, peering down at the squire. Such stillness, she thought. He seemed hardly to breathe and she found herself watching anxiously for the rise and fall of his chest. She pulled the chair closer and sat down.

He looked so old, so unlike the lively man who had come to her uncle's stables only two days ago, full of restless energy and vituperation. His strong-featured, handsome face was sunken now, fallen in upon itself like rotting fruit. She searched for some resemblance between the squire and his son, who slumbered in the next room, and saw none.

Libby noticed the black bottle on the night table. Quickly she picked it up and took it to the bureau, where it was out of the squire's reach. On the bureau was a small mound of coins and keys, the contents of a man's pockets and waistcoat. There was a watch and fob. She picked up the fob and turned it over. Tears came to her eyes as she gazed at the miniature of the little boy, a charming light-haired child with startling blue eyes and cheeks

pink and glowing with health. If there was something vague
about the expression, it was nothing anyone would notice at
cursory glance. He was a handsome child, much like his father.

Libby sat down again by the bed, prepared to hate the man
she watched, the man who had ruined the life of the little boy
in the miniature, blighted the existence of his wife, worked his
mischief daily with his living son, and nearly killed her own
brother. She found that she could not hate him. She took his
hand.

The squire struggled to open his eyes, as if a great weight
were pressing against them. He succeeded finally, through that
sheer force of will that she did recognize as a characteristic of
his son. His eyes were dark and muddied by the drug that
sedated him, and huge in his fallen face. He stared at her,
uncomprehending, and then a flicker of interest came into his
eyes. He struggled now to speak, and she leaned closer.

"Your brother?" he asked.

"He will be fine," she said, speaking slowly and distinctly
into his ear.

The squire tried to say more, but the sedative overcame him.
He nodded and closed his eyes again. Libby squeezed his hand
gently. To her surprise, there was a slight answering pressure
from the squire.

She sat with him for most of the afternoon, watching him drift
in and out of sleep. Candlow came to her after an hour. He
pulled up a chair for a whispered conversation and the good
news that the redoubtable Mrs. Wilcox and her husband, Jim—
"Who can repair anything, I vow"—were on their way to the
Cook estate, plus two stout girls from Holyoke who never let
a cobweb escape them.

"After we have done what we can, we will consider the
situation further," Candlow said. "I put the issue to several
others who appeared reluctant to help the squire, but were
enthusiastic about his son. We shall have all the help we require,
Miss Ames."

"Candlow, you are a wonder," she marveled.

He merely raised his eyebrows, put his finger to his lips, and
left the room, a slight smile on his face that made Libby laugh
softly to herself. In a few minutes she heard voices in the next

room and the sound of water being poured into a tub. She smiled. *Anthony Cook doesn't have a chance. Candlow is in charge.*

Shortly after, Mrs. Weller brought her a bowl of soup and tea, which she drank gratefully.

Mrs. Weller cast her eyes over the squire and then whispered behind her hand. "There's many as would like to see him stretched out that way with daisies on his chest. More like, you must be one of them."

Libby shook her head. "No, I am not, Mrs. Weller," she said.

Tears welled up in the cook's eyes. Libby took her by the elbow and marched her to the door.

Mrs. Weller sobbed in the hallway. "Miss Ames, there is a dragon downstairs, and now you are unkind. I shall grow distracted."

"A dragon?"

"Goes by the name of Wilcox, from Fairbourne," she said, drying her tears. "There she is, telling me what to do and all."

"I trust you will listen to her, Mrs. Weller," was Libby's firm reply.

Mrs. Weller nodded. "I wouldna dare do otherwise, would I?"

Libby shook her head, wondering what this dragon was like that Candlow had found, grateful to him beyond words. *Uncle Ames, I shall bully you until you give him an increase in wages,* she thought, *and even then, he is too good for you and your gouty crochets.*

She stayed where she was outside the door for a moment more, enjoying the sound of splashing coming from the doctor's room. *I only hope he does not fall asleep suddenly and drown in his bathwater,* she thought as she took a deep breath and went back into the squire's room.

The doctor came into the room much later, as she rested her chin on her hand, thinking of Benedict Nesbitt. She sat up, startled, at his hand on her shoulder, and for the smallest moment she thought it was the duke.

He went to the bed, looking down on the squire as she had

done. She watched the doctor, noting with satisfaction that his face was shaved, he wore clean clothes, and he smelled of eau de cologne. He didn't have his spectacles, however, and he squinted at his father.

"I left your spectacles in the surgery," she said. "You handed them to me."

He nodded, feeling his father's pulse, resting his head upon the squire's chest, and then sitting on his bed in silent observation for another moment. "When you go downstairs, send someone back with them, my dear," he whispered. "And if you will, there is a volume on my desk that I would like to peruse while I sit here."

"I can stay," she insisted. "Mrs. Weller brought me something to eat."

He shook his head. "No. I want you to return to Joseph. Take a good look at his cheek. If it is red and swollen, please send for me. If it is not, here is the prescription I have for him . . . and you."

He handed her a folded piece of paper, which she opened and held up to the faint light from the window. "Brighton—July and August until the hops harvest. I will write."

She folded the paper carefully, hurt somehow that he would want her away, but determined not to show it. His advice was sound. She would remove Joseph to the house that Uncle had rented for the summer, and it would be good for him.

"Very well, sir, if that's what you wish," she said, and got up to leave.

He took her hand. "Not so much what I wish, Elizabeth, but what I think you—we—need."

He kissed her hand and said good-bye. She left the room in tears that she did not understand.

Libby found his glasses in the surgery where she had left them. Mrs. Wilcox—it could only be Mrs. Wilcox—had gathered together the bloody rags and crimsoned water from the surgery and discarded them. The room was tidy once again, and a small fire had been laid.

Mrs. Wilcox came into the room, bringing back the basin clean to set on the shelf. She curtsied to Libby and then shook the hand that was extended to her. "A fearsome task you have set us, Miss Ames," she said, her voice brusque, but spoken with a lilt that belied the stern look in her eyes.

"Indeed I have, and you are brave to take up the challenge," Libby said, her voice equally firm. "I only hope that Candlow did not understate the case."

Mrs. Wilcox laughed. "He said the magic word—Dr. Cook—and we knew we would be happy then." She put away the basin and flicked at imaginery dust on the glass instrument case. "Dr. Cook sat through a dreadful bout with Jim's pneumonia this winter." She paused a moment, as if unable to trust herself with words. "We never did feel that we had repaid him enough. This is our opportunity, Miss Ames."

Libby handed her the doctor's spectacles. "He wanted someone to take this to him upstairs, and one other thing." She went to the desk and picked up the book there, turning it over in her hands. *"Anomalies of the Brain,"* she read out loud. "A little light reading for the doctor."

Mrs. Wilcox accepted the heavy volume doubtfully. " 'Twould make a wondrous fine napkin press," she said as she flipped through the pages. "Only think how many flower keepsakes we could press there, Miss Ames."

Libby smiled. "Dr. Cook would be sorely disappointed if we pressed flowers in his medical books, I fear."

The housekeeper rested the book on her hip. "It will do him good to have a little daughter someday who does precisely that, Miss Ames. Flowers in all these books," she said, waving her hand at the whole expanse of the bookcase.

Libby watched her in delight, her own discomfort momentarily set aside. "Mrs. Wilcox, I am sure you are right, but as for now, I recommend a vase of flowers on the doctor's desk in the morning. Think how it will cheer him."

"You pick the flowers, Miss Ames, and I will find the vase," said Mrs. Wilcox, starting for the door.

"I would, but I am off to Brighton tomorrow with my brother," Libby replied, wishing that the thought of a seaside vacation would not bring on that heaviness behind her eyelids.

"Very well, miss, I will see that is it done. Don't you worry about anything. We will take excellent care of your doctor."

"Oh, he's not my doctor," Libby said quietly.

She walked back to Holyoke Green, having refused the loan of the gig. She wanted to walk off some of the agitation she felt and the curious sense of loss that dampened her spirits. Surely Anthony had known that she would gladly have come every day to sit with his father and take some of this complex burden off his shoulders. He had only to ask, but he had chosen not to. I thought we were friends, she thought, and wasn't that what friends did for each other? And aren't we engaged?

Libby thought again about his unusual proposal and felt herself growing cross. If you are such a patient man, then why send me away? she reasoned. Surely we could get to know each other better if I were close at hand.

Ah, well, you said that you would write, she concluded to herself as she walked slowly along the road. And when you do, I will answer your letters promptly, so you will know that I care.

"How much do I care?" she asked out loud, standing in the middle of the road, looking back at the Cook estate. "I wish I knew."

Joseph was still awake when she returned, Aunt Crabtree sitting with him, deep in her solitaire again. Her brother had taken the bandage off and was admiring Dr. Cook's even stitches in the mirror, turning his head this way and that. Libby kissed him and examined the wound, noting with relief that there was very little swelling left. The redness was nearly gone.

She held out Dr. Cook's prescription and he read it slowly, mouthing the words. "Does this mean that we are to go to Brighton?" he asked.

"Dr. Cook decrees it," she said with a smile that she did not feel. "Mama will cry and scold us both, and then she will see that you sit in the sun until your stitches are ready to come out."

"Like she used to do with Papa when he was wounded," he said. "I remember that. Do you know, Libby, I think she enjoys that sort of thing."

"Oh, I am sure of it," Libby replied in round tones. "She will be delighted to see you this way."

Aunt Crabtree looked up from her cards. "She will likely haul me over the coals." She shuddered delicately. "My brother will hear from me if she does. 'A peaceful summer with an unexceptionable niece,' indeed!''

They caught the mail coach in Holyoke the next morning in the dark. Only the direst of threats kept Joseph from climbing to the roof to sit with the other young men, and he pointedly turned away from her and closed his eyes as soon as they started.

The coach traveled back past Holyoke Green and the Cook estate. A light burned in the squire's room. In her mind, Libby could see Anthony sitting there, his eyes and heart on his father.

"You must attend," she whispered out loud, and hunched herself farther into the corner as the tears rolled down her face. Something told her that he would not write. He had sent her away until the hops harvest, when everyone in Holyoke would be too busy for social calls. And then winter would come, with its freezing cold blowing in from the Channel and the steely rains that swept the lands and made her restless. Lydia would likely be married and gone.

The doctor would change his mind and look elsewhere. He would never make her an improper offer, of this she was sure, but when he had time for reflection, calm reason would take over and he would renege. She didn't know whether to be glad or sorry.

"And all because I know you will not write," she said to the glass window of the mail coach. Her words fogged the glass until she could no longer see the house of Dr. Cook or the road the chocolate merchant had traveled away on.

17

◀◀◀

"REALLY, my dear boy, if we had known you would be such quelling company, we could have arranged for you to run alongside the carriage and bark at the wheels."

The duke looked up from his silent comtemplation of his hands into Eustace Wiltmore's vacuous face. He wondered why he had never noticed before how Eustace's voice grated like fingernails on slate, or that irritating way he had of ending each sentence with a little raise of his eyebrows.

Lydia touched the duke and twinkled her eyes at him. "I think he is contemplating the narrowness of his escape, are you not, my lord?"

He turned his gaze upon Lydia, wishing that he had a quizzing glass to stare her up and down. "I have you to thank for so much," he murmured, hoping that Lydia Ames would have the good sense to let it lie there.

She did not. "Eustace, my love, he looks as Friday-faced as Libby. She did not think it a funny joke, either."

The duke rolled down the glass and leaned his head out the carriage window. "Stop this vehicle," he commanded.

The carriage stopped and he got out without a backward glance. The coachman, his eyes alive with curiosity, handed him his shabby bag, while Eustace scolded him from the carriage and Lydia Ames put in her mite.

He merely stood there, face an expressionless study, bag in hand, until the coach rolled on.

He walked slowly toward the next village, ignoring the offers of rides from carters bound for London and farmers and their loads of hay. He knew that his knee would begin to pain him after too many miles, but he wanted to feel discomfort. He remembered lessons of his youth from the vicar, stories of penitents rolling about in sackcloth and ashes to atone for misdeeds that didn't seem half so serious. When did any Old Testament graybeard have to gaze into eyes as beautiful as Libby's and watch them fill up with tears and know that he had been the author of such humiliation?

And yet, it had been a perfectly reasonable offer. He had made it several times before with signal success. None of his previous charming confections had paled at the thought of just such an alliance as he had offered Libby Ames.

"Libby Ames, I have it on good authority that I am a wonderfully proficient lover," he shouted out loud, setting down his bag with a thump. "Women don't exactly beat a path to my door, but no one's ever been dragged there kicking and screaming, either."

No one answered. He stood there in the empty road and realized that if Libby Ames had been standing before him, she would not have answered either. Again he saw before him those beautiful eyes, hurt beyond his comprehension.

He picked up the bag again. And after all, Nez, you block, whose word do you have on your masculine prowess anyway, except those beauties you have kept so comfortably? Were they about to tell you anything but what you wanted to hear? Don't flatter yourself. And they weren't so beautiful, either.

Only one thing would do now, and the thought moved him to pick up his stride. There was a village not far, and what was a village without a public house? He would take off the rough edges with a tankard of ale. His mouth began to water. He would order a pint of Kentish brew so dark it looked black, with the bitter taste of homegrown hops and malts, the ale that peeled the skin off thirst and mellowed the mind.

He came to a village and wiped his lips in anticipation. And there it was before him, the Cock and Hen, a prosperous inn with a thatched roof and sign swaying invitingly in the slight breeze. From the looks of the place, he could procure a private parlor and not be bothered by stares or conversation he didn't wish to partake of.

He set his foot upon the threshold and stopped, pulling out his watch and looking at it. Nine o'clock, by damn. The fragrance of sausage and eggs assailed his nostrils and he wiped his mouth with the back of his hand. He had been too distracted for breakfast at Holyoke Green. He would indulge himself now and have that ale later, when it was hot and he had worked up more of an urge for it.

An hour later, full to bursting with the best sausage this side of the Channel, eggs, and bread so fine that he smiled at the memory, he started off again. The bag he left in a dark corner of the taproom. There was nothing in it of value. He strode along, arms swinging, on the road to London, enjoying the scent of flowers on the breeze and wondering how people managed who never set foot in Kent.

Up ahead somewhere, he knew there was a pub with a pint, and he would find it when he was good and ready.

Women be damned, and you, too, Libby Ames, he thought. Do you seriously think you will get a better offer? Anthony Cook would like to tuck you in his bed, but I don't think his father will approve, and the doctor seems to want the esteem of that prickly man. He chuckled. Not that Anthony Cook is God's gift to females. You had your chance, Libby Ames, and you muffed it.

That bit of self-righteous absurdity was enough to carry him another ten miles closer to London. By the time he arrived at the next promising village, he was more than ready for that pint.

He asked for a private parlor and received it. He sat down in the soft chair with a sigh, flexing his aching knee. In another moment, the keep brought in a tray with a tankard full to the brim with the specialty of the house.

Nez eyed the beautiful brew. "Bring me another in ten minutes," he said. "I have worked up a thirst you wouldn't believe, sir."

The man nodded and left him to his cup. Nez regarded it as
a long-lost comrade and raised the tankard to his lips, more than
ready for that first drop of bitterness to roll down his throat.

There he sat, poised, ready, but unable to swallow. He rolled
the ale around in his mouth and then spit it back in the cup.
Two strides took him to the window, where he dumped the brew
onto the roses blooming below. He leaned on the sill then, the
cup dangling from his hand.

He had stopped drinking under tyranny from Anthony Cook
and then to please Elizabeth Ames. As he watched the foam
froth into the ground, it finally occurred to him that he was now
abstaining to suit himself.

He was still there, smiling to himself, when the landlord
returned with the second pint.

"Sir, are you well?" the man asked when he didn't move
from his contemplation of the roses.

Nez looked up, startled. "Yes, yes, I am fine." He glanced
at the tankard of ale the landlord was setting on the table and
shook his head. "No, sir, I think I'll not have that, after all.
Can you tell me where the mail coach comes?"

He had thought about renting a hack, but the strain on his
knee would likely still prove too much. Better to tough it out
on the mail coach. Likely he would be sufficiently entertained.
He would meet any number of "genuine articles" on the mail
coach and have stories to tell Libby . . . He shook his head
as another wave of desolation washed over him. No stories,
no Libby.

His arrival in London after dark was unheralded by anyone
other than the porters who loitered about the posting house.
When they saw that he had no bags to be hauled somewhere
at an extortionate rate, they ignored him. He hailed a hackney
cab and was deposited at the entrance of the ducal manor.

Luster met him at the door, staring in surprise. "Sir! We have
been wondering where you were," the butler said, not precisely
dancing up and down in excitement, but rubbing his hands
together in evident relish. He eyed the duke's casual attire with
some disfavor, taking in Major Ames' old trousers and the boots
and shirt that had left from Clarges Street two months ago in
much better condition.

"Sir, your clothes appear to have fallen upon hard times," he said. "Cheedleep will probably dissolve into a nervous state if he sees the condition of your boots, so perhaps you will wait in the library while I prepare him, your grace."

Nez smiled at his butler, eager for Luster to take another good look at him. He elaborately ignored the sidelong glances that the butler cast his way as they walked together to the library. Luster opened the door and stood aside while the duke entered.

"Beg pardon, my lord . . ."

"Yes, Luster?"

"Your grace, I can't quite account for it, considering your clothing, but you are looking rather splendid, if I may say so," the butler said. "Not that Cheedleep would agree, if one considers your rig-out. Wherever you went appears to have suited you, sir."

"Thank you, Luster," Nez replied, taking a glance at the stack of letters that had accumulated on the table. "You look pretty well yourself."

"Now, sir, may I get you a drink? Sherry perhaps, or something with a little more hair on it?"

Nez ruffled through the pile of outdated invitations. "There is so much here I am glad I missed. Tea will be sufficient, Luster."

The butler stared, forgetful of thirty years' training. "Tea?"

"You know, Luster, grows in China, comes in a pot?"

"Yes, your grace—certainly, your grace."

The duke looked up from a collection of frenzied dispatches from Gussie. "Luster, one thing else. In the morning, will you see that my wine cellar is cleaned out and the contents sent to the Earl of Devere?"

Luster blinked and swallowed.

"It is a wedding present to my friend. He will be needing it more than I will in the coming years. That will do now, Luster," the duke added kindly when the butler appeared unable to move.

The duke drank tea, laughed over Gussie's messages that grew more incoherent, the more recent the date, and then sat in thoughtful silence as the fire on the hearth turned into glowing coals. He rang the bell to summon Luster one more time.

"Tell me, Luster, earlier this summer, did you receive a visit from a one-legged man by the name of Amos Yore?"

"Sir, we did not," Luster replied.

"Then let me speak for my curricle after breakfast."

"Certainly, your grace." Luster stood there another moment and cleared his throat. "Sir, your sister has been, shall we say, interested in your whereabouts. Might you wish to drop her a message?"

The duke shook his head. "Not until tomorrow afternoon, when I am safely out of here again."

Luster nodded and a well-mannered smile played about his lips.

"If there is nothing more, your grace—"

The duke stopped him. "There is actually, Luster, and it is of a personal nature."

"Sir?"

"Luster, how important is it to oblige one's relatives?"

The butler clasped his hands behind his back and gazed upward. "Sir, I suspect that in consequence it falls somewhere between the burning of Moscow and the Congress of Vienna. More or less," he added.

"I was afraid of that. Good night, Luster."

And pleasant dreams, he thought. From now until the end of my life I can only wish that I would waken to the sight of Libby Ames coming into my room with a pot of tea and two companionable cups. I can dream about the pleasure of watching her at the window in deep appreciation of another summer morning in Kent, the breeze just blowing her hair. When I am old and still dreaming, she will yet be young, sitting beside the bed and asking how I find myself.

I am love's fool, he thought.

He found Private Yore at the same corner on Fleet Street. Nez noticed how the man whisked the begging cup out of sight when he stepped down from his curricle. The man would not meet his eyes.

"Private Yore," he barked, "since when did it become a habit of yours to disregard orders?"

"Sir?" asked the private, sitting up straighter, brushing at a stain on his army-issue cloak.

Nez squatted on the pavement by his former private and looked him in the eye. "When I give you a piece of paper to take around to my residence, I expect it done, Private."

The flush rose in Yore's face, leaving darker patches of color in his hollow cheeks. "I thought I did not need your help, sir," he said, his head high.

"I think you do, Private, and you know how I am when I am crossed," Nez said, his voice low. "I am worse than the Iron Duke himself."

The invalid was silent.

Nez looked about him at the men of business hurrying down the sidewalk, looking everywhere but at the beggar. He sniffed the odor of sewage, observed the dirt on the pavement. "Nice corner, Yore, but your view is somewhat limited. What do you do when it gets cold?"

"We'll find out this winter, won't we, sir?" came the reply. "Last winter I spent in hospital."

"Infamous place, wasn't it?" the duke said, making himself more comfortable, heedless of the stares and not at all concerned, for once, what people thought. "One would think that England could do better for those who defend her."

Yore nodded and held out the cup again to his regular customers on Fleet Street. "You know, sir, if you remain here, it will be difficult for me to earn enough for a meal tonight."

The duke go to his feet. He took up the crutch that leaned against the wall and held out his hand to Yore. "I have a better idea, Private," he said.

The duke dined that night in his kitchen. It was the first time he had ever visited belowstairs, but Yore had become adamant to the point of tears about eating upstairs. Bullying him would have served no purpose. Yore was tired and hungry and his stump pained him. Better to eat belowstairs than make the good man regret that his former commanding officer was out to kill him with belated Christian kindness.

The food tasted better belowstairs. Nez made some remark upon that fact to the cook, who hovered about the table, eager to please, genuinely delighted to see firsthand the effects of his cuisine on the master.

"It is always better when it is hot, my lord," said the cook.

The duke nodded and wondered what kind of eccentric he would be thought if he took all his meals in the kitchen from now on. The idea had merit. *Since I will henceforth be known as the peer who does not drink anything but water and lemonade, I suppose I could hardly suffer any more if the word circulated that I took my mutton family-style with my servants.*

His great pleasure was watching Yore eat. The man was weary to the marrow, but utterly intent upon what was placed before him. Nez could tell by the look in the private's eyes that the modest spread that the chef had created on short notice was more than Yore saw in a week.

Finally Yore had to admit defeat. He pushed back his plate and shook his head regretfully when cook—not unmindful of the preference of soldiers—whisked out a currant duff.

"You could wrap a slice in cloth, sir," Yore suggested to the cook, who nodded. "I could take it with me."

"Do you have any family here?" the duke asked when Yore leaned back in his chair. "Come to think of it, Private, what are you doing in London? I thought you were Norfolk-born and -bred."

"That I am, sir." He frowned and regarded the distant wall. "A mob of us were invalided home. We got as far as London before one of the aides robbed me. I didn't have no choice but to beg, sir, and I am no closer to Norfolk."

There was nothing to say to that artless disclosure. The duke sat in silent contemplation of that same back wall until the private sighed and recalled him to the present.

"What of Sergeant Quill?" the duke asked.

"Dead of fever. He never left Brussels, sir." The private hesitated.

"Go on, Yore, say what you're thinking."

"Sergeant Quill told me you would come for us."

The duke resumed his contemplation of the wall as his insides writhed. "What of Allenby? Wasn't he a Devonshire man?"

Yore nodded. "That he was, sir. The last I heard, he made

it back to Pytch, and his wife was supporting them with laundry while he continued to heal." Yore glanced at the clock. "I have taken up a good portion of your evening, sir."

"Where do you sleep, Yore?"

The private shrugged. "Right now it's a place with five others, each of us paying what we can. Better than the workhouse, so I am told."

"More like," agreed the duke, falling into Kentish talk. He leaned back, crossed his legs, and took a long look at Yore. The man was thin, his eyes tired, but the duke liked what he saw. There was the same air of calm dependability about Yore that he remembered from the frantic afternoon two years ago when they stood back to back in their decimated square and kept each other alive.

"Yore, as I recall, you were a bit of a genuis with weapons."

Yore grinned for the first time, and it cast ten years off his back. "Well, mayhap I was middling good, sir."

"You were very good, if memory serves me." The duke leaned forward and placed his hands palm down on the table. "Yore, I have a gun collection at the family estate in Yorkshire. Well, I say it is mine, but it goes back to the First Duke of Knaresborough. No one has even done it justice over the years. I am wondering—would you like to bring that collection up to snuff and maintain it?"

Yore was silent, his mouth open, as he stared at the duke.

"I mean, plenty of visitors come to Knare each year. They admire the old part of the house, envy my trout streams, and ogle the formal gardens. I would like to really give them something out of the ordinary to stare at. Yore, the job is yours, if you want it."

Yore began to breathe again, but he was still silent.

"There's a tidy apartment off the armory, probably full of cobwebs and mouse nests right now, but it wouldn't take much to make it habitable. A cat would tickle the mice. Your board would be included, of course, and there would be a stipend for all else. Yore?"

Yore stuck out his hand and the men shook on it, neither trusting himself to speak.

The duke broke the silence. He pulled out his watch and studied the face carefully until it swam into focus again. "Yore, it's too late for you to go anywhere tonight. There is a spare bed down here. We can go around tomorrow for any of your possessions. I'd like to start out tomorrow for Knare, if that would suit you."

The private grinned. "I don't know as the other five will miss me much, Major. We can let them have my blanket. There is only my cup," he said, nodding his head toward the tin cup that used to swing from his knapsack through quick marches across the map of Europe.

The duke picked it up. "I'd like to keep this, Yore, if you don't mind."

The private nodded, mystified by the request but too polite to ask why.

I will put it on the mantelpiece at Knare, right up there with the Sevres and the Ming, thought the duke, and it will remind me. I will look at it each day for the rest of my life and let it remind me how close I came to forgetting that I was a civilized man.

The private struggled to his feet.

Luster hurried to his side. "Mr. Yore, I have taken the liberty," he began. "There is a bath for you down the hall, and I remembered some clothing that the duke has outgrown."

"Oh, I couldn't," protested the private. "You've done enough."

The duke took Yore by the hand and nodded, with raised eyebrows, toward the butler. "I never argue with him, man, because he always gets his way. Off you go now. We're leaving early in the morning. Pytch, did you say? I can locate Private Allenby in Pytch?"

"I think so, sir," were the private's last words as Luster led him toward the door.

When Yore had regained his crutch again and was navigating on his own, Luster looked back at the duke. "Sir, do you know, I have been considering your question about obliging relatives."

"And?"

"It may not be so important. After all, your grace, you are the duke. If you can't do what you want, sir, who can?"

"Who, indeed?" Nez murmured. He watched Luster and Yore make their way down the hall as he fingered the tin cup. "I have begun, Libby," he whispered softly.

Tomorrow they would be on their way to Knare. The duke rubbed the cup against his cheek. I have not been home in so long, he thought. Already he saw the rolling hills and busy streams of his childhood. Knare was in need of repair. He would spend the next month seeing to its renovation and making it snug for winter.

Maybe by the time the leaves began to turn, he would have accumulated the courage to go calling in Kent again, bound this time on a different mission.

If he could wait that long . . .

18

ANTHONY COOK did not write. During that first week in the rented house off Marine Parade, Libby had not expected to hear from him. The squire will take all his time, and then there are his other patients, she reasoned as she sat in her room and watched the sun glinting off the sea. She wished herself in Holyoke.

Candlow wrote once, a letter that looked as though it had been labored over at length. He informed them that Aunt Crabtree had fled to London at Lydia's request. ("I anticipate a precarious outcome," he added.). Another paragraph allowed that the squire was much improved and that the Wilcoxes had restored order to the house. "Jim Wilcox is painting the trim on the windows now. I know that his next task is to plant saplings along the lane to the road, for I heard Dr. Cook asking him about that. I would say more, but surely you will hear from the doctor soon and he can tell you better than I how things are going."

Libby waited for the promised letter, but it never came. She knew the mail was delivered each morning around ten o'clock, and always managed to find a reason to be in the hall then, to appear only slightly interested while Uncles Ames looked with maddening slowness at each letter. There was an occasional letter for her mother, but usually Uncle Ames pocketed them all. Libby tried not to show her chagrin, but soon the footman was casting her sympathetic glances and then going about his duties with an equally long face.

From the evening of their arrival in Brighton, Libby had said little about the events that had brought them, beyond the obvious necessity of explaining to Mama how Joseph had come by his interesting scar. She had told the whole story, and Mama had cried, sniffled and gasped "Poor man, poor boy!" as Libby spun the narrative.

After careful consideration, there seemed no point in elaborating on Dr. Cook's surprising offer of marriage and her equally impulsive agreement. With each day that passed without a letter, Libby could only be grateful that she had said nothing.

It became easier and easier to stay in her room—looking out over the treetops to the sea—than to bother to promenade about. She didn't even require a novel to entertain her. It was far more pleasant to doze and gaze at the water and compose dozens of letters in her mind that she never put on paper.

She came to hate the badly spelled letters that flowed out of London from Lydia, letters almost incoherent with news of military reviews and balloon ascensions and picnics al fresco. Lydia begged Aunt Ames to come to London to help her select the material for her wedding dress and guide the hands of the modiste who would be entrusted with that exalted task. "I depend upon you, Aunt Ames," she had written in the last letter, each word heavily underscored.

"Well, I will not go," Mama said at luncheon as she read the letter over again. "She can be guided in these matters by the Earl of Devere's mother." Mother glanced at Libby. "I wish you would eat something, dear. You grow more peckish by the minute, and I fear a deep decline," she teased, waving the letter at her like a fan. "And then we would have to send for Dr. Cook to bumble his way to the diagnosis."

Libby burst into tears and ran from the room, slamming the dining-room door on Mama's gasp of amazement and Uncle Ames' " 'Pon my word." She locked her door, drew herself into a little ball, and gave herself over to mutiny and misery of the worst sort.

Mama knocked on the door. Libby blew her nose and opened

it, averting her eyes from Mama's white face. She waited, miserable, for Mama to scold her for her rudeness.

Mama did nothing of the sort. She settled herself into the window seat that Libby had vacated, and calmly took up the knitting that she had brought with her.

"When you feel like talking, my dear, I feel like listening," was all she said.

In another moment, Libby was on her knees beside her mother, sobbing out the whole story of the chocolate merchant and his impertinent offer, and Dr. Cook's impulsive proposal and his sudden reluctance to have her around. Mama heard it all, interjecting no more than an occasional "Oh, my" into the narrative, her hand resting on Libby's head.

"I wasn't going to tell you, Mama," Libby sobbed, "for I knew how deeply wounded you would be over this matter with the duke."

Mrs. Ames stroked her daughter's hair. "I knew, Libby, I knew," she soothed, "or at least I suspected. Trust Lydia to write pages and pages with the funny tale that the duke had planned to offer for you, and didn't I think that droll?" She pulled her daughter closer. "Well, I did not! I know you are not one to kiss and tease. Your heart must surely have been engaged in the matter, too. I am sorry that it came to what it did." She sighed. "If your Papa and I had been wiser . . ." She kissed Libby. "If we had been wiser, you never would have been born, so cheer up."

Finally there were no more tears to cry. Libby leaned against her mother's leg and waited for some reassurance, some further relief for her mangled emotions. From La Coruña to Salamanca, from Badajoz to Vitoria, Mama had been the regimental mainstay in matters of the heart, a regular font of wisdom. Long after she should have been asleep, Libby remembered Mama dispensing good advice to the men of her husband's command, counseling the lovelorn. Now it was her turn to benefit from this sagacity. Libby waited.

Mama said nothing. Libby raised her face finally from her mother's skirts to observe her gazing out to sea, her eyes soft as she turned the wedding ring on her finger around and around.

Libby plumped herself down across from her mother in the window seat. "Mama, have you listened to a word I have said?" she accused, exasperation just barely edging out amusement.

"I have heard enough, my darling," Mama said quickly, her eyes no less dreamy. "I only wish I had some good advice for you."

Libby stared at her in disbelief. "Mama, you gave advice all across Spain. Have you none for me?"

Mama shook her head and picked up her knitting again.

"At least tell me how to know if I am in love," begged Libby. "Lydia seems so sure about Eustace, but I cannot tell. And who am I in love with, for goodness' sake?"

"Lydia is a pea goose," Mama said decisively. "I love her dearly, and so do you, but she hasn't a clue as to why Eustace was suddenly so enamored of her. Perhaps by the time she realizes he married her for the Ames fortune, she will have a quiverful of children to console her."

"Mama, that is no answer. Who am I in love with?" Libby insisted.

Mama only looked her daughter full in the face and smiled in a way that Libby considered entirely unacceptable. "My dear, you'll know." She looked at the ocean again, her eyes far away. "When you find that you can't bear one more minute without him . . ." She laughed. "Or when you discover that if he does not go away soon, you will spit nails . . ."

"Mama," Libby wailed, and laughed despite herself. "You are no help."

"No, I am not, am I?" said Mama agreeably. "Men can be fearsomely irritating, my dear, totally without wisdom, creatures of random impulse, as I fear your chocolate merchant was. Libby, he probably regrets every word he spoke to you that morning."

Mrs. Ames shook her head. "As for Dr. Cook, I do not know, Libby. He is most definitely a wild card. Somehow I never thought of our fubsy doctor as someone who would be essential to your happiness. Still, stranger things have happened, I suppose . . ."

Mama put her hand to her mouth to smother a laugh that would not be stopped.

Libby joined in, immeasurably refreshed, and put one ghost to bed. She took her mother's hands and said with mock seriousness, "If I should chance to receive a better offer from the duke, I will consider it. At the very least, I will hold out for a manor in the Cotswolds."

"You do that, my dear," said her mama, her voice equally droll. And then she was suddenly serious. "I wish that circumstances were different for you, but this is real life." She kissed her daughter's cheek. "Poor honey! You have had all the real life you can stand for a while, I suspect."

Libby nodded, lapping up her mother's sympathy like a kitten its cream.

"I will go your Dr. Cook's prescription one better. Tomorrow you must venture to the circulating library and get us several good novels. Let us consider them serious research into how others solve problems of the heart."

"And we will wallow on your bed in our shimmies and eat macaroons while we read. I think I will be cured, Mama," Libby said.

Mama's regimen proved to be remarkably efficacious, except that Joseph took exception to it several weeks later and exclaimed over breakfast, in a much-ill-used tone, that it would not do at all.

"Libby, you must walk with me along the Promenade today," he insisted. "There are fine horses at the Pavilion mews, and you must see them."

"My dear, do you think the gypsies have been here?" she teased.

Joseph frowned at her. "I seriously doubt it, Libby." He looked at her and grinned. "You are joking me, aren't you?"

"Of course!"

"Well, sometimes I cannot tell," he said. "Let us leave immediately after breakfast."

It was on the tip of her tongue to withdraw from the expedition that morning because she could not miss the mail delivery. She dismissed the idea. It had been over a month now and nothing had come from Holyoke. Quite wisely, the doctor had reconsidered and had decided to look elsewhere. There was no sense in lagging back anymore.

"Very well, brother, lead on," she said.

"Bravo," Mama exclaimed, and touched her hand. "Let me loan you a new bonnet that Uncle Ames insisted I buy. How free he is with others' blunt."

Libby and Joseph ventured along the Promenade to the mews, where Libby stood in polite boredom while Joseph leaned on the fence, adoring the horses from a distance, pointing out their excellence, and wishing himself closer.

The breeze blew her bonnet back from her face and she raised her chin, enjoying the feeling of the hot sun on her skin. The air smelled of tar and saltwater and sand, mingled with the roasting meat and pasties from the vendors that hawked their wares along the oceanfront.

When she tired of the view, she watched her brother. His wound had healed beautifully, the scar a red line still, but thin and fading. Soon it would be a white scar scarcely noticeable, a testimony to the ability of his surgeon. *And Mama still laughs when I mention Anthony Cook's name,* she thought. *I wish she knew him as well as I know him.*

The thought made her blush, for no reason she could discern, particularly since she had given him up for lost. She was comparing the merits of his kiss in the Caseys' cottage to the duke's kiss in the orchard, when Joseph tugged at her arm and reminded her that the horses had moved off and, besides, he was hungry.

They returned arm in arm to the quiet house on the Marine Parade, chased each other up the stairs, and burst into the sitting room to find Mama serving tea to Anthony Cook.

A twinkle in her eyes, Mama glanced up from the cup she held, checking the flow of tea in midstream. "My dear, must you burst into a room that way? One would think you were being chased by Cossacks, and we know that this is not the case."

While Libby stood still in shocked amazement, Joseph sat down beside Anthony, who took the boy's face in his hands, murmuring, "The lengths I will go to to follow up on a patient's progress. Hold still, lad." He turned Joseph's head more to the light and examined his handiwork with a smile of satisfaction. "Excellent, excellent," he said. "These buried sutures are entirely satisfactory," he told Joseph, who looked at him, a question in his eyes. "Never mind, laddy, so glad you don't remember it. Who removed your stitches?"

"Mama was bound and determined to take me to Dr. Pearman, but Libby beat her to it," he said. "It didn't even hurt, andd we must have saved any number of shillings."

The doctor looked over the tops of his spectacles to Libby, who still stood by the door, too shy to move. "She will likely put me out of business if such quackery is allowed to run rampant. Cat got your tongue, ma'am?"

"No . . . no," she stammered, and came closer, offering her hand, which the doctor held in his own until Mama coughed. "How do you do, sir?"

She could see how he did, and she was pleased. Of course, it was difficult to cast a critical eye over the entire doctor, especially when he stood so close, but she could plainly tell that he had been spending less time at the dinner table. With less overhang in the front, he seemed taller and more commanding, more like the squire. His spectacles still slid down his nose as he looked at her, a slight smile on his face, and his hair was as thick and curly as ever.

"Actually, I do very well, thank you. Father is much better, too. I don't sleep longer than I ever did at nights, but at least Farrell Frink has not fallen down any more wells, and babies have been kindlier, of late. Sit down and take off that hat so I can see how you do."

She did as he said without question and sat, scooting Joseph closer to the doctor until her brother got up and moved to Mother's side. They drank tea together in perfect accord as Anthony told them all the Holyoke gossip he was privy to, mentioning that Eustace and Lydia had returned to Holyoke Green long enough to look over the local church and find it wanting.

"I always thought it a charming place, myself," said the doctor as he shook his head over the sweets Mama offered him. "I think Lydia has her eye on an abbey for her nuptials, or Canterbury Cathedral at least."

Mama snorted in decided unladylike fashion and said something that no one could quite hear.

"Did . . . did the duke accompany them?" Libby asked, keeping her voice as offhand as possible.

"No, he did not," the doctor replied. "I asked Lydia about the duke, and she said that since their return to London, no one has seen much of him. He does not go to the parties and routs and appears to have abandoned Eustace."

"How strange," said Libby. "I thought they were best friends. Oh, I do not hope he has resumed drinking."

"That is my thought, too, Elizabeth. I asked Lydia about that and she gave me a blank stare. She thinks he may have rusticated to the family estate in Yorkshire."

There was no way to keep the duke part of the conversation. Libby nibbled on a biscuit as the subject passed to Uncle Ames' gout. "If you have been physicking him, I wish you well," the doctor declared. He reached in his pocket for a packet of salts and noticed the humor in her eyes. "I will not spread them around the room this time, my dear. I trust the canary recovered."

"That seems so long ago," Libby murmured.

"The beginning of summer," her replied, handing the salts to Mama. "And now it is hops harvest, and that brings me to the reason for my visit." He leaned forward and rested his elbows on his knees, looking Joseph in the eye. "It is a two-part errand I come on. I have a proposal for Joseph and a statement for Elizabeth that I dare not postpone further."

"Speak on, then, sir," said Mama, the light leaving her eyes. She glanced at her daughter and began to twist her wedding ring again.

"Joseph, I have hired a groom to replace the poor excuse that Father sacked. Perhaps you know of him. Granger of Llydd."

Joseph sucked in his breath. "Who doesn't know him, sir? In his day, he was the greatest rider at Newmarket."

"In his day, lad. That day is long over, but he still knows more about horses than any man who ever drew breath, I declare. He has accepted the position and will work out well, but he needs an assistant. Someone young and agile, someone like you, Joseph. Would you consider the position?''

Libby watched her brother's face. She glanced at her mother and looked away quickly. Mama was crying, the tears sliding quietly down her beautiful face. Impulsively, Libby turned to the doctor. ''You're the best man I know, Anthony,'' she whispered.

''I hope you still feel that way in a few minutes,'' was his only comment to her. ''Well, Joseph, I have put it to you. We can discuss salary later with your uncle, if your mother thinks that advisable. Your duties will also include driving me on calls occasionally, particularly if I have been out already and am too tired to do so myself. I recall that was good advice from Nez, and I shall take it.''

Mama blew her nose, composed herself, and looked at the doctor. ''Sir, does your father know of this?''

Anthony smiled. ''It was his idea, ma'am. I wasn't bright enough to think of it.''

Mama began to cry again.

Joseph leapt to his feet. ''I will do it, sir. Then Mama will not be a watering pot.''

They laughed, and Anthony rose, holding out his hand. ''Let us shake on it, Joseph. Very good. Is it too much to ask, or could you leave with me in the morning? Hops harvest is upon us, and we are all needed at home.''

Joseph looked at his mother, who nodded through her tears. ''Yes, sir, I can. I shall go pack right now.'' He ran to the door and looked back at the doctor, his voice filled with quiet dignity. ''Of all things, this is what I wanted the most, sir: the chance to earn my own way. I'll never disappoint you.''

It was the doctor's turn to look thoughtful and rub at the spot between his eyes. ''I know that, lad. Seems to run in your family, doesn't it?''

Joseph was gone, pounding up the stairs. They heard him let out a shout as the door closed to his room.

Mama dried her eyes and managed a watery smile.

The doctor was still on his feet. He held out his hand to Libby, who took it and let him lift her up. ''The second matter requires a different setting, madam. I have something I need to say to Elizabeth that I have been putting off. Will you excuse us?"

Mystified, Mama nodded and went back to her handkerchief. Elizabeth reached for her bonnet, but the doctor set it aside. "No. I can't see your face with that lovely bit of foofraw on your head."

Wordlessly, she followed him into the street and onto Marine Parade, where other couples strolled. He made his way toward the Promenade, her hand clutching his arm rather too tight.

Now he will cry off, she thought, and braced herself for the inevitable. To her surprise, he began to speak of inconsequentials. In another moment, she was at her ease and laughing along with him. And noticing, too, how ladies glanced his way, some peeking around their escorts for a second look.

"Don't look now, sir, but you are being much admired," she said as they strolled along. "Gentlemen and ladies both seem to find you notable."

"Ah, silly you! If it is men, they are admiring you, my dear, as all men always will. It is their nature. If the men glance my way, it is envy."

She laughed and he tipped up his spectacles to give her that nearsighted stare she had been missing. "Envy, dear Elizabeth, envy! I hope that I also give them something to live for. The knowledge that no matter how well-stuffed and homely the man, it is possible to engage the interest of beauty." He kissed her hand. "Heaven knows how, but there you are."

"Knothead," she declared with some feeling. "When it is women who plainly admire you, how do you explain that away, Doctor?"

"Doctor, is it? Simple, Elizabeth, simple! I am surprised that your fine brain did not beat me to the reason. The women admire you first, as all women must. It is their nature. Then they look at me and realize how great is your compassion."

She cast him a speaking glance and he threw back his head and laughed. The sound brought tears to her eyes, which she declared came from sand blowing in from the beach, when he broke off and looked at her with some consternation.

"Elizabeth, what is the matter?" he asked.

She shook her head and refused to look at him. "I think I am just glad to hear you laugh," she whispered. "I didn't leave you in very comfortable circumstance."

He tucked her arm in his again and strolled along the boardwalk, moving away from the crowds that swarmed near the Royal Pavilion. "No, it was not a happy time. Father is better, but he will never be well again, I fear. Curious, Elizabeth, but he looks old now, where he did not before. He requires more of my time, and I give it gladly. I think we have talked more in the past month than we have in twenty-five years." He sighed. "So much to make up for."

And then she understood what he was trying to tell her. There wasn't room in his life for her right now. She turned her face into his sleeve, feeling a physical pain at the thought of what was coming. She couldn't bear a second rejection. Something in her rebelled against it. She would have to beat him to the occasion. She turned to face him, and he stopped walking.

"Anthony, you don't have to apologize or run around Robin Hood's barn."

He looked down at her, surprised. "What on earth are you talking about? Here I am trying to work up the nerve—"

"Don't," she cut in. "I know that proposal of yours was impulsive, and please don't think that I will hold you to it." She held up her hand when he tried to speak. "Now, let me finish. It was lovely of you and I appreciate your kindness more than you know, but I'm not a fool."

"I know that," he murmured, looking at her with an expression very close to love. "You're just a bit tired of being buffeted about."

She nodded and leaned her forehead against his chest as the tears came to her eyes. "Let's go back now. You don't need to say anything. I understand perfectly."

He took her by the shoulders and led her over to a nearby bench, sitting her down firmly. "You don't have the slightest inkling of what I am about to say, my dear."

She looked at him, wide-eyed. "You're not going to cry off?"

"Good God, no," he said, and put his arm around her. "I could never do that." He looked out to sea. "No, no, what I have to say is something of a delicate nature that I tried to put into a letter, but thought better of it each time I tried."

"I waited for a letter," she said.

He smiled. "You'd have gotten plenty of them if thoughts were pen and paper, Elizabeth. I'm sorry."

He stood up then, waited until a strolling couple passed them, and walked to the boardwalk railing, resting his elbows and looking at her. His face grew red. "My dear, when I wore my father down and he consented to frank me in medical school, he sent me off on the mail coach with a valuable bit of advice."

"Yes?" she encouraged when he paused as another couple passed.

"Oh, dash it all," he exclaimed, and took her by the hand, hurrying her along the boardwalk until they came to the end of it and there were no other couples. She sat down and dangled her legs off the walk as he sat down beside her.

"What was this valuable piece of advice?"

He took a deep breath. "Simply this. I was to avoid the prostitutes and devote myself to my studies."

"Oh," she said, her face reddening.

"It was grand counsel, Elizabeth," he said. "Although I must admit that the 'Edinburra hoors' were scarcely tempting. All that wet wool and smelling of oatmeal. Oh, Lord, and when we got them in the infirmary and them so diseased!" He made a face. "I applied myself to my studies and finished at the top of my class."

He took his glasses off, cleaned them, and put them on again, the high color evident in his face. "Well, my dear, what with one thing and another, the years have passed and all my knowledge of women remains theoretical and clinical."

He peered at her and she looked at him. "Anthony, are you trying to tell me that . . ." She couldn't quite think of how to say it.

"That I am totally without experience with women," he finished in one fast sentence. "I am remarkably well-versed in female anatomy and physiology, but, my dear, I remain the veriest amateur." He spread his hands out, palms up, in his lap. "Well, there you have it. I fear that would frighten off any woman. I know such behavior is not the norm in our rather promiscuous society, and from what I hear in the clubs, anyway, women seem to prefer a little experience in their men. At least that is the excuse that men give. How do I know? I hope you are not too disappointed. I wanted you to know." He laughed softly to himself. "You'd have figured it out, in any event. Say something, Elizabeth."

The laughter welled up inside her, but she forced it down. If I go into whoops, he will not understand, she thought. He will think I am making fun of him, something I would not do for the world. I wonder how much sleep he lost over this? Oh, Anthony.

She got up and dusted the bits of sand off her dress. She held out her hand to the doctor and pulled him to his feet. When he was standing up, she threw her arms around him and began to giggle. In another moment he was laughing, too, and it was the most wonderful sound she had ever heard.

She raised her face to his. "Kiss me, Dr. Cook," she demanded.

He obliged her, kissing her slowly, over and over, completely absorbed in the matter at hand, even though couples strolled by, tittered, and hurried on. His glasses fell into the sand, but other than to push them away with his foot to make sure that he did not tread on them, the doctor let them go.

When he stopped finally and retrieved his spectacles, Libby could only regard him with new respect. She took his arm and started him back toward the Marine Parade. "I would say, sir, that your theories are sound, indeed."

"You don't mind that I am so inexperienced?"

"Sir, I am flattered," Libby said simply. "You have paid me such a compliment."

By the time they reached the house, they had agreed upon a wedding date in two weeks' time at St. John's in Holyoke.

"It is not grand enough for your cousin, but I think it adequate," said the doctor. "Such short notice requires a special license, I suppose. Can you have a dress by then?" he asked, and kissed her on the ear. "Not that it signifies. The one you are wearing is lovely."

Her eyes danced. "Yes, and only one shilling, remember? I will be a wonderful economy in your household."

"Thank the Lord for that," he declared fervently, with just a trace of unsteadiness in his voice. "That means I can spend more money on books. Oh, Elizabeth, I love you." He put his arm around her waist. "And the wonderful thing is, I always will."

He left in the morning with Joseph, both of them well-kissed and cried-over.

As soon as Libby's eyes were dry, Mama marched her to High Street and selected yards and yards of white taffeta. "You will rustle in the most gorgeous fashion as you walk down the aisle," she said. "It's a sound I most want to hear." And then Mama burst into tears, to the consternation of the shopkeeper, who hurried over to apologize for the material.

Uncle Ames returned that afternoon from London, grumpy over the division of his spoils with the Wiltmores. "Damnedest family ever," he said, "pockets to let and expenses to choke an elephant. Don't know why I ever agreed to such silliness so many years ago. I must have been polluted." He growled himself into his favorite chair and stifled an oath as Mama pushed a pillow under his gouty foot.

He smiled over Libby's good news and chucked her under the chin. "Good for you, minx," he said. "I don't know that I ever thought Dr. Cook would be the answer to a maiden's prayers, but I'm happy for you. Does this mean I get his services free now?"

Libby laughed. "I shall ask him when is in a good mood."

"And that will be every time he looks at you, puss." He sighed. "I suppose I will have to give out another wedding gift," he grumbled, and then winked at her. "Do you love him, dear?"

"I think so," she said.

"But you don't know? Time will tell, puss, time will tell."

The dress was done a week later, a dream of a dress, low across the bosom and gently gathered into a graceful train at the back. Mama carefully packed it in tissue paper and rested it on the seat across from them in Uncle William's post chaise. When Mama pronounced herself satisfied, the carriage door closed and they began the trip to Holyoke.

They arrived at nightfall, to be greeted by Candlow.

"Madam, what a pleasure to have you home again," he said to Mrs. Ames, taking the dress box from her. He inclined his head toward Libby. "And may I be the first in the house to congratulate you? Dr. Cook told me, and I couldn't be more delighted."

He ushered them into the sitting room. Mama removed her bonnet and fluffed her hair, then crossed to the table where the mail was left. She set aside her letters and held out a package to Libby.

"For you, dear." She looked closer. "Gracious! It has been franked by a lord. I wonder who can have sent that?"

Libby took the package. The handwriting was bold, but unfamiliar to her and she could not read the name. She tore off the wrapping paper and stared down at a box of Copley's Finest Nut Mix. A note was tucked under the ribbon. With fingers that trembled, she plucked it out and opened it.

"Forgive me if you can. Nez."

19

WORDLESSLY, she handed the note to her mother, who read it once, twice, and then sat down. "I knew that the duke would regret his hasty words," Mama said after a moment's reflection. She picked up the box, lifted the lid, and selected a chocolate morsel.

With a sigh of her own, Libby took the note back, crumpled it in her hand, and went upstairs to her room. The room was shrouded in darkness and smelled close with the windows shut. She opened the draperies and raised the window sash.

The moon was full and hazy with smoke from the oasts, the great slow-burning kilns where the hops were stuffed to dry. She breathed deep of the musky fragrance, remembering with an ache that it was the first noticeable thing that had greeted them as they returned to Kent, still reeling from the shock of Papa's death two years ago.

The activity of hops harvest time had taken hold of them then and plunged them into Kentish life. Uncle William had needed their extra arms and sound good sense, and they had needed to be too busy during those days of August and September. When they finally had time to draw a good breath after Michaelmas, they belonged to Kent and were beginning to heal.

And now this season brings another change in my life, she thought, perching herself into the window. Now, in years to come, I will breathe in this bitter, pungent fragrance, this odor

that is making me sleepy, and think about my wedding. Why
did the duke have to send that candy now? Couldn't he have
waited two days when I would have been safely leg-shackled?
Why are men so perverse?

She did not know her own mind yet, if something as harmless
as a box of chocolates could set her off and spinning. The duke
must have heard about her wedding from Lydia and wished to
salve a guilty conscience. He had probably instructed his
secretary to select a box of Copley's, just so large and not any
larger, and address a note to her. She didn't even know if the
note still crumpled in her fist was in his handwriting.

Libby spread out the note on her lap and looked at the words
again. Forgive you, she thought, I should never. You were
untoward and out of line and I should hope that you choke on
your good intentions, for the humiliation you have put me
through. Forgive you? I suppose I can, but kindly remain at a
distance, or else . . . or else I might forgive you too much.

She lay awake until very late, her body worn out with the
journey from Brighton to Holyoke, but her mind talking to her,
whispering, cajoling, and speculating. Long after midnight she
heard a gig trundling down the road, away from the Cook estate.
Is that you, Anthony? she thought as she tried to find a soft
spot on her bed of nails. I wish you would call here. I could
bear this better if I could see your comforting bulk and hear
your reassurance that I am doing the right thing.

Morning brought the doctor to her doorstep, returning from
the call he had made after midnight. Unshaven and heavy-eyed,
he gathered her in his arms, kissed her soundly, set her on her
feet again, and told her to be a good girl for two more days.

"At least come in to breakfast," she coaxed, clasping his
hands to tug him up the front steps.

He shook his head. "I cannot, dearest. Dame Westerfield is
having fits again and prophesying, and I must do what I can
to soothe her and assure the relatives that they haven't much
longer of this tyranny. Give me a kiss, love, and send me on
my way."

She did as he said, clinging to him so tight that he raised his
eyebrows.

"Would that I could stay longer! Two days more and then

you can see me off from our own steps. Elizabeth, I love you."

And I don't know what I do, she thought as she blew a kiss and waved him out of sight.

As the noonday sky shimmered with heat from the oast ovens, Joseph managed to escape from the hops harvest long enough to drop by Holyoke Green. Mama hugged him and cried while he grinned and shrugged his shoulders at Libby.

He was browner, and hungry, and somehow more assured of himself. The scar was obscured by several days' growth of beard that made Mama sigh and remark that her dear boy was growing up.

Libby fingered his chin. "You had better make plans to shave that, and soon, brother," she warned, "if you are to give me away on Friday."

He nodded. "Dr. Cook said the same thing last night." He accepted bread and jam from his mother. "We have been rehearsing the march down the aisle, Libby. I take his arm and pretend he is you, and we walk down the room while he hums."

Libby laughed and clapped her hands while he finished the bread and looked about for more. "We have been almost too busy to eat, Mama. I help the squire out to the hop bines and he stays there all day, watching the pickers." He swallowed another slice of bread. "Libby, the gypsies are all about everywhere. Squire makes sure that I am close by the stables when they are at their lunchtime."

Mama clasped his hands in hers, disregarding the jam on his fingers. "Does the squire treat you well, son? It is a particular worry of mine."

"He treats me well, Mama," Joseph said, "and so does the doctor." He grinned at his sister. "You will like it there, too, I know. Dr. Cook has been trying to move books out of his room so there will be a space for you. I tell him that you would not mind one of the other rooms down the hall, but he only laughs."

Libby blushed while Joseph looked about for something else to eat. Mama took the Copley's chocolate off the sitting-room table and held them out to her son. He plucked out a handful, eating them quickly and eyeing the clock.

"I promised the squire I would be back by the time the bailiff shouts, 'All to work.' " He took another handful of chocolates from the box. "Libby, do you know what? I would not have thought of it, but for these. I saw the chocolate merchant only this morning."

Libby gulped and sat down suddenly while Mama frowned. Unmindful of their reactions, Joseph pocketed the chocolate. "He was riding a neatish bit of bone and muscle as bold as life down the street in Holyoke. I don't think he saw me, but I am sure it was the merchant." He scratched his head. "Or is he the duke? I can't quite remember." He thought about it a moment and then his face brightened. "I suppose it does not matter. Good day, Mama. Libby, you should get in the sun more. You look like something half-dead."

He was gone.

Libby whirled about to face her mother. "What game does this man play?" she asked, her voice full of exasperation.

Mama put the lid back on the chocolates. "I think he means to apologize in person, Libby." She peered closely at her daughter's unhappy face. "I am sure he will attempt nothing more."

"Surely not," Libby murmured, wishing that the high color would leave her face before Mother made some remark upon it.

The duke did not come. The afternoon dragged by as Libby packed her dresses, unpacked them, and packed them again. She heard a horse ride by and ran to the window. It was Anthony. As she watched, his horse leapt the fence in a graceful arc and he disappeared in the direction of Fairbourne. Libby pounded the windowsill in her frustration. Anthony, you don't seem to have a grasp of what is going on, she thought. If you want me, you had better come to me.

Then she was ashamed of herself. The demands of others on his time would always supersede her own needs. He would attend because he was a doctor, and that was that. If you think you cannot bear that kind of neglect, Elizabeth Ames, she scolded herself, you had better cry off right now.

She sent no note, wrote no letter to the doctor, but prowled the house after dinner until Mama put her hands to her head and with an awful expression pointed to the door. Libby grabbed up her bonnet and bolted from the house. She walked rapidly across the field to the place where ashes from a gypsy fire still littered the ground. She poked about with her shoe, raising the ashes, wondering what to do with her life.

Is it fair, she thought, to marry a man I am not entirely sure I love? That Anthony would be faithful throughout his life, she had no doubt. It is I that I question, she thought. Will I find myself lying in his arms one night, wishing myself with someone else? Will I spend sleepless nights regretting what I have done? Will the work and worry of the life he has chosen divide us until we are two strangers sharing a house, a bed, and children?

There was no answers in the field. Her head seemed full to bursting with voices all talking to her at once, setting up such a chatter that she could not think. She wished herself back on the Promenade in Brighton, listening to Anthony's voice alone. Her thoughts did her no credit.

She was walking slowly back to the house as a curricle pulled away from the front drive. She thought for a moment that it must be Uncle William. He had sent regrets from London that Lydia, deep in the anxieties of choosing her wardrobe, would be unable to attend the wedding, but that he would be there. Libby shook her head. It would not be Uncle William. He had never succumbed to such toys of fashion.

She waited until the vehicle was gone down the road before she let herself into the house. Her mother met her at the door, a look of vast disquiet marring the beauty of her countenance. She held a box in her hands that she gave to her daughter.

Libby looked down. "Duke's Delight," she read. "Oh, Mother!"

They sat down in the sitting room. Libby leaned against her mother's shoulder.

" 'It is a special sort,' he told me. The only box of its kind. 'With full measure of rue,' if I recall him rightly. He had it made up especially for you."

"The Duke of Knaresborough," Libby said, thrusting the box to one side.

Mrs. Ames smiled and touched her daughter's hair. "A charming gentleman, Libby. So much address and good manners and everything that was proper. Your father would say he looked as fine as five pence." She paused, hesitated, picking her words carefully, not looking at her daughter. "And I would be inclined to agree with him."

"Did he say anything about that infamous offer?" Libby asked.

"He did. He assumed that you had told me everything. He offered his sincere apologies, and I accepted them for I felt he truly meant it." She hesitated, and then paced the length of the room in great agitation of mind. She took her daughter's hands in a tight grip. "Libby, he was so indiscreet, for all that he means well! He told me that he loves you, will have none other, and means to offer marriage this time. Imagine!"

Libby stared at her mother. "Mama, did you tell him I was to be married in two days? He is too late!"

Marianne Ames nodded, her eyes filled with tears. "Of course I did. I am hardly dead to the proprieties, daughter."

In spite of her own misery, Libby smiled at the idea of her mother countenancing anything improper. "No one could ever accuse you of that. Oh, what are we to do? I suppose he will call again, won't he?"

"He said he would. Problems rarely go away because we wish them elsewhere." Mrs. Ames sat down suddenly, her face set, hard. "I blame myself. Listen to me, talking of proprieties when I was so indiscreet myself so many years ago!" She could not look at her daughter. "A fine muddle this is, Libby. I have learned such propriety over the years. Would that I had exercised it much sooner that first time your father came into the tobacco shop!"

Libby sat down beside her mother and put her arms around her. "Mama! Don't dredge up the past like that. I, for one, am glad you did such a foolish thing. I would not be here, had you not 'forgotten your place,' as Grandfather Ames probably put it."

Mrs. Ames wiped her eyes and allowed herself to be comforted. She kissed her daughter and then looked away. "I have had ample occasion to scold myself, but no, I would not have changed things, no matter how ill it has fallen out for you. I loved your papa. I love him still."

She took another turn about the room and stood before her

daughter again. "And this brings me to a bit of plain speaking. My dear, you have expressed to me your own doubts about your feelings for Dr. Cook. I suspect that this turn of events, however unwelcome, will force you to examine the quality of that relationship."

"Mother, what are you saying?" Libby exclaimed.

"I am saying that you had better know your own mind," her mother persisted. "When the vows are spoken, my darling, you will be a long time married. As improperly as the duke is behaving, you had better study it out carefully in your own mind and be certain that you are marrying the right man."

Libby sat on the front steps and waited for the doctor to appear. When the evening's chill made her rub her arms, she went indoors. Mama had set up the card table and eyed her hopefully, but Libby only shook her head. She sat in silence and growing irritation with Anthony Cook. Tomorrow was the eve of their wedding, and she had scarcely exchanged ten words with him since her return from Brighton.

Are you so sure of yourself, Anthony? she thought as she watched her mother lay out another hand of solitaire, frown over it, and cheat when she thought her daughter wasn't looking.

"Did the duke say when he would return?" Libby asked finally as the clock prepared to strike ten.

"In the morning, my dear."

Libby left the room without another word and trudged up the stairs to her bedroom. She almost cried to see it, books everywhere, clothes jumbled about. She wanted to rush about and put everything back the way it was and forget that she had ever given her impulsive agreement to an equally impulsive proposal. She would put everything in order again and tell Anthony that she had changed her mind. When she finally closed her eyes in exhaustion, she knew it would be for the best.

Libby was awake before the maid tiptoed into the room with her can of hot water. The day was already uncomfortably warm. She threw off the covers, hugging her legs close to her body and wishing that the morning would bring its usual measure of optimism to her. When it did not come, she dressed quickly in her coolest muslin and went downstairs.

Candlow brought her a note during breakfast. "I found this pinned to the front door, Miss Ames," he said, handing it to her.

It was a page torn from Anthony Cook's presciption book. "I was too late. I will be at your house for dinner as planned. Yours as ever, Anthony." He had underscored "will" several times.

Without a word, she passed the note to her mother. "Do you think he will come?"

"I know he will try, my dear."

Libby went into the sitting room, restlessly fluffing the pillows on the sofas, arranging the chairs, and straightening pictures that were already plumb with the room. She sat down, folded her hands in her lap, and waited.

Soon she heard the curricle in the front drive, followed by a brisk knock. In another moment, Candlow stood at the door to the sitting room.

"Miss Ames, the Duke of Knaresborough," he said, his face utterly unreadable as he stood aside to let Benedict Nesbitt pass.

The duke paused a moment in the doorway and then came forward swiftly, hands outstretched, a smile on his face that brightened the whole room. He stopped in front of her, bowed, raised her to her feet, and kissed her hand.

"I was going to ask how you did, but it's perfectly obvious, Libby," he said. "You do well." He touched her cheek.

It was a shock to see him so elegantly dressed. She remembered the sober suit of the London merchant, and then her father's shabby pants and shirts that he had worn during his convalescence. The peer who stood before her with a question in his eyes was slap up to the mark, a credit to his tailor and bootmaker.

He wore the clothes of a country gentleman, and they hung to perfection on his frame, buckskins and buff coat, with gleaming boots tasseled and without a blemish. His neckcloth was an ornament of mathematical precision. As Libby admired his splendor, the thought crossed her mind that Anthony would never have the time or patience to devote so much effort to his person. The duke smelled of some mysterious fragrance that caused her mouth to water. His hair was curled without a strand out of place. He could have come directly from Bond Street without a single detour. He was all that was correct.

"I am well enough," she said when the silence threatened to swallow her whole. "Please be seated, sir."

He shook his head and strode instead to the fireplace, where he rested his elegant shoulders against the mantelpiece. I wonder, she thought as she watched him, does he think he appears to better advantage there?

He stood there a moment and then came back to sit beside her. She moved away slightly to make room, and a look close to pain crossed his face.

"What I did was unforgivable, Libby Ames," he said quietly, looking her in the eye. "I hope and trust that you can forgive."

"I think probably the least said about it, the better," Libby replied honestly. "I am certainly willing to let the whole thing go, if that will assuage whatever feelings of regret you have."

"It's more than that, Libby," he said, moving closer and taking her by the hand.

"I don't think it can be," she replied, pulling back her hand.

He took her hand again and held it more tightly. "I own I was foolish beyond measure, but for the Lord's sake, Libby, why are you rushing into this impetuous marriage?"

"Well, I . . ." she began, and stopped, unable to think of any reason beyond the fact that she was hurt and Anthony had asked her.

"At any rate, my dear, I am only grateful that I chanced upon Lydia only the other day in London. I have been spending time at my estate in Yorkshire." He smiled and looked down at his hand and hers. "Thinking and planning, dear heart—and not drinking, I might add."

"I am so glad for that," Libby said. "We had been wondering."

"We?" His smile turned hard for a moment. "Well, I saw Lydia, and tumbled among all the news about furniture and draperies and modistes was the little item that you were to be married. I knew I had to make it here in time to stop you."

Libby shook off his hand and leapt to her feet. "I have no

intention of stopping anything," she said. "What are you planning to do?" she asked, her voice rising. "Add a hunting box in the Cotswolds, or . . . or a castle in some lonely outpost, to sweeten the pot? Do you think I have any intention of reconsidering your offer? Sir, you delude yourself."

He made his way back to the fireplace, to stand there with his hands deep in his pockets, his back to her. "I was thinking rather along other lines, Miss Ames," he said, his voice quiet so she had to strain forward to hear him. "I was rather hoping you would entertain the notion of marrying me."

He turned around then and watched the confusion on her face with something close to glee.

Her mind a muddle, she opened her mouth to reply when she caught a glimpse from the window of a man on horseback leaping the fence. She ran to watch as he threw himself from the lathered animal and pounded on the door.

In another moment she heard Candlow hurrying down the hall. She threw open the door. "Candlow, what is it?"

"Miss Ames, Preston here tells me that one of the oasting houses in Fairbourne has caught fire. I am to send over whatever servants we have to help with the bucket crew."

"Oh, by all means, Candlow. We will come, too."

The duke look at her in surprise. "I do not think that is necessary, Libby. What good can we do?"

She looked beyond the duke to the butler. "Candlow, was anyone hurt?"

"There are several burned, miss, and some of them children."

Fairbourne was not far from the Casey holdings. All the neighborhood children picked in the hop gardens during the harvest. She felt an icy hand run its fingers down her back. She grabbed the duke by his lapels.

"You will drive me to Fairbourne," she ordered, "and if you do not, I will go anyway, so suit yourself, my lord."

He took her hand as she ran down the hallway. Mama met them at the entrance, a question in her eyes. Tears glistened on her lashes as Libby explained the urgency and hurried down the front steps, impatient to be off.

The duke helped her into the curricle, unable to hide his

distaste. "I do not understand what good you will do there," he said as he spoke to the horses and jumped them off at a trot.

"I have become amazingly proficient in these matters," she said, her eyes looking straight ahead at the smoke rising over the trees.

"Have you ever seen burns before, Libby? I thought not. Let us reconsider."

"No," she said quietly.

Others hurrying before them had knocked down the fence that blocked the shortest way to Fairbourne. He expertly turned the curricle toward the smoke.

"I wanted to speak to you before now, Libby, but I did not have the courage," he murmured as they sped along the road. "The thought of the rest of my life without you is insupportable, and . . . Libby, you're not listening to a word I am saying."

"What?" she asked, her eyes on the smoke. Twin plumes rose above the trees. "It must be two oasting houses," she said. The pungent smell of roasting hops became a gagging, bitter haze that burned the eyes and left them coughing.

Rearing and plunging, the horse would go no closer. Libby leapt from the curricle while the wheels were still turning; she waved a hand at the duke and ran ahead. She put her hand to her nose and gasped as the hot breath of the fire blew her way, bearing with it the overpowering stench of hops and the smell of burning flesh.

She heard the duke somewhere behind her, calling her name, but she ran closer, searching for them among the pickers who had gathered to watch. And then she saw them, Louis, Russell, and Brian and the others, standing with Maud by the hop bines. Libby counted quickly and said a prayer of gratitude.

Libby rubbed her eyes and shouted to Maud. "Where is he?"

"Oh, miss, where do you think? In there."

The oast house was still burning, but a fire brigade snaked its way to the cooling room and onto the roof, where men with blackened faces passed buckets. Libby ducked between the women and children and ran closer, peering through the choking haze that had settled over the entire hop garden.

There they were, Joseph and Anthony, struggling to pull someone from the cooling room next to the blazing kiln.

Anthony's jacket was on fire. She grabbed up a bucket and ran into the smoking room, pouring the water on him and then tugging his coat off.

He looked around in surprise as his smoldering jacket came away in her hands. "Libby, get out of here," he shouted.

"I will not," she shouted back, grabbing up another bucket and pouring its contents over Anthony and Joseph until they were both drenched and in less danger from the bits of flaming hops that popped around them.

By then others had joined them, pouring water on the cooling-room floor to keep it from lighting. Two pickers, shielding their eyes with their hands, rushed closer to the kiln to drag out the last man.

Libby turned away, her hand to her mouth, as Anthony grabbed her and pulled her close to him. "Take this one out," he said distinctly in her ear. "You and Joseph. I'll help with the other."

Gagging at the smell of burning flesh, she grasped the man under the armpits while Joseph, his eyes huge in his blackened face, took the man under the knees. Staggering from the weight, they carried him from the cooling room and set him on the ground, where Libby took a full bucket from Maud Casey and poured it over the man's leg.

"I can help," said a quiet voice at her elbow. She turned to see the duke with a bucket.

"Take it in there," she said, pointing to the cooling room. "The doctor needs it."

He ran inside and in another moment came out with a child overcome by smoke. Anthony walked alongside him, breathing into the child's mouth as they stumbled out together, arms around each other. The duke laid the child down and Anthony continued, breathing and then pausing and then breathing again.

The man with the burned leg moaned and tried to shift himself. Libby rested her hand on his chest and brushed the hair back from his eyes. His heartbeat was rapid, but steady.

In another moment, the child was crying and struggling to rise. Anthony sat back and pulled the boy into a sitting position, looking him over swiftly for further injury and then moving aside as the boy's mother, sobbing and calling his name, gathered her son into her arms.

Anthony crawled over to where she sat, hugging the man in her lap. Silently she pushed the spectacles back up on the doctor's nose and he looked up in gratitude. Joseph was there with the doctor's bag, handing him a pair of scissors. Without a word, Anthony cut away the man's trousers and stared at the leg. He sat there in silence until she wanted to scream, and then he patted the man on the chest."

"Your name, sir?" he asked.

"Tommy Lilburn, from Cratchmore," the man gasped. He reached up and grabbed the doctor's shirt. "Are you going to have to cut it off?"

"Not unless you are wild about being a one-legged beggar, Tommy," said the doctor. "I think I can do you a much better turn than that. It'll be painful, though."

Sweat broke out on the man's face. He nodded as tears of gratitude welled up in his eyes and streaked down his smoke-blackened face.

Anthony patted him. "Good lad. You'll be fine." He called to two hop-pickers, who came closer, their faces pasty under a layer of smoke.

"Take him on a board to the nearest house. I'll be with you in a moment." He held the man's hand, fingers on his pulse, as the hop-pickers ripped the door off the cooling room and brought it back. Lips tight together as the man cried out, Anthony gentled him onto the board and nodded to the pickers.

"What are you going to do?" Libby asked as the crowd parted for the bearers and the wounded man.

"Just clean it up. It's not as bad as he thinks, thank the Lord, but he'll have a few painful days."

She took his hand. "I can help."

Anthony touched her cheek. "You would, wouldn't you? I don't ask it. What you can do is sit with that man over there until his family gets here for him. Just hold his hand."

"No," said the duke, pulling her away and putting his arm around her.

Libby leaned against him, grateful for his shoulder.

"She shouldn't even be here," said the duke. "This is no place for a lady. What's the matter with you, anyway?"

Anthony looked at them. His glance went from the duke to Libby, and his eyes, red from the smoke, seemed suddenly to fill with despair.

"I do ask her help," he said.

"By God, it's the last thing you're going to ask of this lady," said Benedict.

"Is it?" Anthony asked, and then his attention was claimed by a woman clutching his arm. "Maybe I have asked too much."

"No, I don't . . ." Libby began, but the duke only tightened his hold on her.

"I think you have, Dr. Cook."

The two men looked at each other through the haze of the now-smoldering oasting house. Then the doctor turned to grab up his bag. Libby shrugged off the duke's arm and hurried to the man who lay quiet on the cooling-room floor. She hesitated and looked at Anthony, wanting with all her heart to follow him.

He knelt by her, but said nothing.

"Anthony, I . . ."

He tried to smile and failed. "I wish I showed to better advantage, Libby, against that paragon, but I suppose that is not the issue now, is it?"

"You don't . . ."

He did not hear her. "Sometimes when you have done everything you can, you just have to sit back and let nature take its course. That's another rule of medicine. I suppose it's a rule of life, too. I'm sorry, Elizabeth."

His words sounded so final. "Will I see you tonight at dinner?" she asked, her voice unsteady.

"I think not," he replied. "No sense in flogging this dead horse."

He got up and started after the hop-pickers, looking back at her as if he did not expect to see her again. He started to say something, but shook his head and turned away.

20

LIBBY watched him go. The duke knelt beside her, his face set, as she sat by the man on the floor. In a few moments, his wife arrived, her hands smelling of washing soap. She helped him to his feet—scolding her man about taking her away from the washboard—and bore him away from the dispersing crowd.

The fire was out now and a slight breeze cooled them, clearing out the smoke. Both oasting houses connecting to the cooling room were blackened cones. As she watched, the far one crumbled in on itself with a crash, sending up a plume of ash that set them coughing again.

"Come away, Libby," urged the duke.

Maud Casey hugged her and brushed off the front of her dress with a bit of sacking. "Miss Ames, you'll become as ramshackle as we are if you stay around here much longer."

Libby managed a brief smile. She did not look down at the ruin of her dress, but allowed the duke, his arm about her waist, to lead her away.

In another moment he had lifted her into his curricle. "I remember fires like that at Waterloo," the duke said as they started back toward Holyoke Green. "The smell washes out, but you never forget it. Libby, you don't belong in a place like this."

"Perhaps I don't," she agreed, her voice dull as she remembered the look in Anthony Cook's eyes as he turned away from her to follow his patient.

She started to tremble. Without a word, the duke pulled off his jacket and pulled it tight around her shoulders. His arm went around her waist again as he drove carefully down the road.

"Cry off, my darling," he said at last. "All you'll ever have here is hard work and worry."

She started to say something, but the duke was just warming to his subject.

"I can give you everything you want, my dear. You have only to ask and it will be yours, plus my name, of course," he added scrupulously.

She forced a smile. "Of course," she echoed. "Tell me what I will have, Nez."

"I have a beautiful town house on Clarges Street, my love," he said. "You may have your pick of estates for the summer and fall, but I prefer the one in Yorkshire."

"I am sure it is lovely," she said absently, her mind on the doctor.

"Oh, it is! And if you should wish to jaunter over to Paris, now that the monster is on St. Helena, we can do that in a trice, my dear. You have only to ask. I can give you anything."

Libby sat up straighter, listening to him with all her heart for the first time. "Anything?" she asked.

"Anything," he declared firmly.

She turned in the seat to face him. "Nez, tell me honestly. Have you ever had a mistress before? One? More than one?"

Startled, he allowed the horses to break their stride. He slowed the animals to a walk and then stopped the curricle. She watched the flush spread up his face.

"Well, yes, I have. They were pleasant connections which, I need hardly add, have been severed. When we are married, you need never fear such an entanglement again."

"Oh, really? Suppose you tire of me? You seem to be somewhat fickle, my lord duke," she said softly, twisting her hair about her finger.

He took her hand and kissed it, grimacing at the smell of smoke about her. "My dear, I am yours to command. I can give you anything." He laughed, sure of himself. "Even Copley's chocolates."

She laughed too, because he expected it, and took another long look at him. He was disheveled and dirty now, as she was, but everything that a woman would sigh for. Think hard, Libby, she told herself.

"Anything," the duke repeated, nonplussed by the look in her eyes.

She shook her head and sighed. "No, you cannot give me anything I want, Nez. I received a much better offer on the Brighton Promenade from Dr. Cook, and I think I will take what he offered me."

The duke looked at her in amazement and started to laugh. When she did not join in, he sobered. "I admire the doctor. I owe him so much, my dear. But what on earth can he possibly have to offer that I cannot give?"

"Only this, sir: his whole self."

As he sat in stunned silence, she let herself down from the curricle, folded his jacket, and handed it to him. "It's a flattering offer you have finally made me, Nez, but I still do not think we will suit."

"I don't understand."

She smiled up at the duke. "You probably would never understand, my lord."

"I realize Dr. Cook is an admirable human being," the duke stammered, "but surely you cannot love him."

She ducked under the fence that separated the Cook estate from Holyoke Green. "How odd this is," she said. "I do love him, sir. I can only thank you for pointing this out to me. Good day, my lord. Pleasant journey."

He called to her several more times, riding his curricle back and forth along the fence in mounting frustration before he snapped the whip over his horses and disappeared in a roar of gravel. She leaned her arms on the fence and watched him go. Do be careful on that rough stretch in front of my home, she thought. I do not think Mama would tend you with my sure touch, and I will be too busy tomorrow.

She listened to the crack of the whip and the sound of horses trotting. She listened harder, a frown on her face, even as she started to run. He was driving much too fast. He was out of sight now over the little rise, but she closed her eyes.

In another moment she heard it, the curricle sliding across gravel, the horses whinnying. Libby slid under the fence again and up the slope, standing still in surprise and then bursting into laughter at the sight below.

Nez sat cross-legged atop the curricle, which had slid onto its side and slightly into the ditch. The horses, ears laid back, struggled in the traces, but a quick glance told her that nothing was seriously wrong. She stood there in the road, hands on her hips, until the duke looked back and saw her.

When she did not run forward, he placed his hands elaborately on his chest, flopped backward, and slid off the curricle into the ditch.

In another moment, she heard him laughing. "Well, give me a hand at least, you heartless wench. I seem to have wedged myself into this ditch, Miss Ames. Miss Libby Ames, is it? I don't want to get it wrong this time."

She came around the curricle and he held up his hands to her. "This is the damnedest road, Miss Ames. I wonder that anyone has escaped with his life on it."

"Anthony rides it all the time, day and night, rain and fog, and we know how clumsy he is."

The duke fumbled with his waistcoat and raised his quizzing glass to his eye, staring her down. "He obviously has more lives than a cat, and more good fortune than he deserves, damn his carcass."

The curricle was only tipped partway into the ditch. While Libby kept the horses company, the duke managed to push it onto the road again. He walked around the curricle several times, surveying the damage, shaking his head. He stopped in front of her finally.

"This was all I meant to do the first time," he said. "Ah, well, I suppose I must take my name off the lists and retire from Kent. Do you really love him, Libby, I mean, really?"

"I do, Nez."

"I think it will take a bit of coaxing to get him back, my

dear," he said, and his voice was apologetic. "We seem to have hit him when his resistance was low, and no wonder."

"I can manage it," she said, and held out her hand.

"I don't doubt that for a minute," he replied softly. "Libby, I—"

"Goodbye, Nez. Don't make yourself a stranger if you should ever choose to come this way again."

He shook her hand, but did not release it. "I will be back to see you two." He raised his eyebrows. "Of course, I could still threaten to take up the bottle again if you don't marry me."

Libby kissed his cheek. "But you won't, my dear."

"No, I won't. I couldn't." He sighed and released her hand. "Do you love me just a little bit?"

"Just a little bit," she agreed. "But I love the doctor much more. Only think how comfortable I am about to make his life."

The duke groaned. "That is precisely what I do not wish to think about." He climbed back onto his curricle and tipped his hat to her. "Good day, you minx. God keep you both."

In a frame of mind that belied her dismal appearance, Libby strolled back to the house, humming to herself. She knew that Anthony would not come to dinner. He would likely send a polite little note saying that he had told the vicar, and that he wished her well in her new venture.

Well, sir, we shall see, she thought as she mounted the front steps two at a time and burst into the house.

Mama gasped in horror at the sight of her. She took in the stained and bloody dress and Libby's blackened face and arms, walking about her several times and then hugging her tight.

Libby hugged her back. "It was dreadful, Mama." She clung to her mother, thinking how much she would miss her in the coming days, but taking comfort in the knowledge that Mama would only be a field away.

"Where is the duke?" Mama asked finally.

"I sent him on his way, Mama," Libby said, and patted her mother's cheek. "Now, what would I do with a duke? This one didn't wear too well in a crisis, and he is a bit shopworn for me, I fear." She tugged at her hair, smelling the singed ends. "Oh, dear! And Anthony Cook has cried off. I wouldn't expect him for dinner. Tell me, can I find a bath, and soon?''

She sat in the bathwater, humming to herself, dribbling the sponge over the little places on her arms where the hops had burned her, hopeful that they would not show under her wedding gown. Her hair had been singed up the back and she would have to take the scissors to it.

She was still sitting in her bathwater when Uncle Ames arrived from London. Mama must have spent some time with him in the sitting room, because by the time she was dressed and downstairs again, he was drinking sherry thoughtfully.

"Puss, what are you up to?" he asked. "I already sent a wedding gift to Dr. Cook. Figured that under the terms of that abominable trust of my father's, I had better not give any of it to you."

She sat down next to her uncle. "You are a dear, sir."

"It's not nearly enough," he said gruffly, and smiled when she kissed his cheek. "Perhaps if you put it in the funds, it might be the bare bones of a hospital someday."

"What an excellent notion, Uncle William," she said, her voice serene. "We can add to it over the years."

Mama stood up and paced the room. "You are sitting there so calm. You have this day driven away the duke and your other prospect has changed his mind, and you sit there smelling of April and May. If I do not grow distracted with you, then I am an unnatural parent."

Libby laughed. "Mama, trust me. Candlow is lurking about in the hall, ready to announce dinner, and it is getting late. When dinner is over, I fear I am destined to come down with a fearsome case of . . . of something. It will require a hasty note next door. Put all your emotions into that note, Mama." She jumped to her feet, kissed her uncle on the cheek, and danced from the room. "Do your best, Mama. I think I am getting sick already."

After a leisurely dinner that tried her mother to the outmost limits, Libby went upstairs and straightened her bedroom. She finished packing her clothes and boxed the books. She opened the wardrobe for another look at her wedding dress and sighed with delight, shaking out the material and listening to the rustle of the taffeta. Mama will be so pleased as I crackle down the aisle tomorrow.

A look through her bureau turned up a nightgown of ecru lace so impractical that she had stuck it in the back of the drawer years ago and forgotten about it. In another moment, she was out of her clothes and into the gown. She looked at herself in the mirror, blushed, and then laughed.

The bed was softer than she remembered, and she realized it had been so long since she had enjoyed a peaceful night's rest. Likely there would be none in the future, either. There would be a husband to love as well as time permitted, and children to tend, and people knocking at all hours of the night. She put her hands behind her head. *If it gets too uncontrollable, I can kidnap Anthony every so often and drag him to Brighton for a day or two. I doubt we'll ever get up to London.*

Ah! She heard the sound of something crashing over in the front hall and put her hand to her mouth, her eyes merry. Footsteps pounded up the stairs. *Taking them two at a time, are we, Doctor?* she thought as Dr. Cook opened the door and came into her room.

"I came as fast as I could, Elizabeth," he said, and he was out of breath.

He had washed and changed, but his eyes were still red from the oast fire. He carried his black bag and he was giving her the professional eye.

He put the bag on the end of the bed and came closer. "Your mother said you were fearsome sick, Elizabeth. Where does it hurt?"

She patted the bed and he sat down. She pointed to her breast. "Right here. I think there is something wrong with my heart."

He stared at her, vastly suspicious. "There's nothing wrong with your heart, Elizabeth Ames."

"Oh, but there is," she insisted.

"Oh, very well," he said, and rested his head against her bosom. "I do not know what the duke will think of this, Libby. He will call me out," he grumbled, his voice muffled by her gown.

"I sent the duke away, my dear Doctor," she said, and rested her hands lightly on his hair. "Oh, and look, you have singed your hair."

He tensed, but did not raise his head from her breast. "You did what?"

"The duke promised me marriage and the moon and stars. I sent him away because you made me a better offer in Brighton. Now, are we going to do this thing tomorrow or not?"

Her fingers were twined in his hair now. He removed his spectacles and set them on the floor beside the bed, but still remained where he was. He kissed her breast once and then again more thoroughly, and reapplied his ear to her heart.

"Egad, woman, this is serious," he said, sitting up at last. "I've never felt such a racing heartbeat. Let me check that again. There's a good pulse in the neck."

Her arms tightened around Anthony as he kissed her throat and then laid his head on her breast again. "Confirmed. You are in serious trouble. Elizabeth, I love you."

He was silent for a long while. She felt his eyelids close against her breast and she started to chuckle.

"Anthony, are you going to sleep?"

He nodded, sat up, patted her hip, and moved her over so he could lie down beside her. "Yes." He put his arm under her waist and gathered her close to him as his eyes closed.

She knew his habits by now. In a few minutes he opened his eyes and smiled at her.

"Tommy Lilburn?" she asked, her fingers tracing the hop burns on his face, wondering how she could ever have thought the doctor homely.

"He'll be fine. I'm going back there now. As soon as the wedding is over tomorrow, I'll have to be with him, at least for a little while longer. I'm sorry, my heart, but that's how it is."

She kissed him on the mouth, her arms tight around him. "I know how it is. I am sure your father will escort me home."

"The books are still everywhere in my room."

"On the bed, too?"

"No! Elizabeth, you are a bit of baggage. I wonder that I did not see this sooner."

She smiled and rested her head on his chest, listening. "You appear to have the same affliction I do, Anthony. Surely such a racing heart cannot be healthy."

"It is amazingly healthy, you dear one." He sat up reluctantly and put his glasses on again, reaching into his waistcoat for his prescription book. He thought a moment, scribbled something on it, handed it to her, kissed her, and left the room. She heard him whistling down the stairs.

Libby opened the little sheet. "Love in massive doses," she read.

The duke stopped for the night not far from Holyoke, ignoring the stares of the ostler, who whistled at the damage to his curricle. He spoke for a room and dinner, and went outside again to stroll up the slight incline.

He sniffed the breeze, breathing in the subtle fragrance of roasting hops that filled the night air. Tears came to his eyes, and he knew then that he would visit the Cooks occasionally, but never during this season.

The smell of autumn was in the air, too. It would be followed soon by winter in this lovely garden spot of England. Libby would be carefully indoors, caring for her doctor, and watching at the window when he was gone. She would scold him, and bully him, and cry over him, and love him with the fierceness that was her nature. And the damned thing was, the doctor would accept it all in that calm way of his and spend a lifetime showing his appreciation.

Libby will never miss me, he thought, as he swung his quizzing glass round and round on his finger. I hope I am loved like Anthony Cook some day.

He chuckled to himself. I could return tomorrow for the wedding and when the vicar got to that part about "let him now speak or else hereafter for ever hold his peace," I could create a fearful row that Holyoke would cackle about over tea and remember for years to come.

But it wouldn't change anything. Libby knew her own mind now and had found what would make her happiest. I must do the same.

He started back toward the inn. But I do believe I will drop a vulgar load of blunt on the doctor and tell him it is for a hospital and he had better by damn name it after me. That will set the cats meowing in Kent and keep him on his toes with that beautiful wife of his.

Yes, I'll do that first thing I get to London tomorrow. God keep you, Mrs. Anthony Cook.

MISS CHARTLEY'S
GUIDED TOUR

For Rosalind Barrow,
my sister-in-law

Prologue

I f he were a wagering man, he would have bet houses, lands, horses, and hounds that he was the first of his line to ride to his wedding in a hired conveyance.

The thought afforded no pleasure, only a deep washing of shame that flooded his body from face to toes. He closed his eyes against it, only to see himself again as though it were early morning, stumbling into the alley off St. James Square and falling to his knees on the cobblestones, overcome by the enormity of what had happened.

"My God, what have I done?"

It was the first thing he had said aloud in hours, and his words made him jump and then grasp the hanging strap in the hackney. He gripped it tight, retracing in his mind the long walk back to his own flat on Curzon Street, well-wrapped in his opera cloak, head down, praying no one would know him, or speak to him, or wish him congratulations.

He opened his eyes and sobbed out loud, seeing again the pile of bloody clothes he had ripped from his body as if they had burned him, standing naked in front of his mirror and not having the courage to look himself in the eye.

The cold that covered him then, covered him still. He was still shivering, still trembling like an old man with palsy. After he had dressed himself he had tried and tried to pick up the little wedding ring on his bureau. It had taken both hands, and then he had dropped it twice before seeing it into his pocket.

The clothes jumbled about him on the floor he wrapped in his opera cloak and carried down the stairs and into the alley. A quiet walk behind the row of flats and then the bundle was stuffed deep into someone else's ashcan.

There was no time to speak for his curricle from the

stables. He had hailed a hackney and directed the Irishman sitting on the box to St. Alphonse on Wadlington Lane, his fiancée's special choice because she loved the stained-glass windows and the choir screen.

The driver looked at him carefully, and his heart dropped to his shoes and stayed there. "Are ye all right, sor?"

He had nodded, too devastated to speak. If I open my mouth, I will tell him everything, he thought. No one must ever know.

The journey that he wished would take years was over in a matter of minutes. The hackney stopped and the driver sprang from the box and stood by the door, hand on the latch. "St. Alphonse, sor," he said.

"Oh, drive on, please. Just a little farther."

After another careful look and a shake of his head, the driver returned to the box and clucked to his horse. When they were beyond the church, he slowed again, and rapped on the roof.

He had no idea how much money he gave the driver. The man sucked in his breath and bowed, so it must have been more than patrons usually flicked his way. He turned to go, and the man grasped his arm. Again the chills traveled the length of his body.

"You'll not be calling the constable and telling him I robbed you, now, will you, sor?"

He waved the driver away and started back toward St. Alphonse. The clock in a tower several blocks distant chimed twice; he was already half an hour late. He wiped the sweat from his face, unmindful of the cold wind that blew off the river. At least all the wedding guests would be inside. He would be far to the front, next to the altar, and if he looked a little pale, his friends and relatives would put it down to wedding jitters.

He forced himself to hurry. His best man had never been distinguished for his patient temperament and was probably even now wearing a rut in the carpet. And his fiancée?

He broke into a run which ended on the bottom steps

leading to the massive front door of St. Alphonse's Church. Already a crowd had assembled, a collection of children and poor people from the neighborhood, who knew that the gentry inside were inclined to be generous when they came out after a wedding. And failing that, there were pockets to pick.

But the people on the steps were talking among themselves, casting a glance at the church now and then, and laughing behind their hands. Some were already beginning to move away.

He mounted the steps, two at a time, and stood by the entrance with another crowd of more brazen folk, bits of London chaff blown there by news of a wedding. He stood next to a man who balanced on one leg and a peg, a man who nudged him and winked.

"I disremember when ever I saw *this* happen before. And what a crime, I say. Look there at that pretty little lady."

"Yes, look," chimed in the woman on the other side of Peg-leg. "You should have seen her skip up the steps. And such a smile on her face! You could have lit lighthouse lamps from that smile."

He could only groan inwardly as another great tide of shame washed over him.

Peg-leg shook his head. "And now her face is whiter than her dress. There's one gentleman ducking and running in this city who ought to be pulled up sharp-like. See her there?"

He looked where Peg-leg pointed. The doors were open and there she sat in the vestry of the church, flowers drooping out of her hand, her face a study in shock. Her brother was speaking to her, kneeling by her, his hand on her back. She drew away from him. When her father squared his shoulders and started up the aisle toward the altar to make an announcement, she burst into tears, helpless tears that he knew would ring in his mind and soul for the rest of his life.

The clock in the tower chimed the half-hour. From habit he pulled out his pocket watch and clicked it open. Two-thirty. He snapped it shut and shoved it back in his pocket, feeling as he did so the wedding ring.

He couldn't leave London fast enough.

1

When the coachman blew on his yard of tin and signaled their approach to King Richard's Rest, Omega Chartley pulled her mother's watch from her reticule, snapped it open, and examined it. They were precisely on time. The thought pleased her, as all perfect things did, and she smiled to herself.

The loudly dressed fribble sitting opposite her mistook her smile for approval of himself. He sat a little straighter and tugged at his wilted shirt points, smiling back and revealing a mouthful of improbable porcelain teeth.

Omega snapped the watch shut with a click that made the vicar next to her sit up and peer around in fuddled surprise. She fixed the forward young man across from her with the same quelling stare that had reduced many an unprepared student of English grammar to visible idiocy. The man gulped and looked away as the color drained rapidly from his face.

It was high time she squelched his pretensions. Earlier that morning, when she was dozing off as a result of her sleepless night in the last inn, someone (she suspected the man with porcelain teeth) had prodded her feet in a scarcely gentlemanlike manner. It would never have done to call attention to the matter; how nice that she could put him in his place now.

"So the rain has finally stopped," remarked the clergyman on her left as he pulled himself awake and tried valiantly to fill in the awful silence caused by Omega's setdown.

She returned some suitable, if vague, answer and looked out the window. The rain had stopped, but there was no lifting of the gray covering that had settled over the gentle hills and valleys. All was gray. It was not a propitious beginning to her holiday.

Throughout Plymouth's dreary winter and spring, when each day was done and she had corrected papers until her eyes burned, she had treated herself each night to a few moments with *Rochester's Guidebook of England for Ladies*. By the sputter and stink of the work candles that Miss Haversham grudgingly provided for her teachers, Omega Chartley had plotted out the journey that would take her from Plymouth on holiday.

At first the holiday had no plans beyond an excursion to Stonehenge on the Plains of Salisbury ("Entirely suitable for ladies not easily exercised by thoughts of druidical rites," according to the *Guidebook*), and then beyond to the Cotswolds and back again. When, in early spring, a letter had arrived from St. Elizabeth's in Durham with a coveted contract to teach English grammar in the wilds of north England, the holiday turned into a move.

Other than a brief trip to Amphney St. Peter for Alpha's wedding, she had not left Plymouth in eight years. Omega could claim no attachment to the damp seacoast town other than the fact that it was far removed from anyone she once knew. Miss Haversham's Academy for Young Ladies would not bring her face-to-face with any bad memories.

For several years, Alpha Chartley had tried in vain to draw her from Plymouth to Amphney St. Peter. Omega would have none of it; she had chosen her exile and there she would remain. And so she would have, had not the letter come from her own former teacher, advising her of the vacancy and requesting that she apply for it.

And so Omega had applied. She was weary of the gray ocean. She could hide in Durham as well as Plymouth and teach mill owners' daughters instead of the offspring of sea captains. The money was better too. She was on the shady side of twenty-six, and needed to think about her future.

But there was the present to contend with now, and the clergyman who bumped her as he gathered together his belongings.

"Pardon, miss, pardon," he said, his face as red as Mr. Porcelain Teeth's waistcoat.

Omega smiled to reassure him, and made herself small in her corner of the mail coach. She sighed inwardly and wondered if the time would ever come when she would feel at ease traveling on the common stage.

The pretentious young man left the coach as soon as it rolled to a stop, not glancing her way again. The vicar followed and then stood by to give her a hand out.

As she was bending out of the coach and reaching for his hand, a traveling coach rolled into the innyard and dashed past the Royal Mail, spattering the vicar with mud. Omega leaned back inside to avoid the mud, but she was sure she could hear people laughing inside the closed coach.

The vicar sighed a prodigious sigh and extended his hand again. Omega took it and stepped lightly to the soggy ground. Without a word, she helped the clergyman brush the mud off his coat. She was used to tending young girls in similar circumstances and thought nothing of it.

"You are too kind, miss, too kind," said the clergyman, his face redder than before.

"It is nothing," she replied.

The vicar directed his gaze at the traveling coach, which had swung to a stop by the inn door. "You would think that the better classes would set the example for the rest of us, miss," he said darkly.

"Yes, you would think that," she agreed. No purpose would be served for the clergyman to know that when she had been a member of the "better classes" she had never thought of herself as an improving example. Better to let him labor under the misapprehension that his betters really were better.

When the largest chunks of mud had been returned to the innyard, she retrieved her traveling case from the coachman and followed the vicar into the taproom. The inmates of the private coach were nowhere in sight, and the landlady was just returning to her guest register.

Omega spoke for a room, but turned down the offer of a private parlor. Too many of those would end her trip far south of Durham, as much as she would have enjoyed the comfort.

"And may I have my dinner brought to me?" she asked.

"Of course you may, Miss Chartley," said the landlady. "Only you must please wait until I have served the members of that private coach and four."

"I understand," Omega replied. Her head was beginning to ache, but it would hardly have been fair to blame it on the private coach and four.

The room was small and cool, with the lingering scent of cigar smoke. After the landlord deposited her trunk on the floor with a thump, Omega went to the window and opened it, leaning out and breathing in the fresh smell of countryside after a rain. Her room fronted the street, but beyond the busy thoroughfare were the haying fields. She could make out sheep on the hills, and as the wind blew, she caught the sound of their bells, one here, one there, almost an echo.

"I will not miss Plymouth," Omega said out loud, and smiled to herself. If she never again saw the mesmeric swells of greasy ocean or breathed in the pungency of tar and hemp from the ships, she would not mind.

Omega rested her elbows on the windowsill. As she watched, the sky reformed itself, the clouds parted, and the watery sun shone through for the first time since the Plains of Salisbury. The sky lightened, almost as if dawn were approaching, rather than dusk. People on the street hurried home to their dinners, and mothers called in their children.

At the end of the street, where it divided into two roads, men were dismantling a tent and folding it away into an already overloaded wagon. Another Waterloo fair, Omega thought.

She remembered the Waterloo fairs around Plymouth in the early weeks of July, the mad, joyous parades celebrating Wellington's victory in Belgium. Miss Haversham had permitted her to take some of the older pupils into the streets, where they all gazed in wide-eyed wonder at the French eagles and bloodstained battle flags of both sides carried through the shrieking crowds.

After that first night, they did not return. The spontaneous parades where children skipped alongside their parents gave way to vulgar burlesques of Napoleon and Marshal Ney with their trousers down around their ankles, as Wellington beat them with a broken sword.

Here it was, late August, and still the fairs continued, the sideshows moving from town to town, and people in villages more and more remote turning out to hear the stories of the Thin Red Line and the orchard of La Haye Sainte.

Omega refreshed herself with a splash of lavender water on her wrists and forehead, and then sat down with a book to wait for her dinner. Tonight, when the plates were removed and the fire was lighted, she would pull the lamp closer and work on her course outline in English grammar.

Her good intentions slipped away when the empty dishes were withdrawn and she was left alone with English grammar. After all that rain, it was too fine a night to be wasted on the subjunctive. The sky continued to lighten as more and more clouds scudded away like the Waterloo fair.

Omega pulled on her shoes again, gathered her shawl around her, and left the room, tucking in her curly hair where it always seemed to fly out from under her cap. She whistled to herself, looking around to make sure no one was within earshot, and pulled on her gloves as she hurried down the stairs.

She had no knowledge of the village, so she resolved to walk only to the end of the street where the road forked. The wagon was gone now; there would be no fair again until Harvest Home. She sniffed the air. It was late summer, but already there was something in the wind that smelled of winter. And then in January, when the dreariness of winter threatened to overwhelm, there would be that faintest hint of spring in the cold air. Another year would pass.

And I will be one year older, she thought.

She reached the fork in the road, stood there a moment,

and was preparing to turn back when she noticed a boy digging about in the garbage heap left by the Waterloo fair. Surely her eyes were deceived by the dusk. She looked again, squinting against the coming darkness.

The boy, scratching about in good earnest, did not pause in his rapid search through the rubbish. He couldn't have been more than ten years old. Omega stepped closer and watched him. His clothes were grubby about the knee and elbow in the fashion of little boys, but they were of excellent cut and fine cloth. His black hair was trimmed smartly, even modishly, in imitation of his elders. Her eyes caught the sparkle of the buckles on his shoes.

As Omega watched and wondered, the boy stopped and turned around. He looked at her in silence, as if wondering what she would do. Omega was too well-bred to show surprise, but she knew that the face was familiar.

It might have been the way he held his head slightly tipped to one side, or the way he pursed his lips. Whatever it was, she wondered if somewhere she had seen this boy before, or someone very like him.

He smiled at her, the uncertain, tentative smile of someone who knows he should not be pawing about in a midden.

"I thought I could find something to eat," the boy said at last.

He made a motion to leave, so Omega sat down on a tree stump. She did not want him to run away. "When did you last eat?" she asked, leaning forward and clasping her arms in front of her knees.

"Yesterday I found some apples." He grimaced. "They were too green by half, and my breadbox hurt for hours."

"Apples do that to me too," she said. "And do you vow never again to eat a green apple, and then break your promise next summer?"

He grinned. "Something like that," he agreed.

They regarded each other in silence. Omega heard voices; people were coming up the street from the direction of the inn. She did not recognize them from the mail coach. They must have been the contents of the coach and four.

The boy eyed them too. "You see, I am not good at this," he said at last.

"Are you running away?" she asked.

He measured her with his eyes for a moment, as if trying to gauge her response, and then nodded. "And I won't go back," he said. "No one can make me." He scrambled to his feet, as if fearful he had said too much.

Omega put out her hand to reassure him. "How can I help you?" she asked.

When he said nothing, she continued. "Would you like some food?"

He fixed her with that penetrating, naggingly familiar stare again, and then smiled in some relief. "I would like that above everything else," he admitted, "but it did not seem polite to ask."

Omega rose to her feet slowly so he would not bolt. "Then come with me to the inn, and let us find something."

"I should not," he said. "I think my uncle has set the Runners on me."

Her eyes widened. "The Bow Street Runners?" she asked. "Good God."

He realized he had said too much, and began to edge away from her.

"Oh, please don't run away," said Omega as the boy darted away from her.

He did not get far. He ran directly into the arms of the gentleman strolling with his companions toward the fork in the road. The man was thrown backward several paces by the force of the boy against him, but he did not fall, and did not lose his grip on the child, even as the boy struggled.

Omega hurried toward them.

"Was this snatch-gallows bothering you, miss?" asked the man, a bit breathless from the encounter. He gave the lad a shake.

"Oh, no, no, nothing like that, sir," Omega replied. "Please let him go. He means no harm, I am sure."

The man only tightened his grip, whirling the boy about and grabbing him by the hair. He pulled his head back for a good look, and jerked his head from side to side as the boy struggled.

"You'll hurt him," said Omega.

"You can't hurt scum like this," said the man to his companions, an elderly lady who stood a little back, and a younger woman who ignored the boy and stared instead at Omega Chartley.

The man took a firmer grasp on the boy's hair, making him cry out.

"Oh, please stop!" cried Omega, and took the man by the arm. He shook her off.

"And did you say something about the Runners, boy? Did you?" he asked again, shaking the boy. "Answer me!"

The boy sobbed, but he would not speak.

"I'm going to march you back to the inn and we'll see what we see," said the man.

Before he could act on his threat, the boy raked his heel down the man's shin. The man threw him off and into Omega's arms. Without even hesitating, Omega grasped the boy firmly by the shoulders, whispered "Run!" in his ear, and gave him a shove in the direction of the forked road.

Whatever possessed her, she could not explain even to herself, much less to the man who stood glowering at her. For all she knew, the boy was a desperate felon, wanted for crimes she couldn't even imagine.

In her heart she knew this was not so. Omega recognized the look of terror mingled with humiliation on the boy's face. It could have been her own face eight years ago, chalk white and on the edge of tears. No one had helped her then, but that had not stopped her now.

The man could scarcely speak. He worked his mouth open and closed a few times like a hooked fish. "You . . . you let him go!"

"She did more than that," declared the young woman, who had watched the whole incident. "She gave him a push. I saw her." The woman looked back at Omega again. "And *wherever* do I know you from?"

Omega said nothing to her. She squared her shoulders and looked the man right in the eye, even though her knees trembled. "Yes, I let him go. You had no right to treat him so roughly. If the Runners want him, they can find him."

Pulling her skirt closer to her and settling her lips in what Alpha called the "Chartley schoolteacher look," she shouldered her way past the trio on the sidewalk and walked toward the inn. She wanted to break into a run, as though she were pursued by barking dogs, but she did not.

"Did you ever?" she heard the old woman say.

At the woman's words, Omega squared her shoulders again and gave her head a little toss. Instantly she regretted the gesture. She heard the young woman behind her gasp. "I know her now!" she said. "Oh, Mother, do you not remember? I have been puzzling and puzzling where I have seen her before. Oh, Mother! How could you forget? Remember the Bering-Chartley wedding? Oh, Lord, the wedding of the Season!"

Omega sucked in a ragged breath and hurried faster, lengthening her stride and putting distance between herself and the voices and stares. Another hundred feet would put her back at the inn. She could walk calmly inside and then scurry up the stairs and hide in her room until the morning, when the private coach and four would depart. Omega gave herself a mental kick for succumbing to the blandishments of a fine evening and forsaking the safety of English grammar.

A hand reached out and touched her sleeve as she entered the inn, her eyes on the stairs. She whirled around to see the landlord, who stepped back, frightened momentarily by the look in her eyes.

"Miss? Miss? Did you not hear me? I must request your presence in the taproom."

She shook her head. "I have a headache," she managed.

There was another, stronger hand on her elbow, and she found herself propelled into the taproom. "Sorry, Miss . . . Miss . . ."

Omega did not enlighten the man who bullied her into

the taproom. She did not even glance at him as she found herself pushed gently down into a chair.

"I really must protest," she said faintly to the landlord. To her own ears her voice sounded no louder than a cricket sawing on the hearth. Miss Omega Chartley, who by the mere shifting of her eyes could send a whole rank of fourth-form students to the brink of the valley of the shadow, was reduced to complete submission.

Omega stared straight ahead, and a red-whiskered man intruded upon her view. He smelled of cigar smoke and horse sweat, with the odor of greasy leathers thrown in. She could not bring herself to stare at him, but abandoned herself to the perusal of his muddy boots, which, from the looks of them, had never met the acquaintance of a blacking rag.

When he spoke again, his voice was kind enough. "I did not mean to give you a start, miss, but I'm speaking to everyone at the inn, ladies not excepted." He sat down directly in front of her. "It has been my experience that ladies are more acute observers than toffs, any road."

"How, sir, may I help you?" she said in a frosty voice that would have sent her brother, Alpha, into a fit of giggles.

He said nothing, only watched her. It was not an unkind stare, merely a businesslike one.

Omega folded her hands in her lap. "What is it that you wish from me, sir?" she asked again.

He leaned toward her, resting his elbows on his knees. "I'm a Runner, ma'am, from Bow Street. Have you heard of it?"

She nodded and looked down at her hands, unclenching them slightly when she noticed how white her knuckles were. He followed her gaze, but made no comment.

"You have the advantage of me, sir," she said. "What is it that you wish?"

"I'm asking all the patrons at every inn, lodging house, and flea palace between here and Oxford. Have you see a lad about ten with black hair and brown eyes?"

She had. "Sir, you could be describing half the little

boys in England. Does he have a name?'' she temporized, not wishing to answer him if she could help it.

"Answers to Jamie. James Clevenden. He's a runaway, miss."

The sap in a log popped on the hearth and Omega jumped. The Runner watched her. "Have you seen the lad, miss? Answer me, now."

She opened her mouth, but someone else's voice came out.

"Yes, she knows him. Ask her how she let him escape from me."

It was the man from the road. Omega didn't bother to glance around. She wasn't sure that she could have. Her body felt as though it had turned to ice.

The Bow Street Runner said nothing to her, only looked at her. Everyone in the taproom was silent. The occupants of the room did not look at her, but she knew they were listening, judging, forming their own opinions.

"I came across the boy where the road forks," she said in her quiet voice. "He was scraping about in a midden."

"Tell the Runner how you gave that cutpurse a push and told him to run when I tried to do my citizen's duty and stop him," insisted the man.

"You were hurting him," she protested. "I would do the same for anyone."

The silence thickened like pudding. The Runner slapped his knees again and stood up, towering over her. "Could you tell me where he went?" he asked.

She shook her head.

"Does that mean you don't know, or you won't tell me?" persisted the Runner.

Omega stood up to face him. On her feet, she felt as though she were standing in a hole in front of him. What would a big man like this do to a boy like Jamie if he found him? She didn't want to consider it.

"It means, Mr. . . . Mr. . . . ,"

"Timothy Platter, ma'am."

"It means, Mr. Platter, that I do not know where he went," she said steadily. "It also means that even if I did know where he was, I am not sure that I would make it my earnest desire to enlighten you. He was terrified of something, or someone, Mr. Platter. And now, if you will excuse me, I really have nothing more to say."

The Runner adopted a more placating tone. "Miss, it is my charge and duty to return him to his uncle, who misses him surely. He means the boy no harm; nor do I. This is my job, and it keeps my wife and kiddies from eviction."

She could not doubt the sincerity in his eyes. For the smallest moment, she felt a wavering of her own conviction. But only for a moment. "I still have nothing to say, Mr. Platter. Please excuse me."

The Runner put out a hand as if to detain her. She stared him down, grateful that he could not see how her knees were trembling. Omega turned and swept out of the taproom, pausing in the doorway and gazing for a small moment at the two women who stood between her and the stairway. Head high, she stalked past them.

"Omega Chartley," said the younger woman. "Omega Chartley."

"Yes," Omega Chartley whispered back, and fled up the stairs, her courage gone.

In the safety of her room, she could only lean with her back against the door. Omega listened for footsteps, but no one followed. Gradually her breathing became calm again. With steadier fingers she undid the ribbons of her bonnet and set it carefully on the bureau. She looked in the mirror and sighed. Her brown curls were all wild around her face. Absently she twisted one curl around her finger and let it spring back.

"Botheration!" she exclaimed out loud, touching her curls again. There had been a time at the opera when Matthew Bering, bored beyond belief, twisted her curls around his fingers until she was in whoops and the Prince Regent himself stared at them from the next box, his quizzing glass raised.

"Botheration," she said again. Botheration that after eight years, one little difficulty could set off a flood of memories. Omega could still remember his fingers gently twisting the curls on her head. She remembered how she had gone so peacefully to sleep that night, sniffing the

odor in her hair of the lemon-scented Spanish cologne that
he always wore.

Omega moved away from the door and sat down at the
table. The English grammar she had abandoned was open
on the table. She lit the lamp and pulled it closer, feeling as
put upon, tried, and tested as one of her own pupils.

"I wish people would leave me alone," she said, and
copied that sentence in a neat, round hand onto the page in
front of her. She put down the pen and looked at her
handiwork. A reluctant smile came to her lips, and then a
chuckle. "Omega, you are a goose," she said. "You would
have your holiday, so you had better enjoy it."

In another moment she would be telling herself to write
fifty times, "I will not think about Matthew Bering
anymore."

"Or, at least, only five times a day instead of ten," she
amended. "That would be progress."

She went to the open window and leaned her elbows on
the sill. The sky was dark now, and all was quiet on the
street. "Jamie Clevenden, where are you?" she wondered
to herself. The evening was fine enough, but it would be
cool before morning.

"Do look out for the Runner, lad," she said quietly.

As she spoke, someone lit a match below her window.
Soon the smell of cigar smoke drifted to her nose. She
looked down. She could discern the bulky shape of the
Bow Street Runner, standing under her window as calm as
a deacon.

She leaned out further and grasped the shutter. "You
will likely rot your lungs out with that foul weed, Mr.
Platter," she said quite distinctly in her best educationist's
voice.

Omega Chartley pulled the shutter closed with a bang,
but not before she heard Timothy Platter laugh.

Omega took off her dress, shook it out, and draped it
over the chair. Already it was sadly wrinkled from only
two days of travel. Tomorrow she would trade it for her
other traveling dress, and when she arrived in Oxford,
would pause for a general laundering, if the inn was
respectable and the price not too dear.

She pulled on her nightgown and tucked her wayward curls under her sleeping cap. On her knees, she clasped her hands and rested them on the edge of the bed. On a typical night she prayed for the poor mad king, the prince regent, the armies of Wellington, the Archbishop of Canterbury, Alpha and Lydia Chartley, and the little Chartleys.

Tonight she began with the Chartleys and then proceeded directly to Jamie Clevenden. "Keep him safe, mighty God, and for goodness' sake, direct him to return home before he gets all of us in trouble."

Omega paused for a long time and then rested her cheek on the bed. She couldn't bring herself to say it out loud—she never did—but she thought it. And, Lord, please bless Matthew Bering, wherever he is.

2

The sun woke Omega the next morning. She burrowed deeper into her blankets for a moment, and then reached for *Rochester's Guidebook of England for Ladies*. She turned to the chapter on the Cotswolds, running her finger down the list of villages. Bisley, Sapperton. Cirencester, Siege of 1643.

Omega slammed the book shut. How singular it was that the tempting vision of sieges and castles that had kept her going throughout Plymouth's gray winter had so little attraction for her now. She put her hands behind her head and stared at the ceiling. "You're being out-of-reason foolish, Miss Chartley," she scolded herself. Jamie Clevenden was probably curled up in a warm hayloft right now.

She picked up the *Guidebook* again, resolutely shutting out of her mind the picture of a hungry boy scratching about in a garbage heap. She would travel as far as Cirencester today, replaying in her mind the battle of the

Cavaliers and the Roundheads as she wandered through the town. The next day it would be Chedworth, and perhaps a glimpse of the famous Roman mosaic floor. And so on to Oxford, to Amphney St. Peter to visit the Chartleys, and eventually Durham, and then the term would begin.

Omega presented herself in the taproom to request a small breakfast in her room. Timothy Platter was there, dirty boots propped up on the table, head well back, mouth open, snoring.

"Will he *never* leave?" Omega whispered.

"Exactly what my wife is saying, miss," the landlord said. "And he told me he wants to see you again. I told him, 'What can a lady have for you?' and he gave me such a wink. Miss Chartley, we'd all prefer to see his back." He brightened. "Can I have my wife fetch you some breakfast?"

She had been hungry before she spotted the Runner. "No, no, I think not. Tell me. When does the mail coach arrive?"

"Give it a few minutes, Miss Chartley." The landlord glanced over at the snoring Runner. "We'll see you make it."

She thanked him and wandered outside the inn, hoping that Jamie Clevenden would be long gone. The air was cool and Omega wondered if the boy had a coat somewhere.

She turned the corner and found herself nose to nose with the Bow Street Runner. He had come so silently that she had not heard him. How such a big man could move so quietly on his feet provided a moment of marvel that was quickly replaced by anger.

"*Who* would set a Runner on a small boy?" she cried.

"You'd have to ask Lord Rotherford," snapped the Runner, obviously as tired of her as she was of him. He touched her sleeve as if to detain her. "If you have something to tell me . . ."

She shook him off. "You're the last person I would ever tell, even if I did know anything, which I do not!"

She stomped inside, up the stairs, and slammed the door, hoping that Timothy Platter would hear it. Omega sat down on the bed and waited for cold reason to wash over her.

It did not. The more she thought about Jamie Clevenden, the more she wanted to march back down the stairs and slap Timothy Platter silly. And that would never do.

She had seen beggars before. Plymouth was full of them, old sailors too fuddled to climb a ratline anymore; young hard-faced women reeking of gin; children scarcely old enough to walk, sleeping in doorways. Omega had closed her eyes all her life to England's little miseries. Why was Jamie Clevenden so different?

"Because he has a name," she answered herself, "and he reminded me of someone."

And what on earth was such a well-dressed boy doing rummaging through garbage? And didn't that dreadful Mr. Platter mention something about a Lord Rotherford? The name was vaguely familiar to her from those days before she became a teacher.

Omega's agitation increased. She stalked about the room until the landlady scratched at her door.

"My boy will come for your baggage."

Omega nodded and dismissed her.

She was still sitting and staring at nothing when the innkeeper's boy tapped on the door. She nodded to him and he took her baggage downstairs. After another look around the room, Omega settled her bonnet on her riotous curls and stuffed the *Guidebook* in her reticule. She waited in the innyard while her baggage was tied on top of the mail coach.

She happened to glance up at the open door to the hayloft over the stables. Jamie Clevenden crouched there, looking down on the Runner. Timothy Platter stood below, hands in his pockets, rocking back and forth on his heels, puffing on his cigar until his head was wreathed in blue smoke.

Jamie shuffled his feet, and bits of straw drifted from

the open hayloft. She glanced quickly at Platter. The man remained with his back to the stables. Omega stepped away from the coach and made a shooing motion with her hands. Jamie ducked inside.

And then Omega Chartley's mind was made up. Cirencester and the Siege of 1643 would have to wait.

"Remove my bags, please," she said in her clear voice.

Platter turned around, his eyes filled with surprise.

"But they're already tied down," the coachman protested.

"So they are. And they can be untied just as easily," she said. "The yard boy can take them to my room again."

Omega went inside the inn and retrieved the key that still lay on the desk. As she hurried upstairs, the coachman blew his horn and the mail coach left the yard. When her bags were back in her room, Omega retied her bonnet and left the room again.

She knew that Timothy Platter would be waiting for her, and she was not disappointed. With a nod in his general direction, she left the front entrance and walked at a spanking pace up the street. She was certain that Platter would follow her, and again she was not disappointed. Her irritation lessened as she heard his ragged breathing behind her. *I told him those cigars would rot his lungs,* she thought with some satisfaction. A little smile played about her lips as Timothy Platter began to cough and slow down.

Omega let up her relentless pace and stepped smartly into the little bakery she had noticed last night during her twilight stroll. "I'll have four of those rolls, a loaf of bread, and a pork pie," she said, taking the coins from her reticule.

The proprietor wrapped her order in brown paper and tied it with a flourish. Omega took it from him and went into the street again. Platter stood there, red-faced and out of breath.

"Sir, are you following me?" she asked him point-blank.

He blinked and had the good grace to blush. "Do you need to be followed?" was his recovery.

"Of course not," she said briskly. "I am twenty-six

years old, an educationist, and quite capable of taking care of myself."

"From the looks of that package," he growled at her, "you have a prodigious appetite too."

"Prodigious," she snapped, and set off at a rapid stride.

Without lessening her pace, Omega continued up one street, and traveled down the next street. She settled down finally in a small park and unwrapped the package, eating one roll and stuffing two others in her reticule.

She sat there until she was sure Mr. Platter had gone. If he were truly, seriously, looking for a runaway, he would not waste much time on her. He can call me an eccentric and tell his colleagues on Bow Street that he has finally met England's gorgon, she thought.

When the sun was high in the sky, she left the park and strolled back to the inn and went to her room. Leaving her bonnet on, she pulled a chair up to the window, but not too close, and sat watching the field where the roads forked. Nothing moved, and then she saw Timothy Platter, standing next to the entrance of the lending library, out of sight of anyone observing from the empty field.

"Drat you, Mr. Platter," she said. "Why won't you go away?"

She watched him a moment longer. He went inside the library. She stayed at the window, but he did not reappear.

Omega waited several more long moments and then went quietly down the stairs and into the yard, careful not to be seen from the street, where Mr. Platter inside the library might see her. She went into the stables, standing by the entrance until her eyes were used to the gloom.

No one was in sight. Gathering her skirts close around her legs, she climbed the ladder and found herself looking into the grinning face of Timothy Platter. Beyond him, his hands tied together, was Jamie Clevenden, his eyes red from weeping.

Platter held out his hand for her. Wordlessly she took it and he hauled her up into the hayloft. In silence she dusted off her dress and knelt by Jamie.

"Are you all right?" she asked, and brushed the tangle of hair back from his forehead.

The boy nodded. His lips were set in a firm line that again made her think she had seen him before.

"Sit down, Miss Chartley," said Timothy Platter. "You are not quite ready to take on Bow Street."

She couldn't disagree with him. She sat down.

"I could have you arrested, you know," he continued, "for interfering with the law." He took a deep breath, warming himself to the task. "You *knew* he was here, didn't you? And still you marched me all around Robin Hood's barn!"

Again Omega could not disagree with him.

Platter permitted himself a smile. He took out a cigar and stuck it, unlit, between his teeth. "I have the boy, and that's all I want. You can go now; I am prepared to be generous."

Jamie Clevenden began to cry, great gulping sobs that went right to her heart. Omega rose to her knees and turned toward him, taking him in her arms. She patted him, looking beyond him to the ladder, wondering how she could get them both away, when she noticed the ladder moving. Someone else was climbing up.

Omega prayed that it was the yard boy, and burst into noisy tears of her own. Out of the corner of her eye she watched Platter rise to his feet, shift the cigar from one corner of his mouth to the other, and come toward them. Omega cried louder as he approached masking the creak of the ladder.

The yard boy moved fast. Before the Bow Street runner could even turn around, the boy had brought down the muck-rake handle on his head. The cigar flew from Timothy Platter's mouth and he dropped to the hay with a thud.

"Here, untie the lad," said the boy, handing Omega a knife.

She did as he said, and in a second Jamie sat rubbing his wrists. The boy grabbed him by the arm and tugged him to his feet. "I hit that cove smartly, but he won't stay down," he said. "Hurry up!"

Jamie scrambled down the ladder, followed by Omega and the yard boy. Omega thrust Jamie at the boy. "Keep him close a moment more," she said, taking a swipe at the hay on her dress. "My money is with my baggage."

She forced herself to walk into the inn, sighing with relief to see the taproom empty. She walked quietly up the stairs, alert for every squeak and protest of the wood. Her key seemed to scream in the lock as she let herself into the room.

Her luggage was gone. She uttered a cry of dismay and whirled to the door again.

The landlord stood there, his eyes wide. "Mr. Platter ordered us to put your luggage on the noon mail coach that just left," he said. "He told us to address it to Bow Street."

She could only stare at him as her face drained of all color. "But everything I own is in those bags," she stammered.

"He said he was 'authorized,' " explained the landlord. "I'm sure if you explain it to him . . ."

Omega brushed past him. For all she knew, Mr. Platter was even now sitting up in the hayloft with an aching head. She ran down the stairs and into the yard again, grabbing Jamie Clevenden by the hand. She waved her thanks to the yard boy, who was again raking muck from the open stalls, the portrait of innocence.

Jamie needed no urging to keep up with her. Omega gathered up her skirts and ran for the woods, Jamie right next to her, matching her stride for stride.

She ran until her side ached. She stopped and sank to the ground, pulling Jamie with her. He made no objection. The only sound was their breathing. Jamie stretched himself out on the grass and stared up at the sky. He turned to look at Omega, a hint of brightness in his eyes.

"Oh, did you see how his cigar flew across the room?"

She nodded and laughed, taking off her bonnet and fanning herself with it. "I wish he had swallowed it."

Omega handed Jamie one of the rolls she had stuffed in her reticule. As he ate quickly and tidily, with the economy of the hungry, she opened her coin purse. The sight was daunting.

He finished the roll, carefully corralling the crumbs on the front of his elegant, dusty jacket and rolling them between dirty fingers into a little pill, which he popped in his mouth.

"Who are you?" he asked.

"Omega Chartley," she replied. "I am a teacher."

"Oh, you can't possibly be," he disagreed. "You're too pretty." He smiled. "I'm not sure that I would mind you."

She laughed out loud. "Oh, you would! I'll have you know I was the terror of Miss Haversham's Academy in Plymouth."

The dimple showed again. "Are you what my father would have called a 'prune-faced bluestocking'?"

"Most assuredly. Your father is right."

Jamie got to his feet then, as if reminded of the situation. "My father is dead," he said quietly. "We'd better go."

Omega held out her hand. "No, wait. You need to tell me what is going on." She stood up when he did not stop. "Jamie Clevenden, I just helped get you out of an awful scrape, and I've lost all my luggage *and* my money, and goodness knows, Mr. Platter may be preparing a rope for me at Newgate!"

He stopped then and hung his head. "I'm sorry. I never meant to cause you trouble."

A week ago, even last night, the loss of her money, clothing, and grammar books would have sent her into a fit of the megrims that would have consumed the remainder of her summer. Why isn't this bothering me? she asked herself as she came closer to Jamie and touched his shoulder.

"I know you didn't mean to cause me trouble. But please tell me . . . tell me what is going on?"

He did not answer her, but looked over his shoulder. "Do you think he will follow?"

"Oh, yes," she replied. A small shiver traveled the

length of her spine. Timothy Platter was not a man easily dissuaded.

"Then let us walk. I . . . I will talk then."

They walked on in silence. "Is your mother alive?" she asked finally, when he seemed disinclined to talk.

"No. She is dead too."

"And where is your home?"

He would not answer.

"Why are you running away?"

No answer.

Omega stepped in front of Jamie and put her hands on his shoulders. He shuddered at her touch, but he stopped walking. He looked her in the eye, raised his shirt, and bent over so she could see his back.

It was covered with welts, some raw, red, and weeping, others fading to a duller red. The skin was drawn and puckered, as if gouged and left to heal on its own.

"My uncle beats me," Jamie said, his voice calm, as if he were describing someone else. "I will not go back, even if he is my father's brother. He can send everyone on Bow Street after me, but I won't go back." Jamie tucked his shirt in again.

He had allowed her only a quick glimpse of his back, but as Omega walked beside him, she knew she would retain the ruin of Jamie Clevenden's back in her mind's eye longer than she would remember the ruins of Stonehenge or any other amazement listed in the *Guidebook*.

"Then where are you going?" she asked quietly. She brushed off a tree stump and sat down on it.

The boy continued on several paces and then looked back to see her sitting. He waited a long moment, and she held her breath while he considered his strategy and wrestled with the panic within him. To her infinite relief, he walked back slowly and sat down next to her.

"I have another uncle . . . Mama's only brother." He spread his hands out in a gesture of helplessness that lodged in her heart. "Mama said he lives somewhere in the Cotswolds." Again he made the gesture. "I just don't know where, and I'm hungry," he finished with all the logic of a ten-year-old.

She handed him the last roll. "Do you know his name?"

He shook his head. "He is the Viscount Byworth. Mama
. . . Mama always called him B, but that can't be his name,
can it?"

"No. It must be her nickname for him." Her face
brightened. "Oh, but what was your mother's name before
she married? Surely it would be the same as your uncle's."

Jamie's face fell. "I was four when they died, and my
Uncle Rotherford never spoke of her. I mentioned my
Uncle Byworth to him once, and he just laughed."

Omega sighed. "That's hardly a gentlemanly thing to
do."

"I looked in my Uncle Rotherford's atlas one night
when he was drunk, and found this." He pulled a page
from his pocket.

Omega smoothed it on her lap. The page had been
folded and unfolded so many times that the creases were
starting to rip, but she looked where Jamie pointed.

"See there, it says 'Byworth.' At least, I think it does."
Jamie took the page from her lap and cupped it in his hand
like a living thing and then folded it. "That is where I am
going." The assurance left his voice then, and for the first
time he sounded as young as his years. "Do you know how
far it is? Is this the right direction?"

"I . . . I don't know," she confessed. "And see here,
you have torn the section from the book and not left any
references."

Jamie sighed and put the scrap of paper back in his
pocket. "I was so excited just to see 'Byworth' that I didn't
think about that. But I have to find it, don't you see?"

Omega nodded. She took out *Rochester's Guidebook*
and thumbed to the section on the Cotswolds. Jamie gave
her the paper again and she turned it this way and that,
comparing it with the tiny map in the book. "Doesn't that
read 'age'? There, where you have folded it so many
times?"

Jamie squinted at the little paper. "It could."

"Perhaps it is Wantage," she said. "And if it is, then
your Byworth is about ten miles beyond."

"And if it is not?"

She rose to her feet. "We'll just have to try. And when we find your Lord Uncle Byworth or whoever he is, perhaps he'll have some ideas about retrieving my baggage from Bow Street."

"I'm sure he will. Mama was always used to say that there wasn't anything her brother couldn't do." Jamie darted ahead of her on the path.

Let's hope you are right, Omega thought grimly. Maybe he can also tell me what on earth I, a spinster educationist, am doing traipsing about just a jump ahead of the Bow Street Runners.

The thought made her giggle. She crammed her bonnet back on her head and hurried to catch up with Jamie.

3

If Omega Chartley had ever spent a more miserable night, she didn't know of it. They consumed the afternoon and early evening walking in a northeasterly direction that paralleled the main highway but did not come too close to it. Several times they heard the mail-coach horn. Each time, Omega wondered if her money and baggage had arrived in London yet, to be investigated and pawed over.

She had addressed her baggage to St. Elizabeth's in Durham. Suppose one of the Runners went there to await her arrival? The thought of a man like Timothy Platter invading the rarefied atmosphere of a very correct girls' school to inquire after the newly hired English teacher nearly made Omega gasp out loud.

I must devise a wonderful lie, she thought as she trudged along beside Jamie. That thought made her blanch again. It is amazing how rapidly one well-brought-up person can go to the dogs, Omega thought.

Only a day ago she was a proper, well-mannered lady of advancing years. In the course of twenty-four hours Omega Chartley had prevaricated, attempted to outwit an officer of the law, obstructed justice, permitted a wanted person to escape, and done nothing to prevent an assault. The rapidity of her decline made her blink. I have only to steal, commit murder, and perform a treasonous act to be perfect in my ruin, she thought, and smiled in spite of herself. Absurd.

The source of her misery was an unprepossessing barn, constructed perhaps during the late Ice Age of some nameless stone and roofed over with a sieve, which would have been wholly adequate before the rain started. By then, darkness was coming, and no other likely-looking possibilities for shelter sprang into view, which was just as well. An inn would have overdrawn the modest coins that she had in her reticule, and would have meant the scrutiny of a landlord. The barn it would be.

Omega took exception only when Jamie looked at the leaking cavern with a professional eye and then started for the loft ladder. She put out a hand to stop him.

"See here, Jamie," she protested. "Do you not think we would be drier on this lower level, with the overhang of the loft to protect us from that lamentable roof?"

Jamie appraised her with the look of One Who Knows. He shrugged. "I have found that there are more mice on the lower levels, where there is often grain spread around," he commented.

"Dear God," said Miss Omega Chartley faintly, and followed Jamie Clevenden up the ladder, already imagining little cadres of mice snapping at her heels. The prospect of sharing her chamber with rodents was even more daunting than the prospect of teaching gerunds to little girls who wished themselves elsewhere. Had there been room on the ladder, she would have passed Jamie.

They found a corner where the holes had not totally taken over, and settled in. There were vague rustlings in the hay, but Omega resolutely ignored them as she removed her bonnet and placed it in the driest corner she could find.

As the rain pelted down, a chill settled over the loft. Jamie edged closer, until he was leaning against her arm.

He was silent for the longest time, and she thought he had drifted to sleep, when he spoke.

"I like that," he said, and burrowed closer.

"What?" she asked.

"My mother smelled of lavender too," he said.

She smiled into the darkness. "I am surprised you can still catch the fragrance of it."

"Mama kept her dainties in lavender," Jamie said, his voice small under the pelting of the rain on and through the roof. "She would hand me her sachet bags and I would pummel them about until the lavender was properly stirred up." He sighed. "I kept one bag, but it doesn't smell anymore."

He was silent then. Omega wanted to put her arm about him. At Miss Haversham's, there had been numerous occasions, at first, when she had wanted to console a pupil, some of them scarcely more than babies, it seemed to her, but she had been dissuaded by Miss Haversham. "It's a hard world, Miss Chartley. The sooner they realize it, the better for their souls." And so Omega had not cuddled those little ones. Soon she never considered it. She was considering it now.

"I have—had—a pressed flower from my papa," she ventured tentatively. Papa had handed her the half-open bud during their last walk together about the gardens before she made that dreadful trip up the altar. The bud had never opened, but she had saved it.

"Where's your father now?" Jamie asked. He spoke a little loud, and she wondered if he was repeating himself because she had not responded the first time. How easy it was to forget oneself in this place.

"Oh, Jamie, he's dead."

He put his hand in hers.

The rain continued and the cold settled in. Why the rains of August were gloomy, Omega did not know, but it was so. Maybe it was because soon the birds would be flying south to the Azores and the leaves would droop and die.

Jamie sat in silence, doing nothing to solicit her sympathy, but Omega put her arm around him and drew him closer. He sighed and leaned against her, closed his eyes, and slept.

Sleep did not visit Omega so swiftly. No matter how devastating had been some of the events of the past eight years, this was the first time she had been wet, cold, and hungry. Her stomach rumbled, and she shifted slightly, so as not to awaken Jamie. She carefully pulled him over until his head was in her lap, and rested her hand on his arm.

Omega no longer mourned the loss of her trunk; she had no possessions that were irreplaceable. Everything of any value had been auctioned off after Papa's death. Even the loss of her money was less onerous than anyone could have told her it would be. She had only to apply to Alpha for a small loan, and he would find a way to cover it. And knowing Alpha, she believed he would chuckle over her mishap.

But what was she to do about St. Elizabeth's? It was the middle of August. Omega had a month until she was due in Durham. If none of the constabulary from Bow Street contacted the headmistress seeking her whereabouts, perhaps she could contrive to slip through this little detour of her journey. As she leaned over Jamie to protect him from some of the rain, Omega told herself that in the course of a day or two Jamie would be with his uncle the Viscount of Byworth, and the whole adventure would be something to laugh about with the Chartleys.

Provided they found the uncle. Provided Timothy Platter did not sniff them up first. Omega closed her eyes. I *will* sleep, she told herself. Things will appear in a better light in the morning. Omega did sleep then, her head nodding over Jamie.

What it was that woke her toward morning, she could not say. There was no sudden noise, no alarm, no indication of any disturbance. If anything, the night was quieter. The rain had stopped, and it was too early for the birds of dawn.

But something had wakened her. She sat silent in the cool darkness as some strange sense told her that the barn was occupied by others. She could not see them, but they were there. She made herself small in the corner and surprised herself by going back to sleep.

She woke when morning came, woke to find that Jamie had shifted and was curled up next to her, his head resting on his hands, a beatific smile on his lips that belied the dried streaks of tears through the dirt on his face. She listened to the rustle of mice about the vicinity of her bonnet and almost rolled over and went back to sleep again before she remembered the other occupants of the barn.

All was still. Surely her fears of the night were only a dream. She listened and heard nothing, but the feeling settled over her again that someone waited below.

Carefully, cautiously, Omega rose to her knees and stretched herself close to the edge of the loft, mindful not to waken Jamie. Holding her breath, she peered over the edge and into the eyes of a little girl, who lay on her back, looking up directly into Omega's face.

Omega's eyes widened. She watched in amazement as the little girl smiled at her, put her finger to her lips, pointed to the man sleeping beside her, and shook her head.

The man lay stretched out on his back, one arm under the girl's head and the other one placed on his chest. Omega looked again. He had no hand on the end of his wrist. His shirt sleeve had been pulled back, and his arm ended abruptly above his wrist in a mass of scars and rough-looking flesh.

How singular, thought Omega, too surprised to be repulsed by the man's deformity, or amazed by the girl's calm acceptance of her. Omega rested her chin on her hands and stared below. The girl had closed her eyes, her long black lashes sweeping against her cheeks. She appeared perfectly relaxed and not at all nervous under the scrutiny of a strange woman in the hayloft. How singular, thought Omega again, and redirected her gaze at the sleeping man.

He was tall, with several days' growth of beard on his chin. His hair was curly like her own, and richly black. He was dressed in soldier's breeches. His jacket lay nearby, draped on a piece of farm equipment, and he wore a frilled white shirt.

Omega peered closer. The shirt had been torn, bloodied, washed, and carefully sewn together again, but it was undeniably the shirt of a gentleman. Odd indeed, Omega thought as she raised up on her elbows and observed the scene below. She felt no fear, none at all, from these strangers. Omega smiled at the girl, who smiled back, sighed, rustled down further into the straw that was her mattress, and closed her eyes again. The man slept quietly.

That he was a soldier, there was no doubt. Whether he had only recently returned from Waterloo minus his hand, Omega did not know. And the little girl? Omega could only speculate.

For a woman who has spent considerable time in recent years avoiding people, you are surprisingly curious, Omega Chartley, she told herself as she settled her chin on her hands and promptly returned to slumber herself.

She woke with the sun in her eyes, dust tickling her nose. Omega sneezed enormously, prodigiously, making the kind of racket that would have caused her to rain coals of fire on the heads of her students committing such a solecism.

"Jesús, María, y José," said the little girl, who was wide-awake now and sitting up.

"Bless you," said the man, his voice a deep baritone.

"Goodness," said Omega. "Thank you," she continued, remembering her manners.

The little girl regarded Omega a moment and then dipped her fingers into a tin bowl. She took two more small bites, chewing thoughtfully, and then handed the bowl to the soldier. He gestured toward Omega.

"We saved you some. That is, if you'll be coming down . . ."

His voice had a singsong Welsh texture to it that was pleasing to the ears. Coupled with the deep tones that seemed to swell upward from the soles of his feet, the effect was altogether enchanting. Omega waited for the man to say something else, and then realized it was her turn.

"Oh, thank you," she said again. "But there is someone else with me, a boy. I'm sure he won't eat much," she added.

The man smiled. "Boys always eat too much." He cocked his head toward the girl. "Angela, what do you say?"

The child looked up at Omega. "We would not be good soldiers if we did not share," she replied quite seriously.

"Well, then, come down," said the soldier, getting to his feet and extending the bowl toward Omega.

Before she could speak, a shadow fell across the barn's entrance. Omega drew back, praying that she would not sneeze again. There was a space where the boards in the loft had warped and separated slightly. She put her eye to the hole.

Timothy Platter stood below in the entrance, holding the reins to his horse. He dropped the reins, but the horse followed him into the barn and stood cropping wisps of hay. Rumpled and dirty, Platter looked as though he had slept in his clothes. He walked the halting gait of someone who has spent the night in a most uncomfortable place. Nothing about him spoke of ease or contentment. He looked like a man thoroughly annoyed by failure.

Never taking her eyes from him, Angela scrambled to her feet and stood beside the soldier, who tucked the bowl in the crook of his arm and dipped in with his good hand. When he finished, he proffered the bowl to Timothy Platter, who waved it away.

"I'm from Bow Street and I'm looking for a runaway boy and a woman."

Omega held her breath.

Platter continued, coming closer to the soldier, who stood his ground. "The woman is short, with wild-looking curly hair."

Wild-looking? Wild-looking? thought Omega. How dare he?

"But she's not an antidote," continued Platter, "not entirely. She has a trim figure and a brisk way of walking, but she's a bit grim about the mouth." He laughed suddenly. "And such a sharp tongue! You'd know her if you saw her." He chuckled again, but with little mirth. "Or heard her."

"And the boy?" asked the soldier.

"He is ten, has black hair, well-dressed, brown eyes. Small for his age. Name of Jamie Clevenden.

Timothy Platter looked around him, scrutinizing the loft, looking up at the boards until Omega wanted to scream. "Well, my man, have you seen these two?"

"What did they do?"

"Oh, Lord, man, have you seen them? There's a reward," said Platter, softening his voice a bit as Angela moved behind the soldier. "A big reward from the runaway's uncle." The Runner adopted a wheedling tone. "You wouldn't be sleeping in barns anymore. No more soaked corn. That's food for swine."

The soldier was silent for a long minute. Omega felt the tears starting in her eyes. Oh, please, she said silently. Even though you do not know us. Please.

"I haven't seen them," the soldier replied. He rested his good hand on Angela's shoulder and she drew in closer to him.

"You're sure?"

"Didn't you just say to me that I could not forget such a woman?" countered the man. "I lost my hand, not my brain."

Timothy Platter was not satisfied. Omega slowly let out her breath and peered down at him. The Runner took out a cigar and clenched it between his teeth, a gesture she was familiar with. "I know they're around here somewhere," he insisted.

"Then you had better look for them," the soldier murmured. "We swine have to eat now."

Platter looked at the soldier. " 'Twas only a figure of speech, lad," he said more softly. "I meant nothing by it."

"Still and all, you'll be needing to hurry on."

"If you see such a woman and boy, would you let me know?"

"No," said the soldier, and nothing more. He sat down again and crossed his legs.

Timothy Platter said nothing, only looked daggers at the

soldier and chewed on his cigar. He gave a mighty swallow, and Angela gulped.

"I don't know that you're anything you say you are," the soldier explained quietly. "And I'd rather sleep in a barn and eat corn than betray people."

Timothy Platter stomped out of the barn. Omega held her breath a moment, listening, and then heard the sound of a horse riding away. She let out her breath and rested her cheek for a moment on the floor of the loft.

Jamie was awake. With wide eyes he watched her. "Is it over?" he whispered.

Omega nodded and stood up, shaking the straw and chaff off her dress. After another moment's look around, she descended the ladder, careful to keep her skirts tight about her. At the bottom, the soldier helped her down. She looked into smiling gray eyes and had to smile back.

"He offered you a reward," Omega murmured.

Angela still stood with her face turned into the soldier's shirt. Omega touched her gently on the shoulder and she looked around.

"Thank you for not telling him," she said to both of them. "Jamie and I would have been in a real broth then," she added, not even flinching at her own use of slang. How low can I go? she thought as she watched Angela, and smiled at her.

Jamie came down the ladder then, coming no closer than the bottom rung.

The soldier eyed him a moment, and made no move to come closer. Instead, he lowered himself to the ground and sat cross-legged. He handed the bowl of corn to Omega.

"We found a little corn in the feed bin and soaked it last night," he said. "Angela put in a pinch of salt. You'll find it better than you think."

After a slight hesitation, Omega put her hand in the tin bowl and tasted the corn. She chewed it slowly, and then took another bite, and handed the bowl to the soldier. "I am Omega Chartley," she said. "I really don't have a sharp tongue."

"Omega?" asked the soldier. "And were you the last child?"

Omega nodded. "My mother died when I was born. And I actually have an older brother named Alpha. We are both teachers. And this is Jamie Clevenden."

Jamie said nothing, only remained where he was, eyeing them all with suspicion. The soldier held out the can to him and gradually Jamie came closer, sitting down finally to eat.

"Well, I am Hugh Owen, late of His Majesty's Fifty-first Rifles. And this is Angela."

The little girl smiled and curtsied, but all the time her eyes were on Jamie Clevenden. Omega watched, amused and a little touched, as Angela eyed Jamie as though he were some rare species. Omega would not have been at all surprised if the girl had not circled him about.

What is she thinking? Omega wondered as the child continued to stare at Jamie. Finally Angela cleared her throat.

"Pardon me, please," she began, her English heavily accented. "Did that *hombre odioso* say that you were a runaway?"

Jamie eyed her suspiciously. "Yes," he admitted finally.

"You had a home, and you ran away?" Angela persisted.

Jamie nodded, intent on finishing the corn in the tin bowl.

"And you had a bed and more than one meal a day and you ran away?"

The boy nodded again. He put down the bowl and regarded her, trading stare for stare. In her turn, Angela blushed and moved back beside Hugh Owen. She continued to watch Jamie from the soldier's side, as if she could not believe that he was real. She looked to the soldier for reassurance, but the man said nothing.

The awkwardness of the moment did not elude Omega. "We must be on our way," she said crisply, filling in the gap of silence with her schoolteacher tones. "Jamie, be a friend and fetch my hat from the loft, will you?"

Jamie did as she asked, scurrying up the ladder again and rummaging about in the corner where she had stashed her precious bonnet.

"Oh, Miss Chartley," he said at last, "I do not think you want it."

"Of course I do," she replied. "Hand it down now, there's a good boy."

Jamie's head appeared over the edge of the loft. "Miss Chartley, a mouse has delivered ten babies in the crown of it."

Omega sighed. "Well, then, perhaps we should leave the rodents in possession. Come down, then, and we'll be off."

"Where to?" asked the soldier.

"Perhaps it would be best if you did not know," she said. "Then if you should meet with the estimable Mr. Platter again, you will not have to tell him a lie."

Hugh Owen did not persist. "We're glad that we could be of some assistance to you," was all he said as he extended his hand.

The absurdity of the moment overwhelmed Omega, and she didn't know whether to laugh or cry. She shook his hand. "Good luck to you and Angela," she said. Omega felt stiff and formal again. "Your kindness is so appreciated."

The soldier touched his hand to his forehead in a salute.

"Mr. Owen, is Wantage nearby?" she asked.

"We came from there two nights ago. It is about ten miles to the east of us." He smiled, but the smile held no warmth. "If you are a one-armed man, there are no jobs in Wantage."

"And is there . . . is there a place near Wantage called Byworth?" Omega asked. "I do not know if it is a seat of peerage or a village. Have you heard of it?"

"Byworth. Byworth. It sounds familiar . . . but I do not know. Mind you stay off the main roads."

"We shall," Omega said. "Good-bye."

They set off at a brisk pace, heading east, avoiding the roads again and tramping through fields full of the fruits of late summer and enclosed neatly about by stone walls. They skirted a small village and Omega ventured in long enough to buy four rolls with the last of her money. Her eyes were wide open for Timothy Platter, but the earth must have swallowed him whole.

She gave Jamie three rolls, thinking to herself as she nibbled her roll that the extra avoirdupois she had accumulated during her sedentary stay at Miss Haversham's would soon be gone. Her skirt already felt agreeably loose. Hmmm, thought Miss Chartley, this adventure could yield unexpected results.

They ate in the shade of a stone fence, glorying in the coolness of the stone at their backs. As was his custom, Jamie said nothing. His eyes were troubled, but he did not speak.

"And what if you do not find him?" Omega asked at last. She had plied him with several questions, spaced out over the length of their luncheon, and he had responded to none. Her upbringing dictated that she toss in a comment occasionally to fill up the void of profitable mealtime conversation. He surprised her this time with a reply.

"Then I will take the king's shilling and go for a drummer boy," he said, his voice firm with resolution.

"Surely it would be better for you to return to your uncle?" she ventured.

For answer, Jamie gazed at her in that oddly familiar way of his. "I told you that I will not go back."

They were still short of Wantage when night fell, coming swiftly upon them even as they were deciding which road to take.

"If I had a coin, I would flip it," Jamie said.

"Silly, you might lose it," said his companion. "I recommend that we walk toward the river. I am thirsty."

It was more than thirst. Omega wanted to wash her face and see if she could repair some of the damage to her hair. And if she could take off her shoes and just dabble some water over her toes, how good that would be.

There were men fishing along the riverbank. Jamie and Omega sat in the bushes until the men gathered their strings of fish and walked away, talking and laughing, and heading for their homes and dinner.

"I could eat those fish raw," declared Jamie.

Omega shuddered. "I am not that hungry."

"It's not civilized, but we won't tell anyone," the boy joked, and then gasped, pointing to the bushes they had just vacated.

The Bow Street Runner burst through the underbrush, a most determined look on his face. He stood still a fraction of a moment and shifted his cigar from one corner of his mouth to the other.

Omega felt her stomach sink to her shoes and then float free up toward her throat. "Run, Jamie!" she urged, as the boy hesitated, not knowing which way to turn.

And then he was all motion, darting away from the voice, running along the riverbank. Omega started after him, took only a step, and realized to her horror that Timothy Platter had a firm grip on the back of her skirt.

"Let go!" she gasped.

"Oh, no, Miss Chartley," he roared, and took a firmer grip on her dress.

Omega struggled toward the water, tugging Timothy Platter after her, even as he dug into the soft bank with his feet and hung on. She struck at him with her hands, but he had only to lean back to avoid her flailing attempts.

Platter tightened his grip on her skirt. She kicked him in the shins, but the Bow Street Runner hung on like a bulldog.

"I'll see that you're transported for obstructing justice." He made a grab for her waist. "Without you, I'll have that little snip in no time!"

The thought of being shipped to Australia galvanized Omega. She grabbed her reticule by the strings and swung it at him. The paperweight inside—the one Alpha insisted that she carry in her bag—connected with a satisfying thud.

Platter's eyes fluttered and rolled back in his head. He pitched forward against her, his hand still tight in the waistband of her dress, and they plummeted off the bank and into the water.

4

All was dark, all was black, but the pungent smell of woodsmoke convinced Omega Chartley that she was still alive. Mixed with the fragrant smoke was the warm, earthy smell of cow. No, this was not heaven; not even one of its environs. There was nothing to do but open her eyes.

"*Mira*, Hugh," exclaimed a clear, small voice that Omega remembered. "They are blue. You have won the wager."

Omega looked into the brown eyes of Angela.

"But I always wanted brown eyes, Angela," she responded. Omega's voice sounded rusty and ill-used to her ears. No matter; she was grateful she could still talk.

"You must trust me, Angela," said the other familiar voice. "English ladies with that particular shade of brown hair always have blue eyes."

"I have already agreed that you won." Angela pouted.

Now there were two heads leaning over her. Omega looked from one to the other, Angela with her thick black hair and Hugh Owen with his long, friendly face.

And then Omega remembered. "Good God, where is Jamie?" she exclaimed as she tried to struggle into a sitting position. Hugh Owen pushed her back down. She felt his hand on her bare shoulder and realized that she was wrapped in a heavy cotton blanket and nothing more. Her face reddened.

"Easy, Miss Chartley," Hugh said. "Jamie's over there, asleep. As to your clothes, they're drying by the fire. Angela saw to your welfare."

"And Mr. Platter? I think I killed him with my reticule."

Hugh laughed out loud, and then covered his mouth with his hand so as not to waken Jamie. "*Why* on earth do you carry a paperweight in your reticule?" he asked.

"It's Alpha's idea," she admitted. "He says that any

female traveling alone should have some protection. I . . . I couldn't think of anything but a paperweight. It contains bits of shot from the Yorktown Batteries, baked in glass. Papa was there," she added, as if that explained her choice of weapons.

"Well, it certainly gave Platter the rightabout," said Hugh.

Omega reached out for him impulsively. "But tell me, please—that wretched man is not dead, is he?"

"Oh, no. The last we saw, he was floating downstream clinging to a tree branch. He still had his cigar."

"Odious, odious man," muttered Miss Chartley.

"The only real casualty of the encounter appears to be your guidebook," said the soldier. "We're going to dry it out, though, because it could prove useful as tinder for fires." He held up the book with its bloated and wrinkled pages.

Omega settled herself more comfortably. "Well, I wasn't finding much use in it anyway. I seem to have strayed somewhat from my itinerary." Her head ached abominably. She reached a hand around to the back of her neck and felt a rising lump.

"You would not quit struggling, *señorita*," said Angela. "How was I to get you to shore?"

"How, indeed?" murmured Omega.

"Such a useful paperweight," agreed Angela. She rose to her feet and rearranged Omega's clothing by the fire.

"And did she . . ." Omea looked at Hugh Owen.

"Pull you from the river? Indeed she did."

"And Jamie?"

"Oh, you should have seen him racing along the river-bank, calling for help. He ran smack into us."

Omega's brain was spinning. "But whatever were you doing? I thought you were going in the other direction? Oh, I don't understand."

She yawned a mighty yawn then, to her vast embarrassment. To her further chagrin, water dribbled out of her mouth.

Hugh dabbed at it with the corner of her blanket. "You also swallowed half of the River By." He intercepted her

sudden look. "Yes, the River By. The farmer whose cattle
byre this is told us." He continued to interpret her
expression. "And don't worry! He'll not betray us. His
son died at Vimeiro. We're practically mates; he won't give
us up to any Runner."

"I truly don't understand," Omega finished weakly.
She wanted to close her eyes again, but it seemed scarcely
polite.

"Just sleep now, Miss Chartley," said Hugh. "If you
need anything, Angela is close by. I'm going to
reconnoiter."

Against her will, better judgment, and sharply honed
sense of propriety, Omega yawned again and closed her
eyes.

When she woke, there was food, hot porridge—an
island of it in a sea of cream, with a dollop of butter on
top—and a mug of tea smelling discreetly of rum. Hugh
Owen and Jamie were nowhere in sight, so Omega draped
her blanket about her to better effect and rested herself on
one elbow as Angela handed her a spoon.

"It's very good," said Angela, who sat cross-legged in
front of her. "Hugh told me to see that you eat all of it."

She did as she was told, spooning down the porridge,
which settled around all the river water in her stomach and
made her burp.

"Goodness," murmured Omega, her face reddening. As
Angela did not appear offended by such rag manners,
Omega reached for the tea and sipped it slowly, relishing
the way it burned down her throat and into her soggy
insides.

"My papa used to call tea 'English manna,' " said
Angela.

"Where is he now?" asked Omega, handing back the
empty mug.

"We buried him at Toulouse," was her reply. Angela
took hold of Omega's hand, and they sat close together,
watching the cows watching them.

Omega was back in her clothes again when Hugh
returned, Jamie close behind him. Jamie brightened at
once to see her.

"Miss Chartley! This is famous! We are practically on the River By!"

She sat down again and he sat beside her. "I'm sorry that I could not rescue you, but I do not swim."

"Never mind about that," she said. "When you reach your uncle's estate, you must learn. We are both woefully ignorant and have only to be grateful that we fell in with smarter heads than our own. But, sir, where are we?" she asked Hugh. "And should we not look out for Timothy Platter?"

Hugh sat beside her, resting his maimed arm in his lap. "We have executed what General Picton—God rest his soul—would call a 'damned fine tactical maneuver.' I think Platter will not find us immediately."

"You see, we swam the river," said Angela.

Jamie clapped his hands together. "I tell you, it was famous! Angela hoisted you onto Hugh's back, and over you went, and then they came back for me! We're on the other side of the river from where Timothy Platter saw you come out."

It all made sense, and yet it didn't. "I still don't understand," insisted Miss Chartley. "What were you doing following us? I thought you had only just come from that direction."

"It's true," agreed Hugh. "But Angela was worried about you. And . . . and I own, I was too."

The self-sufficient Miss Chartley had no comment, other than the private consideration that the Lord blesses teachers and runaways, even—especially—when they are stupid.

"We've also marched a considerable distance back along the road we followed this morning," added Hugh. "That confused the Frogs any number of times in Spain, and so it should do for a Bow Street Runner."

Omega regarded Hugh with some admiration. "And you carried me on your back all this distance?"

"You're not very heavy," he said, and blushed under her scrutiny. "In fact, ma'am, do they let you out in high winds?"

Omega laughed. Her stomach rumbled, and even Angela

had to smile. Omega tried to suppress another burp and reddened in embarrassment. She began to cough uncontrollably.

"You're going to be doing that all night, Miss Chartley, so you had better get used to it. That's what happens when you swallow a river and live to tell about it. Angela and I have burped up our share of rivers, have we not, *niña*?"

Angela nodded and settled herself next to Omega, who put her arm around the girl's shoulders and pulled her closer.

"Thank you," Omega whispered, and kissed her cheek.

Jamie cleared his throat. "I told Hugh how we came to be together," he said. "I . . . I had to trust him. I showed him my back."

No one said anything for a moment. Hugh Owen's face was serious then. He leaned back against the stall and Omega noticed for the first time how tired he was, how deep the lines in his face. Clearly the effort of her rescue and their march, coupled with his own injuries, had exhausted him. She almost said something to him about that, but thought better of it.

"I don't hold with grown men giving little boys stripes like that to wear around," he said, "but never mind. The farmer says we're still a day or more away from Byworth . . . except he didn't call it Byworth. It was Byford. At any rate, if we follow the river, we'll find it. We will just squirrel away here until you feel like walking, Miss Chartley."

She smiled at him. "My discomfort is little compared to yours, sir. And I wish you would call me Omega. Miss Chartley is a schoolteacher, but Omega is on holiday." She sighed. "And she's a bit of a scapegrace, I fear. Such a holiday!"

She wanted to talk then, wanted to hear their stories, and even wanted to tell her own, but her eyes were closing again. As she drifted off to sleep, Hugh covered her with the blanket and she felt Angela cuddling up close to her. The warmth of the child's body took away the chill of the river, and she slept.

When she woke, the birds were singing, the cattle had

been turned out. Angela was braiding her hair, humming a little tune Omega had never heard before as she pulled her hair back and plaited it carefully.

Hugh came in then, Jamie at his heels, and smiled to see her sitting upright and finishing her breakfast. "Do you think you can walk?" he asked after she finished her tea and dabbed at her lips with the corner of the blanket.

"I can certainly try," she said, and then eyed him in the manner of the suspicious Miss Chartley. "But I'll be keeping my eyes on you, Hugh Owen. You tired yourself dreadfully yesterday, and I refuse to be party to your complete ruin."

"I was tired," he admitted, "but I am fit today. Jamie and I have scouted our march. We will do famously if we march among the trees, stay off the road, and avoid the river." He nodded to Angela. "Does this sound like our Spanish campaigning?"

"You told me England would be different," Angela accused.

"That was before I met Miss Chartley," was his prompt reply. "And her famous paperweight."

"Am I never to be forgiven my paperweight?" she asked.

"No," he said. He picked up the reticule by the fire and hefted it before handing it to her. "Mind you keep that to yourself or we'll all end up on a transport ship, watching the sun rise over the Great Barrier Reef. Come to attention, Angela. We must march."

Jamie stood a little straighter beside Omega and watched as Hugh Owen stood in front of them.

"Old Hookey called us an 'infamous army' not long ago," he said, speaking more to himself than to them. "That was only because he had never seen this file."

"Lead on, sir," said Omega.

They walked into a beautiful Cotswold morning, where dew still decorated spiders' webs and the very ground smelled of summer. Every now and then the sweet, sharp scent of roses teased them as they passed crofters' cottages and skirted tiny villages that probably had not changed measurably since the days of Queen Elizabeth. Hugh ambled into several villages to inquire about Byford. The closer they came, the more information he gleaned.

"Well," he began after his latest side trip, "we now know that Byford is home to well over one thousand souls, is famous for its needlework, and has a church housing the relic of St. Stephen's little finger. Our latest piece of news is that the Viscount of Byford is also the justice of the peace."

"Is that good?" inquired Jamie.

"I hope so. Let's assume that he has a sharp sense of justice, but maybe not too much nicety about law by the books," said Hugh. "Jamie, have you considered what you will do if your uncle turns you over to your guardian? He could, you know."

The mulish look returned to Jamie's face. "I will not stay," he said.

Hugh Owen had the wisdom not to continue the conversation.

Still short of their destination, they paused for the night in an area of heavy woods. "From what I have learned, we could perhaps be there around midnight, if we continued," said Hugh, "but I do not think that rousing the viscount from his bed will further our cause any. Besides, I am hungry."

They all were, but no one complained about the short rations; Hugh and Angela were obviously used to doing without, and Jamie and Omega were too polite. Omega did find herself staring with some longing at a rabbit that watched them from the protection of a bramble thicket.

Hugh must have seen the same rabbit. He halted his little army. "Angela, could you work some Spanish magic?"

She grinned. "*Claro que sí*, Hugh. Come, Jamie."

He hung back. "I've never caught a rabbit before."

Angela stamped her foot. "*Fulano!* And how will you learn if you do not try?"

Jamie could think of no argument to counter Angela's logic. He followed his mentor into the brush by the tall trees.

Omega watched them go, and then seated herself on a

fallen log. "You do not think Angela will go too far away?" she asked.

"She knows what to do."

Hugh's short reply told Omega how tired he was. Without a word he sat down on the ground beside her and rested his back against the fallen tree. He raised his knees and propped his injured arm up on one knee.

"I do not know how it is possible for my hand to hurt when it is not there," he said at last. He shrugged. "And to think I ran away from Wales so I would never lose life or limb in the colliery."

"How did you lose your hand?" Omega asked, cringing inside as she considered all the governesses who had raised her to never ask any question more forward than the time of day.

If Hugh thought her encroaching, he gave no indication. He sighed again. "I'm almost embarrassed to tell you, Miss Ch . . . Omega. I mean, it was a chuffle-headed thing, the merest quirk." He looked at her in embarrassment. "You'll laugh."

"Most assuredly I will not," Omega replied. "This is hardly a laughing matter."

"No," agreed Hugh. He settled back against the tree. "It was about two hours before Boney's Imperial Guard turned about-face and ran from us. Or it might have been ten minutes. Time has an odd way of taking on new meaning during a battle."

He paused and looked off in the distance, hearing something she could not hear, seeing sights she did not want to view.

"Anyway, the Frenchies' cavalry swirled around us, and then they would back off and their guns would roar." He straightened out his injured arm and stared at the hand that wasn't there. "I was so tired. A ball from one of Boney's 'beautiful daughters' rolled into our square. It was just rolling along the ground, moving straight toward my captain's head."

"Your captain's head?"

"Yes. He was dead already and lying on the ground,

half-buried in the mud. We were so muddy. I reached out to stop that ball from slamming into him. Well, I was tired or I never would have done that.''

"Good God," murmured Omega. She touched Hugh on the shoulder. He looked up, as if remembering where he was.

"I didn't even feel anything at first, until I tried to reload my piece and the only thing left was a bone sticking out. Oh, I'm sorry.''

She knew from the look on his face that she was ghastly pale, even under her sunburn. She took a deep breath. He was still looking at her.

"Do you know, Omega, when you turn pale, those little freckles on your nose are quite, quite green?''

She nodded and managed a shaky laugh.

"I was lucky," he continued. "I was able to walk off that battlefield. Some of the wounded . . . some of them drowned in puddles of rainwater." Again he looked into the far distance. "I lost all my friends in that day's work. Every one of them.''

Angela was waving at him from the edge of the clearing. He waved back. "And that is how I came to have Angela.''

"Eh?'' asked the articulate educationist.

"Her mother was a Spanish camp follower. She came to us with a small baby—Angela—and my best mate, Thomas Llewellen, took up with her. She drowned crossing the Duero. Thomas died at Toulouse, and our sergeant and his woman watched after Angela. The sergeant died at Waterloo, and I'm the only survivor of our file. Angela's my charge now.''

"Surely she has . . .''

"Other relatives?'' Hugh shook his head. "Her mother was an orphan. I could have left Angela in an orphanage in Brussels, but that would have been my last night of peaceful sleep.''

Omega understood. If she had gone ahead and boarded that mail coach and left Jamie to his fate, she would have seen his frightened eyes every night she closed her own.

"Besides that, Angela searched every bed in Brussels

until she found someone from the file. I couldn't leave her behind."

"Most assuredly not," agreed Omega. "And I do understand. I seem to have declared myself Jamie's protector, whether he wanted me or not."

Hugh got to his feet. "You've discharged your duty well. Soon we'll be at Byford, and he'll be the viscount's worry."

"I suppose," she said, and wondered why she felt so little enthusiasm for what would have been a wonderful relief only yesterday.

Angela came dancing back into the clearing, followed by Jamie, who walked head down, the picture of failure. When he was quite close, he whipped out a snared rabbit from behind his back, a smile splitting his face from ear to ear.

"Omega, it was famous! The rabbit didn't have a chance. Angela has promised that she'll teach me how to do that."

Omega laughed out loud and clapped her hands together, delighting not so much in what he said as in the joy in his voice. That's what was missing before, she thought to herself as she grabbed Jamie, ruffled his hair, and kissed him on the cheek. He wasn't a little boy before. Now he is. Thank God and Angela and Hugh Owen.

Angela took the rabbit from Jamie. She set it on the ground and extracted two nails from her leather pouch. She looked around for a big rock, and pounded the nails close together into the nearest tree. With quick, sharp motions she forced the rabbit's hind legs into the nails.

Omega watched openmouthed as Angela took Hugh Owen's knife from him. A few quick cuts, a deft slice from vent to breastbone, and in a moment the pelt came off in one wrench. The naked rabbit glittered in the afternoon sun. Omega turned her head.

"Famous!" breathed Jamie. He put out his leg and made a sweeping bow. "Angela, you are a complete hand."

Angela laughed behind her hand like a proper Spanish

lady. As Jamie gawked in admiration, Angela gutted the rabbit and scurried to the river and cleaned her catch. She laid the rabbit carefully on a tree stump. With flint and steel she started a fire. Omega coaxed along the little fingers of flame with selected pages from *Rochester's Guidebook*, while Jamie added twigs. By the time the fire was of respectable dimensions, Angela had divided the rabbit into four parts, like Gaul, and skewered each section onto a green stick. She handed a stick to each diner and motioned them closer to the fire.

"I just hold it in the flames?" asked Omega.

"Up a little bit," cautioned Hugh, "or you will eat more charcoal than rabbit."

The four of them sat companionably close to each other, Hugh making an occasional comment to Omega, Jamie teasing Angela and being rewarded with her bell-like laugh. Mostly they were silent, listening to the wind in the trees and the hiss and pop of rabbit fat on the fire. Soon they were concentrating on the magnificent odor of rabbit almost done.

"I've never been so famished in my entire life," Omega said finally, to no one in particular, as she turned the stick over and over and wished the rabbit would hurry up.

She watched the flames again, wondering at her growing uneasiness in relinquishing Jamie Clevenden to someone else, even if it were a relative. For all his silence and stubbornness, she knew that she would miss Jamie. How much, she would likely discover tomorrow.

But right now, sitting in the little clearing surrounded by people who had become surprisingly dear to her in a short time, Omega experienced another sensation, sharper than hunger. It pierced through her worries about the morrow, and her fear of the future. It was a feeling she had not encountered since the morning of her wedding eight years ago, when she woke up and knew that before nightfall she would be in Matthew Bering's arms.

She felt happy.

During her one London Season, Omega Chartley had attended banquets, routs, teas, small dinners, large dinners, picnics al fresco, and elegant luncheons too numerous to mention. She never enjoyed any of them as much as the rabbit she ate under the trees along the River By in the company of Jamie Clevenden, Hugh Owen, and Angela.

They tackled the rabbit with little nicety, but much enthusiasm. Omega tucked her last clean handkerchief under her chin, grateful for the soberness of her dark gray traveling dress which defied the most obvious stains.

"Angela, have you any salt?"

Hugh paused in his attack on the morsel before him and wiped his chin on his shoulder, holding out the rabbit. Angela dug about in her leather bag and extracted a piece of salt the size of a thimble. Carefully she scraped her fingernail over the gray lump, as Hugh moved the rabbit underneath it. He winked at her and tasted the rabbit.

"Angela! Magnificent!" exclaimed Hugh.

Jamie held out his dinner for a minute scraping of salt. "Angela, this is famous!" he exclaimed.

"It is only salt," said the girl in her realistic Spanish fashion, but her eyes shone with the pleasure of the compliments.

"What else have you in that bag?" Jamie asked, more inclined to talk, now that the sharpest edge of his hunger had been distracted by the rabbit.

Angela took another bite, chewing thoughtfully. "I have a needle and thread—"

"Which has mended trousers and shirts, bullet holes and bayonet wounds," interrupted Hugh. "When the little wounds heal, she pulls off the thread, washes it, and winds it back on the spool."

Jamie made a face.

"I have a rosary."

"Put the cross in your mouth and bite down hard, and then the needle and thread glide along easier," Hugh continued.

"I have a medal of St. Christopher, blessed by the pope," she said imperturbably.

"How else could we swim rivers with swooning schoolteachers?"

Omega laughed.

"Hugh, you should not make a mockery of the pope," reproved Angela.

"Or of schoolteachers," added Jamie, getting into the fun of it. "Especially schoolteachers with prodigious paperweights."

"And I will not tell you what else is in my *bolsa*," said Angela severely, "not even if you have need of it, Jamie Clevenden."

"Fair's fair," agreed Omega. "Angela, let us withdraw now and leave these gentlemen to their port and cigars."

Angela shuddered. "Do not remind me of that mean Señor Platter!"

The two of them went to the river and sat there in pleasant companionship, watching the water and the occasional sparkle as a fish jumped. Angela sighed, and edged closer to Omega.

"Soon we will have to say *adiós* to Jamie, won't we?"

"Yes, I fear so. And you and Hugh will find a place to work and I will teach English grammar to spoiled little girls who couldn't skin rabbits if their lives depended on it. Oh, botheration, let us return to the gentlemen."

Hugh and Jamie had borrowed armfuls of cut timothy grass from the nearby field and arranged it around the fire. The soldier spread out the heavy sheet from his rucksack over one pile and motioned toward it as Omega and Angela came into the clearing again. Angela sank down in the soft hay at once, patting it until the lumps were distributed to her liking.

Omega sat down beside her, her ears tuned to the pleasant rustle of the hay. I must store all this in my memory, she thought as she poked and prodded the hay. I must remember the River By and the porridge in the cattle byre and the good feeling of rough sheet on bare skin. Most of all, when I am lonely this winter, I must remember these people. Tears came to her eyes unexpectedly and she brushed them away.

Angela leaned closer. "Did you hurt yourself?"

"Gracious no," said Omega. "I must have . . . must have gotten some grass in my eye. It's gone now."

She lay down and Angela cuddled next to her. After a moment's hesitation, Omega slid her arm under Angela's neck. Angela sighed and nestled in the hollow of Omega's arm.

"Omega, tell me a story about a handsome prince."

"I don't know any stories like that," she replied, looking up at the stars that winked through the leafing branches overhead like random sequins on a dark gown. "There really aren't any handsome princes."

"I saw one once," said Angela. Her voice was drowsy. "He was William, Prince of Orange. The soldiers called him Little Frog, but I thought he was handsome."

"I'll tell you a story about a prince," Omega said suddenly. "A prince with red hair and—"

"Princes don't have red hair," Angela interrupted. Her voice was faraway.

"This one did," said Omega firmly. "Dark, dark red." She sighed. "And it was gloriously straight, *unlike* my own. And he had brown eyes and absolutely no freckles."

"Was he wealthy?"

"Oh, yes." She giggled. "Rich as Croesus."

"Was there a princess?" asked Angela, long after Omega thought she was asleep.

"Well, no, not really. There was a lady who loved him fiercely."

"Such a strange word," murmured Hugh Owen.

Omega looked over at him, aware for the first time that someone else was listening besides Angela.

She didn't look at Hugh. She hadn't the courage. She stared straight up at the stars overhead. "It is the correct word," she said softly. "Fiercely. Not jealously, not even protectively, for he could take care of himself. Fiercely."

"Like a fox with kits?"

"Yes, I suppose." Omega considered. She would gladly have died for Matthew Bering without a whimper.

She was silent then, until Angela jostled her in the ribs. "What became of the prince?"

"I do not know. One day he disappeared—"

"Was he a soldier?"

"No, no. He was what I suppose you could call a country gentleman."

"And the lady?"

Omega pulled her arm out from under Angela's head and sat up. Angela rested her head on Omega's lap and the woman stroked Angela's black hair. "He left her at the altar. Just standing there holding her little Bible and bunch of flowers."

"Good God," said Hugh in a low voice.

"And that's *all*?" asked Angela in disbelief.

"I'm afraid so. That's the ending."

"Well, it isn't much of a story," said the girl. "I can tell you a better one. Prince William came into our encampment one night in Brussels and I sewed a button on his shirt."

Angela's words recalled Omega to the present. "Imagine!" she exclaimed.

"Yes. It was so cold he did not take off the shirt. I just stood right next to him and sewed on the button."

Hugh laughed. "And blushed the whole time, I own!"

"I did not!"

"She did. And when she finished, Prince William bowed and kissed her hand and she swore a mighty oath never to wash the spot again," teased Hugh.

Omega hugged Angela to her. "That's a much better story than mine. From now on, you are appointed to tell the bedtime tales."

"But not now," said Hugh. "Why don't you follow Jamie's lead and go to sleep? We still have a march before us tomorrow."

Angela was silent. Omega feared she was sulking, but soon she heard the even, deep breathing of the girl. Gently Omega lowered her head back to the timothy-grass bedding and covered her with a small corner of the blanket.

Hugh was quiet then too. Omega thought he had drifted off, but then he spoke. "You see why I could not leave her in a Brussels orphanage."

"I envy you," she said simply.

When Hugh spoke again, he sounded much closer, as if he had raised himself up on one elbow and was leaning toward her. "Come with me down to the river."

She rose and followed him. They sat at the edge of the water. Omega took off her stockings and shoes and put her feet in the water. Minnows darted about and tickled at her feet.

"He just left you at the altar?"

Omega managed a laugh, but it was devoid of any humor. "That was for dramatic purposes. I suppose I must be accurate. I was standing in the back of the church, waiting for Matthew and his best man to walk out by the altar so my father and I could proceed down the aisle. We waited there an hour, until Papa and Alpha escorted me out of the church."

"Did you . . . did you know him very well?" Hugh cleared his throat. "There probably isn't a way to ask such things nicely, I suppose, and see here, probably you would prefer that I get my nose out of your business."

"No, no." Omega paused. There really wasn't any way to tell Hugh that she was relieved for the opportunity to talk. She sensed, somehow, that he understood that fact without having to be told. "Matthew was—or is . . . I don't know—from one of England's finest families. All of Papa's connections told him how lucky I was." The word stuck in her throat. "How lucky . . ."

Hugh touched her hand. "I cannot imagine a worse thing to befall a lady."

Omega laughed again. "Oh, that was nothing; a mere diversion, Hugh. Two weeks later I found my father hanged by the neck in his dressing room." She paused to let that sink in. "It seems there had been serious reverses on the Exchange that Alpha and I were blissfully ignorant of. Papa killed himself."

Her voice broke then and she was silent, waiting for the tears to form so she could brush them away and get on with it. Hugh said nothing.

"Alpha was finishing his third year at Oxford—thank the Lord for that—and he always had a scholarly mind. As soon as everything we owned was sold at auction, he was able to secure a position as a lecturer of English and composition."

No need to tell Hugh of her own solitary ride to Plymouth in answer to an advertisement in the *Times* for a teacher in one of the shabby-genteel schools for the daughters of ship's captains. And the fear that even in that less-exalted hall of learning someone would mention Deardon Chartley and his suicide and the scandal at St. Alphonse's that was the continuing gossip of that London Season.

"But that was eight years ago," she said, "and we have done well enough since then. Alpha married the perfectly lovely daughter of a vicar at Banbury, and he is now head of English at St. Andrew's, near Amphney St. Peter." She smiled to herself in the dark. "And there are three little Chartleys, each as smart as their papa."

"And their aunt, I vow."

"I have managed," she said simply.

Hugh took her hand and held it this time. "And you never heard from Matthew . . . Bering, is it?"

"No. Not ever. Not a word. Alpha and I speculated at length. All we could come up with was that somehow he had gotten wind of Papa's financial misery before we knew of it, and cried off in time to save himself from marriage to a penniless girl without a sixpence to scratch with. . . . Oh, do excuse my language."

Hugh chuckled. "Nor a feather to fly with?"

She could smile at that. "Not a single one." And then her voice was serious again. "I've certainly gotten over whatever silly *tendre* I may have had for that man. I don't expect to see him again. But I do wish . . . I just wish I knew what it was that so disgusted him about me that he could not bring himself to face me again. I would like to know that."

Hugh let go of her hand. "I imagine you would. What does he look like? If I ever see him, I promise you I'll draw his cork for you."

"You wouldn't!" she exclaimed, hugging her arms around her knees. "He's tall. I come up to his shoulder, but barely. And I already told you he has wonderful red hair. He's a serious man, but he could be so diverting. There's something marvelously original about his mind." She sighed. "But that was so long ago. And he's older than I am by eight years. I suppose he would be thirty-four now. Goodness."

"He is probably bald and fat now and loosens his pants at the dinner table."

She laughed, and this time her humor was heartfelt. "I hope so!" She dried off her feet and put on her shoes.

They walked back to the clearing. "I have a question for you, Hugh, and it's quite impertinent."

"Fire away."

"How is it that your English is so good? We had a Welsh gardener once, and he was so singsongy . . . oh, and his grammar!"

"My mama was English, and she had been raised in the home of an earl." He shook his head at the memory. "She would wallop me good if I ever talked like one of the colliery boys. 'How can you amount to much if you sound like a Welshman?' " he mimicked.

"I've never met anyone quite like you," Omega said, "but now, good night, sir."

"Good night, Omega Chartley," Hugh said. "You're a charming lady and certainly deserving of a swift change of fortune."

"The same to you," she said obligingly. "I own that we deserve some good fortune."

When Omega waked in the morning, Hugh Owen was already busy at the fire. One-handed, he had managed to start a fire, and was kneeling in front of it, blowing on the flames. He next went to the river and returned with a canister of water, into which he dumped last night's rabbit bones and set it on the flames.

As the rabbit water turned to broth, Omega marveled

again at their good luck in falling in with such artists. She
said her morning prayers, and woke Angela and Jamie.

They breakfasted on rabbit soup livened with a scraping
of salt, and turned their attention to Byford.

"We should be there soon enough," said Hugh. "I have
an idea. Jamie, you walk with me, and, Angela, you stay
close to Omega. If Mr. Timothy Platter is about, he'll be
concentrating on a woman with a boy and a soldier with a
girl. It isn't much, but it might allow us an avenue of
escape." He grinned. "My captain, God rest his soul,
would call that a master stroke."

"And so would I," agreed Omega. "I shall force my
curls under a cap, so Mr. Platter will not call me a
wildwoman."

"And do try to stand taller," said Hugh. "Add three or
four inches, if you can. Add a stone or two to your weight,
and you'll escape all notice."

A morning's walk, and then Byford spread before them,
cupped in a small valley. The remnants of a wall around
the town indicated the age of Byford, as did the squat-
looking Romanesque church set stolidly in the middle of
the village.

"Well, let us march," said Hugh. He put his arm
around Jamie. "You and I will go in first to reconnoiter.
Omega, you follow in five minutes with Angela."

The man and boy walked ahead. Angela sat down, while
Omega continued to look over the fields and houses of
Byford. The village was tidy to a fault, with a preciseness
that appealed to her sense of order, that sense so badly
scattered in the past few days. To the south, a mile or more
beyond the village, was a large stone house, far larger than
anything in the adjacent neighborhood, shaded well with
tall trees that had probably been mere seedlings when
Ceasar's Roman legionnaires encountered the blue-faced
folk of early Britain. To say that the house was large did
not quite put it in the category of an estate. It was stone
and two-storied, with white shutters and ivy twining up the
walls.

I suppose that is the residence of the Viscount Byford,
she said to herself. Jamie should have a nice home there.

She hoped again that the viscount was a good man, and that his wife would not object to a rather quiet, solemn boy who, every now and then, showed flashes of huge enthusiasm. All he needs is a chance, please, she thought.

"Yes?"

She must have spoken out loud. Omega shook her head and touched Angela's shoulder. And you too, my dear, she thought.

"Let's go, Angela."

They strolled into Byford, crossing the bridge over the River By that looked as old as the church, walking past trim houses close together, and into the town itself. It was not hard to blend with the crowds; an agricultural fair was in progress. Omega walked slowly, keeping Hugh and Jamie in her sight.

Hugh paused to talk to one of the shepherds standing, as well-groomed as his long-nosed sheep, close by the horses. The shepherd leaned on his crook and listened to Hugh, and then pointed in the general direction of the large house Omega had noticed earlier. Hugh nodded to the man and looked behind him. He motioned with his head, and Omega and Angela followed.

A walk of some ten minutes took them across a stream and then beyond the broken wall that had once protected Byford. The way was easy. The cobblestones were as evenly spaced and tidy as the houses, with no weeds sneaking up between the paving.

"I've never seen a better-regulated town," said Omega as they walked along. "It speaks well for the viscount."

Hugh and Jamie were waiting for them at the gates to the viscount's manor. The gates were open, as if someone was preparing to ride through. The gatekeeper was nowhere in sight, so the four of them walked up the curving lane with beeches on either side to the front entrance.

There was nothing pretentious about the house; in point of fact, it was smaller than the former Chartley country house in Lincolnshire. But it was splendid in a kind of magnificence unequaled before in Omega's admiring eyes. It was tidy, with no hint of crumbling mortar between the stones, no buckling of paint on the windowsills, no thin patches in the gravel of the front carriage drive where the ground showed through. The windows were so clean she had to look twice to make sure there was glass in the frames. Each bit of ivy scaling the walls appeared to have been dusted and arranged by hand. It was too clean.

The splendor had affected Angela too. She leaned against Omega. "Do you think people really live here?" she whispered.

Hugh shrugged his shoulders. "I almost hate to touch that knocker," he confessed to Omega as he rapped twice.

Immediately the door swung open on perfectly noiseless hinges. The man who stood before them was as precise as the house, ineffable in his splendor. Angela sucked in her breath but said nothing. Jamie stared in wide-eyed amazement, but he found his voice before the others.

"Are *you* the viscount?" he asked.

The man at the door did not bother to reply. Jamie stepped back and hung his head. Omega squared her shoulders. How dare that man be so insulting, she thought as she looked at the resplendent figure before her. She cleared her throat and pretended that he was one of her pupils, and a particularly ill-favored one, at that.

"Sir, we are looking for the Viscount Byford."

She thought for a moment that he would not speak to her either. She tried to stand a little taller and stare him down. "Are you the butler?" she asked at last.

"Dios mío," whispered Angela behind her back. "He looks like the Duke of Wellington! And you call him a butler?"

"Please tell the viscount that James Clevenden is here to see him," she persisted, placing her hands on Jamie's shoulders and keeping him in front of her.

"I cannot fathom what interest my employer would have in seeing this young person," said the butler, and stepped back to shut the door.

Before he could close the door, Hugh Owen bounded up the steps and stuck his maimed arm in the way. The butler showed surprise for the first time, gasping and stepping back. Hugh spoke over his shoulder to Omega. "I knew that would stop him."

The butler stayed on his side of the door, eyeing warily the place where Hugh's hand used to be. His coloring had gone from sanguine to pasty in a remarkably short time.

"See here, sir," said Hugh as he took another step into the hall. "Is your employer a justice of the peace?"

With a visible effort the butler regained his composure and pulled it about his shoulders like a tattered cloak. "Indeed he is, but he is otherwise engaged this afternoon."

"Is he in residence?" asked Hugh point-blank.

"That, I am *relieved* to say, is none of your concern," said the butler.

Hugh went farther into the hall, and motioned Jamie in after him. "We have a serious matter to discuss with the justice of the peace." He raised his voice, his fine Welsh voice. "And is it not the right of all Englishmen to demand the presence of the justice?" He thumped the door frame with his good hand. "Didn't men and women die at Runnymede for this privilege?"

"Follow me," said the butler, and turned on his heel.

Omega ushered Angela in front of her and caught up with Hugh. "That's the biggest particle of nonsense I've ever heard," she whispered. "Who taught you history?"

"Yes, it was a real hum, wasn't it?" Hugh agreed. "I, my dear, am entirely self-taught."

Omega smothered a laugh as she hurried to keep up with the butler. She looked about her with real delight. The house was magnificent, all warm woods and gently blowing white curtains. An elegant Persian rug traveled the length of the hall, and felt so soft under her shoes.

Adding to the total picture of understated elegance was a pleasant fragrance, one she could not identify immediately, but which nagged at her. The scent, quietly insistent, competed with the smell of furniture polish and fresh-scrubbed carpets. She frowned as she hurried along. The fragrance was sharp and faint at the same time, and the memory of it clanged somewhere in the back of her brain.

Omega hurried Angela along, though the girl wanted to stop at every open door for a glimpse of splendors within. The butler paused at last and opened a door. He peered in and started to open the door wider, but glanced back at the ragged party following him and evidently reconsidered.

"This will never do," he said severely. "Remain here in the hall. Mind you, don't touch anything!" He glared at Angela, who put her hands behind her back.

With a sigh that emanated from a great depth, the butler swept back to the staircase they had just passed on their march down the hall. Omega heard a door close upstairs, and footsteps in the upper hall overhead. They were measured and slow, as if their owner was pausing every now and then to make last-minute adjustments to his person.

"That will be the viscount," declared Omega triumphantly.

The steps came closer. The butler went to the foot of the stairs just as an aproned lady came in another door. Her face was red and she was breathing hard, as if she had just hurried up a flight of steps. With only the smallest glance in Omega's direction, she approached the stairs too.

"I'm first, Mrs. Wells," said the butler, sounding amazingly to Omega like her grammar girls queuing up for treats.

"But, Mr. Twinings," the woman protested, wiping her forehead, "this is truly important. I simply cannot locate a hare for tonight's game course. And I particularly wanted one."

"I, Mrs. Wells, am representing the law in this instance," said the butler. He looked up the stairs. "My lord, there are some . . ." He stopped, wondering how to classify the soldier, two ragtag children, and the woman who was obviously a lady fallen on hard times. ". . . some people below. They seem to require your presence as justice of the peace."

If the viscount made a reply, Omega could not hear it.

"My lord, they insisted. Perhaps if you hurry down, you can clear up this matter at once and be on your way to the judging."

"Very well, Twinings," said my lord, and he began to descend the stairs. He stopped. "The bookroom?"

"No, my lord," replied the butler, and he made no attempt to spare the feelings of the people in the hall. "They did not look precisely . . . tidy, and I feared for the upholstery on the chairs. You can deal with them in the hall, I am sure."

"And, my lord," said Mrs. Wells, wringing her hands together, "your gamekeeper has failed us. There is not a hare to be seen for tonight's dinner."

"Tell Antoine to fix up something or other in one of his sauces. No one will know."

Omega listened to the high drama being enacted right over their heads. Something else about the tone of that conversation set off another bell clanging in her head.

"My lord!" exclaimed Mrs. Wells. "Antoine will have palpitations!"

"Oh, surely not, Mrs. Wells," said Twinings, intruding in the conversation jealously. "This is a trifling matter."

Mrs. Wells fired her final salvo. "Not to your French cook, it isn't," she declared in round tones, addressing herself to the viscount. "And didn't I hear Lord Cabot inquiring after his services last week?"

"Drat! I'll talk to him, Mrs. Wells."

The viscount did not hurry. "Drat!" he said again.

"Heads up, Jamie," whispered Omega. "You're drooping." She smiled at him. She took a deep breath by way of improving example, and the smile froze on her face.

His lordship continued down the stairs. Omega could see his booted legs. She stood where she was and took another tentative whiff, and then another. It was the same odor she had noticed in the front entrance, the sharp citrus tang of lemon cologne.

"Has something gone cock-a-hoops?" Hugh watched her. "You're quite pale, Omega," he whispered.

She opened her mouth, but nothing came out. She knew she looked like a fish hooked and tossed up on the bank. Omega could only stare at Hugh, not daring to turn around.

She looked down at Jamie, who was watching her in that intense way of his, his head angled to one side. As she stared at him, she knew suddenly where she had seen the boy before. Or one very like him.

"Come, come," said the butler. "The viscount hasn't all day, and you insisted upon his presence. State your business."

"Yes, do," said the viscount, "but turn around, please. See here, I don't bite."

Omega closed her mouth, grasped Jamie firmly by the shoulders, and turned around. "Matthew, may I introduce you to your nephew, Jamie Clevenden?"

The viscount paused in the act of raising a quizzing glass to his eye. The glass slipped through his fingers and swung from the end of the ribbon.

It was the viscount's turn to open his mouth and stare. He blinked his eyes and looked from Omega to Jamie and back to Omega, where his eyes remained fixed to her face.

"Omega Chartley," he managed finally.

"The same, Matthew Bering," she said.

Omega was going to say something else—what, she wasn't sure. Every thought, every polite remark that had ever crossed her lips (growing whiter by the second), rushed out of her brain and left it completely bare. The only urge she felt was the instinct, entirely primitive, to pluck up her skirts and run.

Before she could move, she heard a sound behind her. Omega looked back and could only watch in wide-eyed, stupefied silence as Hugh Owen shouldered his way past her. Before she could even speak, Hugh pulled back and smashed his fist into Lord Byford's elegant face.

The viscount's eyes rolled back in his head. Angela scrambled to get out of the way as Matthew Bering, the Viscount of Byford, thudded to his knees and fell forward, sprawling on the carpet.

Hugh stepped back in quiet triumph. "I told you I'd draw his cork, Omega. Who'd have thought it would be so soon?"

"Who, indeed?" said Omega Chartley. "Oh, Hugh, we are in a real broth now."

6

The butler reeled back as if Hugh had struck him too. He lost his footing and stumbled into a small table, upsetting a Chinese vase. The fragile porcelain keepsake teetered back and forth and then fell to the floor, shattering into a pile of antique rubble and scattering roses and water.

With a low moan the housekeeper sat down hard and toppled over in perfect imitation of the vase. She lay in the middle of the roses and gave herself up to a good faint.

"Do you think she was more concerned about the vase or the viscount?" murmured Hugh as he watched the carnage in the hall.

"Oh, Hugh! Do behave!" exclaimed Omega, not knowing where to turn.

Twinings recovered himself sufficiently to run to the door and shout, "Help! Murder! Murder!" at the top of his lungs. His intentions were earnest, but fear had raised his voice one octave and his cry of desperation was scarcely audible.

Omega looked about her. To her mind, the housekeeper was better left alone. And as long as Twinings gathered no more breath, they were in no immediate danger from the constable. Omega threw herself to her knees and grasped Matthew by the shoulders. She turned him over so he was lying faceup, his head in her lap.

"*Dios mio*," exclaimed Angela, "is he dead?"

"No, and more's the pity," said Omega through gritted teeth, amazed at the sudden anger that washed through her whole body. She regarded him with some satisfaction. Blood dripped steadily from Matthew Bering's nose and deckled his snowy waistcoat and the intricate stock he had obviously taken great pains to tie. His nose was pushed slightly to one side, and his eye was already beginning to blacken.

Omega untied the stock about his neck, wiped the blood around his nose, and pinched the nostrils between her thumb and forefinger. "Open your mouth, Matthew, if you have any intention of breathing," she commanded.

He did as she bade him, and opened his eyes too, or at least the eye he could still open. "*Who* is making that unholy racket?" he managed to ask.

"Your butler."

Matthew rose slightly in her lap. "Twinings," he croaked, "stop that infernal noise!"

The butler looked at the viscount and shuddered. "I can have the constable here in an instant, my lord! We have been set upon by thieves!"

"Oh, stow it somewhere!" said the viscount, and flopped his head back. He touched his swelling eye, wincing and muttering something perfectly awful.

The butler remained where he was by the door until Hugh started toward him, a purposeful glint in his eye.

"Oh, Angela, this is famous!" whispered Jamie.

With a shriek, the butler backed up to the housekeeper, stepping over her with a nimbleness Omega would not have thought possible. His eyes never leaving Hugh Owen's face, Twinings grabbed the housekeeper under the arms and towed her toward the open door that led belowstairs. She was soon out of sight; only the flop-flop of her feet on the stairs could be heard as Twinings dragged her to safety in the servants' hall.

Jamie shook his head. He knelt on the floor beside Omega and regarded his uncle. "I don't think this is quite the impression we wanted, Omega," he stated. "But only think how helpful Hugh has been up to now."

Omega didn't know whether to laugh or to cry. "Oh, Jamie," she said as she hung on to the viscount's nose. "This is your uncle and his name is Matthew Bering. You bear somewhat of a resemblance to him."

"Happy to see you, sir," said Jamie, and held out his hand.

Matthew Bering groaned and took his nephew's hand. "Pleased to see you again, James. It has been years . . .

Good God, what *am* I saying? Oh, the deuce take it, Omega, let go of my nose!"

With a little twist that made him yelp, Omega released his nose, wiping around his nostrils to make sure the bleeding had truly stopped. She touched the rising bump on his nose.

"Matthew, you have been reorganized," she said.

Other than the unexpected calamity to his face, Matthew Bering looked much the same to Omega. His hair, the rich chestnut hair she had always thought so handsome, was the same glorious color. He was a little fuller through the chest, but she had previously thought him too lean anyway. Eight years had scarcely altered him. She almost touched the little mole by his eye before she remembered herself.

"How is it that you are the Viscount Byford?" she asked.

"And how is it that you are here?" he challenged in turn. "What the devil is going on?" He turned his head slowly and regarded his nephew, bewilderment at war with indignation in his brown eyes. "And you, James Clevenden, why are you not at your Uncle Edwin's estate?"

Jamie raised his chin and returned the same brown-eyed stare to his uncle. "I ran away, sir. I have come to live with you."

The viscount groaned and closed his eyes again.

Omega watched him for a considerable moment. "Matthew?" she asked finally.

"I'm not going to open my eyes until you all disappear," was his reply, from the depths of the bloody cravat he held to his nose.

"Oh, I like that!" declared Omega as she grabbed his nose again and held it. "I've lost my luggage and my money, ruined my reputation very likely—*if* there was any of it left to ruin—and now I'm hunted by the law, just because I snatched your nephew from a Bow Street Runner."

"Omega," said Hugh, giving her shoulder a little shake.

"Not now. Let Jamie and me help the viscount to hi chambers and—"

Matthew Bering struggled upright, waving awa Omega's hand. "I am supposed to be judging a horse shov in . . ." He pulled out a watch from his waistcoat. "Goo God, fifteen minutes. If you will be so kind as to help m to my feet, I will be on my way."

Hugh helped him up. "My lord, you're in no conditio to go anywhere. I ought to know, because I'm the one tha hit you."

But the viscount wasn't attending to Hugh Owen. H whirled around to stare at Omega. "Did you say the Bov Street Runners? What curious business is this?" he askec no one in particular.

"It is a rather long story, Uncle," ventured Jamie.

Again Matthew was not paying attention. He lurchec over to the hall mirror and looked into it, aghast. H touched his nose in disbelief, and turned around to stare a the people who watched him. "I am supposed to meet twc gentlemen whose influence will weigh heavily on the future of this little village." His voice was rising. "And I look lik some Johnny Raw just come foxed from a cockfight!" H turned to Omega. "If this is your idea of retribution Miss Chartley," he shouted, "you are wonderfully re venged!"

Omega gasped, and tears sprang to her eyes. Before sh knew what she was doing, she grabbed the front of hi shirt. "This doesn't even begin to touch what you did tc me!" she hissed. "How dare you!"

As soon as the moment came, it passed. Omega burst into tears and sat herself down on the stairs, as far away from the viscount as she could manage.

Omega's tears seemed to recall the viscount to himself He sat down beside her, not looking at her, not touching her, his hand still clutching the stock to his bleeding nose. "That was a terrible thing for me to say," he began, his voice much subdued. "Miss Chartley, I have no idea what is going on, not a single clue. I do know that I have to be at a horse judging." He spread his hand out in front of him. "What am I to do?"

"Sir, if I may suggest . . ." began Hugh in his quiet voice.

"Oh, anything, anything," declared the viscount.

"Give me a suit of your clothes. We are much the same size. I will judge that horse show."

"We look nothing alike," said the viscount dryly.

"Oh, I do not attempt a masquerade. Send me with a letter of introduction . . ."

". . . stating that he is a friend of yours, recently returned from the Battle of Waterloo . . ." continued Angela, her eyes lighting up.

"Yes, Uncle, you had a . . . a trifling accident . . . something to do with . . ."

". . . an open door," contributed Omega, blowing her nose in the one remaining handkerchief in her reticule. "Oh, Hugh, do you know anything about horses?"

"No," he admitted. "But I will politely defer to the other judges and admire their taste. When I bring them back here for dinner, if that was your intention . . ."

"It was," said Matthew. "Which reminds me. I have a disgruntled cook belowstairs." He sighed. "And my servants have probably all fled by the back door." He looked about him in disbelief. "This room was so tidy only a moment ago."

"Oh, it was, wasn't it?" said Angela. "I have never seen such a home. Not even in Spain," she added generously.

"It looks like Bedlam now," said Matthew. He looked down with great distaste at his bloody shirt front. "Or perhaps a slaughtering pen."

"Sir, time is passing," Hugh reminded him.

"So it is." The viscount rose to his feet, touching Omega's shoulder for an instant to regain his balance. "Leonard!" he shouted. "Come down here at once!"

In another moment a man appeared at the top of the stairs. He made strange gargling sounds in his throat as he surveyed the scene below.

"Not a word, Leonard, not a word," warned the viscount. "I'll explain everything to you as soon as I know what is going on. Now, help me upstairs and find a suit of clothes for . . . Sir, who are you?"

Hugh pulled himslf together smartly. "Hugh Owen, my lord, former sergeant in His Majesty's Fifty-first Rifles, Picton's Brigade, God rest his soul."

Matthew allowed a tiny smile to come to his lips. "No, not now. You are Major Hugh Owen of His Majesty's et cetera, et cetera. We were classmates at Oxford."

"Indeed," said Hugh, "and I gave it up for King and Country."

"Exactly. And, Leonard," continued the viscount, "find a black silk scarf of mine to use as a sling for Hugh's arm. It will make him appear more romantic."

"Indeed," echoed Omega.

"Miss Chartley, you are to go belowstairs and promise my cook the sun, moon, and stars, or, failing that, a hare for the game course. When this . . . this charade is over, we will discuss the matter of my nephew. And . . . and anything else that comes to mind."

Without a word, Omega went to the open door, motioning Angela and Jamie to follow.

The servants' hall was deathly quiet, for all that the servants were seated around the dining table. Nine pairs of eyes stared at Omega as she came to the head of the table and clasped her hands tightly together so they would not shake.

"There has been a most unfortunate row upstairs," she began calmly, "and I know that you heard it. Your master is well. No great damage has been done, but I know you are all disturbed."

The eyes didn't move from her face. She looked at them all in turn. "Mrs. Wells? Mrs. Wells, there will be a hare for the game course." She put her hand upon Angela's shoulder. "Angela and Jamie will trap one for you." She put her hand on Jamie's shoulder. "This is James Clevenden, the viscount's nephew. He will be staying here." She paused, and for the first time in eight years felt strangely young as the servants continued to stare at her. "As for the rest, you will simply have to trust me."

Still no one moved. Omega's heart began to drift in the direction of her shoes. She held her chin high and looked into each face again. "I am Omega Chartley. Some of you may know who . . . who I am, but it really is of no importance. I will not be here long. Now, please, help your master."

The silence deepened. Finally Mrs. Wells rose to her feet.

"I wouldn't stay another moment in this deranged household," she began, her face red. She opened her mouth to say more, but Omega spoke up.

"Then leave it, Mrs. Wells," she said quietly. "I have managed a household before, and I am certain I can do justice to this one for the short time I will be here."

Mrs. Wells's eyes seemed to start out of her head. After a long second of floundering about for the correct word to express her sentiment, she turned on her heel and stalked from the room.

Omega glanced at Twinings and was quick to catch the gleam of appreciation in his eyes. "You, sir," she said. "Can you delegate the parlormaid and footman to perform a miracle in that front hall?"

"I can," he said. "Come, Tildy, Michael, you have work to do. And bring a broom and dustpan."

The cook rose next. If Omega had had any doubt that it was the cook, he began to speak in rapid French, gesturing wildly, grandly, pouring out his woes to the ceiling. When he stopped for a breath, Angela plunged into the conversation, her French as rapid-fire as his. Omega's eyes opened wide. Angela turned to her at last, a note of undisguised triumph in her voice.

"He will stay for two rabbits and a trout."

"A trout? Oh, Angela, however will you produce a trout?"

"Omega, she probably has a line and hook in her bag," Jamie said.

"You peeked!" accused Angela.

Jamie just grinned and started for the stairs. Angela hurried after him. She said a few more hurried words to the cook, who smiled and kissed his hand at her. Humming to himself, the cook pulled the scullery maid and the potboy to their feet and headed in the direction of the kitchen.

"Omega, we need you upstairs," Jamie called.

Omega hurried upstairs. Hugh stood before her, immaculate in Matthew Bering's clothes. She walked around him. "Well, the coat is large," she said, "but have you not been in hospital for over a month?"

"I did lose weight in hospital, Omega," Hugh agreed.

Matthew had removed his bloody shirt and was wrapped in his dressing gown. He straightened the sling of black silk. "You'll do," he said, handing Hugh a letter. "This should give you the introduction you need. Bring them back here after the judging, and we'll see if my Banbury tale is convincing enough."

Hugh saluted smartly and took the hat from Leonard and left. Matthew shook his head. "This is very odd," he said to no one in particular. His eyes lighted on Omega next; he appeared to be seriously regarding her for the first time.

"Tildy," he called over his shoulder. "I want you."

The maid handed the broom to Michael, the footman, and curtsied in front of the viscount.

"Take Miss Chartley upstairs and find her a dress." Without another word, he went up the stairs, shaking off Leonard, who tried to help him.

"Follow me, Miss Chartley," said Tildy, and started up the stairs. Omega stayed where she was until she heard the door upstairs close, and then she followed the maid.

"Is Lord Byford married?" she asked finally.

"Oh, no, ma'am," said the maid.

They were passing the viscount's room. "Then how is it that he has dresses?" Omega whispered.

"That I do not understand, ma'am," whispered Tildy in turn as she opened a door beyond and stood back for Omega to enter.

Omega went to the window immediately, opened the draperies, and let in the sunlight. The room was stuffy; she opened the window, flinging it wide, and then leaned out to appreciate the gracious flower garden below the window.

"I do recall that my lord specifically required flowers to be planted there. My brother did it," said Tildy. " 'Just broadcast the seed,' his lordship told my brother. 'Let it be like a meadow.' It *is* beautiful, isn't it, Miss Chartley?"

"And so is the room, Tildy," said Omega. The ceiling was low, but this troubled her not at all. There was a coziness that made Omega smile for the first time since she had crossed the threshold of Matthew Bering's house. What a pleasant room this would be in the winter. When the day was gray and rainy outside, this place would be a sanctuary, a place to sew, and read, and just think about things. Omega thought briefly of her damp room in Plymouth that looked over the sound, and then dismissed it forever from her memory.

Again there was that persistent smell of lemon cologne, even in this closed room. How singular.

"Well, Tildy, what have you here?" she said at last.

Tildy appeared not to be attending. "Begging your pardon, miss," she said. "I sometimes wish I had leave to come up here and just sit. Sometimes Lord Byford asks me to dust in here, and then I do sit for a moment, but only for a moment."

Omega smiled again. "I can understand."

"But here is why we have come," said the maid. She passed into the little dressing room. Omega followed, and her mouth dropped open in surprise.

The room was lined with dresses, dresses of all colors and fabrics, walking dresses, morning dresses, sleeping gowns, simple muslin frocks, more elaborate afternoon dresses, cloaks and capes, dominoes. Rows of shoes peeped out from under the dresses, and there were hatboxes on the shelf overhead.

"Oh, Tildy, whatever *is* all this?" she exclaimed.

"I do not know, Miss Chartley." The maid touched one of the dresses. "They're a trifle outmoded, but not by too many years. They were here when I took up my position in this house four years ago." She paused a moment, as if wondering if she should pursue this conversational thread. "It is a subject of some interest belowstairs, ma'am. We have—oh, you'll laugh—we have created our own mythology."

"I would have done the same thing, I am sure."

Omega took one of the frocks, a basic muslin dress, and held it up to her. The hem just brushed the tips of her shoes. It would likely be a perfect fit.

Tildy clapped her hands. "How lucky we are! Oh, Miss Chartley, you can take your pick!"

"It will be something simple," said Omega, "if I am to become the housekeeper for the day."

"As to that, I cannot say that I am sad," confided Tildy as she searched through the dresses. "Mrs. Wells was ever so difficult belowstairs. And none of us could bring ourselves to tell his lordship about the quantities of port she put away when she thought none of us were watching."

"Well, I will not do that. Oh, look, that one, that blue dress. That will be quite the thing, don't you agree? Now, where can I find an apron?"

"I have an extra down in the servants' hall. Now, Miss Chartley, let me see to a bath for you."

"I would like that," Omega murmured. Her last ablutions had been hastily performed in the River By with a sliver of soap that had seen much duty in Spain, France, and Belgium. "And if there is any shampoo . . ."

"I'll find what you need." Tildy handed her the dress. "There are linens and things in the drawers. Do we ask too much . . . do you think the shoes will fit?"

"It's possible."

After Tildy left the room, Omega sat down on the bed. She had no doubt that the shoes would fit. So would the chemise and camisoles. Matthew must have prepared this wardrobe for her eight years ago.

Omega took off her shoes and tucked her feet up under her. She hadn't thought of it in years, but she remembered showing off some of her trousseau to him only days before the wedding, letting her excitement at the beautiful clothes spill over probably where it should not have. Her companion had told her later how improper she was, but she had not cared overmuch. She had been deeply in love with Matthew Bering. She wanted him to see what the Chartleys considered fine enough for such a wonderful marriage.

The trousseau was long gone, sold at auction with everything else. She smiled to herself for no good reason. None of her pretties would have mattered. She could have come to Matthew Bering in her shift, and there would have been this magnificent wardrobe waiting for her.

And there was a time I would have come to you in my shift, Matthew, she thought, if only . . . if only you had told me why.

Such melancholy reflections were not improving the tenor of her mind. When Tildy, Michael, the scullery girl, and the potboy returned with tin tub and buckets of warm water, she was only too grateful to hurry their preparations and close the door on them. The thought of a bath was almost enough to make her mouth water.

Even though she had not time for the luxury of a long soak in the tub, Omega washed her hair, scrubbed herself briskly, and took an idle moment to sit in the warm water, her chin resting on her drawn-up knees, contemplating the strange workings of fate.

She made idle circles in the water. How was it that Matthew was the Viscount Byford? It was a title unknown to her. She looked across her knees to the dressing room and the rows of beautiful clothes. Why would he do such a thing? She sighed and splashed the circles. How little I really know of him. How strange is the human mind.

"Now, if I were a Roman," she said, "I would put it down to the capricious humor of Jupiter. As it is, I must blame dreadful coincidence and awful fate."

It was a simple matter to dress quickly, not dwelling overmuch on the dainty underthings and other personal items in the drawers. She gave her hair a vigorous brushing and wished for the millionth time that it did not curl in such an exasperating fashion. "This is not the hair of an educationist," she told the mirror.

Exasperation always led eventually to resignation. With a sigh that came all the way from her shoes, she found a pretty lace cap and planted it firmly on her curls, resolving to indulge in no more peeks in the mirror. There was work to be done.

Angela and Jamie had not yet returned when she entered

the main hall again. The gardener had brought in an armful of flowers. She followed him downstairs and located a large crystal vase.

"Mrs. Wells was going to place this epergne on the table," said Tildy. "I took the liberty of sending my brother for flowers instead."

"That was a much wiser choice," replied Omega, eyeing the monstrous silver centerpiece. "Rather quelling, isn't it?"

"Yes, and it does not fit our dining room."

Our dining room. Omega liked that. Obviously the servants of Byford's house had taken the place to their hearts. It spoke well of Matthew Bering.

"Beg pardon, Miss Chartley?"

Had she spoken out loud? "Oh, nothing, nothing. Here, Tildy, would you like me to arrange these flowers?"

"Oh, yes, if you would. I'm all thumbs with flowers, and Twinings asked me to hurry with the front hall so I can polish the silver. It has been a long time since we had any company, and some of his lordship's best pieces are quite tarnished." She paused a moment and took a good look at Omega. "And, Miss Chartley, how well that dress fits you! Blue is surely your color."

"Oh, my, thank you," said Omega in some confusion. She had not heard a compliment in years. "Hadn't you . . . hadn't you better hurry with the upstairs front hall?"

Omega arranged the flowers in the vase, wondering how Angela and Jamie were faring, wondering if Hugh could carry off his charade, wondering if Matthew should see a doctor. Matthew Bering. If people had told her at the start of her holiday that she would be arranging flowers in his house, she would have thought them all about in their heads. It remained only to see Jamie safely settled here. And surely there might be a place for Hugh in Byford, and Angela too. Omega kept thinking of Angela's eyes as the girl had looked about the house. Surely there must be a place for Angela.

The chef came to admire the flowers, speaking in his rapid French and gesturing grandly to her. Omega's schoolroom French had been mutinously learned and quickly forgotten. She could only smile and nod as the cook went on and on, and wish Angela were here to interpret.

He paused and looked at her inquiringly. Omega nodded and smiled again, and then squeaked in alarm as the Frenchman grabbed her around the waist, pulled her close, and planted a kiss on her lips.

She looked around wildly for assistance, but she should not have worried. As suddenly as he had grabbed her, the cook released her, kissed his fingers to her, and pinched her as he strutted back to his kitchen.

Omega could only stare after him, resolving then and there to improve her French instead of relying on smiles and nods. She looked about her. No one else had seen the Frenchman's demonstration of affection. Twinings was wiping glasses in the pantry, and Tildy was only now returning to the servants' hall from abovestairs. Omega picked up the vase and beat a hasty retreat up the stairs.

The flowers looked particularly well on the table. Someone—it must have been Tildy—had placed a lace runner the length of the table. The wood contrasted darkly with it and created a dramatic effect. She centered the vase and stepped back from the table to survey her handiwork, moving forward to touch a rose here, a fern there.

She sighed and stepped back again. "Oh, I simply must be on my way to Durham," she said.

"Durham?"

She hadn't heard Matthew enter the room. He was dressed quite casually in trousers and open shirt. And he was fuller in the chest. She hadn't imagined it, after all. Maybe his chest had even dropped a little. She surveyed him as critically as she had looked at the roses, and decided that a little added weight suited his mature years.

"Durham," she repeated. "St. Elizabeth's Academy for Young Ladies. I will be paid a small salary, plus room and board. And there is always extra for private tutoring. Thank heaven English is so mysterious."

Matthew's eye was swollen shut. His nose no longer looked pushed to one side, but there was a bump in it that hadn't been there before.

"Oh, Matthew, your face," was all she could say.

He came no closer, but leaned against the doorframe. "I don't think my guests will fall for any cock-and-bull story about a suddenly opened door."

"I think not," she agreed. "You must tell them that you bent over and caught yourself on an open drawer. Alpha did that once."

"Omega! That's even worse than the door story!" he declared.

"Yes, I suppose it is. Perhaps Hugh has told them something entirely different by now. It only remains for him to return and enlighten you. If you will excuse me . . ."

She wanted to get out of the room. Even after all these years, it was hard to stand there and make polite conversation with the man she had wanted beyond all bounds of propriety and who had left her at the church door.

He made no comment, only stepped aside.

She got no farther than the front hall. Angela and Jamie came in the door, Jamie bearing two hares, their ears threaded through a long cord and draped over his shoulder. Angela carried a trout that threatened to slide from the brown paper wrapped about its middle. Both children dripped water on the carpet.

"Oh, Jamie, Angela!" Omega exclaimed as she hurried to them. "The chef will be so pleased! But how wet you are!"

Jamie looked at his uncle and smiled broadly. "Uncle, I hope you don't mind my saying so, but your hares are remarkably stupid hereabouts. I don't know that there is anything you can do about it," he added generously, to soften the blow, "but it ain't much sport."

Matthew's lips twitched and he laughed in spite of himself. "This is not the best hunting country, lad, for rabbits or otherwise. I go to Northamptonshire in the season. Or rather, I used to."

"My papa was a hunter."

"I remember, lad, I remember." The viscount clapped his hands together. "But see now, Angela is struggling with that leviathan of a trout. Wherever did you find this, child?''

Omega noted with approval that when he addressed Angela, he got down on his knees so as to look into her face. How does he know children particularly like that in adults? she thought.

Angela struggled with the limp fish, which slid out of her grasp and plopped onto the hall runner. She tried to wrestle it back into the brown paper, but the paper was soggy and disintegrated in her hands. Omega thought for a moment she was going to cry.

Matthew must have thought so too. He took a handkerchief from his pocket and wrapped it around the fish. "There, now. My dear, did you purchase this beast?"

Angela nodded, too shy to speak.

Jamie took up the story. "I almost thought we had one for you, Uncle, but it moved before Angela could grab it." He looked at Omega. "And do you know what Angela did then?"

"I have no idea, Jamie, but I want to hear."

"She went to the fishmonger and traded Napoleon's prayerbook for the biggest trout he had!"

"Good God, wherever did you get Napoleon's prayerbook?" exclaimed Matthew in amazement, and then spoke over his shoulder in Omega's general direction. "I wouldn't have thought the Anti-Christ to possess one."

"Perhaps I was not entirely truthful," said Angela scrupulously. "But I did pick it up on the Waterloo battlefield near Hougoumont, and I think it was in French." She lowered her voice. "I do not read. Maybe it was Latin."

Matthew got to his feet and handed the trout to Angela. "Then who is to dispute you? A genuine battlefield souvenir ought to be worth a trout."

"That's what I thought, sir. Come along, Jamie. The cook will be wanting these."

Lugging her trout, she started for the stairs. Matthew touched her shoulder. "And you gave up your souvenir for my dinner?" he asked gently.

She smiled at him, and Omega watched with delight as

the dimple came out in her cheek. "It wasn't hard, sir. We—Hugh and I—we owe you something. I hope you aren't too mad at all of us."

His hand went to her hair. "Perhaps I am not so angry anymore. Now, hurry up, you two. That horse show will be over soon, and my guests will be wanting their dinner, provided they are still speaking to me."

"Yes, hurry, my dears," echoed Omega. "I'll be down in a moment. There's much to be done yet."

Matthew held the door for the children. Omega couldn't see his face, but his shoulders shook slightly, and she knew he was chuckling to himself. He looked back at her and then at the sopping, smelly carpet.

"Come, Omega, let us roll this up. It smells fishy."

She nodded and began at her end of the runner. Matthew began at the other end, but in a moment he waved his hand and sat down on the stairs. "I can't," he said. "Every time I bend over, my face feels as though it is going to fall out on the floor. What did he hit me with?"

"The only fist he has left, sir."

"Am I such an ogre?" he murmured. "What on earth did you tell him?"

Her confusion returned. Omega lowered her head so he could not see her face, and continued rolling up the carpet. "Very little, sir. Truly I am not in the habit of idle chat."

"Then I think he is very protective of you, Miss Chartley. You, uh, you have a way of bringing that out in people, obviously."

"Some people, sir. Shall I leave this here?"

He nodded. "Michael will take it belowstairs."

"I will tell him." The dearest wish of her heart was to leave the hall by the fastest possible route. "I must go help Tildy with the silver."

"Very well. And I will seek my bed again. I am sure Jamie will think I am a granny goose, but my head is still ringing. By the way, Omega, thank you for saving my cook."

"You can thank Angela and her wild game," Omega replied crisply. "Your wretched cook took advantage of my lamentable French and kissed me and pinched me!"

"Oh, did he?" Matthew began, a little light coming into his eye again.

"Yes, and I'll very likely have a black-and-blue mark." She hadn't meant to tell him that.

Matthew rose to his feet. "Well, I shall speak to him later. But you must own, Miss Chartley, that you're much less an antidote than Mrs. Wells, and after all, he *is* French."

"Sir," she burst out, "I am twenty-six and much too old for that sort of thing!"

"I know precisely to the day how old you are, Omega Chartley, and I don't scruple to tell you that you've rarely uttered a bigger prevarication. And if you think that lace cap adds years and wrinkles, you'd better continue to keep an eye out . . . for my cook. Good day, Omega. I am returning to my hunk of sirloin, which Leonard is convinced will help my black eye. Do excuse me."

She watched him go up the stairs and heartily wished him to the devil.

7

Omega remained belowstairs, prudently out of reach of the chef's hands. Tildy had already divested the children of their wet clothing. They sat wrapped in blankets by the fire as the maid spread their clothes in the warmest part of the kitchen.

Before much time had passed, Angela was seated on a stool by the cook, who was speaking to her in French as he cleaned the fish. Omega was pleased to note how eager he was to converse in his own language. Feeling more charitable as she watched him work and talk to Angela, Omega put his impropriety down to loneliness.

She could understand loneliness, she thought as she polished Matthew Bering's silver. No other instructor at Miss Haversham's school in Plymouth had her background; for whatever reason of class or boundary, no one had chosen to pursue her acquaintance, and she was too shy to force herself on others. She had no friends at the school, only colleagues. And probably that is why I have become so used to talking to myself, she told herself. Gracious, it only lacks for me to start collecting cats and knitting useless tea cozies to complete my spinsterhood.

Perhaps that was why she found the company of Hugh Owen so pleasant. How nice it was to talk to someone again, someone besides distant fellow-faculty and fubsy-faced children, pasty from long winters of inactivity and too much heavy pudding. Her admiration did not end with Hugh, but included Angela and Jamie. How much there is to learn from children, she thought. And how quickly they have become indispensable to me.

She finished polishing the salt cellar and filled it, resolving to leave the moment this matter of Jamie was resolved. She stacked a tray with china for the table upstairs and started up the steps, careful to keep a firm grasp on her skirts. How *did* servants manage on stairs?

Omega lugged the tray into the dining room, admiring the effect of the flowers in the crystal vase. Oh, if this were my house, I would place a small table under that window and there would be flowers all summer. And chrysanthemums when the air turned cool, and holly during the cold days of winter.

She arranged the plates quickly, the ticking of the clock on the sideboard reminding her that horse shows don't last forever. She was placing cutlery about when she had a lowering thought: I have absolutely no money. How on earth am I going to get to Durham?

She sank down into the chair at the head of the table and rested her elbows on the arms. If she wrote to Alpha for a loan, he would send her one. He was scarcely a day's drive away in Amphney St. Peter. This thought was followed by a more chilling one. He would do no such thing. Alpha Chartley, beloved Alpha, would demand her direction and insist on meeting her in person to find out what kind of scrape she had got herself into. And if he saw Matthew Bering, Alpha would surely call him out.

Omega closed her eyes and put her hands over her face. Dear, dear Alpha, gentleman, scholar, father, who had never fired a pistol in his life. He must never find out where she was.

She tried to think what to do. The only other recourse was to apply to Matthew Bering, Vicount Byford, for a loan. "Oh, God, I cannot," she said.

"Cannot what, my dear?"

Omega jerked her hands away from her face and opened her eyes. Matthew was standing quietly in the doorway. He was dressed carefully in the elegance of a country gentleman again, stock neatly tied, coat smoothed across his shoulders without a wrinkle. He walked slowly to the other end of the table and sat down. "Cannot what?" he asked again when she did not seem disposed to reply.

There are moments when only the truth will do. "I cannot ask you for a loan to quit this place, Matthew," she answered. "And I dare not tell Alpha my whereabouts, for he would surely challenge you to a duel. I hardly need scruple to describe the outcome of that to you, sir."

Matthew considered her predicament. "If you cannot apply to me to bring you up to scratch, and you don't want to risk Alpha's health, whatever will you do?"

He was teasing her. There was a twinkle in his eye as he leaned back in the chair and regarded her. He was playing with her emotions like a musician with an instrument. How dare he? She rose to her feet slowly, horrified by the intensity of her rage. Had there been a pistol within easy reach, she would have shot him.

He saw the anger in her face. The twinkle left his eye and he sat up straight again. "That was unthinkable of me," he said. "I have no business being unkind to you." He waited a moment. "Oh, say something, Omega!"

She could think of nothing that would do justice to her feelings. There weren't enough words in the language. She could only shake her head and hurry to the door, desperate to get belowstairs again.

There was another look in Matthew Bering's eye that she couldn't identify. A chill settled around her heart. She got to the door first and stepped into the hall in time to narrowly avoid Twinings, who was hurrying to the front door.

Hugh had returned. Thank God. That would be sufficient diversion to allow an escape. Besides, there was much to do belowstairs. Omega Chartley chose discretion over valor, and fled to the safety of the servants' hall.

The dinner was a total success, from soup to fruit. Tildy, Michael, and Twinings had no time to comment as they hurried up and down the stairs, but the look of triumph in the maid's eyes told Omega that all was going well.

Omega continued where she was belowstairs, and Angela and Jamie too, shuttling dishes from the kitchen to the table in the servants' hall, where Tildy and Michael bore them upstairs. Angela's eyes grew wider with each course that passed before her.

"How many people are up there?"

"Four, I believe," said Omega.

"Jamie, there is enough food here to feed a Spanish village," she said to her companion, who had been assigned the task of wiping up any spills on bowls or platters. "And look how much they bring down that is only partly eaten."

Jamie shrugged. It was nothing new to him.

"Jamie, only think how well you will eat here!"

"I haven't heard my Uncle Byford say anything about my staying," was his reply. He looked at Omega for reassurance, but she could give him none beyond a smile and a touch on the head. Omega was past attempting to divine what Matthew Bering would do. She had no expectations. If Omega had had the remotest knowledge of whose estate she had so blithely led Jamie to, she would have kept walking and put him in Alpha Chartley's capable hands, hang the consequences.

I may have done the lad a dreadful disservice, was her thought as she carried empty bowls from Tildy's hands into the washroom, where the scullery maid was already elbow-deep in suds. Her instinct for flight grew by the minute. The only thing that kept her working was a certain determination to see a task through, no matter how distasteful.

Hours passed. "Dear God, will they never go?" she said to Tildy at one point.

Tildy had taken advantage of a rare moment and was seated at the servants' table. "Surely that is a good sign, Miss Chartley," she said. "You know how people always hurry off when they are not happy."

I can well appreciate that, Omega thought.

"This means the business is a success. I can't wait for Hugh Owen to tell us about it," the maid continued. "Think what it will mean for our village!"

"What *will* it mean?" asked Omega. In all the bustle and the anxiety, she had no idea what the issue was.

"Lord Nickle and Sir Martin Dorking are the silent backers of a carting firm out of London," explained Tildy as she scraped plates into a pan. "It's between Byford and Regis as to which of our towns becomes a stop on the route."

"And if it is Byford . . ."

"Goods will travel that much quicker to the markets in Oxford and London. My papa says it is the best thing to happen to us since the old viscount died."

Omega blinked. "Whatever do you mean?"

"He was a dreadful man, always drinking and wenching. Papa would never let me work here if the old viscount hadn't cocked up his toes. Matthew Bering is such an improvement." Tildy eyed Omega. "I . . . we are all so pleased to serve him, Miss Chartley. I must admit . . . I do not understand why you seem to get a little white about the mouth when you have to talk to him."

"Oh, it is . . ." How could she possibly explain what she didn't understand herself?

She was saved from wallowing about for the right words by a step on the stairs. Hugh Owens came down into the servants' hall. Angela ran to him and he gave her a quick hug.

"You look magnificent," she said. "Much better than usual!"

"Oh, I like that!" said Hugh, and smiled over Angela's head at Omega. "There is much to be said for being a gentleman—the best sherry, a truly masterful cigar, clothes that tolerate sitting hour after hour. Angela, I think I will become a gentleman.''

Angela laughed and pushed him into a chair. "Have they gone?"

"Almost. Lord Byford is even now walking them to their curricle. No one seems in any hurry.'' He looked back over his shoulder at Omega. "I think the issue is won, Omega. I impressed them—and me—with my knowledge of horseflesh, our chef here bowled them over—thanks to our wily hunters —and everyone remarked on the sophisticated yet simple arrangement of flowers.''

Omega sat down across from Hugh and rested her elbows on the table. "Whatever did you come up with to explain Matthew . . . Lord Byford's eye?"

"I told the truth.''

"The truth,'' Omega gasped. "And they *stayed*?''

The door opened and Matthew Bering descended the stairs, followed by the butler. From the look Twinings gave the other servants as he followed his master, Omega could tell that such condescension was not an everyday occurrence. The servants began to rise.

"No, no. Stay where you are. You, too, Miss Chartley. Sit, sit.''

The servants looked at each other. Twinings pulled out a chair for his master. Matthew sank into it with a sigh. He glanced at Michael, who was leaning against the dry sink. "Michael, could I trouble you for a rag dipped in cold water and wrung out? My eye feels like the Cyclops' orb.'' Michael did as he was bidden. "That, lad, is *much* better. Yes, Hugh told them the truth. But it's your story, Owen.''

Hugh nodded graciously. "I told 'em I had struck my best friend Matthew a mighty blow when he attempted to wake me from a sound sleep. Forgot myself. I thought I was on the battlefield at Waterloo." He grinned. "Not that anyone was sleeping at Waterloo, but sudden shocks, you know . . . So we have been refighting the battle for the last two hours, Angela. Who would have thought Waterloo would become a dinner-table diversion so soon?''

Matthew shrugged. "It must have sounded plausible to Lord Nickle and Sir Martin. Of course, my good friend Major Owen had already made serious inroads on their affections at the horse judging. Again, Hugh, it is your story."

Hugh smiled modestly around the table. "That was the easiest part, my lord . . . and lady," he said with a nod in Omega's direction. "It was a mere matter of follow-the-leader. I hung back from the lord and the sir, nodding when they nodded, patting where they patted. Oh, Angela, I could read those two like Señora Muñoz read her tarot cards!"

His words were boastful, but accompanied by such a grin that everyone at the table smiled. "I was so agreeable. Happens we made some good choices. There are some devilish fine horses in this country, my lord."

"There are. 'Happens' I own some of them." Matthew took the cloth from his eye. "And thank you, Miss Chartley, for your role in this evening's events. And you too, Angela and Jamie. Angela, what's this? Are you drooping?"

Angela rested her head on her arms. Matthew reached across and touched her head, shaking it slowly from side to side. "And thank you again, child, for surrendering your battlefield souvenir for the good of Byford—and the viscount."

Angela mumbled something but did not open her eyes.

"Tildy, find a bed for Angela . . . and for Jamie and Hugh too. It appears I have houseguests." He pushed his chair back from the table and crossed his legs, giving himself over to an enormous yawn that stopped almost before it started.

"The devil, my face hurts," he said. "Friend Owen, please tell me that I'll feel better in the morning."

"You might, my lord," replied Hugh. He rose to his feet and prodded Angela. "Come along, *muñequita*. Let us follow where Tildy leads. You too, Jamie." He followed the maid up the stairs, pausing at the top step, his face suddenly serious, the smile gone. "I don't really have any regrets about drawing your cork, my lord. Good night, Omega. Don't stay up too late. Tomorrow may be even more trying than today.''

"He is a quixotic combination of parts," murmured Matthew. His face was red with embarrassment, and he made no attempt to look her in the eye. "You have obviously found yourself a champion, Omega.''

"It is of no consequence," she replied, taking off her apron and draping it over the chair. "And, Matthew, I will apply to you for that loan. I need only enough to get me to Durham. I'll repay you after the first quarter. I just wanted to see Jamie situated.''

Matthew reached out suddenly and took her by the hand, compelling her to sit down again. "Omega, you know I can't keep him here.''

She jerked her hand away, but she did not rise. She leaned toward him across the table. "I know no such thing, Matthew Bering! He's been beaten by that . . . that man who is his guardian. Surely you do not countenance such things!''

He shook his head, and she could see, despite her own impulsive fury, how very tired he was. And there was something more, something she could not explain, but which sent shivers down her spine.

"I do not look with favor on such things, Omega, but there is the matter of the law. Lord Rotherford is James Clevenden's legal guardian.''

"Can't you fight for him? Defend him? God, does your nephew have no friends?''

His voice was level, rising a little to compete with hers. "I cannot keep him. And I cannot tell you why.''

"I suppose you cannot tell me why you left me at the altar, either, can you, Lord Byford?'' she lashed out.

"No, I cannot.'' His voice was barely a whisper now.

"Damn you, Matthew Bering," she said, her voice as low as his.

He raised his eyes to hers then. "That's already been done, Omega, rest assured. Good night.''

Without another glance at him, she ran up the servants' stairs, and resisted the urge to slam the door behind her.

Twinings had put out the lights and the hall was dark except for two candles on the table under the mirror. Jamie stood beside the table, waiting for her.

"Jamie," she exclaimed, "I thought you were in bed."

He shook his head. Omega touched his shoulder and felt him tremble. "I came back down for a glass of water," he whispered. "Omega, he's not going to let me stay here? Is that what I heard him say? Oh, I didn't mean to eavesdrop, but I couldn't help it."

She put her hands on his shoulders and drew him close. "Oh, Jamie, I wish I knew what was wrong here. But please, please, don't worry. Go to bed now, and sleep, and in the morning Hugh and I will think of something." She paused and thought of her brother. "There may be someone who will help us."

"But it's not going to be my Uncle Matthew." His voice was the voice she had prayed never to hear again, flat and devoid of hope.

She sighed and hugged Jamie. "We'll . . . we'll think of something. Things always look better in the morning."

Jamie let go of her and stepped back, looking into her eyes. "Do you *really* believe that, Omega?"

There was nothing she could say. She steered him up the stairs and into his room. She sat beside his bed a moment, but when he would say nothing else, but only stared at the ceiling, his lips tight together, she rose and quietly closed the door.

Tildy met her in the hall. "Here, Miss Chartley, you forgot your candle."

She took it. "Where am I to sleep, Tildy?"

The maid looked surprised. "Why, in the room with all the beautiful clothes."

Omega shook her head. "I wouldn't sleep in there for anything. Just . . . just let me get a nightgown and show me where Angela is sleeping. Surely there is room with her."

Omega darted into the room. A fire glowed in the hearth and the chair had been pulled up close to it. The bed had already been turned down and a nightgown lay across it. She snatched up the gown and followed Tildy to Angela's room. Angela was already asleep. Omega blew out the candle and undressed in the dark, crawling in beside the little girl, who sighed and tucked herself close. Gradually Omega felt herself relax. She closed her eyes and slept.

Rain was falling when she woke. The room was still dark, and she feared she had overslept. Angela was already gone. Omega threw back the covers and then hugged them to her again. The room was chilly. She wiggled her toes under the blanket and sank down deeper in the feather bed.

She was drifting back to sleep again when she heard Angela crying in the hall. Omega sat bolt upright, listening. She leapt out of bed and threw open the door.

Angela stood in the hall with Matthew Bering. His hand was on her shoulder, and he was talking earnestly to her, but she was not listening. She raised her face to Omega's wide eyes.

"Jamie's gone," she sobbed. She ran to Omega, who grabbed her and hugged her. "Hugh went to look for him. I wanted to go too, but *he* wouldn't let me!" She raised stormy eyes to Matthew's face and then looked away from him.

"It's too rainy outside, and besides, the river rises when it's like this."

"Angela's not afraid of rain, Matthew," Omega chided, "and she probably swims better than you do. Come, child, let me get dressed and we'll go look for him too."

"No, Omega."

Matthew grasped her shoulder, but she shook him off. "If there ever was a time you could tell me what to do, Matthew, it's gone." Her eyes clouded over. "I can't believe you are so unfeeling. Maybe I never really knew you."

She went back into the room with Angela and locked the door behind her, dressing quickly, dragging a comb through her hair. She thought of the warm cloaks in the pretty bedroom next to the viscount's room, and then dismissed them. It was only an August rain. She wouldn't melt.

Matthew had left the hall. Omega took Angela by the

hand and walked toward the stairs. "Do you have any idea where Jamie might be?" she whispered as they tiptoed past the viscount's room.

Angela shook her head. The door to Matthew Bering's room opened and she jumped. Omega took a firmer grasp on her hand and started down the stairs.

"Omega, wait!"

She turned around to look at Matthew, who was coming down the stairs right behind her. Omega let go of Angela. "Go ahead. I'll find you in a moment." Angela ran out the front door, leaving it wide open for the rain to blow in.

"Omega, you don't need to go look too," Matthew said. His voice was conversational. He came closer on the stairs. "I wish you would be reasonable about this whole matter."

She could match him calm for calm. "I'm not going to abandon someone who needs my help. I have a peculiar habit, Lord Byford. I like to see something through to its conclusion."

He winced at that, but did not stop. "Even if aiding a fugitive is against the law?"

"Yes, if it comes down to that." Little sparks of anger flicked about in her brain. "And I feel responsible. I'm the one who helped him find this place, which has only multiplied his troubles! Excuse me now, Matthew."

She turned to follow Angela, forgetting there were two more steps to go on the stairway. When she hit the first step, she fumbled for the banister. Matthew made a grab for her and missed, and she tripped down the next step and sprawled on the floor, slippery with rain.

Omega cried out as pain laced through her ankle. She felt sick to her stomach and thought for a moment she would disgrace herself entirely in front of Matthew and the servants, who had heard her shriek and were running up from the servants' hall.

Matthew knelt by her and touched her face. "Omega, are you all right?"

She nodded, not sure enough of herself to speak. Tears of frustration and pain came into her eyes and she tried to brush them away. She grabbed the banister and hauled herself to her feet. The pain in her right ankle made her gasp.

Matthew scooped her into his arms. "Omega, you're . . . you're . . ."

She burst into tears.

His voice was more gentle then. Matthew held her closer to his chest. "You're getting my coat all wet." He sighed and spoke into her ear. "Now, how am I going to go look for Jamie if I'm soaked through before I even leave the house?"

She sobbed louder.

"Michael, go get the doctor. Tildy, come with me."

Despite Omega's protests, he deposited her on the bed in the little room next to his. "Tildy, get her into a nightgown. I'm going downstairs to wait for the doctor."

"But you said you were going to look for Jamie!" Omega wailed.

"My tiresome runaway of a nephew can damned well wait until the doctor has seen you, Omega. Lord, but you're stubborn!" He put his handkerchief over her nose and made her blow. "Now, hush a minute and do what Tildy says. And if you don't cooperate, I'll help her."

She grabbed his handkerchief from him and wiped her nose, giving him a speaking look.

He stared right back. "And don't say 'You wouldn't dare,' because I would."

By the time Tildy had helped her into a nightgown, Omega's ankle was swollen to twice its normal size. "Oh, Tildy, what am I going to do?" she said in vexation. The pain was still turning her stomach.

"You're going to let me prop this pillow under your foot and you're going to lie down, Miss Chartley," said Tildy in a firm voice. "And if you feel like you're going to chuck last night's dinner, you'd better let me run for a pan."

"Hurry, Tildy!"

The maid darted for the door, only to be met by Matthew, who had a pan in his hand. He hurried to Omega's side just in time to shove the pan on her lap and hold her hair back while she vomited.

Omega clutched the sides of the pan and retched and gagged until her stomach was empty. She shuddered a few times but didn't relinquish her grip until Matthew pried off her fingers and set the pan outside the door. He came back to the bed.

"Move over, Omega." He sat down beside her and wiped her face with a damp cloth. She lay back in exhaustion on the pillow. Tears welled in her eyes again.

"I'm so embarrassed," she said, and tried to push him away.

The viscount wouldn't be pushed. "Don't be a goose, Omega. Let me raise your head and give you a sip of water."

She did as he said, and he sat down on the chair by the bed. Omega closed her eyes and did not open them again until Tildy knocked on the door and ushered in the doctor.

The doctor poked and prodded her ankle while she hung on to Matthew's hand.

"Young lady, I don't believe it's broken." The doctor shook his head. "Likely you'd feel better if it were." He looked at Matthew. "My lord, I will instruct the maid to keep Miss Chartley's foot elevated, and to apply cold cloths. Two days of that should be sufficient, and then I'll look at it again and we'll see where to go from there."

"Two days!" said Omega. She released Matthew's hand. "But I plan to be out of here this afternoon at the latest!"

The doctor laughed. "You're a funny one, Miss Chartley. Tildy has a sleeping powder here for you. Take it like a good girl."

"I won't."

"She will."

She did. After the doctor left, Matthew watched her a moment longer. Her eyelids began to droop and he appeared to grow larger and smaller, and then to disappear altogether. But he hadn't vanished; he was kneeling by her bed.

"Omega, can you hear me?"

She nodded.

"I'm going after Jamie now."

She nodded again. Her lips felt dry, and his voice was so far away.

"And when I bring him back, Omega, we'll talk."

She nodded again. She thought he kissed her on the forehead, but the room was dark, the rain thundered down, and she was so tired she couldn't be sure.

8

The rain continued throughout the day. After the sleeping powders took effect, Omega dozed and wakened, only to have the sound of the rain drumming on the windowpanes pull her back to sleep. She was conscious of a dull throb in her ankle, but she was too sleepy to care.

She woke finally in the afternoon. Tildy had pulled back the end of the coverlets and was applying another cold cloth to her foot. The pain was intense and she cried out.

Tildy nearly dropped the pan of water. Her eyes filled with tears. "Oh, I so hate to cause you pain," she said.

Omega struggled into a sitting position and pulled back the covers entirely. Her ankle was swollen beyond twice its size now. She touched it. Despite the cold compresses, her flesh was hot and red.

"Oh, Tildy, what a mull I have made of things," she said as she lay back down and the maid tucked the blankets around her again. "Has anyone returned yet?"

"The master returned several hours ago for his horse, and I have not seen the others. I sent my brother off to look too. They'll find him, Miss Chartley." She brushed back the hair from Omega's eyes. "But then what?"

"I wish I knew," replied Omega, closing her eyes again.

The rain stopped as night fell. Omega awoke to the silence of the house, and then to the welcome sound of Angela's voice.

"Omega! Omega!"

"Hush, Angela, you'll disturb Miss Chartley."

The voices were right outside her door. "Angela?" she called. "Oh, do come in."

The girl came into the room, followed by Tildy. She was soaked through, and shivering in her light dress and shawl, but a smile covered her face.

"Omega, we have him! Or rather, Lord Byford has him!"

"Thank God," said Omega. "Is he all right?"

"Just angry. And he's not speaking to anyone. You know how he is. Lord Byford rained a regular peal over his head. It was a royal scolding." Angela came closer to the bed, but was careful not to drip on Omega. "I think he's secretly relieved that we rescued him. I shall ask Jamie tomorrow, when he is not so angry."

"And now, my dear," said Tildy, "you will follow me. There is a hot bath in your room for you. Miss Chartley, you'll pardon me, but I took the liberty of taking one of the nightgowns from this room. It's for a small lady, and almost fits Angela."

"Anything for that little scapegrace," said Omega. "It's not mine, so I can be generous," she joked.

Angela came closer again. "I like it when you tease me, Omega. Are you feeling better?"

"Oh, yes, wonderfully," lied Miss Chartley. "Now, where is Jamie?"

"The master is bringing him."

"I want to see him."

"You're sure, Miss Chartley?"

"Positive. Now, help me sit up, please."

A few minutes later, Omega heard footsteps at the door, familiar footsteps, and then a knock. "Come in, please."

Matthew entered the room, followed by Jamie Clevenden, who was soaked to the skin and shivering like Angela. Omega shook her head at the boy. "Jamie, you have caused us no end of trouble."

Jamie hung his head and said nothing. Matthew came closer to the bed, carefully removing his cape, which dripped water on the floor. "I've already delivered a blistering lecture, Omega," he said.

Omega raised her eyes to him, secretly delighted with Matthew. It was only a small defense, but he was taking Jamie's side. Good for you, she thought.

Omega reached out her hand for Jamie. He looked at her then, his eyes twin pools of misery. Without a word, she held out her arms and Jamie hurled himself into them, sobbing. She stroked his wet hair and rocked him in her arms until he was silent.

"Jamie, all I ask is this: please do what Matthew says. We're simply going to have to sit down together and figure out what is to be done. Running away won't help."

Jamie wiped his nose on his soggy sleeve. "But, Omega, I've been seen!"

The words chilled her heart. "Mr. Platter?"

Jamie nodded. "It was at the Regis and Byford crossing, I think." He looked at Matthew, who nodded. "Uncle Matthew swooped me away, but I know Mr. Platter saw me. How soon before he figures out where I am?"

She kissed the top of his head. "All the more reason for you to do exactly as your Uncle Matthew bids. You must promise me, word of honor, that you will not run away again. I have no power to keep you here. I cannot chase after you. You must give me the word of a gentleman, Jamie Clevenden."

"I shall not run away again, Omega," he said finally.

"And that will do for now, lad," said Matthew. "You've soaked Miss Chartley's gown. Come, lad. Did I heard Tildy say something about a bath? And then to bed with you. Run along, now."

Omega gave Jamie another hug and touched his cheek. "Come see me in the morning, dear," she said.

Jamie hurried from the room. Matthew sat down wearily in the chair. "I found him at the crossing, waiting for a carter, I suppose, or a farmer going to market. Platter must have been watching from the inn." He leaned back in the chair. "Omega, I started to give Jamie the scold of his life, and he put his hands up to his face as if to shield himself from a blow. Omega, I would no more strike him than I would strike you!"

"But he doesn't know that," Omega said slowly. The implications of Matthew's words sent tendrils of cold down her spine.

"How true. I think I begin to understand how his other uncle has been treating him. Well. It was a revelation to me."

The air was heavy with unspoken words. "Where . . . where is Hugh?" Omega asked at last.

"He is here too. He did not wish to disturb you." Matthew ran his hand through his wet hair. "No more do I." He raised the coverlets off the foot of the bed and looked for a long minute at her ankle.

"Not a pretty sight, is it?" she said.

He shook his head, and tucked the covers in again. "Perhaps I should summon the doctor in the morning." He patted her other foot. "Between us, we have three eyes and three feet. Is this what my late father used to refer to as 'damned old age'? A lowering thought."

"Lowering indeed," agreed Omega.

"Well, I must change. Twinings said something about dinner. May I bring my plate up here and eat with you?"

"Oh, no, please, Matthew. I'm not up to dinner yet. I'm afraid even the smell of food would make me long for that pan again."

"Very well, then, I'll be back in a little while." He stopped, and she could see the indecision on his face. "Omega, I know you're in pain, and I know you're tired, but I simply must talk to you before I lose whatever nerve remains. Please."

She nodded, her eyes on his face. And soon you'll know, Omega Chartley, she thought as she watched him, her eyes touring for a brief moment the face she knew so well, and, before yesterday, had thought never to see again. The swelling on his nose was going down; his eye was black and blue, but he was Matthew Bering. She realized with a wrench that nothing had changed: she loved him as much as she had ever loved him, even as he exasperated and unnerved her.

He tried to smile, but it went nowhere. "Well, Omega, now that you have memorized my face, I'll go . . . and return before you chance to forget what I look like."

She closed her eyes when he left. That short interview with Jamie had exhausted her. How wearing pain is, she thought. I will only rest my eyes this minute before Matthew returns. The pain is so great I surely will not sleep.

Omega woke hours later. The house was still, her room dark, except for the light that glowed from the fireplace, and the lamp dimly flickering beside the bed. She thought for a moment she was alone in the room, but she heard Matthew's steady breathing. As her eyes became used to the gloom, she saw him in the chair by the window, the draperies pulled open and his feet propped on the sill. The rain had begun again and the room was chill.

She regarded him from her bed, bemused all over again how little, really, he had changed in eight years. How is it possible for him to be handsomer? she asked herself. I only wish that I had fared as well.

And then his breathing changed, and she knew he was awake.

"Matthew?"

"Yes." He yawned and put his feet on the floor. "Don't breathe a word of this to Angela or Jamie, but I swear I am too old for adventuring." He laughed softly. "My chief delight in the world is to sit in a dressing gown by my fire with the London *Times*. That is slow work indeed to you mettlesome folk who seem to have attached yourselves to my household like barnacles."

He was silent another minute, and then he turned the chair around to face her. "But this is idle chat, my dear." He spread his hands out in front of him. "Where am I to begin, Omega?"

"You can prop me up and put another pillow behind my head."

He did as she said, plumping the pillow behind her head and adding another one. "Now where do we go?"

Omega closed her eyes. It was easier somehow not to look at him. "First you must tell me how it is that you are

Viscount Byford. I never knew there was a title due to you."

"I seldom thought about it, and it was almost a surprise to me, Omega," he said, pulling his chair closer. "My mother had a cousin, Rufus Laws, who was the Viscount Byford. He died without issue, and indeed, without anyone really to mourn him. You may have heard the servants mention him. No young girl was safe here during his tenure." He laughed dryly. "Things have changed with a vengeance," he added in almost an undervoice. "Well, I succeeded to his title and land. This was . . . five years? . . . six years ago, almost." His voice was lighter as he continued, and she could sense the affection in it, even as his words were deprecating. "Believe me, it is no great honor. I find myself justice of the peace and called upon to settle the pettiest of differences and to participate in hurried-up weddings. It is a curious fact, Omega, my dear, but when you have a title and money, people seem to think you know everything. I do not understand the correlation. I am called upon to be wise, impartial, and above reproach, rather like the Archbishop of Canterbury." He sighed. "And now?"

She opened her eyes. "What I want to know is probably a very small thing to you. I suppose it doesn't really matter, after eight years, and maybe it is just my female vanity. Please don't think me foolish . . . but I must know: did you . . . did you feel some . . . some great disgust for me all of a sudden?" Her voice faltered. "If you did . . . if you do . . . just say so, and I'll not plague you further."

Her words sounded silly to her own ears, and stilted, and altogether nonsensical, rather like the whining of a child. A look of great sorrow came into Matthew's eyes, and she almost wished she hadn't said anything. She could have gone to her grave gladly without seeing that look of pain cross his face.

He reached for her hand. "Omega, I loved you almost from the first moment I saw you." The look of anguish left for a moment, and he seemed almost young again. "I would wager you don't even remember when that was, do you?"

She shook her head. He took her hand and rested it on his knee. "I remember so well. You and Alpha were at the Kensington Hall Gallery, both of you poring over a guide book and looking genuinely interested."

"But we . . . we *were* interested!" she protested, and took her hand from his knee.

"Exactly so. You two and no one else. Didn't anyone ever tell you two country children that one goes to the gallery only to see and be seen? And there you were, both of you enjoying yourselves so immensely. I was struck by your . . . your integrity, I suppose, for want of a better word. I think that if one of us Bond Street Beaux had strolled over and said that such enthusiasm was not at all the thing, it wouldn't have mattered a straw to you. You were there for the paintings." He touched her hand again. "You had on a dress of the palest pink muslin and carried the most useless-looking parasol. And your hair was everywhere at the same time." He laughed, and again the years melted away. "I wanted to sneak up and tweak one of your marvelous curls, just to see if it was real. You probably would have slapped me."

"I would have."

"I found out who you were, and discovered immediately that you had far too few years in your dish for me. But somehow, I couldn't stay away from you."

She remembered. Scarcely a day had passed without a little note, a handful of violets, or a funny drawing from Matthew Bering. She remembered his visits to Alpha, when they discussed Oxford and laughed over dons who were ancient when Matthew was there, and were still lecturing on. Almost before Omega had realized what was happening, she was in love with him. Not all the long walks in the garden, or quiet afternoons sitting in contemplation in one gallery or another had sufficiently convinced her that at eighteen she was too young for this man who had been on the town for years. He had never seemed too old for her then. He did not seem too old now.

"I told myself over and over it was foolish beyond reason to be struck dumb by a chit barely out of the schoolroom." He shook his head, the wonder still in his voice. "I don't understand how such things happen, but I felt comfortable around you, at peace, completely free to be myself. You had not an ounce of pretense in your whole body. I've never met anyone so utterly without guile. Or a woman so intelligent. You were the kind of person so utterly suited for me . . . and for children."

"Then why, in heaven's name, did all this happen?" She couldn't look at him, even in the dark, and turned her head away. "If I know, then I won't trouble you further."

It was the question she had asked almost daily for eight years, even when she wasn't consciously dwelling on the matter, as she had not in recent years. During the oddest moments—when she was grading papers, or listening to her pupils recite—her mind would take a leap back to that morning's work in the church, and then move forward again, almost as if memory had parted for an instant and let her glimpse inside.

"There are two reasons," Matthew said slowly, "two reasons that have given me cause to regret every day of my life since then." He rose suddenly and went to the window, opening it a crack and letting in the cooler breezes. "One is terrible and the other no better. I shall begin with the terrible one first."

He wouldn't look at her. "I was the guest of honor at a bachelor party that night before our . . . that night. Do you remember?"

She did. They had dined together, her father and Alpha, with Matthew, making last-minute plans, laughing about one thing and another. "You left early. It must have been before ten." She regarded him thoughtfully, pulling the memories up from eight years. "I seem to recall that Alpha was to accompany you, but he begged off."

"Thank God that he did," said Matthew fervently. "It was the worst night of my life." He laughed, and there was no mirth. "Or perhaps just the first night of eight years of worst nights."

He took a deep breath and plunged in. "My brother-in-law's brother had arranged a party. That was Rotherford."

"Rotherford? You mean the one who is hounding Jamie?"

"The very one. Edwin Clevenden, Lord Rotherford. You never met him. He was older than I by a few years, and scarcely ever in from the country. Indeed, I was surprised and a little flattered that he would plan this party. I did not know him well. Jamie's father was there—at least he was for a little while. I do not perfectly remember. There were three others of my closest friends there."

"Where was this party?"

"Oh, I do not know. Rotherford had rented rooms near St. James Square. I probably could find them again if I looked hard enough, but I never had the heart to do so."

Matthew was silent then. He left the window and paced in front of the fireplace, hunkering down for a moment to stir at the coals. Omega said nothing, only watched him.

He paced again, and then stood still. "This is devilish hard, Omega. I've never discussed this with anyone, and most assuredly not with a woman. You will think so ill of me." He laughed his mirthless laugh again. "Well, what am I saying? I'm not precisely in your best books, am I?"

"Oh, Matthew, don't."

He took another deep breath. "I was the main attraction at the party, and destined to become the entertainment. We drank ourselves practically into a state of catatonia, and then Rotherford fetched in the *pièce de résistance*. Oh, God."

It was as if he were seeing the whole event again. He sank down into the chair as if his legs would not hold him. "She couldn't have been more than fourteen. Just a prostitute from Covent Garden. Someone scarcely older than Angela."

He looked at her. "I am glad it is dark, Omega. It was always so easy to tell precisely what you were thinking, only by looking at your face."

She held out her hand to him. "Pull your chair closer, Matthew," she said. When he did not move, or reach for her hand, she folded her hands in her lap again.

"Rotherford invited me to remove my clothes and

partake of some Covent Garden honey. I was so foxed I don't know how I got my clothes off, but there I was, ready to take on that poor little whore, surrounded by my best friends, everyone cheering me on.''

Omega took a deep breath. There was a sour taste in her mouth, a churning of her stomach again. She gritted her teeth against it.

"So while you were sleeping the sleep of the innocent, and perhaps dreaming about your loving husband-to-be, I was trying to lay a London drab.''

"Matthew," she began, but couldn't speak.

"We're not a very good lot, Omega, we *bon ton*." Matthew got to his feet again and crossed the room. "But remember, dear, I haven't gotten to the terrible part yet. And there is worse beyond that. I'm not a performing bear, Omega. I vaguely remember everyone cheering and clapping and encouraging me, but I was totally unable to satisfy either that whore or my friends. It was mortifying, all the more so because I really didn't want to be there.''

"What . . . happened then?''

"She laughed at me and I struck her so hard I bloodied her mouth. Then I remember someone putting me to bed. When it was—earlier? later?—I'm unsure. I heard her screaming and crying, pleading with someone, and then I didn't remember anything else until morning.''

Matthew shuddered and the chill seemed to pass into Omega's body too. He went to the window and flung it open wide, leaning out, breathing in the cold and the rain. He remained that way, elbows on the sill, until Omega wanted to cry. She made no sound, only wished she was able to cross the room to him. What he was telling her was abhorrent and evil, and alien to every code of conduct she knew, but Omega Chartley knew what it was to hurt, and to see Matthew hurting was the worst thing of all.

He turned around and sat on the window ledge, distancing himself from her. "When I woke in the morning, I was not alone in bed. Oh, God, that girl lay beside me, and she was dead.''

"Dear God," Omega said, and swallowed.

"Her face was practically transparent, drained of all

blood, but everywhere else was covered with blood. The sheets, the floor. We were both awash in it. The room stank of blood. It was the worst nightmare you could imagine, except I was not dreaming."

"What of . . . the others?" Omega's voice sounded far away to her own ears. Her heart was pounding so loud she put her hand to her chest to quiet it.

"There was only Rotherford. He told me the others had fled. He alone remained. He assured me that he would get me out of the mess. Promised that no one would ever hear of it. My secret was safe with him."

Matthew closed the window and pulled two blankets from the chest at the foot of the bed. He covered her with one of them and wrapped the other around himself and sat down in the chair again. "I had time to bathe and dress and show up at St. Alphonse."

"Oh, Matthew." Omega reached for him again, but he would not let her touch him.

"I rode past St. Alphonse in a rented hack. Everyone was already inside, waiting for you to walk down the aisle. I tried to go in, but I fled. I kept going until I was home in Shropshire."

A heavy silence seeped between them. I must say something, thought Omega. I must continue this until it is done.

"Why did you not write to me later, or communicate somehow? Couldn't you imagine my distress?"

He winced at that and settled the blanket high on his shoulders. "I was so ashamed, so utterly devastated. Someone had died because of me. Someone no one would ever miss, someone so expendable. Someone my name would never be connected to. Her life was . . . so cheap, and I was afraid I had ended it."

"Your friends?" she asked in the stillness. "What of your friends?"

"One of them wrote to me. I did not answer. Another came to Shropshire. I refused to see him. The third rejoined his troops immediately. The only one I ever saw again was my brother-in-law. Even he seemed happy enough not to mention the workings of that evening."

"But that poor child!"

He laughed but there was no mirth, and the sound drilled into her brain like an awl. "You have said it, Omega. She was poor, and she was a child." He clapped his hands together in frustration, and she jumped. "Did you never look about you in London? In Plymouth? It is not we wealthy men who ever suffer. No, Omega, we were all of us glad enough to overlook the doings of that night. God damn us."

The rain stopped. Somewhere far below in the house a door opened and then closed. Morning was coming. Soon the servants would be about. Omega's ankle throbbed but she said nothing, unable to bring herself to interfere with his train of thought. She dreaded what he was saying, but she had to hear it, and he had to tell it.

"I thought later of writing to you, I really did. Then I began to reason that you would be better off with someone else. Surely there could be no lack of suitors. Your life would go on." He sighed. "Imagine my further dismay when I learned that your father had killed himself over his reverses on the Exchange. I knew then that you would not have a pleasant time of it, after all. But it was too late for me to make any amends. Not only had I ruined two lives; I had ruined yours too, and that was unforgivable."

Dawn was lighting the sky outside now, and she could see his face. He looked old and tired, the fine lines around his mouth and eyes more deeply etched, his eyes as hopeless as Jamie's. He would not allow her to touch him.

"I'm not done yet, Omega," he said, his mouth twisting into a caricature of a smile. "I told you it gets worse. I thought long and hard about seeing you, but I did something unforgivably stupid instead. I procured myself another whore and tried again. And failed again. And again. After that, I tried no more. The next two years were spent deep in my father's wine cellar. I have been through some very good years, Omega, down-cellar in Shropshire."

He leaned forward suddenly and wiped her face with his fingers. She hadn't realized that she was crying. His fingers were so cold.

"So you see, my dear, even if we had found a way to overcome the simple matter of a brutal murder—excuse my sarcasm . . . I can only almost bear it when I am sarcastic—we still could not have made much of a marriage, considering my inability."

He stood up and went back to the window, the blanket tight around him. "And that was what I wanted to tell you. Have you ever known a greater sinner?"

She couldn't help herself. The tears streamed down her face. She tried to stifle her sobs, but it was useless. She sank lower on the pillow and cried into the blanket.

Matthew stood with bowed head by the window. He opened it again and breathed deeply of the fragrance that the breeze of morning was bringing up from the flower garden below. He closed the window again and stumbled like an old man to the door, the blanket still tight around his shoulders.

"I'll leave now, my dear." He looked at her. "I suppose you have been frightfully compromised by my presence in your room all night. I might add that you have probably never been in less danger from any man."

He opened the door. "Good night, Omega, or good morning. There's more to tell you, and it touches on Jamie. Perhaps if we ever feel up to it . . ."

He closed the door quietly behind him, not looking back.

9

Omega cried in earnest until her pillow was soggy, and then she turned it over and tried to sleep. It was day now, the air cool and smelling fresh after the long rain. The birds that had been silent yesterday made up for the lack, and right under her window, too, singing, quarreling, and shrieking at each other until she wanted to throw something.

Her ankle ached amazingly. It hurt so badly that no amount of discipline that Miss Chartley possessed could convince her to fling back the covers and have a look at it. If my leg is turning black, with shooting red streaks, she told herself grimly, there is not a single reason in the world for me to watch it happen.

Her mind could dwell on nothing but the pain, and the anguish of Matthew Bering's disclosure. Somehow she knew that when all this was over, as everything must end eventually, she would always associate the two.

Omega wished he would come back into the room, wished that he felt like talking more, and she like listening. That he had made a shocking mull of a terrible situation was not lost on her. And what would I have done in a similar circumstance? she asked herself as she gritted her teeth and tried to find a comfortable position. Had I been Matthew Bering, could I have faced me?

She concluded that she could not. How could anyone have dropped such a disclosure into an eighteen-year-old's lap? The thought brought the only comfort available to her.

There was a scratching at the door. Two heads peeked in.

"Oh, come in," Omega said gratefully.

Angela and Jamie entered the room, Jamie edging along the wall, half-dreading another scold from her, and Angela eyeing her with worry of another kind. She came close to the bed.

"Lord Byford said we were under no circumstances to bother you. But . . . but he doesn't understand!" Angela's eyes filled with tears.

In her surprise, Omega forgot her own hurt for a moment. She put out her hand and drew the little girl closer. "Why, Angela, what is the matter?"

Angela knelt down and rested her head on the bed, her voice muffled. "He doesn't know what it's like to wait outside a hospital and wait and wait and then be told it's too late or told to run along and not bother the wounded."

Without a word, Omega rested her hand on Angela's
hair, smoothing it back from her face. "No, he doesn't
understand, my dear. I'm glad you came to see for
yourself." She managed a smile for Angela's benefit. "I'll
be fine in a few days." She put her fingers to her lips,
kissed them, and touched Angela on the cheek. "And
that's all you needed to know, wasn't it?"

Angela nodded.

It was Jamie's turn. "Omega, I'm sorry for the trouble I
caused. It's my fault, isn't it?"

She held out her hand and he came closer, standing
beside Angela. "It's no one's fault but my own that I was
clumsy. Don't be a goose, Jamie. Come here, you scamp,
and give me a kiss." He laughed and did as she said.
"Now, my dears, I would recommend that you hurry
belowstairs and see how very helpful you can be today.
Lord Byford is not precisely . . ."

Angela's eyes opened wide. "Oh, miss. I've never seen
anyone with such a case of the megrims! And all because
Jamie was such a *fulano!*"

Omega considered. Perhaps there would be no harm in
prevarication. No good would be served for the children to
have even an inkling of Matthew's agony. "Jamie, Angela.
Lord Byford is not used to having children in his house. I
am sure he will come around. Now, run belowstairs before
you find yourself in trouble."

"It is already too late," came a voice from the doorway.
"Omega, you know you should not encourage these
graceless beggars."

His voice was light, but there was nothing light about
Matthew's demeanor. Omega had to admit that he looked
better today than yesterday; his blacked eye was open now,
and the bump on his nose scarcely noticeable. It was the
lack of expression in his face that was so disconcerting.
Upon hearing Matthew's voice, Jamie shrank back against
the wall again, watching his uncle's every move.

Matthew noticed Jamie's fright. He knelt by him with
that wonderful instinct of his that Omega so delighted in.
Jamie drew away, closer to Omega.

Matthew put out his hand slowly, as if he were trying to

touch a skittish colt. "Jamie, Jamie, if we are to rub along together in this household, there is something you must know. It is something that will never change."

Jamie was too terrified to raise his eyes to his uncle. He continued his minute examination of the grain in the wooden floor until Matthew slowly reached out his hand, raised the boy's chin, and forced him to look in his uncle's eyes.

"Jamie Clevenden, I will never strike you. I do not hold with beating children, no matter what the provocation. I mean what I say. It is more than a promise, Jamie; it is a covenant." He rested the back of his hand against Jamie's cheek for a second. "Now, run along. Tildy is waiting downstairs to take your measurements. Yours too, Angela. I can't have such ragged children in my household. How on earth am I to puff up my consequence in Byford if you look like workhouse brats?"

Jamie smiled then, and took Angela's hand. "Let us hurry! Do you think the cook will teach me some French words? Papa used to say some, and Mama would scold him."

"Jamie, let me warn you, I have no objection whatsoever to soap applied to the mouth," said Lord Byford.

Jamie laughed and tugged Angela out of the room with him.

Matthew waited until the children were gone. "I was afraid they would be bothering you, Omega." He came to the foot of the bed. "But see here, you look hagged."

Without a word, he took the blanket off her foot and stood another long minute looking at it. "I've already summoned the doctor, Omega. I'll be gone with Angela on our errand as soon as he arrives. There is a fair nearby in Templeton, and Tildy informs me I can find secondhand clothing for children."

He left her alone then. Omega lay back and stared at the ceiling, biting her lip to keep the tears back. He hadn't once looked her in the eye.

The minutes shuffled by like hours. Omega was ready to gnaw her knuckles against the pain when Matthew returned with the doctor. He ushered the man in, but did not leave the doorway. "I'll be off now, Omega."

Omega pulled herself upright. "Matthew, don't you dare leave me!" she cried, and then looked at the doctor in embarrassment. "Can't you just . . . can't you just hold my hand again?"

The doctor looked from one to the other, and then discovered a fascination with the beech tree outside the bedroom window, strolling over to it and gazing at each leaf in turn. When the doctor's back was turned, Matthew knelt by the bed. "You . . . you truly want me here? After everything I have told you?"

"Oh, shut up!" she whispered back fiercely, clutching for his hand. "You cannot fathom how doctors terrify me! How am I to bear it if you are not here?"

The doctor did not turn around, but he seemed to have taken his mind from things arboreal. "May I be so bold as to suggest, my lord, that you do as the lady wishes? I, for one, never argue with women."

Without a word to either of them, Matthew pulled the chair nearer and laced his fingers through hers.

The doctor bade her bend her leg at the knee, commanded her to wiggle her toes, and then turned her ankle this way and that, as Omega drew her lips into a thin line and clung like death to Matthew. The doctor desisted finally, looked at her over the tops of his spectacles. "I am finished. Miss Chartley, I recommend that you turn loose of the viscount before you quite curtail all circulation in his fingers."

Matthew covered her fingers with his other hand too. "She's all right. But tell us, please."

The doctor shook his head. "I still cannot see that you have broken your ankle, Miss Chartley. I believe the application of cold cloths will eventually do the trick. I hold that sprains are worse than fractures." He cleared his throat. "I trust you have changed your plans about quitting this place immediately?"

"She has," replied Matthew for her. "I'll make sure that she does not exert herself in any way."

"You will be doing her a great favor, my lord. Miss Chartley, I will place this wire frame over your ankle. It will keep the blankets from weighing too heavily on it. I can do little else until the swelling goes down. I expect you will see a change in the next day."

He shook some powders into the glass of water beside the bed. "Drink this like a good girl. That's capital, my dear. I will bid you both good day."

The doctor took up his bag, pausing only to peer at Matthew's face. "My lord, your eye . . ."

Matthew managed the smallest of smiles. "It was a mere accident."

"I heard how it happened. News gets about fast in Byford." The doctor allowed himself a chuckle. "Lord protect us from our friends, eh?"

"Indeed, sir. Good day to you."

"I can communicate with a London surgeon, if you wish," said Matthew after the doctor had gone. His fingers were still laced through hers.

"No. No." Omega scooted herself down lower in the bed, but she did not release her hold on him. The medicine was already making her drowsy. "No. I think all that I need is time."

Gently Matthew let go of her hand. "Omega, I did not think that after last night you would ever want me about."

She sighed. The bed was warm and soft, and Matthew smelled wonderfully of lemon cologne. The pain in her ankle felt farther and farther away, as if someone were stretching her out to a great length. "I think . . . I think I am tired of groping my way through muddles alone," she said, and then shook her head. "I suppose I am not making a great deal of sense right now, but, Matthew, can we not be friends?"

He was silent so long that she feared she had said the wrong thing. He chose his words carefully. "Of course we can be friends. And when you're feeling more the thing, we have a matter to discuss that has given me considerable food for thought since last night's conversation. I want to try it out on you."

She could not understand what he was saying, but little was making sense to her. Her eyes were closing when the children came into the room again.

"Ah, Jamie," said Matthew, getting to his feet. "I particularly wish you to remain right here with Omega until I return. If she needs someone to hold her hand, you have been appointed, nephew."

"Yes, sir," said Jamie. He leaned toward Matthew. "Is she . . . is she. . . ?"

"Half-dead?" Matthew chuckled. "No, just medicinally foxed, a little bit to let. Angela and I are leaving now to visit the fair. It probably would be best if you did not show yourself about Byford just yet. We must discover if Mr. Platter is lurking about."

Jamie nodded. "I will not leave the room. Only, sir, there is one thing."

"Yes, Jamie?"

"Could you get a bottle of lavender scent?"

Matthew stared at him. "Jamie, I don't perfectly understand. Are you partial to lavender scent?"

"Oh, Uncle, it is not for me, but Omega!" His expression was earnest. "She smelled of lavender when I first met her, and do you know, it reminds me of my mother."

Matthew looked down at Omega. "Yes, I seem to remember Diantha and her lavender." He touched Jamie's shoulder, his eyes remembering. "And Omega and hers." He recalled himself. "Nephew, Angela and I will find the biggest bottle to be had and Miss Chartley can dribble it all over herself if she chooses."

"Matthew, don't be nonsensical," Omega said. She wanted to say something else, but her words were slurred.

Matthew leaned closer. "My dear Miss Chartley, you are the one making absolutely no sense. Do be quiet and go to sleep. In less than a month you will have an entire class of eager pupils looking to you for guidance and syntax. Now, just hush, hurry up and heal. Come, Angela."

Angela skipped out of the room and the door closed quietly behind them. Omega made a great effort and turned her head toward Jamie. "Hugh?" she asked, reduced to one-syllable sentences.

"Oh, it is famous, Omega!" declared Jamie as he settled himself into the chair. "He is out in my uncle's stables, just sitting in one of the stalls, memorizing a horse! I cannot imagine what he is about, but he told me that perhaps he ought to learn something about horses. Do you think he expects to continue his masquerade?"

Omega thought of a number of things in reply, but none of them reached as far as her mouth. She closed her eyes and abandoned herself to the doctor's sleeping powder.

When she woke, the shadows had changed places in the room, but Jamie was still sitting beside her. Hugh was there too, sitting on the blanket chest at the foot of the bed. She looked about her with a feeling of deep comfort, and less pain. She wagged her ankle experimentally. The sharp pain seemed more dull; it was still there in abundance, but the edge was gone.

"Are you feeling in better spirits?" Hugh asked.

She nodded. "A little." She looked at him. "Did Jamie tell me something about horses? Something about memorizing horses?"

Hugh laughed. "You have hit on it. Lord Byford told me that as long as I am about Byford, I should continue my masquerade. And he seems to think I will not quit the place until you are gone." He paused to reflect. "He could be right."

He stood up. "I think he is a bit smitten with Angela too, if you want the truth. And even your guardian angel here. Come, Jamie, Tildy told us to scatter when Omega woke up."

Tildy entered the bedroom with sheets draped over her arm and summoned Hugh back. "Please, miss, could Hugh pick you up while I change your sheets?"

Omega nodded and held up her arms for Hugh, who picked her up carefully, wincing when she winced, and sat with her in the chair. Tildy was just tucking in the blankets again when Angela bounded up the stairs, followed by Matthew.

Why she felt shy as she rested against Hugh's chest, Omega couldn't have said. Something in Matthew's face made her blush. Whatever it was she saw there was quickly gone. Matthew motioned to Angela, and when she came close, whispered in her ear. The girl glanced at Omega, covered her mouth with her hand to stop the laughter that bubbled in her, and darted down the hall.

"What is it all about?" Omega asked Matthew when he seemed not disposed to offer any information outright.

He shrugged. "You will have to wait until she returns. Jamie, we have purchased a large bottle of scent which will probably keep Miss Chartley reeking of lavender until she is in her dotage."

"Matthew!" declared Omega in her best teacher's voice. "You are an outrage at times, you know."

His returning smile was genuine. "You used to say that. My dear, it is nice to hear it again. And now, Hugh, if your arm is tired, I will relieve you of Miss Chartley."

Hugh shook his head. "I carried far heavier burdens over the Pyrenees Mountains, my lord."

"That strikes me as a dubious compliment," said Omega. "But really, Hugh, I do not wish to tax you."

He shook his head. "It is a small matter, and look, Tildy is finished."

He set her carefully down in bed again. Tildy straightened the covers as Angela pranced into the room again.

"Angela!" exclaimed Omega, and clapped her hands. "How magnificent you look!"

Angela stepped forward, her hands on her hips like a Gypsy dancer, and twirled around at the side of the bed. Her dress was deep blue Egyptian cotton, with a row of bone-white buttons that marched in file down the front from neck to ankle. It was simple and serviceable. The light that shone in Angela's eyes told Omega that it was much more.

The girl executed one more twirl and flopped against the bed. "Oh, think, Omega, this one is almost new! I was going to ask the woman at the booth if it belonged to

someone who had died, but Lord Byford told me that
would be rag-mannered. See, it has not been cut down.''
She leaned closer and Omega took her hands. "And do
you know, Lord Byford bought me another one, a green
one! And that is not all. I have two petticoats on, Omega.
And other things . . .''

Angela flashed her magnificent smile at Matthew, who
had pulled up a stool next to the chair Hugh sat in. "Lord
Byford, I've never had *those* other things before.''

"Angela, spare my blushes,'' he murmured. When
Angela stood up again, he winked at Omega.

"Angela, you are a lucky girl,'' Hugh said.

She was serious then, touching the folds of the dress,
gathering them to her, stroking the fabric as if it were a
living thing. "The lady said the dresses were taken apart at
the seams, washed, and sewn together again. I did not have
to check for lice! *Mira*, Hugh, I never suspected England
would be like this.''

"Nor did I,'' the ex-soldier said softly, the same wonder
in his voice as in Angela's.

"Miss Chartley, there is a cloak too, and a bonnet, and
even shoes, which *no one* has ever worn before. But I will
save those,'' Angela added. "The shoes are too beautiful
to wear.''

"Don't be a goose, Angela,'' said Matthew. "If you
save the shoes, you will outgrow them and they will never
fit you.''

Tears stood in Angela's eyes then, as if suddenly the
excitement was too much. She burst into noisy sobs. Jamie
snorted and made a face, muttering something about
Angela not being any more fun now that she had dresses.

Omega yearned to pull Angela close to her, but before
she could act, Matthew gathered Angela to him and set her
on his lap. She sobbed into his jacket while she rested her
head on his chest and he toyed with her black curls.

"Angela, between you and Omega, I'll not have a single
coat without watermarks. Hush, child.'' He looked over
her head to Hugh. "Every soldier deserves some reward,
and this is yours, Angela. I only wish they were new

clothes." He winked at Omega. "However do parents manage without a seamstress on permanent duty? This abominable brat will grow too fast."

Angela cried a moment more, and then her tears vanished as quickly as they had come. She pulled herself away from Matthew, looked at him for a tiny moment, and then kissed his cheek before hopping off his lap and hurrying from the room.

It was Matthew's turn to struggle within himself for a moment. Omega had the good grace to look away and invite Jamie to open his parcel, which he did, sitting cross-legged at the foot of her bed.

"Omega, this is famous!" he exclaimed. "I have never had clothes like these! A person could really *do* something in these clothes!" He pulled out ordinary working clothes from the brown paper, shaking out the shirt of heavy cotton and pants of nankeen. "I could climb trees in these," he declared, and spoke to Omega confidentially. "Lord Rotherford used to tell me that I must always set a good example for the lower orders."

"There is scarcely anything more tiring than being a paragon," said Matthew, his voice controlled again. "I expect to see you in a tree before nightfall. Only please, I beg, do not break your arm. I am certain the doctor already thinks we are raving lunatics."

Omega noted with some gratification his use of the word "we." Almost as if he were a part of this, she thought, noting how happy he seemed at that moment and how young it made him look, how like the man she'd fallen in love with years ago.

"And what, pray, are you smiling at, Miss Chartley?" Matthew asked.

She said nothing, but succeeded in annoying herself by blushing fiery red. Hugh laughed and got to his feet. "I always leave the room when women blush like that," he said as he went to the door, motioning Jamie to follow.

Matthew had the diplomacy not to say anything else right away. In her confusion, Omega wished he would follow Hugh, but he moved from the stool to the chair and pushed the door closed with his foot.

"I saw Timothy Platter again." He shook his head. "We both took each other's measure, nodded, and walked on. How strange."

Omega forgot her embarrassment. "Matthew, what are we to do?"

Lord Byford spread his hands out in front of him. "I have no legal power to keep Jamie . . . Now, don't interrupt me, Omega! Don't rip up at me! How can I think when you nag? I shall have to think of something. I am tired of being such a coward."

He left the room before she could say anything else. She watched him go, mentally kicking herself, wondering at what point in the last eight years she had ceased being a young lady of gentle manner and had become a nag and scold. She berated herself until she was thoroughly out of sorts, and until there was nothing to do but sleep, and resolve to do better at their next meeting.

As dinnertime approached, she woke and began to feel frightfully ill-used. She also discovered how hungry she was. Delightful odors were drifting up from the dining room. She imagined everyone sitting around the table laughing and joking, and she longed to be part of it.

How many years have I sat wallowing in my own company? she thought. How many meals have I eaten, book in hand, moving food from fork to mouth, finding no pleasure beyond the thought that it was one less meal to contend with? She stirred restlessly. It would never do to think of such things, those things she had so resolutely put out of her mind, but she lay there and remembered evenings around the table with Alpha and her father, and later Matthew, talking and laughing until they were all a little silly.

Omega stretched out her foot tentatively. It throbbed, but some of the pain was gone. "It will be different in Durham," she said out loud. "I will seek out the other teachers." Her former teacher would be there for advice and company, too. And surely there would be pupils about Angela's age who would care to spend an evening discussing good books and great ideas. "And if they should chance to ask about me," she said softly, "I will tell them, and not hide within myself anymore, wasting my time wondering what they are thinking. So much time I have wasted."

She heard Matthew's step in the hall then, and put her hand to her hair, patting the odd curls under her cap. He opened the door without knocking, and brought in her dinner tray, which he set on her lap.

"Antoine told me to hurry up with this."

She looked at him in surprise. "Your chef orders you about?"

He nodded. "Of course. And I pay him outrageously. But the results, madam, the results."

She was hungrier than she thought, eating quickly as Matthew watched. He made only one comment as she worked her way through the delicious dinner. "Antoine told me to pay close attention to what you did not eat, and he would try to remedy your paltry appetite tomorrow. I have the happy task to inform him that the only thing you did not eat was the gold border around the plate. I am sure he will try to correct that oversight."

Omega laughed and waved him away. He sat back with a smile on his face and closed his eyes, his hands folded across his stomach. When she finished, he took the tray from her and set it outside in the hall.

She expected him to leave then, but he did not. "Let me tell you something curious about this whole nasty business, Omega. I haven't ever really considered it before, mainly because I did not want to—as you can well imagine. But now that Jamie is here . . . well, I must speak of it."

"Are you sure you want to talk about it?"

He nodded. "Positive. Omega, I have never spoken to anyone about this matter before. It seems easier, now that you know. Do you recall that I told you four of my best friends were present at that . . . that party?"

"Yes." Omega's eyes were on his face.

"Three of them are dead now, and one I have not heard from in years. I fear that he is dead too. Don't you see, there's no one alive to relate any of the events of that night. I have only Rotherford's word for what happened."

He leaned forward and looked her straight in the eyes.

"I am beginning to wonder if I am part of a huge blackmail, Omega." He paused to let that disclosure sink in.

"But . . . but, Matthew, why would Rotherford do this to you? Did he dislike you? Did he want to destroy my happiness too? I don't even know him."

Matthew sighed. "He doesn't hate me and he didn't know you. But the thing I have not considered before—before you and your entourage barged in on me—is Jamie . . . Jamie and his fortune."

"I don't understand," said Omega.

"Then I shall tell you. Play devil's advocate, my dear." He took off his shoes and propped his feet on the bed. "My friend Colonel Merrill Watt-Lyon, Lord Mansfield, was at the party, and he died in Spain during the Peninsular campaign."

"Matthew, that is war," she said.

"Ah, but he did not die in battle. His troops found him and his horse at the bottom of a ravine outside Ronda. Word got about that he had been drinking, but Merrill seldom drank. Liquor made him sick. I remember how sick he was that night."

"Friend number one," murmured Omega.

"Friend number two was David Larchstone. I believe you remember him?"

She nodded. "He was the first person I ever danced with at Almack's."

"And let me tell you, that was only because he got in front of me and had no scruples about loping across the ballroom floor!" said Matthew with a smile. "I had a certain reputation to maintain then. Dashed if I can remember why, now."

"And is he dead?"

Matthew nodded. "About six months after Merrill. He was a bruising rider after hounds. He went to take a fence that his horse could not jump. It didn't yield when he struck it, and he died after a day and night of the most acute agony."

"Dear God," said Omega. "But it was a hunting accident, was it not?"

"The top rail on the fence—a fence he had jumped many times—had been raised and nailed quite firmly into place. There was no way he could have avoided what happened. I learned these particulars from the solicitor whom our families share." Matthew started to reach for her hand, and then thought better of it. "I remember wondering at the time who could have had a grudge against that charming scapegrace. And then there is my brother-in-law, Marchant Clevenden, Lord Rotherford's younger brother and husband to my sister Diantha."

"I knew so little of him," said Omega. "Was he not in business with the East India Company?"

"He was. What you probably did not know—because goodness knows, such things never seemed to interest you— March was a very wealthy man. He took to Indian trade and intrigue like a duck to water. He amassed a magnificent fortune." Matthew chuckled. "It makes mine look like I'm only a stagger away from the workhouse. Lord, but that man had a talent for raking in the ready! It used to send Diantha into whoops when she considered how Rotherford sneered at his little brother's 'smell of the shop.' "

Omega sighed and rubbed her arms.

"I am tiring you," Matthew said.

Omega shook her head. "I am cold."

Matthew got up and pulled the blanket up from the foot of the bed until it was arranged comfortably around her. He sat down again and put his feet under the edge of the blanket. "I am cold too. I am also frightened. Omega, March and Di were visiting the Clevenden estate in Somerset about five years ago when their carriage tipped them into the ocean. They drowned."

Omega opened her eyes wide. "I never knew. And what of Jamie?"

"He was supposed to have been with them, but at the last moment Di left him behind at the house because he was napping. The fortune is his." Matthew looked away from her. "And the guardianship fell to Rotherford, as somehow I think he had known it would. Do you see what has happened?"

He was looking at her so earnestly then, his eyes searching deep into hers, almost pleading with her to understand.

"Is Rotherford an improvident man?" she asked slowly, feeling her way through this puzzle.

"Yes, or that is the rumor. Again, my source is my solicitor, who keeps me well-informed." Matthew clapped his hands together in frustration. "I would give my whole stable right now to find out if Rotherford has been dipping into Jamie's trust. But I was never included in any dealings regarding Jamie's guardianship."

And then Omega understood clearly. "And he knew you would never contest his guardianship. Oh, God, Matthew, you owed him his neat little wrapping-up of that dreadful evening's work!"

"Exactly, or so I am beginning to believe. And to think I was so grateful to him for protecting me in that mess!" he said bitterly.

"Don't berate yourself, my dear," Omega said.

He looked at her quickly then, but made no remark on her address. "For all that I have behaved stupidly, I am no fool, Omega. All the witnesses to whatever happened that night are dead, or at least far away. If I were to make any motion to challenge his guardianship—Clevenden left no will—Rotherford would have trussed me like a Christmas goose and delivered me to the hangman. He *knew* I would say nothing."

"But, Matthew, that would mean he has been planning this for . . . for years!"

Matthew took her by the hand. "Yes, it does, doesn't it?" He shook his head. "Rotherford has one virtue that I used to admire. He is a patient man. You should see him with his horses, how he trains them carefully and slowly. He would think nothing of patiently weaving a web of this kind."

"Is it possible?"

"Yes, indeed, my dear. Time was on his side. He knew I would do nothing. At some point in this dirty business he examined my faulty character and *planned* it that way."

Omega shook her head. "It is hard to imagine that

someone would be so cold-blooded. I cannot take it in.''

"Well, my dear. I can understand how you would feel that way. You have no guile. You never in your deepest nightmares could have imagined that anyone would leave you standing in the church, exposed to the ridicule of the world, did you? So how are you to believe this?''

He was silent then. Omega scooted herself to the edge of her bed and leaned against his arm. He started, and then looked at her in surprise. "Omega, my dear, I obviously do not understand women. I tell you this terrible story, and you only seek to give me comfort.''

He did not touch her, but he did not move away either. Omega put her arm through his. "Matthew, don't you think you have berated yourself enough in the past eight years? I know that I have scolded and railed against fate and excoriated myself until I am sick of it.''

Matthew stirred himself and put his hand over hers again for a brief moment before he moved farther away from her. "One thing remains for us to do, my dear. I had better locate Timothy Platter. Do you think . . . could we possibly ask him to help us?''

10

Matthew did not bring her breakfast in the morning. It came direct from the kitchen in the hands of Antoine, who was followed by his interpreter, Angela. After Angela tucked a napkin in the top of Omega's gown, Antoine set down the tray with a flourish, exposing several ladylike slivers of Yorkshire ham, crepes nestled in raspberry sauce and topped with a spoonful of clotted cream. There was tea in the pot, and a small basket of pastries.

"Antoine, *magnifique*!" she exclaimed, exhausting her French.

Antoine beamed and dabbed at the corners of his eyes.

He spoke rapidly to Angela and then folded his arms.

"I am to tell you that if there is any little morsel that he can create for you, he will be so grateful," Angela said. "He begs to tell you that he will prepare a small restorative to be eaten around ten o'clock."

"Oh, tell him that will not be necessary," Omega replied, her eyes on the crepes.

"I cannot do that!" Angela protested. "It will wound his feelings. He is so dreadfully sensitive, and besides, Jamie and I will eat the goodies at ten o'clock."

"Very well then, dear," Omega said, "although I do not believe for a moment that you are being a martyr."

After staying long enough to watch Omega eat one of his crepes, Antoine dabbed at his eyes again and left the room, overcome with strong feeling.

"You have made him the happiest Frenchman in England," said Angela.

The dignified Miss Chartley snorted and poured herself some tea. "That is a whisker, Angela! Only wait until I cross him on some issue about dinner or luncheon. Then he will rain rapid French down on my head until we are all quite weary."

She finished the crepes. "Tell me, what of Lord Byford? Is he about yet?"

"Oh, long since. He took Hugh with him into the garden and they walked about for some time and talked. And then Lord Byford walked into Byford by himself. I do not know what it is about. I teased and teased Hugh, but he would not tell me."

Omega sipped her tea. So now Hugh Owen is acquainted with the whole sad story. She sighed. It is better so, she thought, even as she colored faintly with embarrassment for Matthew.

Jamie came into her room dressed in his new clothes. He said hello politely and paused only long enough to claim Angela. "She has promised to teach me to trap rabbits, Omega. Besides," he added, looking darts at Angela, "didn't Uncle Matthew make us both take an oath not to disturb Miss Chartley?"

"I was merely telling her the news," answered Angela

with great dignity. She collected Omega's tray and suffered
Jamie to tow her toward the door. "Boys have no sense
about anything."

When they were gone, Omega pulled back the bedcovers
and swung her legs over the edge of the bed. Her ankle was
still puffy and angry-looking, but she could tell that much
of the swelling had subsided. I wonder if I could stand on
it? she thought, even as she grabbed the bedstead and
pulled herself to her feet. She was reaching for the chair,
with her eyes on the dressing table across the room, when
Tildy came in, shrieked, and hurried to her side.

"Miss Chartley! Oh, should you be doing this?"

"Yes," said Miss Chartley through gritted teeth. "Help
me to the dressing table. Be a good girl, Tildy."

Tildy shook her head in vast disapproval, but took
Omega by the elbow and steered her to the dressing table.
Omega surveyed herself in the mirror. "Do you know,"
she said in shocked surprise, "I really *do* look green when I
am pale."

Her hair was wild about her head, reminding her of
Medusa, but it was nothing compared to her pallor.
"Tildy, Miss Haversham, the headmistress at my last
school, used to tell the pupils that fragile women were
'interesting.' That is a great hum. It's hard to believe that I
could go downhill so rapidly."

"Now, Miss Chartley," said Tildy, "let me brush your
hair for a minute. A bath would do you wonders too. And
then, when you are done, you can sit in the chair by the
window and look 'interesting.' " Tildy giggled and
reached for the hairbrush.

Tildy's recommendations were all accomplished by
noon. Her hair neatly composed under another lace cap,
and wearing a fresh nightgown and robe, Omega sat by the
window, her foot propped on a stool. She seldom sat
without something to do, but it was pleasant to feel the
warmth of the noonday sun on her face, with no thought
of a task that needed to be done. I could grow used to such
indolence, she thought. Tildy had turned down the covers
on the bed and fluffed the pillows, "for when you feel like
a nap, Miss Chartley."

Miss Chartley felt like looking out the window, listening to the birds and the faint sounds of cow bells in distant fields. Until she was surrounded by the peace of Byford, she hadn't been aware of Plymouth's noise. For eight years she had accepted the racket of the busy seaport, listening with resignation to the sounds from the docks, the screechings of the fishmongers as they exhorted their customers block by block, the gruff talk of sailors, and over all, the deep sounds of harbor bells.

There was none of that here in Byford, only a blissful sort of quiet that was more restful than a hundred naps. She hoped that Durham would prove like this, even as her heart told her that it could never be as special as Byford, and her head reminded her that she was leaving as soon as she could.

Omega was dozing in the chair when she heard voices in the hall. Tildy was talking to Matthew. Omega answered, "Come in, Matthew," to the firm knock on the door.

He stuck his head in. "Ha! I told you she would see me!"

Tildy pursed her lips and stepped aside. "My lord, she needs her rest."

Omega started to rise from the chair. Matthew hurried across the room and picked her up, depositing her on the bed. She put her hands on his chest. "Matthew, I think I would rather be downstairs."

"In a moment," he said. "Tildy, I'll carry her down to the parlor in a moment, if you will arrange the pillows on the sofa."

Matthew turned back to Omega, looking at her ankle carefully, comparing it with the other one, and then nodding. "The doctor was right, Omega," he said as he spread the blanket over her. "It looks better." He leaned close to her hair and sniffed. "And you smell of lavender. As Jamie would probably say, 'This is famous!' "

She smiled and looked at him in turn. "Your eye, Matthew. My goodness."

He bowed. "Yes, I have reached that dreadful green-and-yellow stage. Whereas you, my dear, may languish and appear mysterious, I look as though I keep low company." He grinned. "Come to think of it, perhaps I do."

But that was not what he had come to say. "Setting all this aside, I must tell you that I have searched for Mr. Timothy Platter and he is nowhere to be seen."

"This is vexing," she said. "Do you suppose . . . could he have returned to Lord Rotherford's estate with his intellligence?"

"He could have."

"Where is his estate?"

"Somerset, near Taunton. I believe that Platter is still about, but don't ask me why. I just don't think he would have left the area, especially as we are closer to London, where Mr. Platter will surely be repairing soon."

"You don't think he would spirit Jamie away, do you?"

"There is that possibility. I will set a strong watch about the house. Still, I expect we will hear from Mr. Platter when he feels the time is right." Matthew rubbed his hands together. "Let us hope it is soon."

He carried her down to the parlor, admonishing her to hold tight to his neck. "For if I should stumble on the stairs, my dear, neither of us will be fit for a midden. I am already convinced that Jamie and Angela consider us two of the most decrepit people of their acquaintance."

The sofa was ready for her, with pillows to prop her back and a basin of cool water and epsom salt for her foot. Tildy was there with her mending; Twinings came to bring up roses for the vase at her side and to assure her that her time was his, should she need any assistance. Jamie raced through with another snared rabbit ("Omega! This is famous! *I* snared it!"), and Angela followed more sedately, pausing to ask Omega how she did. Soon Antoine ascended from the kitchen bearing a pot of tea and yet another French pastry for Omega's weakened constitution. Hugh wandered by with several drawings of horses and a distracted look on his face.

Matthew watched the stream of people through his parlor with a combination of exasperation and amusement. "Before your precipitate arrival, I could have sat here all day and never seen another living soul," he said. "Now, Omega, if I want a private word with you, I will have to fill out a card and wait my turn, just like an Assembly Room ball!"

His tone was censorious enough, but the effect was mitigated when he grabbed Angela around the middle as she drifted about and set her on his lap.

"I am too old to sit on your lap, my lord," she said gravely.

"I think not. I will release you on one condition: that you go upstairs and see what is on your bed."

She leapt off his lap and ran up the stairs. The next sound was a scream of delight, and then loud crying.

"My God," said Omega, "what have you done?"

"Do you suppose that Spanish females carry on in such fashion whenever they are overcome with emotion?" he murmured. "It's a wonder Beau Wellington did not wash his hands of the whole Peninsula."

"And what have you done, Matthew?" she asked again.

"A small thing. I also bought some muslin at the Templeton fair yesterday, and promised one of our local seamstresses a ridiculous stipend if she would make a dress from it by this morning. You know, a church dress, a fancy dress." He looked at her for a reaction. "Do you know, Omega, I like the way your dimple shows, even when you are trying to be stern with me. Ah, there it is!"

"You are so good to Angela."

"It is purely selfish, Miss Chartley." He took her hand and raised it to his lips. "You resist taking a loan from me so you can get on your way to Durham. I shall spoil Angela out of spite . . . and also because I have become fond of both children." He rose and went to the window. "Almost as if they were my own."

She could think of nothing to say, and was spared comment when Hugh came through again, and Angela, red-eyed and smiling, came downstairs and threw herself into the viscount's arms. He hugged her. "Just tell me one thing, Angela: are you happy?"

She nodded and burst into tears all over again. Matthew threw back his head and laughed. "Is she always this way, Hugh?"

Hugh grinned. "I wouldn't know, my lord. Up to now she has been content with one meal a day—on a good day—and a castoff dress. You've probably ruined her forever. How can we leave this place?"

Matthew rested his arm on Angela's shoulder. "Perhaps you will not have to, Hugh. When this . . . this issue is settled, perhaps there will be occasion for another discussion."

By the time Matthew carried her upstairs that evening, Omega Chartley was ready to go. How a healthy woman could become so tired from sitting in a comfortable parlor and doing nothing was a thing she did not understand. She wanted only to sleep now, to sleep and not worry about the disturbing past, her uneasy present, and her uncertain future. She would try to walk in the morning, try to be of some use in the household where she was treated with such kindness.

"Can I do something else for you?" Matthew asked after he blew out the candle by the bedside and arranged the blankets on her legs again.

You could love me, she thought. Even if you thought you could not, you could try.

"No. I am fine. Matthew, thank you again for all you are doing for us. I know I am such an imposition. As soon . . . as soon as I am able, I'll accept your offer of a loan and be on my way to Durham."

"Suppose I should withdraw my offer?" he teased, his eyes on her face in the dark.

"Then I will apply to Angela to instruct me in the art of snaring rabbits and catching fish, and I'll be on my way in any case," she said calmly, wishing that he did not look so good to her, even with his eye decorated in moldering shades of green and his nose slightly swollen. Did he have to wear that marvelous lemon cologne? Why did he not wear bay rum, like other men? What a nuisance he was. How much she would miss him.

He touched her face. "And will you think of me occasionally when you are grading papers and listening to recitations?"

"I will not, my lord," she said firmly. "I shall

concentrate fully on my duties, and have time to wool-gather only during vacations and holidays.''

He smiled. "Well, spare me a thought, then. And now, good night. Call me if you need me.''

Omega fell asleep promptly and slept soundly all night, paying no heed to the creakings of the old house as it settled itself, and ignoring the cats orchestrating by the back wall of the garden.

In that period of dawn just as the light was beginning to stream in the window, she opened her eyes, suddenly alert. Nothing discernible woke her; it was just a feeling, a feeling that she was sharing the room with someone else. Her heart leapt to her throat as she opened her eyes and slowly turned her head toward the window.

At first she could see nothing, but she waited and watched and her vision cleared. The curtains rustled. As she watched them, a man threw his leg over the windowsill. She opened her eyes wider and held her breath as the man straddled the windowsill and just sat there, as if wondering what to do.

That he had come recently from the flower garden was amply clear to her; his coat was sprinkled with pollen. A pair of morning glories from the climbing vine outside her window had caught on his pocket, a dapper, if somewhat unlikely, buttonhole flower.

Omega raised herself on her elbows, careful not to make a sound, and regarded the intruder with more amazement than fear. His face was still in shadow and she could not make out any features, but there was something deliciously funny about her unexpected guest. I should name him Floribunda, she thought, or perhaps Glory. She opened her mouth to scream, mainly because it seemed like the thing to do.

Before she could scream, the flowery man in the shadows reared back his head suddenly, "Ah . . . ah . . . choo!''

His sneeze was so powerful it seemed to circulate around the room, making the air vibrate. He sneezed again and again, even as he tried to brush the offending pollen off his coat.

This was a mistake. He lost his balance and fell out of the window, maintaining a tenuous grip on the sill even as he sneezed and cursed and beat with his feet against the side of the house.

Omega lay back and surrendered herself to laughter. "Matthew!" she gasped. "You'd better come in here, Matthew!"

Even before she had finished shouting, the door slammed open and Matthew stood there, clad in his nightshirt, pistol in hand. "Good God, what is that caterwauling?" he asked, and then stared at her as she sat up and clutched at her ankle.

"Oh, it hurts when I laugh! Matthew, you must help that . . . that man at the window!"

Openmouthed, Matthew dropped the pistol on the bed and ran to the window, leaning out. "Oh, hold on." He peered closer. "I do believe you are Timothy Platter, are you not? Pleased to meet you, sir. Perhaps we should shake!"

Omega's laughter gave way to occasional hiccups as Matthew grabbed the Bow Street Runner by the pants and the back of his coat and hoisted him in the window. The morning glories were wrapped around Mr. Platter's ear by now, and Omega decided that he looked quite lovely.

He sat down with a thump inside the window, gazing about him with a dazed expression. Matthew held his hand out in front of him. "Don't move. Don't even think about moving. I'm going to get my pants on. Omega, point this pistol at him if—and only if—you think you can collect yourself enough to be useful."

She took the pistol from him, trying not to smile, and failing miserably. Matthew glanced down at his exposed legs and snatched the blanket off the end of the bed. "I'll have you know that in some circles these are considered quite shapely," he snapped. "You need only ask Gentleman Jackson or any number of my fellow inmates at Oxford!"

He exited with as much dignity as he could muster, returning moments later stuffing his shirt into his pants. He leveled a withering glance at her that did nothing to foster her sobriety, and pointedly turned his back to her as he hauled Timothy Platter to his feet.

"And now, you will explain yourself!" he said as he pushed Mr. Platter into a chair.

Mr. Platter removed the flowery vines from about his ear and muttered something about "bleeding roses." Matthew winced. "Sir, remember yourself," he ordered, looking with no sympathy on Platter.

"You see, Lord Byford, if that is who you claim to be, I thought I was in your room. I climbed the trellis."

The viscount sat down on Omega's bed. "I have a front door, Mr. Platter. At least I did the last time I checked."

"Happens you do, sir, but I am no flat. Timothy Platter's mam raised no half-wits."

"Words do not express how relieved I am to hear that. Pray continue," said the viscount. "It is early, and I fail to see the connection between your mother and my front door."

"Do you know that your place is devilish well-guarded?"

Matthew nodded, a trace of a smile on his face.

"I thought I would try the window."

"I am incredulous. Is this something new in law enforcement?"

Platter took exception to Matthew's tone. "Sir, when a gentry mort searches the pubs and scatters about messages that he wishes my presence, I get leery."

"So you thought the window would be best."

"I did. I thought this was your room."

"As you can see, it is not." Matthew glanced at Omega, who had regained her composure. "If this room were occupied by anyone less . . . shall we say . . . lively of mind than Miss Chartley, you would probably be pitched on your head by now."

"I like that," said the lively Miss Chartley.

"I thought it was your room," the Runner insisted. "I stayed in the flowers until the guard went away, and then I climbed up, and there *you* were, sitting in this very chair! It was dark, but I could see your face."

Omega stirred. "Matthew, what are you up to?"

"That's what I'd like to know," declared Timoth
Platter virtuously.

"I come in here every night to make sure you are well,
he said softly.

"But you sat and sat!" said Platter in triumph. "And s
I thought this was your room. An honest mistak
gov'nor."

"I must have fallen asleep," Matthew suggested, mor
for Omega's benefit than the Runner's.

"Your peepers was wide open, my lord. I watched you.
couldn't make a move in the window however, becaus
that guard came back." Platter attempted a diversior
"Your guards would have been the first to drop a
Waterloo, sir."

The tactic failed because Matthew ignored it. "In futur
dealings, Mr. Platter, if we are so blessed, be assured tha
you may approach my front door with temerity."

The men eyed each other. "And now I am here, my lord
Where is your nephew?"

The men eyed each other for a moment in a room fille
with silence. "It must be the early hour that troubles m
again, Mr. Platter," said Matthew slowly. "I canno
understand the connection between my nephew and you
ante-dawn climb. Is there one?"

Platter said nothing for a moment. Omega watched hi
face grow redder and redder. When she thought that h
would burst, he pointed a finger at Matthew. "Don't bai
me! Don't be calm and well-bred!" When Matthew said
nothing, he turned his attention to Omega. "And you! I
was you who nabbed Jamie out from under my reach, righ
when I had him. Don't give me that wide-eyed missish
look," he shouted. "You know where he is, and it's my
commission to find him and restore him to his uncle."

"You'll have to do better than that!" snapped Omega
"If you think I would willingly turn over a child to an ogre
who beats him, then you've got windmills in your head!'

"Speaking of my head," Platter snapped back, "I'
give more than a shilling to know what you spiked m
with."

"A paperweight," she hissed, "and I'd do it again in a minute."

"I could ruin you," he said, his voice quieter. "You gentry morts may not think we Runners are much, but I could ruin you."

"I have already been ruined, sir," she replied, her voice matching his. "I haven't a thing to lose by defending James Clevenden."

"Here, here, now," interjected Matthew. "You don't need to mill each other down." He looked at Omega first. "My dear, pull your claws in. The boy is in no immediate danger." He turned to Timothy Platter. "Yes, my nephew is here, and here he will remain until I am absolutely satisfied about his welfare. If this disturbs Lord Rotherford, he can come and tell me himself."

"He'll likely do that, my lord. I have already sent for him."

Omega sucked in her breath. She knew it was unreasonable to hope that Platter would not fulfill his commission, but she had hoped that he would wait a bit.

There was silence in the room again, broken at last by Matthew. "Would you believe me if I told you that you have made a terrible mistake?" he said quietly.

Platter passed a hand in front of his face. "I might believe anything, my lord. You can't imagine what a summer this has been. My boss, he told me, 'Tim,' he says, 'this will be a regular holiday for you. A chance to breathe the air of the country again.'" Platter sighed and shook his head. "Like a gull, a real flat, I believed him. And what have I done except get sacked by an ostler's yard boy, clobbered by a paperweight and nearly drowned, and . . . and generally just been discommoded."

"At least you still have your clothes," Omega began.

"Omega, please!" said Matthew.

She allowed him to wave her into silence, but sat, arms folded, lips tight, in grumpy silence.

Matthew regarded her a moment, as if to assure himself that she would behave. "Setting all this aside, Mr. Platter, I would like to accompany you to London. I have a matter

of business that might interest you. I hope that it wi
explain some of our reluctance to release Jamie to his othe
uncle."

"Anyone can travel on the common stage," said Platter
not about to be placated by Matthew's gentler tone. H
looked pointedly at Omega. "I *had* a horse, but it departe
my company when I found myself floating downstream."

Omega opened her mouth, but Matthew glared at her
She closed it.

"You have my word—and Miss Chartley's word—Oh
yes, Miss Chartley—that Jamie will remain here," said
Matthew. "I will happily provide you with one of th
mounts from my own stable, and we—"

"I can't be bought," interrupted Platter.

"I'm not buying," said Matthew evenly. "When we ge
to London, I expect my horse back. I need to acquaint yo
with a story that might arouse your interest, particularly i
you denizens of Bow Street have a file of unsolve
murders. I must engage your services, Mr. Platter."

"I'll consider it," said Platter. "But no promises, d
you hear?"

Matthew clapped his hands together. "Excellent. Tha
means that I will likely not be required to engage in a bit o
real unpleasantness and have the constable incarcerate yo
for breaking and entering, coupled with possible attemp
to do bodily harm to a female invalid."

Omega sputtered and Platter fumed.

Matthew smiled at the Runner. "Our constabulary her
is so efficient. I could have an officer of the law here
in—could it be?—five or ten minutes."

The silence was heavy in the room again. Platte
thoughtfully brushed the rest of the pollen off his coat. H
sneezed several more times, and then slapped his knee
"Let's go. I've had all the peace and quiet of the country
that I can stomach, my lord."

"I knew that you would understand, Mr. Platter," said
Matthew, his voice filled with cordiality. "Let me show
you to my stables." He winked at Omega before he left the
room, his hand on the shoulder of the Bow Street Runner.

Matthew Bering and Timothy Platter did not even wait

until breakfast to leave. Two horses were saddled and
ready to ride even before the children woke.

"It's better this way," said Matthew as he pulled on his
gloves. While the impatient Mr. Platter waited in the hall
below, Matthew had requested Hugh's presence in
Omega's room. "Hugh, I would ask that you resume the
role of Major Owen." He buttoned his glove. "Rotherford
may be here before I get back from London. He's more
likely to be intimidated by a major. My dear Omega, you
must continue your role as housekeeper, I fear, and that
means a return to the company belowstairs. Keep Jamie
close by you."

"By all means." Omega held out her hand to him, and
he took it. "But, Matthew, what are you going to do in
London?"

"Something I have avoided for eight years," he replied
grimly. "I am going to see what I can learn about what
happened that night. It could be that I am innocent of all
that Rotherford has led me to believe. It could also be that
I am quite guilty." He sighed and sat down on Omega's
bed. "And if that is the case, we'll have to devise another
course of action for Jamie. Or, rather, I will," he
amended. "At any rate, Omega, after you see this little
masquerade out, you should be on your way to Durham
soon enough, whatever the outcome."

"Yes," she agreed, keeping her voice steady. "I don't
have much time left, do I?"

"Neither do I, likely," said Matthew. "Hugh, could you
go below and see if there is anything Mr. Platter needs? I'll
be right along."

When Hugh left the room, Matthew went to the window
and stood there looking out at the flower garden, hands in
pockets, rocking back and forth on his heels. "I have so
enjoyed it here," he said at last. He turned around to face
Omega. "Do they, as a rule, hang murderers who happen
to be members of the peerage, or merely transport them?"

"Matthew, please!" she said, and held out her arms to
him.

Without a word, he knelt by the bed and wrapped his
arms around her. She hesitated only a moment, and then

hugged him to her, resting her hand on the back of his neck, running her fingers against the nap of his hair. With an ache more immense than any pain she had felt in the last few days, Omega remembered that the last time she had fingered his hair was the night before her wedding, when she said good night to him.

He pulled himself away from her. "No one's done that for ever so long, Omega." His voice was strangely altered. "I can't tell you how good it feels."

She pulled him to her again, fiercely this time, as if she did not wish to let him go. "Matthew, be careful!" she whispered in his ear, and then kissed his cheek.

He sighed and gently disentangled himself from her embrace. "And even if I do win this one, my dear, dear Omega, it doesn't change anything between us. I wish that it could."

"Good-bye, Matthew," she whispered. "God watch you."

"And you, Omega."

11

The first few miles to London were covered in silence, neither man disposed to address the other. Matthew stole a glance at his traveling companion several times, the last time to find him staring back. Both men smiled. Matthew spoke first.

"I have become somewhat of a recluse in these past eight years, Mr. Platter," he apologized. "If I am silent, it is out of habit, and also because I am trying to work up my courage to acquaint you with this delicate subject. My dear sir, murder is hard to skate around."

Platter made a motion with his hand. "Murder, is it? Sir, I have probably heard all of these things before, so you may proceed whenever you feel like it. And by the way, his is a fine horse. What a pity that I cannot be bought."

Matthew laughed. "Yes, isn't it?" He sobered quickly. "Well, sir, lend an ear now. I seem to be making a habit out of telling my story in these past few days, but you are the first person who has the power to have me hanged because of it."

Riding along past the haying fields and the August harvest of the Cotswolds' bounty, Matthew Bering described the events of eight years ago, including every detail that would show him at his worst. He tried to keep his voice calm, but it was difficult. Many times he struggled and looked away, aware all over again of the magnitude of the crime committed, and acutely aware that he was confessing to an officer of the law. Matthew knew the road to London well, but he concentrated on keeping his eyes straight ahead on the highway before him, preferring not to see his crimes reflected in the face of the Bow Street Runner.

His hands shook and he tightened his grip on the reins as he told of that morning of his wedding when he woke up with the pale dead woman beside him. Matthew could not resist; he glanced quickly at Timothy Platter, and then found himself even more deeply disturbed. The Runner was struggling with emotions of his own. Platter was gnawing on his lower lip, even as he frowned. The very attitude of his body was tense. In response, his horse danced along, skittish and upset too.

The moment quickly passed, and Platter brought the horse to rights again. The Runner managed a tight smile. "My lord, for all that there is nothing new under the sun, this is interesting."

"That would not have been my choice of words, sir. You are kind," was Matthew's reply.

"No, I am not, sir," said Platter firmly, his own feelings submerged again. "Pray continue. I do not see the connection yet between you and Rotherford and the nephew you share in common. So far, your story does not fadge."

"I was sure it did not. Let us pause first, Mr. Platter," said Lord Byford with a sigh. "There is a tolerable inn ahead. They have a way of toasting cheese that is quite superior. My horses need a rest.''

They dined in silence, Platter concentrating his thoughts upon the blank wall beyond his companion's shoulder, and Bering regarding his plate and wineglass as if he had never seen such utensils before. The viscount looked around occasionally at the others in the room, and couldn't help observing that the other diners were glancing his way in curiosity.

''We seem to be exciting some interest,'' he murmured finally to his fellow traveler.

''Runners seldom travel ordinary-like with toffs,'' said Mr. Platter as he reached for another slice of bread, which he tore in half and mortared together with apple butter. ''I have a suggestion, my lord. If this village has a ready-made store, I would recommend that you visit it. We stand out like blackamoors in Glasgow.''

The village, which boasted a large population of the farming society, indeed supported such a store. Nodding to his companion, Lord Byford visited it, returning to the innyard a short while later, his clothes in a bundle, clad now in shirt, trousers, and rough boots of a much-less-distinguished Englishman.

''I left my beaver hat with a somewhat mystified hay-wain driver. Will I do now, Mr. Platter?'' he asked as he stuffed his other clothes into a saddlebag, and wondered what his tailor would think if he could see him.

''Decidedly,'' commented the Runner. ''I should not be ashamed to travel with you now. My reputation, Lord Byford, my reputation.''

Matthew looked at him sharply, and then caught the gleam in the Runner's eye. He bowed and managed a smile of his own. ''Then, sir, pray let us continue. My horses have no more patience than their owner.''

Matthew continued his story immediately they had left the village behind, wondering to himself for the thousandth time if the whole thing sounded false. Maybe it *was* foolish above half to suppose that Rotherford would have planned such an event with patience. Perhaps Omega was right; surely no one was so careful, so willing to wait.

He only wanted to believe it, only wanted to assure himself that he never could have killed someone.

Matthew finished and was silent, looking straight ahead again, not trusting even a glance at his companion, who sat in silence of his own.

"These friends of yours . . . all dead?" asked Platter finally. His question was spoken deliberately, as if he asked it in a court of law.

"For sure, only the three that I mentioned. The fourth one, Sir Horace Billings, I have not heard from since . . . since . . . I don't know . . . 1810 or 1811. I have written to him several times. The letters were neither returned nor answered."

"He could be alive."

"He could be. Horace never was one to take chances like the others. He was a bit of a priss and a dandy. He lives . . . or lived . . . in the wilds of Suffolk. 'A drafty castle, fit for Vikings,' or so he used to tell me."

The Runner considered this piece of intelligence, and sought another. "Was anyone else aware of the evening's events?"

Matthew shook his head, and then looked at Platter. "There was the landlord of the building. I remember him vaguely."

"Then we must find this set of rooms, Lord Byford, must we not?"

Matthew reined in his horse, turning it slightly to stop the Runner's also. "Then do you believe me?"

Platter would not look him in the eye. "Let us say that your story is intriguing, and I feel sorry for you, my lord."

The Runner raised his glance to Matthew for a second. Again there was that look in his eyes that had so disquieted the viscount earlier. Again it passed, leaving instead the calm and rather sour expression of a professional officer of the law.

"It's a discomfiting thought to be considered an object of pity," said Matthew finally.

"Go on, sir, finish your thought," said Platter, his voice rising slightly, and then lowering again to its professional tone. " 'An object of pity from one of my class.' " Platter

sat straighter in the saddle. "But I do feel pity for you.
More than your life alone has been affected. Other men
may have died because of this. And there is a woman
deeply hurt. And as a justice of the peace, you are aware of
the laws of our land, my lord. It remains for you to prove
yourself innocent. But I will say no more on that subject,
my lord."

He was true to his word. Not another sentence was
spoken during the rest of that long day. The silence greatly
embarrassed Matthew at first, but then he grew used to it.
He glanced occasionally at the Runner, and decided finally
that the man was deep in thought. It would not have been
polite to disturb him. Matthew's lively brain was fully
occupied with his own predicament.

They reached the metropolis as the sun was setting.
Neither man would admit fatigue to the other, but
Matthew had watched Platter stand in his stirrups several
times in the last few hours, as if weary of his seat.

The houses drew closer and closer together as the men
rode in silence. Soon the houses were joined by stores and
grog shops and the road grew even narrower. Smoke and
fog of a most disagreeable consistency rolled down the
street.

Platter took a deep breath and sighed. "It's good to be
home," he said, breaking his great fast of silence.
"London air."

Matthew took a whiff and wished himself immediately
back in the country. "To each his own," he murmured.

Platter turned toward him with a faint look of surprise.
"My lord, don't those early-morning birds ever drive you
to Bedlam? Or the way it is so damned quiet the rest of the
day? I wonder anyone can endure the country. Not this
cove, any road."

Matthew smiled. "*This* lord's ways are mysterious,
then, my good man. And perhaps since I am traveling
incognito, it would be best if you were to call me
Matthew."

"Certainly, my lord."

They continued deeper into the city down roads that

Matthew was unfamiliar with. It was a part of London he knew nothing of, for all that it teemed about him: people spilling into the noisome streets, beggars, maimed soldiers with begging bowls (he thought of Hugh Owen), and women, girls merely, standing on street corners leering at the men who passed, calling out to them. His face reddened and then he felt that familiar sickness in his stomach.

"Matthew?"

"Yes?"

"I was asking you, would you prefer to put up at your own establishment?"

"I have no house here. I sold it eight years ago." He looked down at his blue shirt, with the dark perspiration stains under the armpits. "And I do not think I would get past the doorman at Claridge's."

"Then come home with me, sir."

"Oh, I could not." Matthew noticed that look again in Platter's eyes. "And don't get your back up, man! I mean nothing other than it is not my wish to disturb your family. You need only recommend an inn."

"I'd like you to come to my lodgings, sir."

Matthew thought it over. "Very well, Timothy, I will." He paused, wondering how to frame his next question. "And . . . do you go to Bow Street first to make your report?"

Platter shook his head. "I do not. I think I have not finished this particular assignment. My master is a nitpicker. He likes everything tied in neat bundles. My report can wait a few days."

"Thank you."

They passed through another street and turned into an alley, which led into a warren of narrow houses, each more decrepit than the one before. They stopped at last before a building that Matthew knew he could never find again, even if he wrote down explicit directions. Platter dismounted stiffly and threw the reins to a young boy standing by. He bade Matthew to do the same.

Matthew did, but he looked at Platter with some

trepidation. "And will my horses still be here in the morning?" he asked in a low voice. "Not wishing to offer insult, but still, sir, I worry."

Timothy measured him with a long appraisal. "I would not have taken you for such a flat, my lord. Do you think the gulls in this alley will tinker with the mounts of a Bow Street Runner?"

"Of course they will not," agreed Matthew. "How foolish of me."

Stiff-legged, the men climbed the stairs, going past landing after landing, until they were near the top, lacking one. Matthew stood on the landing and clutched the banister, trying to regain some rhythm to his breathing. "Was there ever a truer indication of my rapid decline than the purgatory of that saddle, and now these stairs?"

Platter laughed. He went down the hallway and knocked on the door, listening as the bolt was thrown back. A woman not much older than Omega stuck her head out and broke into a smile. She took Timothy by the hand and pulled him into the room. She noticed Matthew then, and stepped back shyly.

"He can come in too, Maeve," said the Runner. "He won't bite."

"If you are sure." She opened the door wider. "But I must say, sir, that my Timothy has brought home all manner of strays in his career." Her voice had an Irish lilt that was altogether delightful.

Matthew wondered what Omega would say to such an address. He stepped inside. The room was small, but it was clean. A little boy, finger in mouth, stared at him and clutched at his mother's skirts. Over by the hearth, a baby lay in a cradle, contemplating, with the majesty of few months, the miracle of fingers.

Platter was watching him. "There are others of my calling who live much finer, Matthew. I believe I have already told you that I cannot be bought. We live well enough, and by God, my conscience allows me to sleep nights."

"I have come to expect nothing less of you, Mr. Platter," murmured the viscount. "My congratulations."

"And here are my wife, Maeve, and my children, Davey and Sarah," Platter said, his arm around his wife's waist. "Maeve, this is Matthew Bering. He will be staying with us a day or two."

She nodded, as if this were nothing new to her, and turned her attention back to the pot on the hook over the fire. Platter sniffed the air appreciatively. "Irish stew. Maeve, I am fair gut-foundered."

There were insufficient bowls for all of them to eat at once. Matthew and the lord of the house sat first at table, Davey on his father's knee, eating every other bite, as Maeve stood by the fireplace stirring the stew, holding the baby, and telling her husband in her pleasant brogue of the events of the neighborhood since his taking leave of it.

Platter nodded at the appropriate times and steadily ate his way through two bowls of stew. When Matthew finished, Maeve filled his bowl and stood by the fireplace eating out of it. Matthew took the baby from her and insisted that she sit down. He pulled the stool out for her, and she looked back in surprise.

Platter flashed him a warning look. "Not too fancy, Matthew, my friend. Think what attention Maeve will demand when you leave."

Matthew put the baby to his shoulder and let her rest her head in the curve of his neck. Her hair was brown and wild about her head. He sighed and thought of Omega as he fingered the curls.

When Maeve finished, she refilled the communal bowl with a little more stew for her son. Matthew watched as she helped him, and mentally resolved to order a whole set of crockery for the Platter household. His lips twitched. Wouldn't that be a surprise for Maeve? He wouldn't even tell her it was from Platter's latest "stray."

The baby fell asleep in his arms and he stood where he was, leaning against the wall, enjoying the pleasurable weight of the child, and the sudden knowledge that he would sleep well too, this night. He had told his tale; his fate was in the hands of this strange man. He could only surrender himself to the acceptance of the fact and enjoy the moment.

Bedtime came quickly, dictated by the sputtering of the tallow candle. "I could light another one," offered Maeve as she looked at her husband.

The Runner shook his head and put his arm around her, drawing her close. "No. Maeve, my dear, regard our guest there. He will fall on his face and black his other eye if he stays awake much longer."

"Am I that decrepit?" Matthew asked as he handed over the sleeping child to her mother. "Or do you merely want to look good, compared to me, Timothy?"

The Runner grinned. He pulled a pallet away from the wall and dragged it in front of the fireplace. "You'll find this soft as angel hair, my boy, and Davey will keep you excellent company."

Davy was too sleepy to object to his strange bedfellow. He allowed Matthew to help him into his nightshirt. After Maeve pinched out a candle, Matthew took off his pants and arranged himself on the pallet next to Davey, who hesitated only a moment before curling up next to him, sighing once or twice and surrendering to sleep. Matthew put his hands behind his head. The Runner and his wife retired to their bed on the other side of the room.

Breakfast was toast dipped in sweet hot tea and laced with cream. Maeve buttered each slice of thick-cut bread, humming to herself. The children were still asleep, so she sat with her hands folded in her lap, content to watch her husband as he ate.

"Mr. Bering, do you have a family?" It was the first question she had addressed to him.

He shook his head, touched by the look of real pity in her eyes. She gave him another piece of bread, and left more butter on it this time. Matthew took it with thanks and went to stand by the window, looking out on the dingy alley as Platter and his wife conversed in low tones. Gazing on the refuse-filled square far below, he reflected that it was a poor place to raise children, and wondered what he could do about it. He leaned against the windowsill. If he was unable to prove his innocence, he could always put a codicil in his will and provide Platter and his little ones with a place in the country. The thought was hardly comforting, even for a budding philanthropist.

At length Platter joined him at the window. "Well, sir, let us be off. We can reclaim our—your—horses and get a little closer to your part of London."

They rode carefully through streets already crowded with the commerce of a typical summer morning. Milkmaids and knife grinders competed with butchers and bakers as they shouted their wares to all about them, and screamed at the stingy.

The horses were left in a public stable off Piccadilly and the men continued on foot. The crowds were no less, but the quality of the people had changed. Instead of looking over his shoulder and staying closer to Platter, Matthew found the quality looking over their shoulders at him. Several women went out of their way to avoid him. He knew that he didn't smell good and that there was a day's beard on his face, but he smiled all the same. "Timothy, we do not precisely shine in the company of these men," he said.

The Runner snorted. "If you consider these fops and popinjays men, my lord."

"I did at one time," Matthew confessed. "I can't imagine why. I may even have looked like them."

Platter was silent a few more moments, and then he changed the subject. "Think, my lord. What do you recall of that evening?"

Matthew stopped in front of Eyestone's Bookstore and rested his back against the wall. He was hurried on his way by the proprietor, who stepped out of the door swinging a broom in front of him like a broadsword.

"I used to be his best customer," said Matthew. They walked a few paces. "I remember that we first went to Watier's, where I had another dinner—Omega had already fed me—and we played cards."

They reached the corner of Bolton and Piccadilly and stood in front of Watier's. Matthew looked about him. "We must have left after midnight. The air was cold and it hit me like a bucket of ice water. Ah, but you're not interested in that."

"Happens I am, my lord. Sometimes if you just walk backward in your mind, you think of things. What then?"

"We walked along to St. James Square," said Matthew, and turned in that direction, with the Runner following. "The house was on one of the streets off the square. Lord bless me if I can recall which one, but perhaps when we're standing in the square . . ."

They walked without conversation to the great square, where Matthew stood for a moment in silent contemplation. "Do you know, sir," he said at last, his voice soft, "I have not seen this square since that night. Sometimes in the years since, I have almost convinced myself that the whole thing was a bad dream." He looked at Platter. "Standing here again, I know it was not."

"Very well, sir, and what did you do then?"

Matthew shoved his hands in his pockets, a frown on his face. "It was the oddest thing . . . you will think this silly beyond measure, but my friend Merrill Watt-Lyon began to sing." He smiled. "What *was* it? Oh, I do remember! It was 'The British Grenadier,' only he had made up the most amazingly vulgar lyrics." Matthew glanced at the Runner again, and saw nothing but patience on that impatient man's face. "What made this something to remember was that he sang through four dreadful verses, and at the end of the fourth one, we were standing in front of the house."

The Runner nodded. "Then all we need to do is walk down this street humming the tune, and when we reach the end of the fourth verse, we will be there?"

"Something like that," agreed Matthew, "if I have not taken total leave of my senses. The trouble is, of course, that I am not sure which street. We shall have to try them all."

He looked about him and then pointed to Alistair Street. "That is as good a beginning as any other, Mr. Platter. Let us be off."

Humming to himself, Lord Byford strolled down the street, and came to a halt at the end of the second verse. The street was a dead end. Matthew stared before him at the stone wall covered with ivy that blocked his forward passage. "Obviously this is not the street. Come, my good man, let us do an about-face and try again."

They tried again and again, and nothing looked familiar, and nothing matched the song. "You're certain that it was St. James Square?" ventured Platter at last.

"Oh, yes, oh, yes," insisted Matthew, even as he felt the edge of doubt creep into his brain like a London fog.

"This is the last street then, my lord," said the Runner. His voice was matter-of-fact, but Matthew heard the beginnings of skepticism.

He shrugged off the gloom that threatened to settle over him and hummed his way down the street, looking about him intently, willing the house to appear, praying for some recognition, some lifting of that veil he had so deliberately drawn across the events of that night.

Nothing.

"Damn," he exclaimed when he came to the end of the fourth verse and no house materialized. They stood before a row of shops. Matthew couldn't bear to look at the Runner as they started back in silence toward the square again. Eyes to the pavement, he stepped off the curb and glanced idly down the alley, and stopped short.

He took hold of the Runner's arm. "I think I can do it now, sir," he said softly. "Let us return to the square and try this street again."

The Runner followed him without a word. Matthew hummed a little louder this time and stepped off the paces. When he reached the curb where the alley intersected, he turned instead of continuing straight ahead.

Matthew began the third verse. The alley was narrow, but well-tended, with a clean roadway. It was an ordinary shopkeepers' neighborhood.

The song ended. Matthew stopped and looked up. He had found the house. A shiver traveled down his back as if a cold wind had suddenly whipped through the alley. "This is not a place I wished ever to see again."

"You're certain this is it?"

"I'm certain."

They faced a long flight of stairs up to the front door. A

row of trash barrels, lids on straight, hugged the staircase
wall. The shutters on the first floor were closed tight, but
the windows higher up boasted window boxes filled to
overflowing with petunias. The flowers formed the only bit
of brightness on the building's facade. All else was dark
stone, darkened further by the smoke of London's many
fires. A curtain was drawn aside for a moment on one of
the upper floors, and then brushed back again by an
unseen hand.

The Runner looked inquiringly at Matthew. Matthew
nodded. What he had not remembered, he remembered
now: the many steps up to the door and the heavy brass
knocker in the shape of a dolphin. He remembered with
startling acuteness how Sir Horace Billings had picked up
the dolphin's tail and knocked on the door, and then
tittered about it.

And there it was again. He mounted the steps—
wondering if this was how Louis XVI had felt when he
climbed up to the guillotine—and knocked on the door.
The Runner was close behind.

The door was opened a crack, and Matthew could just
barely see into the long hall, dark with wainscoting. He
saw two eyes, a nose, and a mouth, and little else against
the darkness.

"I have no rooms to let."

"I am not here to rent a room, sir, but merely to ask for
some information."

The door started to close in his face, except that
Timothy Platter opened it wider and pushed his way into
the hall. "See here!" sputtered the landlord, retreating to
the stairwell.

Platter dug into his pocket for the small emblem all
Runners carried. The man looked it over. "Close the door
behind you," he said to Matthew, who obliged.

The man made no move to show them into a parlor. He
stood there, his arms folded. "I have nothing to hide," he
declared. "This is not a place where we are acquainted
with the likes of you."

Platter bowed. "I'll not require much of your valuable

time, gov'nor,'' he said. ''What I have in mind is a history lesson.''

The landlord stared hard at the Runner, but added nothing to the conversation.

''Dredge your mind back to the early spring of 1808, sir,'' said Platter. ''There was a party here on the night of . . .'' The Runner looked at Matthew.

''April 9,'' said the viscount. ''And it was in that set of rooms at the top of the stairs . . . the ones looking out onto the street.''

The landlord laughed. ''My, but that is a faradiddle! Me old mam has lived there these fifteen years and more! Laddie, you'd better take yourself off. You've got the wrong house.''

''No, I have not,'' said Matthew quietly. He turned to Platter. ''Sir, have you any jurisdiction to search those rooms?''

''Certainly I have,'' said the Runner. ''And if Mr. Landlord here has other ideas, why, he'll soon be pissing in a bucket in Newgate.''

''Well put, Timothy,'' said Matthew. ''I do so admire your way with a phrase.''

Platter smiled grimly and directed his attention at the landlord again. ''Well? What's your pleasure, sir?''

The landlord removed a ring of keys from his pocket and climbed the stairs. He crammed the key in the lock and growled over his shoulder, ''Me mam is visiting me sister in Kent. And it's a good thing for you!'' he concluded, shaking the keys at the Runner.

''I'm all atremble,'' said Platter as he opened the door.

The room was as neat as a pin, with furniture carefully arranged and smelling faintly of roses. It was the room of an older woman, with one or two portraits badly in need of cleaning, and cheap landscape drawings here and there. The furniture was exactly as Matthew remembered it, right down to the doilies on the chair backs, and that lingering odor of roses. He felt the hairs rise on the back of his neck.

Matthew walked into the next room and stopped short in the doorway. It was the same; everything was the same. He recognized the brasswork on the bedstead that rose in a fanciful ogive in the center, with a smaller ornamentation echoed in the foot. He closed the door behind him over the protests of the landlord, preferring to be alone.

The viscount approached the bed and stood there staring down at it, almost hearing again his friends gathered around it, clapping and cheering him on, and then laughing. He shook off the fright that was settling around him and came closer, raising the coverlet until he exposed the mattress.

The bed rested on ropes. It was as tidy as the rest of the room. Matthew wiped off the sweat that had suddenly popped out on his hands and then picked up the corner of the mattress and looked under it. Faint rust stains speckled the edge of it. He raised the mattress higher and then dropped it. The rust stains merged into a larger pool of rust that covered the center of the mattress like a gigantic poppy. Someone had scrubbed and scrubbed at it, and then carefully turned the mattress over.

The room swam before his eyes. Matthew leaned against the bed, then ran to the window, slammed up the sash, and put his head out, gulping the cooler air, until he felt less light-headed.

He heard the door open, and he knew the Runner and the landlord were watching him, but he was powerless to do anything except stay where he was, taking deep breaths of air, and resting his arms on the ledge, filled with a fear greater than he had ever known before.

Finally he closed the window. "There was murder done here eight years ago," he said quietly to the landlord. "A drab was raped and killed. And you know nothing of this?"

The landlord's eyes never wavered from the viscount's face. He shook his head and smiled. "Laddie, I tell you, you're foxed. Maybe you're even crazy. Better get your keeper to take you back where you came from."

"There were six gentlemen in this set of rooms," continued Matthew inexorably, "here to celebrate the coming wedding of one with a last-night lay. And you remember nothing of this?'' He looked closely at the landlord. "Or were you paid to remember nothing?''

The landlord returned him stare for stare. "You'll have to leave. This is a respectable establishment. My mam has lived here fifteen years. Anyone in the neighborhood can tell you that.'' He laughed then, a peculiar laugh that sent chills down Matthew's arms. "And she never had a party like the one you're describing. That's the kind of parties 'gentlemen' have.'' He spat the word out.

"Perhaps it is,'' said Matthew heavily. "We're wasting our time here, Timothy. Let us go.''

"Yes, let us go,'' agreed the Runner. He took Matthew by the elbow and propelled him from the room. They hurried down the stairs and out into the sunlight. The landlord followed them downstairs and watched them. He slammed the door finally, and they could hear his laughter receding down the hall.

"There were bloodstains all over that mattress. Someone had turned it so they wouldn't show. God, Platter, is there no one who remembers anything? No one who will help me?''

"And I suppose the old lady will swear up and down and cry and carry on, and no judge will doubt her,'' said Platter. "I've seen it in too many trials. The one who pays the most wins.'' He put his hand on Matthew's shoulder. "And I think Rotherford must have paid a lot. How curious this is, to hush up a murder and yet use it to keep you forever in his debt.''

The front door opened again. Matthew looked back expectantly. The landlord stood there with a bundle in his hands. "Ashman!'' he shouted. "Ashman, come out!''

A small door opened by the ashcans and a little man ran out onto the walkway until he could see the landlord. He held his arms up and the landlord threw down the bundle and then slammed the door again.

The ashman staggered under the weight of the bundle and Matthew moved to steady him. The man looked at him, nodded his thanks, and then looked again. Instead of putting the garbage in the cans, he carried it in through the small door, looking over his shoulder one more time at Matthew.

Matthew shook his head. "Well, now what do we do?"

"I'm not entirely sure, my lord," replied Platter with more uncertainty in his voice than Matthew had ever heard before. "I need to think about this." He sighed. "And I need to go to Bow Street and check some records. Make a report. Dammit, but this is a difficult thing!"

"I think I can well imagine," said the viscount dryly. "I can't charge Rotherford with murder. I do not know all the circumstances. For all I know, I killed the girl. And if I make the slightest move to object to Rotherford's claim on my nephew, he will shout long and loud, and the landlord will have a miraculous recovery of his memory, and he will slip my neck through a noose."

The Runner took up the story. "And then in a year or so, when your nephew meets a mysterious end, there will be no one alive to even suspect. Rotherford will become one of the richest men in England, and there will be such a trail of dead bodies behind him that any respectable person would wonder how such a man sleeps nights."

"But people like that always sleep like babies," Matthew finished bitterly.

The Runner stopped walking. "We need someone who can tell us what happened. And, my lord, it appears there is no one."

Matthew nodded and pulled out his watch. "Mr. Platter, if you trust me, I would like to go to Hyde Park. It is almost time for the strut, and I have not seen it in years. Have no fear that I will elude you. All I want now is to get back to Byford and protect my nephew as long as I can. But I want to think. When you have finished at Bow Street, come for me."

"Very well, my lord," said Platter. "I am sorry about this."

"So am I. You can't imagine."

The men parted company at Piccadilly and Matthew walked to Hyde Park. He paid little attention to his surroundings, but hurried along, his long strides eating up the blocks until he came to Rotten Row. The horses,

curricles, and high-perch phaetons were assembled there as
he remembered them. Ladies and gentlemen were
assembled there too, some walking back and forth, some
riding around and around, seeing and being seen. It was
the highlight of the day for many a young miss in her first
Season or a lieutenant back from the wars. There would be
balls and routs and drums and assemblies, and the opera,
and dinners where people only toyed with their food and
lived for the next *on-dit*.

All of a sudden it was the silliest society he had ever
heard of. He longed to be back in Byford with Omega and
her fidgets and scolds. Or, failing that, he yearned to
retrace his steps to the Runner's house, where Maeve
would butter him some bread and let him hold her baby or
dandle Davey on his knee. Nothing else really mattered.
He was shattered and filled with hope at the same time.
After eight years of hiding, he wanted so much for himself
and those he loved, even as he knew things were coming to
an end.

He was desperate to get back to Byford, but there he
remained, watching the men and women riding by and
flirting, until the Runner came for him.

12

The Runner had both horses. Matthew took the reins
the man handed him. "Where to now, sir? Bow Street
for me, and then Newgate?"

With a look of surprise on his face, Platter shook his
head vigorously. "Not a chance, my lord. I still don't have
sufficient evidence either way."

"You are being kind," replied Matthew as he swung
into the saddle. "Don't deny that you have arrested others
on less evidence."

"I don't deny it," admitted Platter frankly. "You seem
to forget, however, that I have only your word for the fact

that a crime has even been committed. No one else has ever come forward. This is a singular case.''

They rode in thoughtful silence, broken by only one remark from Platter. ''I have forwarded Miss Chartley's trunk, valise, and box of books to Byford, sir.''

''She'll be glad to see them. And was her money returned also?''

''Certainly, my lord. She's quite free to leave.''

Dinner was a continuation of last night's stew, and it was no less welcome to Matthew. Maeve proudly set her bowl before him and he ate, thinking of his own table. *Maeve would never believe me if I told her how much we waste in a single day*, he thought as he carefully wiped out the inside of the bowl with a piece of bread as large as his plate.

He watched Maeve as she sat on the floor with Davey by her and the baby on her lap. *How is it that I have reached the age of thirty-four and never been aware of these people before? England is full of them, and they might as well be invisible, for all that I have seen them.*

He could not sleep that night. He lay on the floor staring at the ceiling, thinking of the landlord, wishing he could remember more of the events of that night.

Finally Matthew sat up. ''Timothy, are you awake?'' he whispered.

The mattress rustled. ''Aye, sir.''

''I'm going back to Quallen Lane. There must be something I have overlooked. At any rate, I cannot sleep.''

''Mind you are careful, my lord. You may have noticed that this is not a savory neighborhood.''

He reclaimed his horse with no trouble and saddled it himself, keeping his back to the wall, watching the men who watched him. He had few illusions about the fact that he was far from his fighting trim, and only hoped that his height and general bearing would keep them from getting any untoward ideas.

The streets were still populated, but it was a quieter crowd. Many slept in doorways, others wove down the streets in various stages of disrepair from grog and Blue

Ruin. The drabs unlucky enough not to find a bed for the night were still on the street. They eyed him with some hope and then shrieked at him when he rode on past, casting certain aspersions on his manhood that only made him chuckle. Oh, if you jades only knew, he thought as he navigated the streets and kept open the eye in the back of his head.

The horse he left in the stable again. The square of St. James was empty, except for a few peep-of-day boys. He avoided them, walking in the shadows of the great buildings. They looked to be students mostly, lads finishing the long holiday. He knew that they liked to shout out challenges and break the heads of those less worthy, so he made sure he was not seen.

Quallen Lane was empty and silent, the very model of propriety. Matthew looked up at the windows on the second floor. Doubts again assailed him. How could he have hoped to find the place again, and, even finding it, how could he be so naive as to think that anyone would help him?

Quietly he mounted the stairs and sat down halfway up them. The air was suddenly cool on his face as a little breeze picked up bits of trash and sent them sailing around the foot of the stairs.

A door opened. He sat, alert and silent, as the ashman tiptoed out of his room from somewhere under the steps and collected the paper. I have seen all this before, he thought; I have felt that rush of cold air, and it was right here on these stairs. He stirred and wished he could remember more.

The ashman glanced up, stepped back in surprise, and dropped his papers. To Matthew's surprise, he sank to his knees as if overcome. Matthew hurried down the steps. "See here, man," he whispered, "are you well?"

The ashman drew in a deep breath, and clutched at Matthew's arm, feeling up and down from wrist to shoulder, and then managing a weak chuckle. "You're not a haunt, laddie," he said at last. "Oh, my boy, if you had been a late-night devil, old Thomas Grissam wouldna be here now, and that's a fact!"

"I don't understand you, man," said Matthew. "Here, let us sit down."

The ashman looked over his shoulder at the house again. Satisfied, he settled himself on the bottom step. "I wouldna be doing this if the master were watching. He's devilish particular about the steps." The ashman peered down at Matthew more closely. "You gave me a fright, laddie, a real start. I remember another time when another cove sat right where you were sitting. I asked my master about him once, and what did he do but laugh in that way of his and say something about the man being 'snug as a fish in a bottle.' "

"Might that have been . . . about eight years ago?" asked Matthew finally, when the old man looked as though he would not bolt.

"It might have been entirely just then. My daughter was newly leg-shackled to a sailor and I was by meself again." He rubbed his chin, scratching at the days-old growth. "And now my daughter is a widow with a small boy to feed. And doesn't he eat a lot?"

Matthew sighed inwardly, but patiently pulled the thread of the story back. "And what happened here eight years ago?"

The ashman looked more closely at Matthew, taking him by the chin and turning his face this way and that. "You was here this afternoon, or someone like you. You look much like that man, that man on the stairs, but that man was a gentleman." He sniffed the air in Matthew's general vicinity. "Gentlemen smell better than you, laddie, and they look better too."

Matthew prepared to pull the conversation back again, but he stopped as the ashman continued.

"And we know about gentlemen here on Quallen Lane." He chuckled at some great private joke. "The joke's on my master's old lady, it is. She doesn't have a clue what happens in her flat when she goes to Kent to visit her daughter." He rocked back and forth in the clutch of silent laughter.

"What does happen here, Grissam?"

The ashman stared at him and tightened his lips as if he

had said too much. But his mirth caught up with him. He leaned close to Matthew, resting his head for a moment on the man's shoulder. "Oh, laddie, my master sows and reaps and never misses a penny." He put his hand over his mouth and chuckled. "He rents out that flat to gentlemen as want to have a sporting evening with no questions asked." He nudged Matthew. "And then by Sunday evening everything's all right and tight again, and nobody's wife or father is ever the wiser."

Matthew put his arm around the old man, his voice low, as if he were involved in the conspiracy too, even as his heart pounded loud in his chest. "And was the old lady gone that night . . . that night you saw the man on the steps?"

The ashman nodded. "She was, laddie, and it was a good thing. That was a wild evening, sir." He slapped his thigh, nearly carrying himself over backward. "I think it was even more than my master reckoned for." He sat up and shoved his face into Matthew's again. "We never had a murder before nor since, laddie."

"A murder?" echoed Matthew. His heart was thumping painfully loud now.

The ashman looked about him. "But I am not to say that, laddie, not to anyone, and not until it is in a court of law." He frowned. "And then I am to say only what my master tells me to say." He leaned closer again. "And that *wasn't* what happened."

The ashman was silent then. He leaned back against the steps, his elbows propping him up, and stared up at the stars as if they were a new experience to him.

"Ah, Grissam, you have my interest up now," said Matthew when he could stand the silence no longer. He tried to keep his voice casual, as if he were merely idling away his time. "What . . . what did happen?"

"You promise not to tell?"

Matthew nodded.

"Cross yourself, laddie."

Matthew crossed himself.

"That man on the steps. He sat there all evening. But I'm supposed to say that I found him in bed with a dead whore when I went in the room to clean up." He looked at Matthew, faintly puzzled, and then his eyes clouded over. "But it was not so!"

His anger subsided as quickly as it came. "But if I wants my rum, that's what I say." He nudged Matthew again. "And laddie, I wants my rum."

"The man on the stairs," started Matthew. "Was he very drunk?"

The ashman chuckled out loud this time, and then clapped his hand over his mouth and looked around. "Oh, laddie, I've never even seen a sailor any farther to the wind than that poor one. When the other toffs took their leave, he just grins at them like an inmate of Bedlam, bless my soul."

" 'The other toffs'? Was one of them tall and thin . . ."

"And with the silliest giggle?" finished the ashman. "Yes, laddie, and the other was a military man, leastwise he looked like one. Walked like he had a poker up his ass."

Matthew grinned in spite of himself. Never had he heard a better description of Merrill Watt-Lyon. Too bad his friend was not alive to enjoy it. "And the others? Was one of them a quiet man with a limp?"

The ashman stared at him. "The very him! And didn't he even look a bit like . . . like *that* man, the one inside. They could have been brothers. . . ." He stopped, and when he spoke again, his voice was shrewd. "And how would you know these things, laddie? You're too old to be the man on the steps, and besides, he was much trimmer."

Matthew shrugged. "I'm just guessing. Was there another man?"

"There was another cove, any road, and he didn't even look faintly pizzled. O' course, some men hold their liquor wondrous well. Happen *I'm* one of those. Well, that man, he patted the drunken laddie on the head and wished him happy. Said he would see him at the wedding in the morning, and reminded him about hunting in the fall."

There was no wedding in the morning, and there was no hunt in the fall. David Larchstone, that rascal in tight pantaloons, was dead before the hunting season was half begun. His dead friends, all of them accounted for except one, paraded before Matthew's eyes.

The ashman was speaking again. "There was one more. He paid me." Grissam stirred as if the step was suddenly uncomfortable. "He threw some money down the steps and told me to . . . to . . ."

He stopped, resting his hand on his chin, scratching himself and then staring at nothing in particular. "But I am not to say that, laddie."

Matthew stared ahead too. "I can buy you a bottle of rum, Mr. Thomas Grissam," he said softly. "As many bottles as you want. Your story . . . interests me."

Grissam said nothing, but held his hand out. Matthew put a coin in it. Without looking at him, the ashman bit the coin, grunted in satisfaction, and pocketed his wealth. "The man on the steps went to sleep, just right out there in the cold."

"Was he covered with . . . with blood?"

Grissam started in surprise. "No, no, laddie! He had on a frilly shirt and them short pants that gentlemen wear, and he wasn't tidy, but . . . bloody? No, not him. It was t'other one."

The same chill covered Matthew, the chill he had felt in the upstairs bedroom earlier that day. "Which man was it?"

"The cove who paid me. Lord, he came running out of the house, his mouth open, ready to scream. My master grabbed him from behind. And then . . . then they noticed the sleeping man, and just looked at each other. Lord, I thought I was dreaming. Without a word between them, they picked up that sleeping man and carried him into the house."

Matthew sat forward on the steps so the ashman could not see his face. He needn't have bothered. The ashman was so overcome with his own tale that he was paying no mind.

"Ah, laddie, it was such a night! Be glad you were not there. They carried that poor sod inside, stripped him, and arranged him nice-like next to the drab."

"You . . . you saw this?" Matthew asked. His voice didn't sound like his own.

The man nodded, and glanced back at the house again. "I followed them in and just stood there in the door of that bedroom like a Bermondsey boy. The man, the one with the bloody shirt, told me that if I ever breathed a word, even in my sleep, he would cut my throat from ear to ear." Grissam shuddered. "And don't doubt that he would. I went to sea once, laddie, and saw glimmers like that on a shark. Shark's eyes."

Carefully Matthew let out the breath he had been holding. It was no one but Rotherford.

"And so I should not tell anyone. And I will not, laddie," he said, filled with resolve that quickly melted away when Matthew pressed another coin in his hand.

"And then what?"

"The bloody man, the one with the shark eyes, he took off his cravat and shirt and threw them at me. Told me to burn them."

"And did you?"

The ashman smiled, showing a mouthful of gums and few teeth. "Lord love you, laddie, I can tell you're not an ashman!"

Matthew shook his head, faintly amused. I have called myself any number of things over the years, he thought, but not that.

"I took them bloody, reeking things, bowing and smiling me way out of the room. I even stoked up a good fire out back, but, laddie, I couldna do it. Do you know what a good shirt like that brings on the market?"

"I . . . I can't imagine," said Matthew faintly.

"I washed it and washed it, thinking I would sell it. But do you know, laddie, I couldna do it." He shook his head sorrowfully, as if chagrined at his own weakness. "I couldna bring myself to think that gentry mort's leavings would be on some other man's back. It didna set right with me. The shirt's belowstairs, laddie. Would you like to see it?"

On legs that had turned to rubber, Matthew followed the ashman down the stairs and into the little room under the front steps. Strange scurryings and rustlings heralded their entrance, but Matthew could see nothing for a moment. He lived in momentary dread that a rat would run across his foot, but followed his leader into the room, which was no more than a pathway through the discarded throwaways of years and years of tenants.

"Ah, laddie, I can't throw out a thing, as you can well see. Some of this is surely worth a ransom," cried the ashman, fondling a splintered chair leg as if it were a holy relic. "My precious jewels," he crooned as he worked his way back into the room to the cot where he slept.

With a grunt he threw himself down on his knees and reached under the bed, pulling out a wooden box. "Laddie, light that lamp over there."

Matthew did as he was told, scarcely able to take his eyes from the box, as the ashman tugged at the dirty string around his neck and produced a key. He fitted it into the box and clicked it open. Matthew leaned forward, holding the lamp high.

With a crow of delight Thomas Grissam took out the shirt, shaking out its folds and petting it. "Pretty, pretty linen, my laddie," he said, and his voice was soft and reverent. "Now, wouldna you like a shirt of this quality?" he asked. "And look at this cravat." He laughed. "I stood myself in front of that mirror scrap behind you and tried to tie one of them fancy bows." He gave a growl of disgust. "That's for them gentry morts as has time for folderols. Look at this, laddie."

He spread the shirt out on the cot. The material had faded to a pale yellow, and it was ringed here and there with the faintest outlines of rust spots. It was a large shirt, large and long, the shirt of a tall man. Matthew picked up the cravat. The stickpin was still in it, a gold fancy in the shape of a horseshoe. He thought of Rotherford's expensive stables and the horses he prized so highly. Anyone who saw the horseshoe pin would know it as Rotherford's.

"I wonder you did not sell this, Mr. Thomas Grissam," he said. "You could have bought lots of grog with it."

The ashman shook his head. "No, laddie. I took it to a

tavern once, and even plunked it down on the counter, but no, laddie. It's blood money I would have gotten for me troubles, and sure as the world, I would have choked to death on me rum that night. No. Better to leave it in this box.''

Matthew traced the lines of the horseshoe with his finger. "I would buy this from you, and the shirt and stock too.''

The ashman grimaced and grabbed them back. "You'd have nothing but bad luck, laddie.''

This would be nothing new, thought Matthew. "You won't consider it?'' he asked out loud. When the ashman only clutched his treasures tighter and shook his head, Matthew adopted a soothing tone. "Mr. Grissam, would you do something for me, since you won't sell me these things?''

The ashman quickly shoved his treasures into the box and locked it. "I might,'' he said grudgingly.

"Would you let me write down your story, and then would you sign it?''

"I can't write, laddie.''

"Then would you make an X?'' persisted Matthew.

"I might. I might. But you wouldna tell a soul, would you?''

"No,'' said Matthew. "There might even be another coin, sir.''

"Then sit you down, laddie. What can it hurt if no one sees it? And you have an honest face, my boy.''

"Thank you,'' said Matthew without a blink.

"I'm sure I have a pen and paper here somewhere.''

"I'm sure that you do,'' agreed Matthew.

The room was becoming lighter when the ashman neared the end of his retelling of the story. "What became of the . . . the body?'' Matthew asked, the pen poised over the ink bottle.

"Oh, laddie, that was my task.'' The ashman glanced slyly at him. "Remember how I told you I never throw anything away?''

"Good God!'' exclaimed Matthew, looking about him wildly.

The ashman threw himself backward across his cot in a peal of silent mirth, his hands folded across his stomach as he laughed without making a sound beyond a gasp and wheeze for breath. When he could collect himself, he sat up and thumped Matthew on the knee, causing the ink bottle to rise in an arc and bounce against the bed. Matthew made a grab for it before the ink entirely spilled out.

"Just wanted to see if you were paying attention, laddie," said the ashman as he wheezed a bit more. "No. No. I dumped that little whore in a laundry bag and took her down to the river for a little swim. No one ever paid me any mind." He became serious again. "Just a little thing, she was, for all that she was a favorite of the men. I used to see her about the neighborhood. Name of Millie Platter."

The ink spilled again and Matthew made no move to right the bottle. His whole body went numb. He stood up and rested his forehead against the dirty pane of glass that served as the ashman's only window. The glass was cool. As he stood there, ignoring the ashman's loud questions, he understood Timothy Platter's look of anguish on that ride to London, when he had confessed everything. The look had struck Matthew then as unprofessional for a Bow Street Runner, but he understood now, and his purgatory was complete. His cup ran over and there were no words left.

When he was able, he sat down again, dipped his quill in what remained of the ink puddle on the floor, and finished the ashman's curious deputation. He dipped it one more time and wrote "Thomas Grissam" in large block letters. Once more, and he handed the quill to the ashman. "Make your mark, sir," he ordered.

There was command in his voice that he did not feel, but that communicated itself to Grissam, who took up the quill without a word and made his X.

"You'll not show this to anyone?" asked the ashman again.

Matthew shook his head. He reached in his pocket and spilled out a handful of gold coins. The ashman's eyes

widened. "Coo, love," he breathed, "you're a bank
robber."

"That's it," said Matthew. "You have hit upon it."

Grissam picked up one or two coins and pushed the rest
back toward Matthew. "Oo, don't I seem to run with
irregulars?" he said, more to himself than to his guest.

Matthew allowed himself a laugh. "Oh, I'm an
irregular, sir, make no mistake. But what should I do with
this money? It should be yours."

"No, laddie, not mine. If I start spending the
ready—and I will, you know—my master will get wind of
it, and I'll be in a vat of trouble. Send it to my daughter in
Bristol, her what has the little boy. That'll do." He looked
closely at Matthew. "And don't let on as it's bank money.
My daughter is wondrous prune-faced about such as
that."

"Not a word from me, sir," said Matthew. He wrote
down the direction of Thomas Grissam's daughter as it
was dictated, and rose to go. He held out his hand to the
ashman, who stared at him.

"No one's ever shook my hand before, laddie." The
ashman wiped his hand on his filthy pants. "Even if you
are a thief and a bank robber, I'll shake with you."

Matthew folded the ashman's history and pocketed it.
He threaded his way back through the maze that was
Thomas Grissam's castle to the doorway. The sun was
almost up, although the street still lay in shadow. He took
a deep breath. Even London air smelled like Omega's
lavender scent after his sojourn in the ashman's home.

"Good day to you," he told Thomas Grissam, and
started up Quallen Lane.

He had gone no more than a pace or two when he heard,
"Ashman!"

He looked up to see the landlord standing at the top of
the stairs, a bag in his hands, watching him.

Matthew hurried on. Surely the street was still deep
enough in shadow that the landlord would not know who
he was. He touched the document in his pocket, turned the
corner, and nearly ran into Timothy Platter.

The Runner had both horses with him. He leaned

gainst the building and snuffed out the cigar that Omega
o despised. " 'Twas a long night, my lord,'' he
ommented.

"It was," agreed Matthew. "Timothy, he has told me
verything."

The Runner's eyes opened wide. "Surely not the
andlord!"

"The ashman. It is a long story, and I haven't time to
ell it. Can I hire you on commission?''

"Perhaps."

"I want you to find my friend Sir Horace Billings. I'll
give you his last direction in Suffolk. I want you to
produce him in Byford, or have a statement from him,
igned and notarized. Can you go right now?''

The Runner nodded. "If you'll trust me with this fine
piece of horse again, my lord."

"Timothy, I'd trust you with my wife, if I had one." He
ook some coins from his pocket. "Take this too. And
don't stare at me that way! You can't imagine the trouble
'm having getting rid of it. It's to speed your journey.
Come to Byford as soon as you can." Platter took the
coins without a word and swung into the saddle. "I'll see
you soon, then, my lord.''

Matthew put his hand on the horse's bridle. "One more
thing, Mr. Platter. Do you . . . could you arrange a break-
n for me?"

"Sir, we are the law," said Timothy in shocked tones.

"I know all too well," Matthew replied. He did not
loosen his hold on the bridle. "If you had known of a, er, a
free agent who could have been inclined to remove a box
from under the bed of the ashman at 10 Quallen Lane, that
would have been a good thing. But it is no matter, I
suppose, particularly since you are the law." He released
the bridle and stepped back. "Godspeed, Mr. Platter. Let
me see your face soon."

Platter tipped his hat to Lord Byford. "You will, sir.
And about that other matter: I'll see what I can do."

"I knew I could depend on you."

Matthew Bering, Lord Byford, shook the dust of
London off his feet, but not without a visit to his

solicitors, where he revised his will and signed it, and the
directed a respectable sum of money to be sent to on
Varinda Grissam Talbot of Chatting Crossroad, Bristo
He next ordained his solicitor to send a very junior clerk o
respectable girth into the backwaters of Limehouse t
deliver a set of crockery to the household of Timoth
Platter.

"And mind that the lady of the flat has no notion o
where it came from. You just make sure that it gets there
Mr. Pitney," ordered Matthew. "And now, sir, I am of
to Byford. I think my presence will soon be greatly i
demand in that spot."

His solicitor produced another document that had bee
requested. "And let me wish you happy, my lord," sai
Mr. Pitney. "Do I know the fortunate lady?"

"You did at one time, sir. She is an opinionated
fractious, meddlesome, irritating educationist who fight
hammer and tongs if you happen to get her back up."

"My lord, I know of no one that meets such a descrip
tion!" said the solicitor, disapproval written all over hi
face. "Whatever can you be thinking of?"

"Marriage, Mr. Pitney—at least, some sort o
marriage."

"Sir you are bamming me!"

"I, sir, do not 'bam' solicitors. Good day."

13

After Matthew and the Bow Street Runner left so early
that morning, Omega took herself back to bed. She
toyed with the notion of taking another swallow of the
good doctor's sleeping powders, but decided against it
With Matthew gone, the weight of the household fell on
her shoulders, and the responsibility of Jamie. She needed
to have her wits—or what was left of them—about her.

She spent another luxurious hour stretched out flat on

he comfortable bed, listening to the birds outside the win-
ow, her hands folded across her stomach, the picture of
epose. Soon she would be back in the classroom, which
neant early dawns and constant distractions. How plea-
ant it was to rest and not think much beyond the prospect
f breakfast.

Angela's arrival in her room ended the peace and quiet.
Without even knocking, the little girl hurled herself into
he room and onto Omega's bed. "Oh, Miss Chartley,
ou'll never guess who is below!"

No, she could not. Her first thought was Rotherford,
ut she dismissed it. Surely even he could not arrive so
uickly.

"It is those two gentlemen from the horse judging! They
ave come to take Hugh"—she giggled and put her hand
o her mouth—"Major Owen to another horse judging in
Claybrook, a town not far from here."

"Dear me," said Miss Chartley, and she threw back the
covers. "Angela, help me find something to wear."

Clad in her blue housekeeper's dress again, and leaning
against Angela, she hobbled down the hall to Hugh's room
and knocked. The soldier came to the door, his cravat
dangling from his neck. He sighed with relief when he saw
t was Omega, and pulled her into the room.

"Here, you must do it," he commanded, extending the
end of the cravat to her. "I cannot do this with one hand,
and Matthew has sent his man Leonard off on holiday now
that he is gone up to London."

She tied his cravat, grateful that Matthew was not there
to laugh at her efforts. "Can you . . . can you judge
another horse show, Hugh?" she asked.

"I had better," he said grimly as she helped him into
Matthew's blue superfine coat and smoothed the wrinkles
out across the back. "I am taking Jamie with me. He
claims to be an expert."

As if to verify his words, Jamie bolted into the room.
"Omega, this is famous! I get to help judge the horse
show!" He looked at her, his eyes wide. "Omega, you are
feeling better?"

"Yes," she said, "if you do not woosh by me again and

make me lose my balance. You may go, of course." She
looked at Hugh and lowered her voice. "Please, pleas
keep Jamie close by. Rotherford may be nearer than we
know."

He nodded. "I'll be watching."

She smiled her gratitude, and then considered the
business at hand. "And now, should I go below and gree
the guests? What *does* the housekeeper do?"

"Twinings is serving them some coffee and biscuits,"
Angela said. "If Hugh is overlong, I will volunteer to
sing."

"At nine in the morning?" scoffed Jamie. "Angela, you
are daft."

She stuck out her tongue at him and flounced from the
room. Hugh turned to Omega. "You will be all right here?
We have been invited to be overnight guests at Lord
Nickle's manor in Claybrook . . ." His voice trailed off.

Omega grinned. "You are certainly traveling in fine
circles, Major Owen," she said, twinkling her eyes at him.
"Just remember, always start with the fork that is farthest
out and proceed toward the center, and you should acquit
yourself admirably."

"Excellent, excellent, Miss Chartley," he said. "You
never fail me."

"Certainly not," she agreed. "I have Tildy and Twin-
ings to help me get belowstairs again, so we will do well."
Omega sighed. "I expect we will have to entertain Lord
Rotherford when he arrives. Perhaps Angela will sing."

Hugh and Jamie went downstairs, while Omega limped
back to her room. The pain in her ankle was growing
strong again. "This will never do," she said out loud, and
hobbled into Matthew's bedroom.

The room was as neat and tidy as she would have expected, nothing out of place. The fragrance of lemon cologne made her sigh. She went to his dressing room and
opened the door, marveling at how organized he was, and
knowing that if they had ever married she would have been
such a trial to him. For I am *not* tidy, Matthew, as you well
know, she said to herself.

"And now, sir, do you have a cane?" she asked. "If you ever professed to be a gentleman of the first stare, you must have had at least one."

He had several. They were lined up like soldiers next to his boots and shoes. She found one to her liking, and discovered that it would serve the purpose.

The cane was an improvement, Omega decided as she took herself from the dressing room. She looked about Matthew's bedroom with some interest. She could imagine no other room for him. It was simple, with plain furniture, a narrow bed and an overstuffed chair that looked well-sat-in. She glanced at the book on the table by the chair: Plato's *Apology* in Greek, with his favorite passages underlined. She picked up the other book and smiled. "So you are also reading *Tom Jones*," she said. "How relieved I am that you enjoy a novel now and then."

She replaced the book on the table and her eye was caught by an oval miniature lying facedown. Omega turned it over and tears started in her eyes. It was her miniature, the one she had given Matthew after the announcement of their engagement. She was wearing the pink dress he had so admired, and her hair, wild as ever, was loose around her face.

Omega had almost forgotten the miniature; Matthew had not. She realized with a guilty start that Matthew had given her a miniature in his turn, which she had pitched in the ashcan after her return from the church. And here was her portrait, eyes twinkling up at the artist, still gracing his table after all these years, all this pain. She set the miniature upright and left the room quickly.

Omega descended the stairs and gingerly made her way down to the servants' quarters, where Angela was engaged in helping Tildy arrange some of the clothes from upstairs into the former housekeeper's room.

Tildy flashed her a smile. "Miss Chartley, I took the liberty of taking some of the plainer dresses from the dressing room upstairs for your use down here. And I have loaned you my best apron."

"Thank you, my dear." Omega looked around her at

the other servants, who had gathered in the servants' hall.
"And thanks to all of you. I realize what a dither we have
dumped you all into. I am sure that things will be back to
normal soon, and I will be on my way to Durham before
too many more days."

If anyone was delighted with her disclosure, no one
showed it. The butler sighed, the footman frowned, and
Tildy swallowed and looked away.

"I have a position to fill at St. Elizabeth's in Durham,"
she said. No response, beyond a sniff from the chef when
Angela translated for him. "Someone must educate
Britain's young females, wouldn't you agree?"

No one agreed. With an inscrutable expression Twinings
turned back to decanting the wine, and Tildy dabbed at her
eyes before hurrying into the housekeeper's room again.

There was nothing for Omega to do belowstairs,
particularly with everyone so Friday-faced. She resolved to
write a letter to Alpha, and then one to St. Elizabeth's, in
case anyone was wondering yet where she was. She would
keep her letter to Alpha light, describing the national
treasures she had seen, and also those she had not. No need
for dear Alpha to know that she had strayed somewhat
from her itinerary. She hobbled down the hall to
Matthew's bookroom, searching for paper.

The room was spotless, nothing out of place. The
ledgers and account books were lined neatly according to
height in the bookcase behind the big desk. From curiosity,
she removed one and opened it, marveling at the careful
script and precision of the numbers. Matthew had
accounted for everything on the property, and on his other
properties as well. She opened another book, and another,
not so much to put her nose in his business as to get a
better grip on the life he had lived for the past eight years.

Every sum was correctly totaled, no column left
unfinished. She ran her fingers down the neat file of
numbers. "So this has been your life, dear Matthew?" she
asked. "Instead of wife and children, you have lavished
your care on records." She sat down and rested her chin on
her hands. "And I have devoted myself to literature and

rammar that little girls forget the minute they are berated from the ogre's classroom. How sad we are.''

Omega remained a moment longer in contemplation of he sterility of their lives and then closed the ledgers and eplaced them, giving herself a mental shake. This would ever do. She opened a deep drawer in search of paper, nd pulled out a large stationery box.

She opened it and quickly closed it. Matthew had begun letter to someone, and she had no right to pry. Without ooking at its contents, she would reach underneath for a resh piece of paper. She pulled out another sheet, sucked n her breath, and extracted another and another.

"My dear Omega," headed each piece of paper, receded by the date, and nothing more. With trembling ingers she pulled out all the sheets and flipped through hem. "Dear Omega," "Dearest Omega," "My beloved)mega," headed each sheet. The dates went back to 1808, he first one April 11, the day after she was to have been narried.

Hundreds of pages rested in her lap. She was too tupefied to cry, and scarcely remembered to breathe. For eight years, daily at first, and then fortnightly, Matthew had begun a letter to her, to get no farther than the salutation. While she had been agonizing in Plymouth, trying to forget, and very nearly succeeding, he was tearing open the wound every day of his life.

"Matthew, how could you do this to yourself?" she asked as the tears started down her cheeks. She made no move to brush them away, but let them fall on the pages gripped so tightly in her hands. She cried for the waste and the sorrow, and when she was done, she wiped her eyes, gathered up the papers, and threw them all in the fireplace. With fingers that were steady, she struck a match to the whole lot and watched it go up in a blaze.

When all the years were but a pile of ashes, she found one sheet of paper unwritten upon and pulled herself up to the desk. She dipped Matthew's pen in the inkwell and carefully wrote, "Dearest Matthew, I love you." She signed it, dated it, wondered at her audacity, and put it

away in the box. He would likely not find it until she was
on her way to Durham, but perhaps it would convince him
to stop tearing at his insides day after day. It was the least
she could do for him.

Omega sat in silence through the long afternoon in the
bookroom, shaking her head when Tildy tried to bring her
luncheon on a tray. She gazed out the window at nothing
in particular, comfortable in Matthew's chair. It had
molded itself to his shape, and she felt almost that she was
sitting on his lap. It was nothing but pure foolishness, but
she felt better when she finally picked up the cane and left
the room.

Dinner was another silent affair. Angela had begged
permission to share Tildy's half-day at her mother's house,
and Omega had consented, wishing to be alone and not
have to be clever or wise or accommodating. She pushed
the food around on her plate, and then scraped it out the
window into the flowerbed, knowing that if she sent a full
plate belowstairs, Antoine would be up in a minute, to
wring his hands and rail at her in French.

She would gladly have shared the evening with Matthew,
and they would not have had to exchange a word. She
remembered many such quiet evenings in her father's
London house, after their engagement, Matthew with a
book, she with her needlework, content, both of them, to
leave the plays, operas, and routs to others. A case-
hardened bachelor and his little schoolroom lady—how
curious everyone had deemed it, and yet how well they had
suited.

Omega talked sternly to herself and went belowstairs to
bed. There was no point in doing this to herself. Dredging
up those tranquil moments was no better than writing
"Dear Omega" over and over. "And if this is really and
truly over, and it must be, then I must forget him all over
again," she finally told herself as she crawled into bed,
carefully arranged the blanket around her throbbing ankle,
and surrendered herself to sleep.

She slept long beyond a housekeeper's hours, oblivious
of the sounds in the servants' quarters. She woke, stared
guiltily at her bedside clock, and wondered at the air of

tension that seemed to fill the room. She dressed quickly, brushing her hair and then stuffing it underneath her housekeeper's cap. Something was terribly wrong, and she could not identify what it was.

She left the housekeeper's room. The servants all sat at the table, no one speaking. Omega looked around her in surprise. Twinings rose to his feet when she entered the room, all dignity gone. The look in his eyes frightened her.

"Twinings, whatever can be the matter? Has something happened to Jamie or Matthew?"

He shook his head. "Miss Chartley, it is Lord Rotherford. He is waiting in the parlor."

The other servants looked at her. Omega managed a feeble laugh. "Surely he is not a seven-headed Hydra!" she exclaimed. "I trust you made him comfortable."

"A man like that is never comfortable," said Tildy with a shudder. "I won't go back in the room with him alone! I'll leave my job first." She leapt to her feet, clutching at Omega's sleeve. "Miss Chartley, we daren't turn Jamie over to him!"

Stifling the fear that was rising in her, Omega touched Tildy's hand. "My dear, that was why Matthew went to London. He is trying to resolve this thing. I had better go upstairs and face the wrath." She smiled, attempting to put them at ease. "What name have you given me? Am I Mrs. Wells?"

"Yes, Miss Chartley, we thought that best."

"Very well, then. Angela, whatever are you doing sitting over there in the corner? Tell Antoine to prepare a luncheon worthy of a lord."

She grasped the cane firmly and hauled herself up the stairs. No one, she told herself, is such a dragon that he cannot be reasoned with. She would simply have to make it perfectly clear to Lord Rotherford that there would be no discussion of Jamie's removal while Matthew was away.

The hall was empty, the front door open. She closed it and entered the parlor, tucking her unruly hair under her cap.

Lord Rotherford stood with his back to the door in front of the fireplace, contemplating the little blaze that took the

morning's chill off the room. He appeared to be of
Matthew's age, perhaps a little older. He was dressed as a
gentleman, in riding pants and boots, with a coat as
elegant as any she had seen. His hair was dark like Jamie's
and he was tall and lean. Nothing to disgust one, she
thought, and then cleared her throat.

"Pardon me, Lord Rotherford."

He turned around, and she understood.

Her quick glance took in a handsome face with regular
features, even if his nose was a bit sharp. But all attraction
ended at his eyes, and she could look no further.

They were eyes totally without expression, eyes without
any sense of depth to them. Nothing sparkled from them,
no warmth, no censure even, no inkling that anyone lived
behind them. Omega Chartley had never seen eyes like that
before. As she stood in the doorway, and then closed the
door behind her, she hoped never to see such eyes again.

She curtsied, leaning on her cane. "Sir, I am Mrs. Wells,
the housekeeper. How may I help you?"

He took her in with a long stare, even raising his
quizzing glass. Omega felt her blood grow cold, as if
chunks of ice were clogging her veins. The hairs on her
arms rose and remained upright.

"You cannot possibly be a housekeeper," he said at last.
His voice was warm, silky, totally at odds with his
unfathomable eyes, which, in their unblinking way, took
in every detail of her face, hair, dress, deportment, and
character. She felt utterly stripped of all clothing. Even her
thoughts seemed to have been scooped from her head.

This will never do, she told herself, and moved deeper
into the room, forcing herself to come toward Jamie's
guardian. "Lord Rotherford, I am Mrs. Wells and I am
the housekeeper."

His eyes flicked to her cane and he smiled. "Matthew
has taken to hiring the infirm? I never would have thought
him a philanthropist."

Hot words rose to her lips, but she swallowed them and
managed a slight smile. "I met with an unfortunate
accident on the stairs and sprained my ankle. I do not, as a
rule, require a cane, my lord."

He made no move to sit down or suggest that she take a chair, and she remained standing, shifting the weight off her foot, wondering at his ability to put her completely at a disadvantage. She gripped the cane tighter and regarded him with what she hoped was a hospitable air.

Rotherford came closer, and she fought down the urge to step back. "My dear Mrs. Wells—if that is what you choose to call yourself—I am here for my nephew, James Clevenden. Please tell him to come to me at once."

"Alas, I cannot do that, my lord."

He came closer. "But, Mrs. Wells, I insist." His voice was so warm that he practically purred.

Omega raised her chin a little higher. "I cannot produce him, my lord. He has gone to a horse-judging show with Major Hugh Owen, a guest of Lord Byford's. He is not expected back until tomorrow."

"Then I will speak to Lord Byford. Don't tell me that he is not here either?"

"He is not, my lord. He has gone up to London."

"To London? Surely not! And for what purpose?"

She returned him stare for stare. "Lord Byford does not see fit to acquaint me with his schedule. Indeed, sir, I do not ask. I am not even sure when he will return, my lord."

There was no show of emotion on Rotherford's face beyond the slight twitching of a muscle in his cheek. "You, madam, are a singularly valueless housekeeper," he said at last.

She couldn't help herself. "And you, sir, are singularly rude."

The muscle in his cheek worked a little faster. "I cannot imagine why Matthew keeps you on, unless he gets some other satisfaction from your services, madam, and I know that is not the case." He allowed himself a small chuckle at this, and turned back to the fireplace. "I will wait here for James, even if it takes all day and night, Mrs. Wells."

Nails digging into the palms of her hands, Omega struggled to maintain her composure. "I regret, my lord, that our guest rooms are all in use. May I suggest you consider the Ox and Bell in Byford? The food is well-recommended and the sheets are clean."

He turned around to face her again, and Omega stared into his eyes. She knew that her great anger showed in her own eyes, but she was equally determined that she would not be the first to look away. How dare you think to frighten me and the staff of this household, she thought as she gazed at him.

To her intense gratification, Lord Rotherford was the first to look away. He came closer, walking around her, tapping his quizzing glass on one of his waistcoat buttons. When he had completed his circuit, he stopped in front of her.

"You claim he is in London?"

How smooth his voice is, Omega thought. He sounds so wonderful. I wonder if the devil is like this. "Yes, my lord."

"I would not have thought anything could get him back to the city again, Mrs. Wells," he mused, speaking as if to himself, but goading her to reply.

She did not rise to the bait. "I have no notion of his intentions, my lord."

He walked around her again, this time pausing behind her. He let out a deep sigh, and she felt his breath on her neck. "Why is it that I do not believe you, Mrs. Wells?"

"My lord, I cannot imagine," she replied. She turned to face him, wishing that he was not standing so close, but refusing to back down. "We are preparing luncheon, Lord Rotherford, if you would wish to remain. Lord Byford's cook is quite good."

"I will, Mrs. Wells, on the condition that you eat with me," he answered.

He was so close that she could see clearly the pores on his face. Omega managed a smile and a nod in his direction. "How kind of you, sir, but I fear, sir, that you are doomed to disappointment. The housekeeper never dines with the guests. Lord Byford would be deeply chagrined with me. May I show you out now?"

She stepped around him and made her way to the door, wishing that she could sweep out elegantly instead of limping across the room, which seemed to grow longer and longer with each step. She knew he followed, even though he was uncannily silent.

Omega put her hand on the doorknob, and Lord Rotherford leaned his hand against the door, preventing her from opening it. She calmly took her hand away. "Sir?"

"One more question, my dear Mrs. Wells. Does the mail coach stop in this pleasant village?"

"It does, my lord."

"And postal service is rapid to London?"

"Very."

"Ah, that is excellent."

He removed his hand from the door and she opened it, grateful beyond measure to see Twinings standing in the hallway. Omega nodded toward Twinings. "Could you please see this gentleman out?"

The muscle in Rotherford's cheek worked more quickly, but he bowed to her and laughed. He had a pleasant laugh, but it sent waves of goose bumps up and down her back. "My dear Mrs. Wells, I will return this evening and see if you have, ah, learned anything more about your master's bolt to the city. Perhaps you'll find that your memory has improved by nightfall."

"That is unlikely, my lord. And now, let us not detain you any further. Twinings?"

Lord Rotherford allowed himself to be led to the front door. Twinings opened it with a flourish, handed him his hat and cane, and bowed. Rotherford ignored the butler. "Mrs. Wells, one more thing. If you are thinking of sending any kind of a message to James Clevenden, be assured that I do not ever travel alone, and several of my men are quite, quite interested in the architecture of this lovely old home. They may even remain here to observe it."

"You can't do that!" she burst out.

"I would wager that I can, my dear, dear Mrs. Wells. If you summon the constable, Matthew would be so chagrined at your rag manners. Good day, my dear Mrs. Wells. Until this evening? And you *will* dine with me this evening. I absolutely insist."

"Very well, sir," she said through clenched teeth, "since you asked so nicely."

Twinings closed the door and leaned against it. Omega walked as fast as she could to the door and slammed the bolt into the lock. "I hope he heard that!" she said savagely. "God, what a terrible man!"

"Miss Chartley, what does he mean to do?" asked the old man. "I cannot fathom what is going on."

She touched him on the shoulder. "He means to spirit Jamie away. And he means to keep us prisoner so we cannot warn him. The devil take him!"

"What are we to do?"

She took him by the arm. "Twinings, just . . . just go downstairs. I'm going to sit in the bookroom and think. You might . . . you might direct the footman to lock all the doors and windows."

The bookroom was quiet. She sat down in Matthew's chair and rested her aching ankle on an open drawer. "Oh, Matthew, what am I to do?" she said out loud.

Somehow she had to warn Hugh and Jamie. The thought of Hugh brought tears to her eyes. He would know what to do.

"Drat you, Matthew Bering," she said, "it seems you are never around when I need you."

She was ashamed of her uncharitable words as soon as she spoke them, and was grateful Matthew was not within earshot. She opened another drawer and pulled out a sheet of paper.

The letter was soon composed, sealed, and directed. It would startle Alpha and send him up into the boughs, but he would do what she said. On this head she had absolute reliance. Another moment's quiet reflection, sitting at Matthew's desk rubbing her ankle, and she had her answer. She smiled rather grimly and got to her feet. Lord Rotherford was not going to win this time. He had ruined enough lives already.

Twinings waited for her outside the bookroom door, as if afraid to let her out of his sight. "Twinings, you're just the person I need," she said, her voice filled with decision.

"Bring Angela up here. And . . . and if any of you have any money, please let me borrow it."

She sat down on one of the low window ledges outside the bookroom and looked over the flower garden to the back gate. A strange man stood there, hands on his hips, looking back at her. She had little doubt who his keeper was. She turned her back to him.

Angela came running. Omega made her sit down on the floor where she would not be seen from the window. "Angela, we must warn Jamie not to return here tomorrow."

Angela nodded.

"And once he has been warned, we must do something else. He must be taken to my brother Alpha's house just outside Amphney St. Peter."

"I can do these things, Miss Chartley. *Mira*, Twinings gave me all this money!"

It was a paltry sum, but it might provide a meal or two.

Omega smiled and rested her hand on Angela's shoulder. "I have no doubt that you can do all these things I have asked of you. I think the difficult part of your journey will be getting out of this house to take a message to Hugh at Claybrook. Twinings tells me Claybrook is a small village not ten miles from here to the north."

She looked out the window again. The man had shifted his position but was still guarding the back gate. "I don't doubt there is a guard at each gate, my dear. Can you get out without being seen?"

Angela thought a moment and then leaned against Omega's knee. "Do you know, Miss Chartley, that Hugh told me England would be boring and stuffy and not a bit like Spain? But so far, it is very much like campaigning with Picton." She clapped her hands together. "Omega, this is famous!"

Omega threw back her head and laughed. "Oh, I wish Jamie could hear you, my dear! What will you have me do?"

Angela scampered downstairs for her leather campaigning bag and ran up the stairs again, tying it around her waist. She helped Omega to her feet. "Do you know there is a little door off the breakfast room that no one uses? It gives out onto a grape arbor that leads to the gardening shed."

"Oh, but surely you will be seen, Angela! Let's wait until dark."

"No, no. The grape leaves almost cover the walkway. I can get to the gardening shed, and Tildy said her brother will get me out from there and point me in the right direction." She eyed Omega. "Do you think you could create some sort of diversion, just to make sure?"

"What would Sir Thomas Picton do?" said Omega.

"Oh, he would have sent the sappers ahead to pick off a few Frenchies."

"I'll think of something, Angela." She held out her arms. "Now, give me a hug, and don't let anyone see you. Tell Hugh to come quickly, and get Jamie to my brother."

Angela wrapped her arms around Omega, who kissed her and held her tight for a moment. "Do be careful, my dear," said Omega.

They walked arm in arm to the breakfast room. "I wish I knew what to do, Angela, to distract the guards."

Angela twinkled her eyes at Omega and put her hand to her mouth. "Once my mother took off her shirtwaist and washed her hair in a stream while the rest of us escaped. I remember that."

"Oh, I couldn't do that!" Omega said, and then reconsidered. Well, she told herself as she let Angela out the little side door, I've already lied, broken the law, committed assault, and practiced all manner of deceit.

The thought of Lord Rotherford stiffened her resolve. She limped to the door that led out to the garden, threw the bolt, and walked onto the tree-covered pathway. She noticed out of the corner of her eye that the guard was looking her way. She proceeded down the path and stopped before the climbing roses. Taking a deep breath, she allowed herself to stumble into the roses, and soon found herself trapped by the brambles.

"Oh, dear," she said out loud. The guard, still on the other side of the wall, came closer to watch. Her eye caught a flash of movement as Angela started for the gardener's shed. Omega began to cry, loud noisy tears. "Oh, dear," she sniffed again, and then unbuttoned her dress and carefully stepped out of it, leaving it behind on the thorns.

By now the guard was intent. Clad in a camisole and petticoat, Omega turned around and carefully began to remove the dress from the thorns, bending over so the guard would have plenty to look at, and wondering as she did so what Miss Haversham in Plymouth would say if she could see the meek-and-retiring Miss Chartley now.

When the dress was almost undone, Omega looked up and into the eyes of the strange man. She screamed and pointed at him, and then collapsed in a picturesque heap on the walkway. She opened one eye just a crack, watched him scurry away, and sat up, smiling in grim satisfaction. "I hope that was worth it, sir," she said out loud, retrieved her dress, and put it on before the servants came running.

Tildy was quick to see the humor of the situation, but Twinings was not so charitable. "Lord Byford would have been horrified, Miss Chartley," he scolded. "Can you imagine what he would think?"

"Yes, I can," she said, not the least repentant. "I will ask him when next I see him. And now, sir, if you would invite Antoine to prepare a sumptuous dinner, I believe Lord Rotherford will be dining here tonight. Let us show him every courtesy."

"I hope he chokes on it," declared Tildy.

"So, my dear, do I. But that only happens in novels."

14

O mega brushed her hair and arranged it carefully, wondering if it would be quite gray before the evening was over. It shone out, as rich brown as ever, as she tweaked her curls here and there, and then gave up in disgust. Tildy found her a dove-gray silk dress from the closet upstairs and helped her into it, buttoning it up the back. When she finished, she looked over Omega's shoulder into the mirror.

"Miss Chartley, it is perfection!" Then her face fell. "What a pity to waste it on that horrid man."

"Indeed," agreed Miss Chartley. "But it can be worn again, Tildy."

The maid regarded her a moment and then spoke softly. "Begging your pardon, Miss Chartley, but was this dress . . . was it meant for you?"

Omega nodded. "I think so, Tildy." Her smile was a little wan. "Matthew always had impeccable taste." She turned around and took hold of Tildy's hands. "My dear, I know all of you are wondering. It is enough for me to say that Lord Byford and I had a terrible falling-out eight years ago."

"Oh, but could you not resolve it?"

"I . . . I think not, my dear."

Tildy draped Omega's other dress and apron over her arm. "The house will be so strange when all of you leave, and Lord Byford will retreat to his bookroom again, and not speak above ten words a day to us, for all that he is kind."

"I'm sorry, Tildy. Truly I am." Omega squared her shoulders. "There, now. Do I look sufficiently matronly and dignified? No? Well, it will have to do. Let me know when Lord Rotherford arrives."

Tildy went to the door and hesitated. "This is forward of me, Miss Chartley, but do you love Lord Byford?"

It was forward, it was encroaching, but Omega was touched by Tildy's evident concern. "I do, my dear," she replied softly. "I did not think it possible that he could be dearer to me than he was eight years ago, especially after all we have been through, but he is. I wish that I understood such things." She made a small gesture. "Perhaps education and books do not really make us wise, Tildy. I once thought they did."

"Good luck, Miss Chartley," said Tildy as she quietly closed the door.

It was Twinings who summoned her upstairs when Lord Rotherford arrived. "The footman and I will serve tonight," he said. "Tildy is afraid."

"Very well," she said. And I am afraid too, she thought. "Have you shown him into the parlor?"

"Yes, Miss Chartley. Or rather, Mrs. Wells."

Her courage deserted her as she mounted the stairs and approached the parlor door. "Oh, Twinings," she whispered, "do not delay dinner long!"

"No, Mrs. Wells."

Rotherford was resplendent in evening dress. He turned when she entered the room, and bowed mockingly to her. He raised his quizzing glass. "You are magnificent, Mrs. Wells. How honored I am that you have indeed chosen to dine with me."

She nodded in his direction. "It would be rude to ignore my master's relatives."

Twinings summoned them into the dining room. Lord Rotherford offered her his arm and she took it. She could hardly help from noticing how nicely muscled his arm was. Oh, Matthew, I fear you are sadly out of shape, she thought, compared to this paragon. I hope this affair will not come to blows.

Dinner was a challenge. Rotherford's conversation was a smoothly flowing river, a fountain of clever information about London doings and gossip that held little interest for her. He was amusing, he was charming. She listened to his cleverness, forced herself to smile into his dead eyes, and wondered what was going on in his brain.

Course after course came and went, and still Rotherford carried his end of the conversation and hers too, laughing at his own witticisms, nodding at his sagacity. He began to fascinate her in a way that drew her even as it repelled her. Omega decided that listening to Lord Rotherford was rather like running her tongue over an abscessed tooth. It was painful even as it was compelling.

Dinner over, Rotherford pushed back from the table. "Now, my dear Mrs. Wells, my, er, friend at your back gate tells me that you had an encounter with a rose bramble this afternoon."

She colored prettily and looked away. "I fear my ankle is still a trifle unsteady. I should have stayed off that uneven path."

"Oh, come now, my dear. My short acquaintance with you—and I don't scruple to say that I swear I have seen you before—my short acquaintance tells me that you would never do such a thing."

"My lord, you know what a trial roses can be."

"I bow to your greater knowledge. Why is it that I think you may have been attempting a rather clever diversion?"

Omega raised her eyebrows and widened her eyes. "My lord, whatever can you mean?"

He leaned forward, moving almost quicker than sight, and grasped her by the wrist. "If you have somehow alerted James that I am in the neighborhood, it will not be a pleasant thing for any of us."

Just as suddenly he released her arm. Omega remained absolutely still.

"And because I feel some . . . slight suspicion, I intend to remain here all night." He smiled at her. "I am not going to let you out of my sight. And when morning comes, we will see who arrives."

Omega rose to her feet, and Rotherford handed her the cane. "Mrs. Wells, is the parlor more comfortable? Or do you recommend another room?"

"The library, my lord." Her words were calm, even as her thoughts bounded about the room. The library was at the back of the house. Surely one of the servants would alert Hugh before he found himself in the middle of something terrible.

Rotherford bowed and offered her his arm again, which she took. "Lead on, then, Mrs. Wells. We will go to the library."

Omega started down the hall and realized her mistake. That there was a library, she was sure, because Tildy had mentioned it. But where was it? She moved down the long hall as the taste of defeat grew in her mouth, and opened the first door she came to.

Rotherford opened the door wider and peered inside. He looked back at her, his eyes showing absolutely no emotion. "My dear Mrs. Wells, I believe this is the billiards room! Fancy that. Shall we try again?"

Omega tightened her lips and opened the door across the hall. It contained a piano, a harp, and several easels, all in holland covers.

Rotherford laughed. "Mrs. Wells! Such a forgetful housekeeper you are! Let me help you. Could *this* be the library?"

He opened the door and ushered her in, closing the door behind them. Enough daylight remained for him to light the lamp and set the candles around the library winking in their sconces. He raised both arms in a flourish. "*Voilà*, Mrs. Wells, the library! How lucky that we found it!" With each word, his voice grew a little harsher. "Since you have obviously never been here before, you may want to note its location, so you can dust here in the morning."

She said nothing, but sat in a chair gripping her cane. Rotherford quietly pried her fingers from it and set the cane out of her reach. He knelt by her chair. "My dear, we have certainly established beyond all doubt that you are not the housekeeper. Who might you be?"

When she did not speak, he stroked her under the chin. "I have my suspicions, but that is so farfetched that I will not bore you with it. Rather let us remain here and await the arrival of . . . who knows? I am filled with anticipation."

She sat silent, her hands clutched tightly together in

her lap, as Rotherford crossed to the globe and set it spinning. He selected a book off the shelf and handed it to her. "If you read to me, I am sure the time will pass more favorably."

Omega glanced down at the book. It was Defoe's *Journal of the Plague Year.* With fingers that trembled, she opened it to the beginning and then slammed the book shut. "Sir, I refuse to be bullied further by you. We will remain in silence, for I have nothing to say."

He bowed to her and took a seat nearby. He turned toward her and rested his chin on his hands. "I, then, shall study you, Miss Whoever-you-are. Perhaps it will occur to me where I have seen you before."

She bore his scrutiny in silence, willing herself to think of other things. The first hour dragged by, and then she began to conjugate verbs and then to parse sentences in her mind. Rotherford continued to stare at her. When the clock in the hallway chimed eight times, she smiled. It was one more hour that Jamie and Angela were farther away from this terrible man. She could stand anything if only they were even now hurrying toward the home of her brother.

Another hour passed, and another. Thunder rumbled in the distance, coming closer and closer. Soon it began to rain. Omega sighed. Perhaps some friendly farmer returning late from market would pick up Jamie and Angela.

And then, as she was resting her cheek on her hand, struggling to keep her eyes open, she heard voices in the hall. Rotherford sat up straight, but he continued to watch her. He noted her expectancy with that bloodless calm almost more frightening than outright rage. "Please remain seated, my dear. I wouldn't want our latest arrival to think I have been boring you."

The door to the library banged open and Hugh Owen stood there, soaking wet. He opened his mouth to speak to her, but Omega put her finger to her lips and shook her head. Hugh glanced from Omega to Lord Rotherford and nodded in complete understanding.

"Lord Rotherford," he said pleasantly, extending his

hand. "How disappointed Jamie will be to have missed you!"

Rotherford leapt from his chair, all pretense of civility gone. "Where is my nephew?" he roared.

Omega made herself small in the chair. Hugh walked deliberately toward Rotherford until he stood in front of Omega, shielding her. "He is not here. You're not going to find him easily, either, my lord. In fact, I think you may not find him at all."

With a cry of rage, Lord Rotherford slapped Hugh Owen with the back of his hand, slamming the sergeant to the floor like a felled tree. Hugh's check was slashed open by Rotherford's signet ring, and suddenly there was blood everywhere. With a cry of her own, Omega dropped to her knees and reached for the sergeant. Before she touched him, Lord Rotherford grabbed her by the hair and dragged her backward. He shook her like a dog with a bone, bending her back over her sprained ankle.

"Oh, God," she shrieked. "Let go of me!" Little starry lights flickered around her eyes as she clawed at Rotherford's hand, which had a firm hold on her hair.

Dimly she heard someone else screaming in the hall. It must have been Tildy. Omega called to her, but her voice was the barest whisper. As Rotherford shouted terrible things at her that she could not even understand, Omega heard the door slam again. She hung on to Rotherford's hand and prayed that Tildy had run for the constable. "Oh, sir, let go of me!" she begged.

"Yes, Edwin, I suggest that you do as the lady says, and quickly too, before God," said Matthew from the doorway.

Omega tried to slew herself around, but Rotherford held her tight. She sagged to the floor, scratching and clawing to free her hair, when Rotherford let go of her. She crawled to Hugh again and held on to him, afraid to look up.

She felt a hand on her shoulder and cringed. "Omega, it's all right," she heard, and opened her eyes. It wasn't Matthew as she had ever seen him before, with a days-old growth of beard, and dressed in the clothes of a farmer. Like Hugh, he was wet from the rain, his hair plastered to his head. She reached for his hand; he clasped hers for a moment, and then stood up again.

"Edwin, I challenge you do a duel," he snapped in a voice she had never heard before. "Tomorrow at dawn."

Rotherford laughed. "Pistols at ten paces then, you fool."

Matthew moved closer to Rotherford until they were almost nose-to-nose. "Make it five paces, please. I don't want either of us to miss."

Rotherford stepped back involuntarily, his eyes holding in them the first glimmer of expression that Omega had seen. It was replaced quickly, smoothly, by that blank curtain. He spoke again in his calm tones, as if he were placating a noisy child.

"My very dear Matthew, you forget yourself. All I desire is that my nephew be restored to the bosom of my family." He moved toward Omega as if to raise her to her feet. She hugged Hugh closer to her and ducked her head over his limp body. "Here, now, my dear, I meant you no harm!"

"Get away from me!" she muttered through clenched teeth.

Rotherford straightened up, a wounded look darting across his face and disappearing. "Really, Matthew, you know you do not wish to duel with me!" He managed a small indulgent laugh. "Have you never seen me shoot, dear boy? I will be pleased enough to forget all this in exchange for my nephew."

Matthew sat down on the arm of the chair close to Hugh and Omega. "I will duel with you, Edwin," he said softly.

As Omega watched in alarm, terrible, murderous anger overtook Rotherford again. He struggled against it, his face growing red and then white. Matthew watched him imperturbably, his leg swinging slightly.

Rotherford took a deep breath. "You forget that I can ruin you, Matthew. And now I will."

Matthew only smiled and looked down at Omega, who stared at him wide-eyed. "Lord Rotherford —Edwin—I would appeal to your nobler instincts, but you have none. You can't threaten me with ruin; I am already ruined. You have destroyed my happiness, and that of the woman I love. What else is there? You can kill me, and welcome to it, Rotherford." He leaned closer. "Who cares?"

Rotherford looked from Omega to Matthew. His eyes traveled to her again, and she curled up closer to Matthew. "This . . . this little scrap is Omega Chartley," he said, his voice filled with a curious combination of amusement and wrath. "Of course! You described her to me that night at Watier's, didn't you?"

Matthew nodded. " 'A waist small enough to span with two hands, and hair like a dandelion puff.' And did I say she was liable to speak her mind? Sorry, Omega," he said, looking down at her with a smile. "But you must agree, it is apt."

She nodded and relaxed slightly, although she did not release her grip on the unconscious sergeant.

"Edwin, she knows everything. I told her the whole wretched story. You can't threaten to tell her, because she knows. So does that very fine man you slapped silly. So does your own Bow Street Runner. I'll run a column in the London *Times* if you choose. I'll stand up in the House of Lords and declare it. You can't frighten me anymore."

"But you could hang for that murder," Rotherford reminded him.

"Could I? I have a signed statement from the ashman at 23 Quallen Lane, and he tells a different story than you do. And besides, whoever said there was a murder in the first place? You hushed all that up." Matthew got to his feet suddenly. "You studied my rather casual courage and *knew* I would do nothing to contest your guardianship of Jamie. You played me like a harp and put me in your *debt*." He spat the word out. "I discovered in London yesterday that I owe you nothing, Rotherford." He looked away from Rotherford then, as if he were bored with the whole conversation. "Tomorrow at dawn on the knoll behind Byford Common. Anyone can tell you where it is." Matthew made a final gesture with his hand. "Now, get out of my sight, Edwin. You sicken me."

Rotherford regarded Matthew for a long moment, rubbing his chin in a meditative fashion. "Matthew, you are overlooking the most pertinent fact of all: I am a wondrous fine shot and you are not. I'll kill you tomorrow."

Matthew laughed and walked to the door, flinging it open wider and gesturing toward the hall. "Edwin, don't you *ever* listen? I don't care! Get out of here."

Rotherford stalked to the door and looked back. "But if you are dead, Matthew, I will have Jamie."

Matthew laughed again and shook his head. "Dear God, Edwin, you have no idea how amusing you are! I place all my trust in Omega and Hugh Owen, even after I am dead. You'll never have Jamie as long as they are about. I do wish you would leave. You're so tiresome, and I am sleepy." He smiled at Rotherford. "I'll see you in the morning."

Rotherford swore roundly until Omega put her hands to her ears, and then left, banging the front door so hard that something in the hall crashed to the floor.

"Temper, temper, Edwin," said Matthew softly, and then got down on his knees beside Omega. "Well, my dandelion puff, you look a bit hagged, but infinitely better than this stalwart soul." He touched Hugh's slashed cheek. "Is that the work of Rotherford's ring? Good Lord."

Omega dabbed at Hugh's bloody face with the train of her dress. "We should summon a doctor, Matthew."

Matthew rested his hand on the back of Omega's neck. "We cannot, my dear. The good doctor would demand an explanation, and scream loud and long for the constable, and there would be no duel. No, Hugh will have to yield himself up to our mercies. He's seen much worse, Omega, I needn't scruple to tell you." He touched his forehead to hers. "Can you walk?"

"I think so." She tugged at his sleeve as he bent over Hugh. "Is Rotherford really such a marksman?"

Matthew nodded, and there was no smile this time. "He is, Omega. I'm probably looking forward to my last dawn. Oh, here, now, don't start that!"

Omega grabbed his arm and sobbed into his sleeve. "At least you're not crying all over my best coat this time," he said softly, and rested his hand on her head while she cried. "Look now, Hugh is coming around. Let's help him into this chair."

Hugh opened his eyes and stared from one person to the other. "I was going to challenge him to a duel, Matthew," he said finally, his words slurred.

"Bless you, Hugh, I beat you to it," Matthew replied. "We're going to get you upstairs and see you to bed. I can't summon a doctor, at least until after . . . after tomorrow morning. Omega, don't you dare start in again."

She swallowed her tears with a great effort and helped Hugh to his feet. In the hall, Twinings took over for her, an apology in his eyes.

"My lord, we were so afraid. I'm sorry." He could not look his master in the eye.

"You were wise not to get involved, Twinings. Rotherford is a nasty customer." He glanced at Tildy, who stood near the stairs wringing her apron through her hands. "But, my dear, I am glad you screamed. It certainly put a spring in my step." He sighed then, and turned Hugh over to the footman beside her. "It has been a long, long day."

He watched the butler and the footman lead Hugh Owen upstairs, and put his arm around Omega. "Let us go into the parlor, my dear. I feel quite old, all of a sudden."

Matthew shut the door and sank down onto a sofa. "Omega, could you pull off these boots? I've been in the saddle since early morning, and everything aches."

She did as he asked, and then sat beside him.

"As the estimable Timothy Platter would say . . . Oh, no, I will not repeat it. Omega, I have added greatly to my vocabulary in the last forty-eight hours. Lord, is that all it has been? But see here, you're not paying attention, my little educationist."

She shook her head as he tried to lift her chin. "And you need to pay attention, Omega. I have a proposition to set before you that would make me most happy, on this last night of my life."

She closed her eyes and leaned against him. Matthew settled himself more comfortably and put his arm around her. "It's a simple thing. I have in my pocket—and it is likely soaking wet—one special license for the marriage of Omega Chartley, spinster, to Matthew Bering, Lord Byford, bachelor. I propose that you marry me this night without any more delay. I have named you beneficiary of my lands and estates, and I mean for you to collect. If it comes to probate, it will be easier if you are my wife."

Omega pulled away and stared at him. "Matthew, I wish you would not talk this way!"

"But I must," he declared, taking her by the shoulders and giving her a little shake. "If Rotherford survives me, as he surely will, he will find a way to get all of Jamie's fortune. Of this I have no doubt. But if you inherit my estates, while they are not as grand, you can at least provide Jamie a comfortable living, and one for yourself too. I'm the author of your eight-year misery, my dear, and it's time to make what amends I can. Now, hush and give me no chat."

Sitting close to Matthew in the early-morning hours, Omega faced what he was saying squarely and without tears. He was right, of course. With his legacy, she could see that Jamie was well-cared-for, educated, and fitted for a position of use in the world. There would be enough for Angela too. And there would be Hugh to manage the estates.

Matthew seemed to divine precisely what she was thinking. "Omega, there will be sufficient money and then some for you to start an eccentric project or two, say, something like providing education for Byford's daughters. Something that will keep them . . . keep them from the streets of London. It's small compensation, but—" He could say no more.

Omega put her finger to his lips. "Let it rest now, Matthew. You've punished yourself enough."

When he could speak, he turned to her. "Omega, will you marry me?"

She looked right back at him, wishing for a small moment that her hair was tidy, her face not tear-spotted, and her dress clean and free from bloodstains. "Yes."

"Very well, my dear. Let us hobble down to the bookroom and—"

"But who is to marry us?" she interrupted as she allowed him to pull her along.

"You forget, Miss Chartley. I am a justice of the peace. I'll do this myself. If I were able to consummate this and we were to live together as husband and wife, I doubt it would hold up in a courtroom, but for now, and for our purposes, it will suffice. We can rely on Tildy and Twinings to witness."

Tildy made an excellent attendant, holding Omega up and taking the strain from her ankle, as Matthew held her other hand and read the marriage lines. His voice was firm. He looked at her with great love, and in the middle of her complete misery, Omega felt a tiny tugging of hope that she knew would betray her at dawn.

She knew there would be no ring, but Matthew surprised her. "I had left this with my solicitor, dearest," he said as he slipped on her wedding ring. "The date inscribed inside says 1808. We were merely . . . a little slow."

Matthew declared them man and wife, and he kissed her to seal the bargain. Tildy wept into her apron as

Twinings inspected the row of ledgers behind the desk as if searching for dust. He sniffed once or twice, and then blew his nose hard.

Matthew closed the book and replaced it on the shelf. He signed the license and handed the pen to Omega, who signed. The witnesses affixed their signatures, and Matthew stamped the document to make it legal.

"I will not . . . not likely be able to register this with the proper authority, Omega," he said. "You'll have to see it is done as soon after . . . as soon as you can. Don't neglect it."

"I won't," she said, her voice tiny.

"And now good night," he said. "Twinings, Tildy, thank you for your services. Twinings, make sure that I am summoned by five o'clock. Come, Omega."

They went upstairs arm in arm. "My dear, this is a shockingly informal kind of marriage, and one that you know I am unable to consummate, as much as I would wish it. But if you please, let us lie together tonight. I do not really wish to be alone." She felt the slight shudder that ran through him. "I confess to some trepidation."

She did not answer, but hugged him tighter around the waist. In her room, she thoughtfully removed her dress as he sat on the bed watching her but not seeing her. Her heart ached and she wondered what was on his mind. She found a nightgown and put it on, crawling into bed with a sigh. The bed was so comfortable. If she were not so numb, Omega knew that she would fall asleep in an instant.

Matthew went into his bedroom and returned in his nightshirt. He stopped at the side of the bed, looking down at her. "You do not mind?"

Omega blew out the candle and settled herself again. "Don't be a goose, Matthew."

She heard him chuckle as he got into bed. He held out his arms for her and gathered her close. Omega curled up against him, resting her head on his chest.

"I always did like the way you just fit under my arm," he said. His voice was close to her ear, and drowsy. "How pleasant this is. How I envy myself." She felt his chuckle again. "Dear God. I have less than five hours until my morning appointment. Wouldn't a sane man spend the time talking and talking, and trying to say everything there was to say?"

"Please, no," she said. "I can't bear it."

"But I only want to drift off to sleep in your arms. To me that is heaven, my dearest, beloved wife. Good night."

She listened as his breathing grew deep and regular, and even the beat of his heart slowed. She knew that she would never sleep, but she did, safe in her husband's arms.

15

The room was cool when she woke, cool and dark. Omega sighed and moved closer to Matthew and then opened her eyes. He was gone. His warm spot in the bed was already turning cold.

She sat up and threw back the covers, hurtling out of bed, gasping when she stood on her ankle, and then reaching for her robe. The hall was deserted. She descended the stairs, moving carefully, feeling for the last step so she would not fall.

Omega limped to the front door. It was still bolted, so she knew he had not left. "Matthew!" she called. "Matthew! Oh, please don't leave me like this!"

He came out of the breakfast room with Hugh. With a sob she ran to him and threw herself into his arms, hugging him to her, grasping all of him that she could hold. Dimly she heard Hugh say something about waiting outside, as Matthew picked her up and carried her back upstairs. He sat down with her on the bed, making no attempt to extricate himself from her fierce embrace. He stroked the

back of her neck, his lips on her hair, and she gradual[ly]
relaxed her grip.

"Better now?" he asked at last.

She shook her head and burrowed closer to him.

"I just sat in the chair and watched you for an hour, m[y]
dear," he said, speaking into her hair. "It was the prettie[st]
sight I have ever seen. That was how I wanted to rememb[er]
you, utterly at peace. I don't think I can bear any mo[re]
tears, Omega, so please, please don't cry."

She shook her head again but loosened her grip on hi[m,]
sitting up finally in his lap.

"That's better. Now, kiss me like a good girl and let m[e]
go."

Her eyes still closed, she raised her lips to his and kisse[d]
him. His lips were soft and warm. Omega put her hand[s]
behind his neck. He did not break off the kiss, b[ut]
continued to taste her warmth and softness, as if he coul[d]
not get enough. Finally she released him and leaned he[r]
cheek against his shoulder again.

"That will . . . last you awhile?"

He smiled. "I think so. Don't follow me downstairs."
He deposited her on the bed, putting the blankets u[p]
around her shoulders. "It's getting cold again. Soon it wi[ll]
be autumn, Omega." He leaned over and kissed her on[e]
last time. "The people here are friendly, my dear. The[y]
will help you with whatever schemes you come up with fo[r]
their betterment. And I think Lord Nickle and Sir Marti[n]
will move on that carting route. It is something I hav[e]
worked for. I leave it for you to see it through."

He went to the door and opened it, looking back jus[t]
once. "I have a favor, dearest."

"Anything, anything."

"Just this. Put your wedding ring on my little finge[r]
after . . . after this is over. Eternity is a long, long time[,]
Omega, and it will be easier if part of you is with me."

"I will," she whispered.

He nodded to her, blew her a kiss, and closed the doo[r]
behind him. Numb with sorrow, she hugged Matthew'[s]
pillow to her breast and listened as they rode away fro[m]
the manor.

She would have to begin forgetting him all over again, but this time it would be different. Before, she had loved Matthew Bering and lost him. This time, she had loved Matthew Bering and lost him, and lost herself in him. This one would be infinitely more difficult; it would be impossible.

When it was barely light outside, Omega dressed and found her cane, negotiating the hall with more assurance, now that she could see where she was going. She looked at the window. It was still too dark for the duel, but she was sharply aware that the Byford Common knoll would receive the first strong light of morning, and there would be a killing. The thought snatched the breath from her body. It isn't fair, she told herself. It isn't fair.

She went downstairs again. None of the servants came up from their quarters, although she could hear them talking in low tones. She couldn't have faced them anyway. Moving quietly, Omega opened the front door and sat down on the steps, waiting for the sun to rise. She wondered if she would be able to hear the shots.

Omega listened, and heard only a horse approaching, galloping too fast to make the slight curve where the lane circled in front of the manor. She sat up, alert, and sucked in her breath as a horse and rider leapt smoothly over the low stone wall and came to a halt right in front of her.

Omega jumped up, praying that it was not Hugh already, come to tell her that it was all over. "Oh, please, what is it?" she begged.

And then she smelled the cigar and heard the rough voice of Timothy Platter. "Miss Chartley, what're ye doing out here? Haven't you gentry morts a particle of sense?"

She hurried down the steps and grasped the stirrup. "Mr. Platter, oh, please, can you stop Matthew and Rotherford? They have gone to duel."

The Runner swore and threw away his cigar. "Damn fools," he exclaimed. "Where are they?"

"Byford Common, the knoll. But I don't know where that is!" She hurried to the front door and shouted, "Tildy! I need you!"

In a moment the maid stood beside her. Without a word
the Runner grabbed her hand and pulled her up behind
him. "We're going to Byford Common, miss," he
growled. "If you know a short way, don't be shy about
it!"

"Across the field is quicker, if you can jump the
fences."

The Runner grabbed her hands and pulled them together
across his stomach. "Hang on, girl. Tell me the direction
as we go. If you should fall off, I'll not stop, mind."

They were gone. Omega shivered and rubbed her hands
over her arms. She sat back on the steps. In a few minutes
she was joined by Twinings and the footman, and then
Antoine, the potboy, and the scullery maid. They were all
quiet, and silently she blessed them, drawing strength from
their presence.

Omega willed the sun to remain below the horizon, but it
rose anyway, with all the promise of a beautiful day. Men
would go about their haying, women would continue their
preparations for harvest, not even aware that Omega
Chartley's heart was broken and would never mend.

"Can we hear anything from the knoll?" she asked
finally.

"Depends on the wind, Miss Chartley," said Twinings.

They sat for an hour, until the sun was well up and the
roosters had settled down to a new day. Twinings was the
first to stand. "I believe I should see about breakfast," he
said. "Come, Antoine."

They got no further than a step inside the entrance when
Omega stood slowly and shaded her eyes with her hand. A
carriage was tooling down the road. Tied to the back of the
carriage was Matthew's horse. She sobbed out loud, and
then looked again. Rotherford's horse was tied next to it,
and overseeing them both was the Bow Street Runner,
cigar clenched in his teeth, a big grin on his face. Tilda
waved to Omega from her perch behind the Runner, and
Omega felt her heart begin to beat again. She walked down
the steps.

The carriage swept into the circle drive and stopped by

the steps. The door opened and out stepped the constable, looking remarkably displeased. He tipped his hat to Omega. "I don't scruple to tell you, miss, that both of these gents are too old for this sort of dandified nonsense. And our own justice of the peace, too! Now, how does it look when our betters carry on in such a ramshackle fashion, I ask you? Stand back, miss."

The constable swung down the steps and Lord Rotherford descended, tight-lipped and grim about the mouth. He was followed by Matthew Bering, equally dour.

All of a sudden, it was too much. For the first time in her life, Omega Chartley quietly fainted, caught at the last minute by the potboy.

When she opened her eyes, she was stretched out on the lawn, her head in Matthew's lap. "You're alive," she said.

"Indeed, my dear. And under arrest for dueling, for which I have Timothy Platter and the constable *I* hired to thank."

She turned her head slightly and regarded the two men, who squatted on the lawn close by. "Thank you, Mr. Platter. I don't think you ever made a better arrest, Constable."

The constable merely grunted, but the Runner tipped his hat to her. "Someone had to stop these two fools." He held his hands out in front of him. "There they was, in all their magnificence, already stepping off the ten paces. D'ye know I've never seen a duel before?" He grinned. "I was almost of a mind to let them continue, except I feared our laddie would likely get the short stick." He glanced in Rotherford's direction. "Now, had the wind been blowing the other way, why, I might have been inclined to let them continue. But fair's fair, eh, my lord?"

Rotherford only looked straight ahead, no expression in his eyes. "I'll take you to court for this, Matthew," he said. "You've had your chance to lie low these many years, but no, you had to stir up the water."

"Yes," agreed Matthew dryly, "wretched of me to show a little spine after all this time. Can't imagine what I was thinking."

"I will make you wish you had not."

Matthew shrugged. "Suit yourself, Edwin."

Omega reached for his hand and clasped it to her stomach. He smiled down at her. "I can't say that I'm disappointed Platter showed up."

"You should not be!" Timothy said indignantly. "And me riding all night from Suffolk, with a tiny stop in London." He motioned to the constable. "Sir, you've done a spanking fine job, a fine job. Now, if you don't mind, I'll take over."

The constable bobbed his head up and down. "You'll get no complaint from me. 'Tis the haying season, my lord, and I'll just have to trust the two of you until we are done in our fields."

Platter clapped his hands together as the constable drove off. "And now, Lord Byford, if you would, let us go into the house. I have a matter of business that should prove of great interest to you and your lovely relative over there."

They adjourned to the bookroom, Platter seating himself behind Matthew's desk after a gesture from Lord Byford. Rotherford took his chair as far away from the others as he could. Matthew stood behind Omega's chair, his hands resting lightly on her shoulders.

Platter heaved a sigh and leaned back in the chair, hands across his belly. He took out a cigar, looked at Omega, and thought better of it. He eyed the cigar for a moment, bit off a hunk of it, and started to chew. He regarded Matthew speculatively.

"My lord, do you know what happened the other night in London?"

"I can't imagine, Timothy. Please enlighten all of us."

"A curious robbery. I don't pretend to understand it. A bloke of the thieving population pinched a wooden box from under the bed of a stinking, reeking dustman on Quallen Lane."

"Fancy!" exclaimed Matthew.

Rotherford raised his head, and then elaborately ignored the rest of them.

Timothy sucked on the bit of cigar. "I don't know

hat's happening to the thieves of London. Silly man runs
raight into the loving arms of one of my fellow Bow
treet Boys.''

"How fortuitous," declared Matthew, ignoring Omega,
ho was regarding him suspiciously.

"Indeed. And do you know, there was only an old shirt
nd cravat in that box, my lord, plus a curious stickpin. I
on't know who it belonged to, but it's so distinctive that
'm sure we'll know its owner soon enough." He leaned
oward Matthew in a conspiratorial way. "And, my lord,
here were the faintest rusty brown stains all over it." His
yes shifted from side to side. "Blood, my lord."

Rotherford appeared more interested. If Platter noticed,
e gave no sign.

"Now, why, I asked myself, would a cove pinch
omething like that, and only that?"

"I'm sure you were curious," agreed Matthew affably.
"Pay attention, Omega."

"I was so curious I set a guard to watch that house. He
ad watched for only a moment or two when a messenger
ode up all of a lather and handed the landlord a note."
Timothy Platter leaned back and patted his stomach.
"That horse was so lathered, why, it could have come all
he way from Byford, bless my soul."

"I'm sure it's possible, although we have excellent mail-
oach service. Perhaps it just wasn't fast enough.
Whatever could the note have said?" asked Matthew, all
nterest.

Platter clicked his tongue and shook his head. "I'll
ever know, my lord, for do you know what happened
ext?"

"No, what?"

"In ten minutes, the whole house was on fire! Why, you
would have thought there was something in that message
hat scared the landlord."

Matthew's hands tightened on Omega's shoulders. "The
devil, you say."

The Runner slapped his knee. "What a blaze!"

"And did it all burn down?" asked Rotherford, making

his first contribution. A smile of satisfaction played about his lips.

"Oh, I'm afraid it did, laddie, my lord," Platter said mournfully, but then he brightened up. "But do you know, the Runner watching the house was able to dash inside and save some possessions!"

"Good for him. My faith in London justice grows by the minute. What did he save?" asked Matthew. "Or shall I guess?"

Platter grinned and took another bite off his cigar. "Guess if you want, my lord."

"He saved a mattress, didn't he? From the second floor. One with bloodstains like the ones on that shirt?"

"You've hit upon it, my lord," exclaimed Platter. "And do you know, when that mattress hits the pavement, the strangest little ashman from belowstairs comes up and begins singing such a tune!"

Rotherford slumped forward, his face drained of all color.

"The landlord tried to shut him up, but no, no, the ashman was still talking when I left the place. I wonder what he was saying. Do you think it might have had something to do with the bloodstains?"

"No one believes a drunk," said Rotherford, recovering himself.

Platter nodded. "That's what I say, my lord Rotherford, that's what I say. It would never hold up in a court of law. But do you know, sir, I heard the very same story from Sir Horace Billings of Suffolk. Now, do you think a court of law would believe him?"

Rotherford leapt from his chair and Omega jumped. Matthew stood in front of her, shielding her from Rotherford, who pounded his fist on the desk under Platter's nose. Platter did not move.

"That's impossible!" Rotherford shouted. "Billings is dead!"

The Runner looked at him for a long minute. "Now, how would you know that? Are you friends?"

Rotherford sat down, poised to leap to his feet again. "He is dead, I tell you!"

Platter sighed and crossed himself. "You're so right, my
rd. Thank you for pointing that out. I have a bad habit
f livening up my tales."

Rotherford smiled and looked around him. Platter
ulled open his coat and rummaged among the papers
side, humming to himself. "Ah, here we are. I have a
ttle document, stamped and sealed right and tight, that
ight be of interest to you, Lord Rotherford, particularly
' you were a friend of the late departed."

"He was merely a slight acquaintance. Matthew knew
im well."

Matthew nodded. "He was a friend of mine from
)xford. And he is dead?"

"Alas, dead these five years," said Platter sorrowfully.
'Died of the damp, he did, my lord. Such a drafty place is
uffolk." Platter rested his elbows on the desk. "But
omething was weighing heavily on his mind, my lords and
ady. Some deep, dark memory." Platter crossed himself
gain. "Told his younger brother he would sleep better if it
lidn't weight so heavy."

Rotherford sucked in his breath. Matthew took a seat
eside Omega and clasped her hand so tightly that she
ilmost cried out. She squeezed his hand in turn and leaned
:loser to him.

Platter lowered his voice. "Sir Horace dictated a sorry
ale to his brother, a tale of rape and murder, of an
·vening's jest gone awry, a wedding eve turned sour."
Platter turned to face Lord Rotherford, who sat with his
·yes closed. "I'm sorry to have to tell you this, my lord,
)ut Sir Horace said some dreadful things about
rou. It seems you were not precisely the perfect host."

Rotherford rose to his feet slowly and went to the
vindow. He pounded on the frame in sudden violence, and
hen was silent. The silence stretched into long seconds and
hen minutes. His voice was soft when he finally spoke.

"Matthew, what will you have me do? I'm too old for a
·oyage to the Antipodes in the hold of a prison ship, and I
lon't fancy a noose around my neck."

"Release Jamie to me, Edwin. Sign a statement
·esigning your guardianship. And then you never, never

show your face around my home again. Not ever."

Rotherford did not turn around. "You will discover, Matthew, that there are funds, large funds, missing from Jamie's trust."

Matthew considered this. "I think Jamie's trust can stand the nonsense, as long as this ends it."

Rotherford turned around. "Very well, I agree."

"Then let me encourage you to leave Byford as soon as you can pack."

Rotherford went to the door, looked back as if he would speak, and then thought better of it. He bowed to them all, his eyes still expressionless, and left the room. They waited, silent, until the front door closed.

Matthew let out a sigh. Platter rose to his feet and reached across the desk. "Give me your hand, my lord—we've done the thing." The men clasped hands across the desk. Matthew smiled for the first time.

Platter tucked Billings' statement inside his coat again. "Me for London, then, my lord. Do you know, Maeve is in such a dither. It seems that someone left a box of dishes outside our door. Happens Maeve's name was on it, but she can't imagine who would give her such a legacy." He grinned and took another bite of his cigar. "Particularly since our only company recently was a down-at-the-heels farming laddie without a sixpence to scratch with!"

"Fancy," murmured Matthew. "Some farmers save their money for rainy days, I suspect."

"Happens they do," said Platter.

"Before you go," said Matthew, "could you fetch Hugh Owen back here?"

"Before God," said Omega, "where *was* Hugh all this time?"

"He was my stalwart on the dueling field, offering all manner of advice. Why, I think he was vaguely disappointed when the constable and our Runner materialized out of the gloom. Well, at any rate, he is in the custody of the doctor, who is repairing the damage done by Rotherford last night."

Platter tipped his hat and whistled his way down the

all. Omega shook her head in amazement. Matthew gathered her in his arms and pushed the door shut with his foot.

"We have one more matter to discuss, my dear," he said. "One that you will find painful, but which I cannot avoid, as much as I would wish."

He released her, sat her in a chair, and went to his desk, where he took out the special license again. As she watched open mouthed, he tore it into small pieces and threw them into the fireplace.

"I will not bind you to a man who wouldn't be much of a husband, my dear."

"Matthew, I don't care about that," she whispered, afraid to trust her voice.

He sat down on the desk. "You would eventually, my dear. You're too young to be leg-shackled to someone who would be an excellent conversationalist but remarkably ineffective in that other kind of companionship. Now, hush, and listen to me! There's likely someone in Durham who will love you in ways that I can't."

When she said nothing, he sighed. "Now, excuse me, Omega. I stink as badly as that ashman. I haven't gone so long without a bath since I took a dare at Harrow. When I am done, I am going to take my carriage to your brother's and retrieve those wandering children."

He bowed to her and left the room.

She sat there until she heard his footsteps overhead and his door closing. With eyes as blank as Rotherford's, she walked slowly downstairs to the housekeeper's room, lay down on the bed, and curled herself into a ball. She ignored Tildy's questions, closing her eyes. She thought she heard Matthew in the servant's hall, speaking to the others. When he finished and went upstairs, no one bothered her again. She wrapped her arms around herself and slept.

When Platter returned with Hugh, she roused herself and helped the soldier to his room. She tucked him in bed, reminding him in her best educationist's voice to lie still so he would not tear his stitches. She bustled about the room,

closing the draperies and feeding a small fire on the hearth
The room was cool with autumn. She sniffed the air; fal
was here. It was almost time to begin the term at St
Elizabeth's, her first term in a new school.

"Omega," said Hugh suddenly, "I haven't told you,
have I?"

"What?"

"When Jamie and I were in Claybrook, Lord Nickle
asked me to manage his horse-breeding farm in Ireland."

"Oh, Hugh!" she exclaimed, and her pleasure was
genuine. "And will you do it?"

"Of course. Only think of the opportunity . . ." His
voice trailed off as the doctor's famous sleeping powders
prepared to claim another victim in Matthew Bering's
house. Hugh struggled to the surface one last time before
sleep overtook him. "We brought your trunk and your
valise from the mail coach, Omega. In your room . . ."

She let herself out the door and into the room upstairs.
There they were, her shabby trunk, the leather valise that
had been Alpha's at Oxford, and her bundle of books. She
looked in the valise and sighed with relief. Her money was
all there. She untied the cord about the books and sat
down, turning the pages of her old friends.

The term would begin in a week. She found a sheet of
paper and a pencil and began to outline her first course.
The business occupied her thoughts and she almost did not
hear Matthew leave in his carriage. The pencil tightened in
her hand and her glance wandered to the window for a
moment, but then she bent her head over her books again,
putting him out of her thoughts.

16

O mega's eyes did not close that night, no matter how hard she tried to sleep. She tossed and turned until the bed was a tangle of sheets and blankets. Toward morning she gave it up and retreated to her chair again, hugging her pillow until her head nodded forward and she slept.

She woke in midmorning, startled by the pounding of feet on the stairs. She sat up, putting the pillow behind the chair as the door opened and Angela and Jamie dashed in. With a happy cry she held out her arms for both of them and they hugged her in turn.

"Oh, Angela, you are such a hand," she exclaimed, smoothing back the child's curls from around her face. "Thank you for getting Jamie to safety."

Angela allowed herself to be held for a moment on Omega's lap. "Oh, Miss Chartley, I got lost once. It was Jamie who found the right road."

"Jamie! You are a complete hand too!"

He dropped his eyes modestly for a moment, and then remembered his news. "Omega, this is famous! Uncle Matthew says I can stay and stay and never leave this place. We have been making such plans."

"I am sure you have," said Omega quietly. She looked at Angela, who was suddenly silent. "And, my dear, has Hugh told you his good news?"

She nodded, but there was no light in her eyes, no indication that her friend's good fortune was anything she wanted. Her eyes filled with tears and she clung to Omega. "Miss Chartley, I don't want to leave Byford! It feels like I thought home would, if ever I had one. What am I to do?"

Omega ached for her little friend. I don't want to leave Byford either, she thought as she hugged Angela closer. She bowed her head over Angela and closed her eyes.

"Angela."

Hugh stood in the doorway. He was dressed in

Matthew's good clothes again, his arm arranged in a sling. How long he had stood there listening, Omega had no idea, but his face was serious.

He came into the room and knelt beside Angela. "*Munequita,* do you want to stay here? Don't . . . don't think you'll hurt my feelings by whatever you say. Just tell me the truth."

Angela rested against Omega. "Hugh, I want to stay here with Jamie and Omega."

Omega winced. Perhaps Matthew could explain it to Angela when she put her own bags in the stage again and left for Durham. She knew she could not.

"It's a home, Hugh," Angela said, attempting to explain something for which she had no words. "Are you really angry with me?"

Hugh held out his arm to her. She came to him and leaned against his knee. "Angry? Why should I be? I've already talked to Lord Byford about this. And do you know what he says?"

Angela shook her head.

"He says he would be happy as a grig if you stay here. Only he promised me that both you and Jamie will spend your summers in Ireland . . . if everyone is agreeable."

Angela burst into noisy sobs. Hugh smiled over her head to Omega. "Now, that's the Angela I know." He kissed her on the forehead. "We've traveled some long roads on foot, *amiga*. We'll get together every summer and refight any battle you say."

"Omega, have you become such a lady of leisure that you sit in your bedgown until noon?"

Omega looked up in surprise. "Alpha!" she shrieked, and hurried to her brother, who whirled her around and kissed her heartily.

He held her off at arm's length. "Such a tale Matthew has told me! And I thought I could trust you on the roadways of England."

"Obviously you cannot, my dear," said Omega. "I've had a world of adventure, even though I missed my whole itinerary and fell in with some of the most *eccentric* people. Alpha, this will keep me warm for many a winter."

"Good. I am here to drag you back onto the straight-and-narrow path and take you directly to Amphney St. Peter, where Lydia awaits with broths and hot packs and good advice, which you can select from at your leisure."

"Alpha," she sighed, and leaned against him. "Let's go as soon as we can."

Hugh stood up. "Not until I leave," he said. "Lord Nickle wants me in London tomorrow for some instructions and information from his solicitors. I expect all of you to see me off this afternoon."

Omega shook her head. "Not I, Hugh. I find that I cannot . . . cannot abide farewells anymore." Her voice broke and Alpha looked at her with some concern. "It is somewhat lowering to see one's friends cast to the four winds."

Alpha hugged her to him. "We'll go in style tomorrow morning in Matthew's carriage. *You* may prefer the common stage, but I think I will enjoy this bit of luxury again."

She dismissed them all, dressed hurriedly, and joined them downstairs for luncheon, served by a somewhat subdued Twinings and by Tildy, whose eyes were red. Matthew presided at the head of the table. He looked tired, and he said little, but the conversation traveled along at a clipping rate from brother to sister, over to Hugh, and back to the children.

Omega could not bring herself to look at Matthew. She steeled herself for the ordeal of eating, and was grateful when the meal ended. If he doesn't come too close to me, or say anything of a personal nature, I can rub through this day and leave with Alpha first thing in the morning, she thought as she stood on the front steps and waved as the others set off in Matthew's barouche to take Hugh into Byford. She blew a kiss to her sergeant and waved both hands until they were out of sight.

The servants hurried down the steps and climbed into the gig that the footman drove. Tildy leaned over the side. "Miss Chártley, Hugh said he would write to me. Do you think I will find something to say?"

Omega touched her arm. "You will find plenty to write

about. I'm so glad. Now, hurry, or you'll miss his good-bye!''

Omega trudged up the stairs, wishing that her ankle did not ache so, and wondering if a visit to a London surgeon was in order, after all. Perhaps Alpha could spare a day to take her there. Her mind a purposeful blank, she knotted her books together, tying a neat bow. Before he left with the others, Matthew had spoken to her quite formally and invited her to take any or all of the clothing in the dressing room. She had decided against it at first, and then changed her mind. If she did not take the dresses, they would only hang unused. There had been too much waste already; no sense in adding to it. She would take only the more useful gowns that would suit in the classroom.

And then when she had packed them, she changed her mind, flinging the dresses from her trunk and putting them back in the dressing room. They would only serve as a reminder, and she was determined to forget this time. She would teach and commit herself to the classroom. Maybe someday there would be someone else. She couldn't imagine such a thing, but perhaps in a few years it would be possible.

Omega was repacking her valise when she heard a noise next door in Matthew's room, the sound of drawers being opened. She stopped and listened. The noises ceased and she continued her packing, berating herself for being such a goose. And then she heard the sound of drawers again.

She frowned. One of the servants must have remained behind. But surely they knew better than to invade his privacy like that. Without a thought in her head, she left her room and went next door on tiptoe, carefully and quietly opening the door.

Lord Rotherford stood before her, one of Matthew's drawers in his hand, the contents spilling on the floor. She gasped and stepped back, and suddenly became aware that she was all alone in the house.

Rotherford put down the drawer. ''Miss Chartley, I had no idea you were here.''

She was silent, unable to think of anything to say, her feet rooted to the carpet.

"Cat got your tongue, my dear?" he said. "Devilish inconvenient for a teacher, eh?"

"What . . . what are you doing here?" she managed finally.

Rotherford picked up another drawer and pawed through it. "An excellent question, my dear. I thought I would take a look at that letter from Horace Billings. It's not downstairs in the bookroom. I just want another look, my dear, nothing more."

Suddenly she was furious. "Can't you leave Matthew alone? Can't you just go away and cease your meddling? Haven't you done enough? Good God, Rotherford, you are a menace to society!" She wanted to beat him, to flay the flesh from his bones, or at the very least to murder him. She could only stand there in the doorway and rail at him.

He took all of this in, and then began to smile at her wrath. "You are lovely when you are angry," he said. "You would be such a challenge. Not like that little drab on Quallen Lane. You could be such a pleasant farewell for me from Byford. God knows Matthew hasn't any means to do anything with you."

Fear greater than anything she had ever known rose in her eyes. She backed away. "I'll scream, my lord, if you come one step closer."

He crossed the room in a bound. "Scream away, Miss Chartley. I believe we have the house to ourselves." Before she could move again, or even raise her hands to defend herself, Lord Rotherford took the front of her dress and ripped it down to her waist. She screamed as he pulled her sleeves down, pinning her bare arms to her sides.

She screamed again when he touched her. "Oh, scream away, my lovely. That will make it so much more—"

She had no idea what he intended to say next. He uttered a strange groan and a puzzled look pierced his inexpressive eyes. They opened wider, and the look in them was a horror she would never forget. He knocked her off balance as he sank to his knees and then fell forward at her feet, a knife deep in his back.

Struck dumb with fear, Omega struggled to right

herself. She pulled her arms from her sleeves and raised the front of her ruined dress. She crouched in the corner, covering herself as best she could, when she looked up and gasped.

Timothy Platter was sitting in the window, the cigar still clutched between his teeth, his coat covered with pollen again. Without a word beyond a sneeze and a grunt of satisfaction at his handiwork, he tossed a blanket to her. She pulled it around her body and sat there on the floor, her teeth chattering.

"I've been watching him, Miss Chartley," he said finally as he stubbed out his cigar. "Something told me this case wasn't quite over yet, miss. Happens I was right. Maeve always tells me, 'Timmy boy, trust your instincts.' "

In a surprisingly gentle fashion he raised Omega to her feet and sat her down. "Now, tell me, what was he doing here? He couldn't have known you had remained behind."

When she remained speechless, he reached inside his voluminous coat and detached a bottle, which he uncorked and passed to her. She took it without a murmur and downed a good swallow. The liquor made her eyes water, but it put heart back in her.

"Timothy, he came for the letter, you know, the letter from Sir Horace Billings. I think he still intended to do Matthew harm."

Platter nodded and produced the letter from his pocket. Omega's eyes widened. "But didn't you give that to Matthew?"

"I took it back again." He broke the seal on the document and spread out the page so she could see.

The page was blank. Her eyes even wider, Omega took a deep breath and reached for the paper, turning it over and over in her hands, as if she expected to see magic writing suddenly appear. She looked up at Platter. "Oh, Timothy, I do not understand. Not at all."

"I do."

Matthew stood in the doorway. He took in Rotherford dead at his feet, and Omega, white-faced and wrapped in a blanket, and then closed the door behind him and locked it. "It wouldn't do the children any good to see this," he said, and then touched Omega's cheek. "He didn't hurt you, did he, my dear?"

She shook her head. "Timothy . . ." She couldn't collect her thoughts.

Matthew bowed to the Runner. "I remain in your debt, sir," he said. He plucked the paper from Omega's nerveless fingers and handed it back to the Bow Street Runner.

"There never was a letter, was there, Platter?" he said.

"No," Timothy said simply, "although that part about Sir Horace and his nightmares was true. His younger brother told me how deeply troubled he was. I merely supplied the text."

Matthew sank down on the bed next to Omega and stared at the Runner. "You broke the law for me?"

"Happens I did," said Platter gruffly. "Happens sometimes you have to bend the law to preserve it. Don't stare at me like that!" He put the paper back in the envelope. "Was it a bad idea?" When no one said anything, Platter looked Matthew in the eye. "And I did it for Millie Platter."

"You knew," Matthew said simply.

"I knew. She wasn't a good girl, but she was my sister, Lord Byford."

A curious range of emotions passed across Matthew's face, a mixture of sorrow and shame, coupled with respect. The expression yielded to a quiet calm that Omega had been wishing to see for eight years.

"Timothy, thank you. Thank you from the bottom of my heart. For everything."

Platter nodded, and coughed, wiping around his nose, with a swipe at his eyes. "Too much of that treacle, Lord Byford, and I'll not be fit for duty. Give me a hand with this rascal. Let's wrap a sheet around him. No sense in giving the little ones the blue devils. Miss Chartley, Omega, my dear, I suggest you find another dress. You'll catch your death in that one."

By the time the house was cleared of the constable, the doctor, and the undertaker, and the Bow Street Runner had at last taken his leave, dinner was long over. Omega left Matthew and Alpha in the dining room discussing the events of the day over brandy and what remained of Antoine's mousse.

She had to complete her packing. She and Alpha would be away at first light for the drive to Amphney St. Peter. She would see her nephews and Lydia would laugh and cry over all her misadventures, and then it would be Durham for her.

After she had finished, Omega took one last look in the dressing room, running her hands along the frocks, wishing there had been time to try on the really elaborate ones. She closed the door then and put them from her mind.

The window was open and she went to it, leaning out for a last smell of roses. Winter would sweep over this lovely land, and then spring. Her life would go on with the same regularity as the seasons. The thought brought Omega no pain now. She was almost content with the way things were. Matthew would have the children to comfort him, especially since he would likely have none of his own, and she would be busy enough. She would not think of him beyond four or five times in an hour, and with any luck, by the time another eight years had come and gone, she would only recall him to mind once or twice a day.

She closed the window and shut the draperies. She turned back the coverlet, aching for a good night's rest. Someone knocked. Her heart rose for a moment, and then resumed its normal rhythm. It was not Matthew's knock.

"Alpha?"

"May I come in?"

She opened the door and drew him in. He surveyed the trunk and books, all tidy and bound together. He rubbed his hands. "You can almost smell winter in the air already." He flopped on her bed and put his hands behind his head. "Well, dear heart, you remind me of something."

"What?"

"I have become a reader of nursery rhymes. You may

credit your nephews. Remember the one about St. Ives, and the kits and cats and sacks and wives?"

"And 'how many were going to St. Ives?' " she finished for him, a smile on her face too. "I confess I feel that way." She sat down beside him. "A soldier, a runaway, a Spanish orphan, a Bow Street Runner, a true villain, an almost-husband . . ." The light left her eyes. "But I was the only one going to St. Ives after all, wasn't I, Alpha?" she asked, her voice small.

He took her hand. "I'm afraid so, my dear." His voice was soft. "We're teachers. What did you learn from all this?"

She lay back next to him and he put his arm around her. "Alpha, I learned to toss away itineraries and just let things happen. I feel as though I haven't looked at a clock in years. Is that enough?"

She sat up. Suddenly it wasn't enough, not nearly enough. "Alpha, it won't do."

He watched her from the bed, his eyes bright.

"Alpha," she said slowly, "what would you say if I went to Matthew Bering's room tonight?"

He considered the question. "You're old enough to make your own decisions, dear heart."

"That's no answer," she said crossly.

"It's the only answer you'll get from me. I just don't want to see you hurt any further, Omega. You mean too much to me. So there."

"Won't you give me some advice?" she pleaded. "Alpha, I don't want to leave him. I simply don't know what to do!"

He got up and kissed her. "I think you do know what to do. You want advice? I'll tell you this: nothing is worse than regret. There's no hell greater than asking yourself: 'What if I had done this, or that?' Good night, Omega. Pleasant dreams."

"Alpha, you are worse than useless," she said after he closed the door.

Omega climbed into bed, examined her ankle, decided that she would likely limp for the rest of her life, and pinched out the candle. There was no comfortable spot anywhere in the bed that only two nights ago had felt so wonderful. She might as well have slept on rocks or sharp-pointed sticks. She folded her arms resolutely and willed her eyes to snap shut.

They would not. She listened to the clock in the hall as it chimed, and then chimed an hour later.

"This is impossible," she said at last, and got out of bed. She paused with her hand on the doorknob. "Oh, I can't do this," she said out loud.

It sounded almost like whimpering. She berated herself and almost retreated to her bed. Courage, Omega, she thought, and let herself into the hall.

There was no light showing under the door of Matthew's room. He had probably been asleep for hours. Heaven knew it had been a tiring day. She raised her hand to knock, and then lowered it again. I can't possibly do what I'm contemplating, she thought, and started back to her room.

She was almost back to her door when she thought of Alpha's words and turned around. Matthew could tell her to go away. But if she never knew for certain what he would do, she would only spin out her hours and days and years in endless circles of regret.

She gritted her teeth and knocked on the door, steeling herself, already turning to go.

"Come in."

She opened the door slowly. "Matthew?"

He didn't say anything, and all heart left her. The tears welled in her eyes and she started to back out into the hall. But then Matthew lit a match, and a small point of light shone in the room. She couldn't see his face, but he was there and he had lit a candle.

"Matthew, I would like to stay with you tonight."

Again the long silence. Again her heart failed her.

"Omega, don't you remember anything I've told you? I'm impotent. That's as plain as I can make it."

And then she was angry with him. She came into the room and shut the door behind her. "Matthew, you cod's head, I love you! Did those . . . those ladies—"

"Scarcely ladies," he interjected.

"Did those ladies you tried—did they care for you?"

"Hardly."

"Then I wish you would take a chance with someone who loves you!" She gestured in the dark, warming to her subject. "And I've been feeling in the last week that you're not entirely indifferent to me."

"That's true enough. Good God, Omega, I love you. I never quit doing that."

"Then you'd better show me, Matthew, or I'll just go on being a teacher who never takes a chance, and you'll wither away."

"Omega, you are absolutely daft."

"Oh, good night, Matthew!" She blew out the candle and went to the door.

Her hand was on the knob when he spoke again, and this time his voice was softer. "Omega, it's a narrow bed."

"The most paltry excuse," she said, and leaned her forehead against the door.

"But it's comfortable, my dear, if you don't mind sharing a pillow."

She smiled to herself. She was silent, waiting.

"And the floor is cold, and you're not getting any younger standing there."

She laughed. "Neither are you."

She heard him sit up and light the candle again. Her smile deepened as he pulled back the coverlet. "Come on, Omega. Let's . . . let's throw out the itinerary."

She got in bed, feeling a tingle of fear mixed with her joy. This was different from the other night, when they had clung together for solace. She needed something more this time, and so did he.

Without saying anything, Matthew touched her tentatively, running his hand down her body. She relaxed and moved closer. In another moment they were in each other's arms, and Omega couldn't tell where she ended and where Matthew began. She was afraid for a moment, but no more than he was. Without a word spoken, he gave himself to her, and she welcomed him into herself, her hands tight across his back, loving him fiercely as she had always wanted to do.

He was her lover, and she was his, and there was no room for regret or pride. They were the only two people in the world, and it was a world they knew they would never tire of, now that they had found it.

Omega refused to let go of him.

"See here, my dear, I'm not going anywhere!"

"Promise?" she whispered, and then ran her tongue inside his ear until he groaned with the pleasure of it.

"Good God, Omega, I fear we are going to be exhausted by morning. And you have to leave with Alpha. Hold still, we're going to fall off."

She giggled. "Silly, I'm not leaving with Alpha."

"Oh, yes you are! In a week's time I will arrive at Amphney St. Peter with another special license clutched in my hand. And Alpha will give you away, and Lydia will cry, and Jamie will say, 'Oh, this is famous!', and Angela may give you a Waterloo souvenir, for all I know."

She considered this. "No more than a week. If something should result from this evening's sport, and heaven knows, it could, I wouldn't want your—our— neighbors counting the months back on their fingers."

He settled himself beside her. "A distinct possibility, now that you mention it. Two days?"

"Much better, Matthew."

"Excellent. Oh, do that again. Good God, Omega. Where was I? Oh, yes, we will leave our darlings with Lydia and bolt to the city for a week or so. I want to renew some old acquaintances, and I have a proposal for Mr. Timothy Platter."

"Which is . . ."

"The constable, I fear, is sorely displeased with me, and in truth, he has been thinking of retirement. Do you think Timothy Platter would give up London's beauty and safety for the boredom of Byford?"

"Oh, Matthew, I love you."

"And I love you. Of course, the Platters will have to get used to the birds yelling, and fresh water, and all manner of evils, but I will put it to Maeve."

He kissed her. "And there was something else. Omega, you are such a distraction! How can I think? Oh, yes. Dear Omega, it has come to my attention that you are not entirely indifferent to me. Can I . . . oh, have I reason to hope that—"

"Yes," she interrupted, and kissed him.

"Hush, Omega, I'm not through, and I'm only going to propose this last time in my life. Do I have reason to hope that you might consent to joining your life with mine?"

"Yes," she said again, and touched his face. "Matthew, you're crying."

"I am. Older men get funny. Omega, you'll have to send a letter of regret to St. Elizabeth's."

"It will be my only regret, dearest."

Read on for a peek at
One Good Turn
by Carla Kelly,
available from Signet
in December 2001.

"Damn my eyes. I am a grown man, veteran of war, and justice of the peace in my own shire. Why can't I just forget Libby Cook?"

Earlier in that endless winter of 1817, he would have looked around, wondering if any of his servants had overheard him talking out loud in the book room. It was March now, a rainy, dreary March. After a winter with snow to the rafters, and for all he knew, wolves carrying off his crofters' small children, he didn't care anymore who heard him talk out loud.

Benedict Nesbitt, the seventh Duke of Knaresborough, knew that his servants already thought him eccentric. He had been taking his meals belowstairs all winter. He told them it was because the food came hotter to the table, but he sensed they understood his loneliness. Amos Yore, his former private of the 20th Foot that he had installed as curator of armaments, never felt comfortable eating off the crested china in the breakfast room, so it was an easy matter for Nez to eat belowstairs, where they could talk about weapons and Amos's plans for the estate's extensive collection. Even then, Amos had felt uneasy, until Nez asked him one evening, in all apparent seriousness, if he had found the stones that his relatives lobbed at Julius Caesar when family members painted themselves blue and threw rocks at the Roman legions. "Amos, I depend upon you to see that they are properly numbered and labeled," he had warned. His reward was a blank stare, and then Amos's delighted laugh. Dinner belowstairs was never a problem after that.

His own friends had finally stopped twitting him about his abstinence from the bottle. He had promised Libby he would never drink another drop, and he was scrupulous in his vow. The promise had been hard to keep at first, never more so than when he first returned to London from Kent, knowing that Libby, a married woman now, was surely giving herself regularly to her dear Tony, that bumbling doctor with nothing to recommend himself except a huge heart and a gentle nature. His pleasure should be mine, he told himself over and over in those first awful weeks. He went to bed too many nights desperately unhappy.

He even went down to his wine cellar one morning after an especially bad night, just to stand there and stare at the empty racks. He had sent the bottles—some of them dating back to the time of England's first George—to his friend Eustace Wiltmore, who had married Libby's cousin Lydia. He wanted them back, wanted just to sit on the floor in the cellar and drink, and not come upstairs until he was cured or dead. His butler had found him there, miserable and silent, and had done something unthinkable in a butler. Nez smiled just remembering. Luster had stood there watching him a moment, then knelt down with a creak of his knees—he wasn't young anymore, if he ever had been—and touched his master's cheek. That was all. It was the smallest gesture, but it kept him from the wine cellar again.

Even in the middle of Nez's misery and his disgust at his inability to let go of that glorious creature now married to her dear doctor, he resisted. He ignored his friends' laughter when he toasted King and Country with water, shook his head over their insistence upon including him in rack punch after an evening of cards, or even eggnog to herald winter's solstice. After a while, they did not even include him in their festivities; he felt only relief at their distance.

His mother died after Christmas, but there was no reason to mourn her from inside a brandy bottle. She had outlived many of her contemporaries, and much of her usefulness, according to his sister Augusta, who could be even more censorious than he. *Sic transit glorious* Mumsy, he thought from his own apartment on Clarges Street at the time of his mother's death. He closed his apartment, moved into the family house in Half Moon Street, and assigned his footman the task of refurbishing the place. He accompanied Mama's coffin back to Knare and placed her beside his late father. The sixth duke had died five years earlier while Nez recuperated in Portugal from a concussion received during the second siege of Badajoz. He remembered still the odd sensation of reading the letter from his solicitor over and over again as he lay on his cot, trying to get his eyes to focus.

And now Mama was gone, too, where all good Nesbitt-Knares went, and where he would rest someday. Aye, he thought, eventually we're on the wall in the gallery, fit only to glare down on future generations, and to turn into worm's meat in the vault. He stayed at Knare then to organize Mama's tangled accounts, and stare out the window that overlooked the formal gardens, his mother's last bit of extravagance, if he could believe the neighbors when they came to offer condolences.

He remembered with a pang the empty feeling inside him when he settled the last of her accounts, and put her ledger back on the shelf in the book room. There was no reason for him ever to open it again—no more gambling debts to pay, no more tears over *modistes* who would not wait another quarter, even though he had continued Papa's generous allowance. She was gone from his life, and now that it was too late, he wished he had known her better.

Even though the snow was deep that winter, he remained on the estate, eating belowstairs, helping Amos Yore catalog his gun collection, and enjoying the tranquility and freedom from his sister Augusta's suggestions that only set his head to humming. In the high cynicism that had been his nearest companion since the Spanish wars, he also knew that he was finding too much pleasure in the parental absence. When he forced himself to think about his mother's passage, he felt sorrow finally and grieved in silence, unable to cry because he knew it would bring on a storm of emotion he doubted he could tolerate in himself.

In the stillness of late January, when the estate was quiet under snow, he sat down at his desk and wrote a lengthy letter to the Cooks. He told them of his mother's death, and asked them to name that hospital for her that Tony was building in Holyoke with his wedding gift. He included another large bank draft, wincing at its vulgarity, even as he applauded the rightness of the cause, and sat back for a letter in return. He almost dreaded a reply, but he had to hear something from the Cooks, or he knew he would run mad.

He didn't need to wait long, which was a good thing, because the rain that followed winter's snow was getting on his nerves. Less than a week later Luster, his face solemn but his eyes lively, bore in a letter on a silver salver. "I took the liberty of slitting the seal," his butler told him, "so you would not have to waste your time."

He grinned for what must have been the first time in months. "Luster, you're an old scoundrel," he said, trying not to snatch the letter from the tray.

"Very well, your grace," Luster said, and bowed himself out.

He had received a Christmas letter from Tony Cook and a small note from Libby wishing him the best of the season. Three months ago! It seemed like years. Holding the letter in front of him, he kicked off his shoes and lay down on the sofa, resting his head on the upholstered arm and shoving a pillow under his lower back. Thank God Augusta was not there to scold him for his slovenly ways. He opened the letter and smoothed it out upon his knee. With a small sigh of disappointment, he recognized Tony's handwriting, a doctor's scrawl written in haste.

My Dear Duke,
    Thank you is a paltry expression, when it runs alongside your handsome and welcome gift. While we express our sorrow at the news of your mother's death, we are touched that you would choose to honor her with such a memorial as is being constructed in Holyoke. Simply put, it is a magnificent way to keep her memory lively.

He put down the letter and laughed, unable to help himself. Oh, the irony, he thought; Mama never went near a sickbed if she could help it. I do believe I will compose a paeon to her generous nature and constant concern for the infirm and halt of our sceptr'd isle. I can have it bronzed and placed in the entrance. Oh, it is delicious. Imagine: people a hundred years from now in 1917 will revere the memory of that lady of charity. "And so legends are born, Dr. Tony Cook." He murmured and picked up the letter again.

    May we invite you to our estate? We have heard weather reports from your part of the realm and would like to assure you that pansies are already blooming in Kent, even if winter is a bad guest that will not depart from your own Great Plain of York. That is not all that is blooming. My Libby is blooming, too. I know she would like to see you, even if she protests as I am writing this. I don't know why she is so shy right now. I know her well; she will protest, blush perhaps, but he delighted to see you, in any event, even as I will. Don't stay away long, Nez. Something in your letter tells us both that you would like to visit.

Come soon, dear friend.

With gratitude for your kindness and love for yourself alone,

Tony and Libby

" 'My Libby,' " he said. "Yours to have and to love, Tony damn you. And you know her well? I suppose you do." Lying there, he crumpled the letter and threw it toward the fireplace. Luckily his aim was off, because in a moment he was retrieving it to smooth upon his knee again and reread. I wonder, does she blush and protest to see me because she really loves me? he asked himself. Reason told him no. He was the first to acknowledge the rightness of Tony Cook for Libby Ames, as much as the idea pained him.

He read the letter again, and then he set it on the fire, standing there to watch it catch flame. So, Dr. Cook, something in my letter tells you that I would like to visit? He smiled into the flames. Well, at least I did not sob into the rag linen and use it to blow my nose! The image made him laugh. He was still smiling when Luster brought him tea.

He looked up at Luster and accepted a cup and saucer from him. "Luster, it was from the Cooks in Kent. But you knew that!"

"Your grace," was all Luster would own.

"They are well, and have invited me to Kent. What do you think of that?"

Any other butler would have made no specific comment, but he knew that the man who had patted his cheek so tenderly months ago in his wine cellar would have something to say. Luster did not fail him. "Excellent! Will you need one traveling case or two, your grace?"